AF264902

DOCTOR MARGARET
In Delhi
(Book 2 of The Azadi Series)

By

Waheed Rabbani

*** This novel received a Bronze Award in the 2018 Global eBooks Awards Competition

Doctor Margaret In Delhi
Copyright © 2015 by Waheed Rabbani All rights reserved.
Cover Art by Stonepatch Design

This is a work of fiction. Names, characters, places, and incidents either are the product of the author's imagination or are used fictitiously. Any resemblance to actual persons, living or dead, events, or locales is entirely coincidental.

All Rights reserved. No part of this publication may be reproduced, stored in a retrieval system, or transmitted, in any form or by any means without the prior written consent of the author, nor be otherwise circulated in any form of binding or cover other than that in which it is published and without a similar condition being imposed on the subsequent purchaser. Except by a reviewer who may quote brief passages in a review.

First Edition: May 2015

Published by Historical Fiction Novels Publishing

ISBN-13:978-0993863509
ISBN-10: 0993863507

[Note: Translation of non-English words are in the Glossary]

DEDICATION

For my wife, Alexandra, without her love, help and continuing support this work may not have been possible.

Also

In fond memory of my beloved mother and father, who unfortunately did not live to see this book in print.

CONTENTS

ACKNOWLEDGMENTS

I am most grateful to all my lecturers at the McMaster University's Creative Writing Program, who taught me everything about writing fiction. I am thankful for their constant encouragement and suggestions in the evolution of this novel. I am indebted to my writing circles' partners: those in the McMaster class groups; the HisFicCritique Group (moderated by Anne Whitfield); Historical-Fiction-Writers-Critique Group (moderated by Mirella Patzer); and the CAA-Virtual Branch (moderated by Anne Osborne). Thank you all for your wonderful critiques that were of invaluable help to me in developing this novel.

I am truly appreciative of my skillful editors, Victoria Bell and Judyth Hill, for not only their superb edits, but also for the many helpful suggestions.

I found the McMaster University Library's historical volumes collection stacks a most valuable source for reference material and am thankful to the Librarians for their prompt attention to my many inter-library loan requests. I am grateful to Mr. James Capodagli, Head, Health Information Center Library - SUNY Upstate Medical University, for information on the Geneva Medical College during its early period, 1853 – 1857. I am also indebted to Ms. Lisa Grimm, Assistant Archivist, Drexel University College of Medicine, for very useful information and help in directing me through their digital collection archives on the Female Medical College at the time of its inception in 1850.

Although this is a work of fiction, the following sources, among many others, were of particular value during research, in setting the historical backdrop of this novel.

Bayley, Emily. *The Golden Calm: An English Lady's Life in Moghul Delhi,* London, 1980.

Dalrymple, William. *City of Djinns: A Year in Delhi*, Penguin Books, New York, 2003

Dalrymple, William. *The Last Mughal*, Alfred Knopf, New York, 2007

Kaye, Sir John William. *A History of the Sepoy War in India, 1857-1858*. W. H. Allen, London, 1880.

Lowrie, John. *Two Years In Upper India*, Robert Carter and Brothers, New York, 1850.

Parkes, Frances. *Wanderings of a Pilgrim In Search of the Picturesque*, Pelham Richardson, London, 1850.

Pernau, Margaret (ed.). *Delhi College*, Oxford University Press, New Delhi, 2006.

Spear, Percival. *The Twilight of the Moghuls*, Cambridge, 1951.

Sen, Surendra Nath. *Eighteen Fifty-Seven*. Ministry of Information and Broadcasting, Government of India, 1957.

Walsh, John Johnston. *A memorial of the Futtehgurh mission and her martyred missionaries: with some remarks on the mutiny in India*, J. Nesbit and Co., London, 1859.

Wilson, Leighton and Lowrie, John. *The Great Revolt In India: Its Effect Upon The Missions Of The Presbyterian Board*, New York, Board of Foreign Missions, 1857.

The translations from Urdu to English of Bhadur Shah Zafar's couplets (at the beginning of Prologue and Epilogue) are my own efforts.

I am most grateful for all the love, help and support of my wife, Alexandra, in enabling my thoughts to transform into this novel.

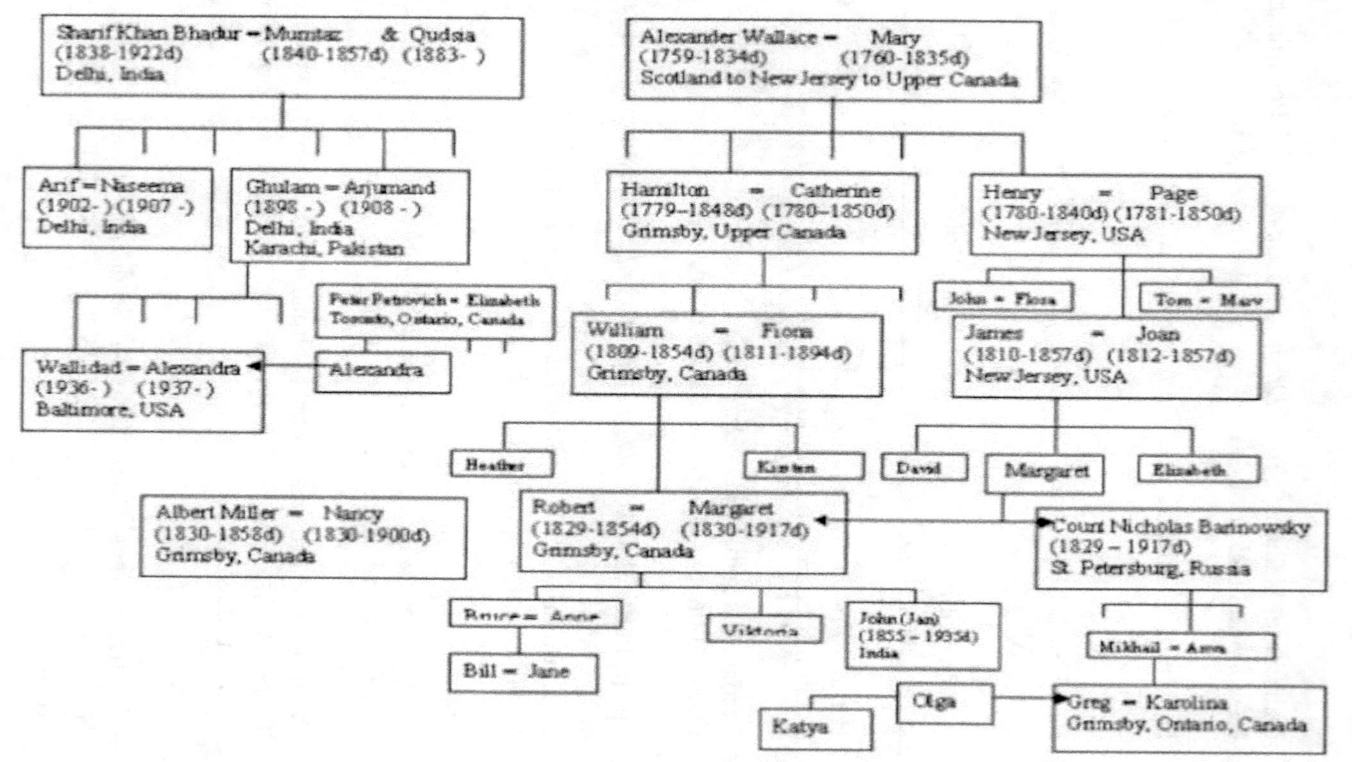

FAMILY TREE: Wallaces, Barinowskys and Sharifs

Prologue

[Aik shakh-e-gul pe baith ke bulbul he shadman]
Sitting on a branch of flowers, the nightingale sings,
[Kanthee bicha diye mere dil-e-lalazar mein]
Thorns are scattered in my heart's leas
--Bhadur Shah Zafar, Delhi (1775 – 1862)

IT SEEMED AS IF I was back in Delhi, on another assignment from Johns Hopkins Hospital. However, on this visit at the insistence of my aunt and uncle, I was staying with them at our family's ancient *haveli*, Sharif Mahal, in Daryaganj.

It being a stifling night, and unable to sleep, I decided to go out for a midnight stroll. The full moon shone in the cloudless sky, lighting up the foggy laneway, from the *haveli* towards the Jamuna River, like a path into a mysterious destination.

Stunning mansions cast giant shadows onto impressive gardens that lay on either side of the street. But something seemed strange, for the houses had somehow warped back into their former glory, during the Mughal era. Paying no heed I glided forward, effortlessly. Finding the Daryaganj Gate of the city wall open, I hurried through it and was amazed to see water flowing in the Jamuna River's branch that had dried up a long time ago.

Nobody was around. I walked up to the *ghat,* and stood by the riverbank watching the gentle waves lapping on the stone steps. The moon reflected in the water, as if bathing in it, scattering moonbeams. Suddenly, I heard footsteps, as if someone, no, two persons were running. I saw a woman, unmistakably European from her Victorian dress and long blonde hair flowing behind her in the wind, run out from the Daryaganj Gate. My heart skipped a beat when I recognized her to be the same lady of my dreams. Next to her was a darker woman, possibly Indian, except she wore Western clothes, and a shawl over her head and shoulders, likely her maid, no, her ayah, for she carried a fair haired child in her arms.

I waved at the women to stop, for I wanted to ask them, if I could be of any assistance. However, they ignored me, as if they did not even see me, and continued jogging along the river bank. They soon faded into the distance.

I wondered if I should follow the women, but I heard rhythmic footsteps, as if a group of soldiers were running in unison, on the double. A troop emerged through the gate. Their leader, a European officer ran at the front, a revolver in hand. He was followed by six sepoys carrying rifles with fixed bayonets. I cowered behind a tree, lest they spot and shoot me. They trotted away in the direction the ladies had vanished.

Troubled by what I observed, I trembled. I was trying to control myself, when I saw a lone figure emerge from the gate. He was a young Indian man, dressed in the Delhi style: kurta-pajama, black waistcoat, and a white *topi*. When he drew closer, I thought I recognized him, but still searched my brain for where I had seen him. It then dawned on me, he was the person in the painting that hung in my uncle's Connaught Place jewelry shop, but he looked much younger. He was ... I shouted, "Sharif-*Dada*!"

On hearing his name, he looked surprised, and drew nearer. "*Arrey ... beta ...* it's you ... Wallidad?"

"*Ji, Dada.* It's me." We embraced and tears of joy ran down my cheeks.

We parted, but he still held me by my shoulders, and stared at me with his fierce eyes. "Where have those women gone? Did they not come this way?"

Overcome with emotion, I could not speak.

"Tell me. We have to help Doctor Margaret."

When I tried to speak, but could not form the words, he shook my shoulder.

*****

"Wake up, Walli dear. Are you dozing again?" It was my wife, Alexandra, squeezing my shoulder as she stood beside my chair.

"Oh! Sorry, darling. Looks like I had a little nap. What time is it?" I took the coffee cup she held towards me.

Alexandra and I had finished our round of golf, at the Baltimore's Twin Oakes Golf and Country club, and while I rested in an easy chair on the club's outdoor patio, she had gone to the washroom and returned with drinks from the coffee shop.

"Nearly one o'clock. Our friends should be finishing their round soon." She sat on an adjacent chair. "They do move around well, even in their senior years."

"Thanks, dear. I hope I can walk as well, in my old age." I sipped the coffee and stretched out my legs. It being a fine summer's day, I felt hot but refreshed from my little nod-off.

"Look, there they are." Alexandra pointed in the direction of the four players.

I gazed out onto the green and saw our visitors from Grimsby, Canada, walking towards us, their golf caddies in tow.

Chapter One

Visitors from Grimsby, Canada

1967, July: Baltimore, Maryland

I STARTED MY BUICK station wagon and drove towards the golf club's exit; Alexandra sat next to me. Our visitors from Grimsby—Jane and Bill Wallace, and Karolina and Greg Barinowsky—were in the two bench seats at the back. I envied our friends' freedom; they were in their retirement years and on their way to a vacation in Florida. It being a Sunday, I was happy to have time off from my busy schedule at the hospital, and I imagined my wife was as well, from her law practice. We had just finished a round of golf and, while it had been an exhilarating afternoon, from the silence it seemed we each were engrossed in our own thoughts, likely about what had transpired in the club's parking lot earlier that morning.

"Thank you, Doctor Sharif," the gatekeeper said, as I rolled down the window and handed him the prepaid, stamped parking slip and a tip. He raised the barrier and waved a goodbye.

I nodded to him and, exiting through the golf grounds' gates, continued onto the Beltway that would take us to our house. Mindful of the passing cars, I wondered what to make of Greg's prearranged meeting that had taken place earlier in the parking lot with my patient Richard—who worked for the CIA—and his division chief. I was intrigued, just as surely Greg had been when he informed us of the CIA's offer to help bring his daughter, Katya, out of the Soviet Union. What made their proposal more interesting was that in return, they only wanted him to locate dealers of Soviet-made arms. We had wondered—and Alexandra, the lawyer, had conjectured—that the arms were very likely destined for Afghanistan to be used by some rebel groups. But against whom? I could not believe that the rumored Soviet invasion of that country, which Alexandra's father had mentioned, could be true. He had heard of it within the Russian émigré community in Canada.

While steering the Buick, rather sharply, from the highway onto a smaller road, I remembered the incident in Grimsby where, following a car chase, I had managed to evade some Soviet agents. That was when Alexandra and I had travelled to the Wallace Estates to deliver their Grandmother Doctor Margaret Wallace's sea chest, which I had brought back from Delhi. As we learned from her diaries—found in the trunk—she had worked as a physician for the Rani of Jhansi around the time of the Indian Rebellion of 1857. The Rani's exquisitely jeweled crown was also discovered in the sea chest. Upon the Canadian Soviet Embassy agent's interference, Margaret's other grandson, Greg, had handed the crown over to them, in return for a visa to the USSR and a promise of some reward upon his arrival there. However, then again, why were the Soviets so keen on possessing Margaret's journals, as well? The Wallaces had lent those to me for reading and safekeeping, along with a request to write a biography of Doctor Margaret Wallace.

"So, Walli, how far along are you with Margaret's journals?" Jane asked, from the seat behind me.

"We've just finished reading the first two volumes. They covered her life in North America and Europe. You may have those back. We are about to start on Volume III, in which I believe she wrote about her experiences in India."

"Yes, we're looking forward to reading them, and are most anxious to learn what she wrote about her time in Grimsby," Jane said.

Greg cocked his head within range of my rear-view mirror. "Walli, what about Katya's book, *Lara's Story?* The one you bought from her in Delhi. What does she have to say about Grandmother?"

"I haven't read it yet, Greg, just glanced through it. It seems to start after Margaret's arrival in St. Petersburg."

"May I borrow it?"

"Yes, of course. I'll read it after you," I said.

Just then, the laneway to our house appeared and, turning into it, I parked on the driveway, next to the Wallaces' shiny blue Cadillac with Ontario plates.

*****

After a quick wash, we gathered in our backyard and sat on cushioned patio chairs under a shady umbrella. Colorful summer flowers were in bloom in the bushes dotting the garden. Jane said something about the fragrance of the roses to Alexandra. I served them drinks: white wine for the ladies, and red for the gents. While Alexandra was setting up the table with appetizers, salads and condiments, I fired up the propane barbecue and proceeded to grill steaks and sausages.

Having piled up our plates, we settled around the table. Still absorbed in our thoughts, but hungry, we ate in silence at first, but soon—following sips of wine—we relaxed and the conversation flowed gradually. There were compliments all around on my barbecuing skill and at having done the steaks exactly to everyone's preference.

Alexandra, who had looked rather pensive for a while, said, "Jane, you asked earlier about Margaret's diaries. Yes, we did learn quite a bit about her and her husband, Robert's, life in Grimsby, but there is scant information about Albert Miller. You know, the one who accompanied them to Crimea. Do you know much about him or his wife, Nancy?"

At Alexandra's question, I cringed a bit, for I didn't think it was a good idea to discuss Albert. I was certain neither the Wallaces nor the Barinowskys knew what Albert had done to Margaret and Robert during the voyage and in Crimea. But I said nothing and continued to chew my food.

Jane replied, "No, not much, Alex. All we know is that he was a bit of a ladies' man and died somewhere in Crimea or … India, did you say, Greg?" She sipped her wine and looked towards Greg.

Greg swallowed his mouthful and nodded. "Yes, it was in India. At least, that's what I heard from one of his grandsons. But no one knows where exactly Albert was killed." Then he turned to me and asked, "It was likely in the Mutiny, or how did you call that war, Walli?"

"Indians prefer to speak of it as their First War of Independence, although most call it a Rebellion," I replied. "However, the British still refer to it as the Indian Mutiny." I noted amusement on everyone's faces.

Alexandra put her knife and fork down and pushed her plate

forward. "So, tell me, Greg, did Nancy go to India as well, with Albert?"

Greg took a gulp of his drink. "I believe she did. And you know what, she survived the war and returned to Grimsby. From what I heard, she never remarried and used to live alone in a mansion up on the Grimsby Mountain."

Jane, joining in the conversation, said, "Yes. Well, you know her father, Colonel Mitchell, was quite an influential man in our town. Not only was he the commander of the cavalry regiment, he held several important political appointments as well."

Bill, who had remained silent all this time, having finished his meal, put his plate aside. "I detest that man," he said in a loud voice. "He was responsible for sending Grandfather Robert off to war and to die in Crimea."

Jane quickly took Bill's hand. "Now, now, Bill," she said in a soothing voice. "There is no need to still be resentful about those events. They happened more than a hundred years ago. True, we do not speak to the Mitchells, but now with this wonderful return of our dear Margaret's sea chest, through the kind efforts of Alexandra and Walli," she waved her hand towards us, "perhaps it is time to make amends with Nancy's family. Don't you think, dear?"

"Do whatever you wish. Just don't include me in it," Bill replied and sipped his drink.

"Oh, I forgot to tell you, Bill," Jane persisted. "One of Nancy's granddaughters called the other day. She'd heard about the arrival of Margaret's sea chest and wanted to come look at it. I told her we would see her, when we get back from this trip."

Alexandra, likely trying to ease the tension, started picking up the empty plates. "Why, that's marvelous, Jane, for the Mitchells to have contacted you. I'm sure you'll have much to talk about. But you know, I've been wondering … perhaps … could you ask them if Nancy left a diary or something?"

"Yes, I will ask, for I'm certain they'd wish to see Margaret's journals."

Bill took a sip of his wine. "Oh, I'd let them wait. We've asked Doctor Walli to write Margaret's biography. Let them buy a copy and read it."

Jane patted Bill's arm again. "Why not, Bill? Asking if Nancy had a diary seems like a good idea."

Bill said in a gruff tone, "Why? What good would that do? What could *her* diary tell us we don't already know?"

Alexandra put out the dessert plates. "Bill, it may not say much, but it would be interesting to get Nancy's side of the story."

I was glad that Alexandra hadn't elaborated on what "story" she referred to. It looked certain that, not having read Margaret's journals, the others did not know what had transpired in Crimea. I felt it was not the proper moment—might spoil their vacation—to go into a discussion about it. It seemed more appropriate for them to learn the details of the incidents surrounding their Grandfather Robert's death in the privacy of their home and to grieve in their own way.

I quickly finished my meal and asked if anyone wished to have another steak or a sausage. All declined, saying they had overeaten, except Greg said, "The filet mignon is delicious. I'll have another small piece, please." I got up, served him, and refilled everyone's drinks.

Alexandra, with help from Jane and Karolina, cleared the table and brought out a freshly baked hot and aromatic apple pie, and a bowl of whipped cream. I rushed in and carried out the tray of percolated coffee and cups. While we nibbled on the tasty dessert and sipped coffee, my thoughts turned towards Greg's daughter, Katya, whom I'd met in Delhi.

"Greg, when did you last see Katya?" I asked.

Greg, although he seemed hesitant at first, replied, "Oh, it must have been about forty years ago. It was just before Karolina and I left St. Petersburg." He glanced towards Karolina and continued, "She was about ten then … lived with her mother. Of course, I didn't tell her I was leaving. You said she worked for the Soviet Embassy in Delhi?"

I nodded. "She'd contacted the Delhi hospital, offering that their government, would be happy to take over Margaret's sea chest."

"Did she say why the Soviets wanted the trunk?" Greg reached for his coffee cup.

"I don't believe so. My chief surgeon, Doctor Rao, inquired with the hospital's Board of Directors and they refused. They wished the trunk to be returned to the rightful descendants of Doctor Margaret. Therefore, I ended up bringing her trunk all the way from Delhi to

Grimsby."

"And we are ever grateful to you for it, Walli," Jane said, sipping her coffee.

"Greg, when did Katya join the Soviet foreign service?" I asked.

"I don't really know. It must have been after she finished university. Her heavily censored letters were few and far between. However, I was astonished when you mentioned that she'd written a book! Where was it published?"

"She said she'd had it translated, into English, and published in Delhi. I'll fetch it." I quickly went up to my study and, locating the hardbound volume—which had a red dust cover and title in golden letters, *Lara's Story*—brought it out and handed it to Greg.

He took the book in his hand and, turning it around, examined it with a look of admiration. He flipped through the first few pages and said, "Yes, Walli, you were right. It starts in her great-grandmother's house in St. Petersburg. It seems Lara is unhappy because her husband is leaving on a journey. An interesting beginning, don't you think?"

"Yes, quite so," I replied. "I'm sorry that I've been very busy at the office, I haven't had the time to read it."

Greg sipped his coffee. "Did Katya say it was a true story?"

I thought for a moment and tried to recall what Katya had told me. "I believe she said it was based on her grandmother's life. When I asked her if it was anything like *Doctor Zhivago*, she laughed and said it was much truer than that novel."

Alexandra seemed puzzled. "Bill, now why did Margaret choose to go to India, from Crimea? Why did she not return to Canada or to … New Jersey? Wasn't she originally from there?"

Bill took a sip of wine. "Oh, I'm sure Robert's parents would have wanted her to come back to Grimsby. You know her two children were with them. But her parents had gone to India as missionaries to work at the American Mission at Futteh … how is it called, Walli?"

"Futtehgurh," I answered. "Her father was a Presbyterian minister, was he not?"

Bill nodded. "Yes, and Margaret's mother had taken up a teaching position at the school there."

While finishing dessert and sipping coffee, the conversation moved on to other matters. We discussed current events and other issues concerning the United States, Canada and the rest of the world—particularly the conflict still brewing between India and China.

In the late afternoon sun, it was getting a bit hot, even under the shade of the umbrella in our quaint garden, and I noticed Bill was nodding off. Alexandra suggested he might go inside and rest a bit? Bill readily agreed and getting up walked towards the backdoor; Jane followed him. Greg refilled his wine glass, saying that he would go in to the living room and start reading his daughter's book. Karolina helped Alexandra and I take the empty dishes into the kitchen. While the two ladies washed the dishes, I retired to my home office to look over the files of my patients I was to see on Monday.

*****

The next day our guests departed, to continue on their journey to Florida. They left promising to visit us again, and we undertook to call on them soon in Grimsby. They had taken back Volumes I and II of Doctor Margaret's journals. As requested by the Wallaces, I had drafted in a narrative style, from these volumes, the story of Margaret's life in North America and Europe into a manuscript giving it a working title, Book I: *Doctor Margaret's Sea Chest.* My Book II would cover her life further, and I was anxious to start reading Volume III of her diary.

That evening after dinner, Alexandra and I, wineglasses in hand, sat snuggled together on the living room couch. The journal was in our laps. It was written in flowery, Victorian-style handwriting and started as follows:

Volume III
My Life in India
By
Margaret Wallace

Chapter Two

Arrival in Calcutta

1855, January: Calcutta, India

IN THE MIDDLE OF THE NIGHT, the stillness of the ship woke me. I lay on the narrow bunk bed in the tiny cabin, wondering what could be the matter. After spending weeks—which had seemed nearly a lifetime—rolling and pitching about, and trying to keep my belongings secure in the cupboards, the eerie tranquility was unbelievable. Were we there already? I did not think so, for just that morning the grey-bearded Captain had said, "It's still one more day to Calcutta, ma'am."

Throwing off the covers, I jumped out of bed and peered through the small porthole. In the foggy darkness, I could only discern the outline of some thatched-roofed huts and flickering lights on the shore. Indeed, we had reached our destination! Unable to contain my excitement—and taking care not to awaken the lady who slept snoring on the opposite bed—I put on a petticoat, a dark gown and a bonnet. I made sure that I tucked in my long, fair hair, for I did not wish to get it wet in the mist. I tiptoed out of the cabin and proceeded towards the companionway. Despite the late hour, I could not wait to take a first look at India, the land I had read and heard so much about; the country of my dreams.

As I stepped on deck and walked up to the railing, the warm, misty night air and a rotten eggs like stench, from the floating sewage, engulfed me. Sailors bustled about, shouting instructions to each other, doing the chores needed to anchor the ship, while I stood with my elbows propped on the handrail and gazed out into the steamy, gloomy night. Where were all those lovely buildings I had heard some of the passengers talk about?

"Is Calcutta out there?" I asked one of the sailors.

"No, ma'am. We be just at the mouth of the 'Ooghly. A bit o' the ways to go yet." He touched his cap and hurried along.

So, it would still be some time before I would see my dear parents, sister and brother again. I sighed. While I believed the Calcutta Government House would have informed them of my arrival, I wondered if any of them might be at the docks to receive me. Likely not. For one thing, the American Mission at Futtehgurh was quite a distance up the Ganges River. I was not certain whether even Papa would be able to come all the way down. My thoughts turned to the last time I had seen them.

It was about five years ago, when I had just graduated from the Women's Medical College in Philadelphia. My husband, Robert, had come down all the way from Fort George in Niagara, Canada, to take me back to our first home. He looked very smart in his cavalry officer's red jacket. What is more, he had spared no expense and rented a carriage; we were to travel in style! I had protested that I could have ridden a horse, but he would hear none of it, saying that I had far too many portmanteaux, books and other paraphernalia. Indeed, there was quite a collection of medical books. Although, I suspected he was mostly considering my condition, for I was expecting our first child.

Robert helped me up onto the carriage and followed to sit beside me.

"Shall we go by Elizabethville?" I asked.

"Are you sure?" Robert looked at me with raised eyebrows. From his eyes I knew he wondered if I still wanted to see my parents, even though they had not replied to my letters and attended neither our wedding nor my graduation.

I nodded.

"Well, all right. Going via New Jersey won't be much of a detour. About time we made peace with your parents." Clucking his tongue, he slapped the reins on the horses' flanks and we were off with a jolt.

The next day, by mid-afternoon, we reached Elizabethville. The town did not appear to have changed much during my nearly two-year absence, but tears came to my eyes when I saw the familiar tree-lined street and my childhood home loom ahead. We passed by the Presbyterian Church, where I had listened to countless sermons delivered by my father, the pastor. People were going in for the evening service. My teenage sister, Elizabeth, wearing a faded old dress, stood outside the entrance gate to the house, talking to some friends. I waved to her. Upon seeing me, she immediately turned around and ran along the front path, up the porch steps and into the house. She was just the same.

Robert pulled on the reins and stopped the carriage in front of the gate. We alighted and as we walked on the path up to the house, Mamma and Papa emerged and stood on the porch. Mamma looked her usual tired self, her golden hair all disheveled, wearing an apron over her old blue dress. Papa looked well, dressed in his customary black suit and white collar. He was holding his dark coat in one hand and started to put it on. David and Elizabeth stood next to them, looking curiously at me.

While Mamma did smile and called out our names, Papa said nothing. His stern face said it all. He came down the porch steps.

I hurried to him, and put my arms around his broad shoulders. "Papa!"

"Excuse me, Margaret. I'm late for my sermon." He pried my arms from his shoulders and proceeded to walk towards the gate.

I stood aghast, staring at his back.

"Good afternoon, Uncle," Robert said with a bow, as his father's cousin walked by.

Papa stopped, put his black hat on, and nodded. "Robert." He then calmly strode out of the gate towards the church.

Robert remained motionless, in stunned silence.

Mamma flew down the porch steps and embraced me. I sobbed on her shoulder and she ran her hand over my head, as she used to when I was little. After I calmed down, she led us inside. Ushering us into the parlor, she darted into the kitchen, saying she would put the tea kettle on.

The parlor looked the same. While the furniture showed its age, its arrangement had not changed. On the back of the couch, I saw some rips in the fabric and proceeded to smooth them.

Mamma must have seen me when she came in and said, "Oh, not to worry, Margaret, I'll sew them up soon."

"It looks beyond repair, Mamma. Isn't it about time you got a new set? Look, their legs are about to collapse."

"Yes, dear. We will soon. It's just that your Papa is a little short …" She trailed off, realizing Robert was in the room.

"What's the matter?" I asked. "Are you in financial difficulty?"

"We're not exactly in the poorhouse," she said, looking apologetically at Robert. "It's just that everything costs so much more, and your Papa's salary hasn't increased …" She again grew quiet and stared out of the window.

"But what about your school?" I remembered it had a large enrolment during the time I was a teacher-cum-charwoman there. "Surely there is some income from it?"

She looked at me blankly for a while. "Oh! I suppose you haven't heard. I had to close it. With the opening of much larger institutions around us, there isn't much room for small establishments—" The kettle whistled and she hurried off towards the kitchen.

Now I stood at the railing, wiping the tears that had welled in my eyes from those nearly five years ago recollections, and remembered that it was a year or so later, in Canada, when I had received a letter from Mamma. It was not really a surprise to read that Papa had decided to accept a position at the American Mission at Futtehgurh, India. I was not certain if his decision was entirely due to economic circumstances, for he had been considering serving as a missionary for some time. What was more interesting, Mamma had added that she would be teaching at the orphanage school there. Hence, the whole family were to depart for India shortly.

I was taken out of my reverie when I heard, "Good morning, Margaret. Goodness, you are up early!" A tall person wearing a British officer's uniform—complete with the cross belt and holster—and smoking a cigar, approached me.

It was Colonel Humphrey, an elderly gentleman who, having spent years of service in India, had gone back home and was now returning on another assignment. Being a widower and having daughters in their twenties—about my age—I dare say he had taken a fancy to me. I had not minded his attention, for he was good company during the long voyage. He used to engage me in pleasant conversation and provided me with valuable insight into India, the land and its people. Also, since his constant addressing me as "Mrs. Wallace" was getting rather tedious, I had suggested he call me "Margaret."

"Oh, I couldn't sleep any longer. How about you, Colonel? What brings you up on deck at this hour?"

"I'm usually up early." He stood beside me and took a puff on his cigar. But then, lifting it in the air, asked, "Do you mind?"

"Not at all. The air is much worse than your smoke, Colonel."

He guffawed and, after taking another puff, threw the nearly finished cigar into the water. "Won't be long now before we reach Calcutta."

"I just can't wait. Why are we anchored here?"

"For the tide and daylight, and the pilot, I suppose. You'll see how crowded the river will become. It should be much busier now, with the change of the Governor General about to take place."

"Is Lord Dalhousie leaving?"

"Yes. Being replaced by Viscount Canning, the former Postmaster. I am sure many Indians won't shed a tear on seeing old Dal depart!"

"Why, is he that unpopular? We admire him in Canada. His father served there, you know. How long has he been here?"

"Nearly seven years. To give him credit, from what I've heard, the fellow's a work-hound. Toils at his desk from morning till late into the night, and on other days rides around all over the country. On top of it all, he's waged several wars against the Sikhs and the Burmese."

"Then why is he so disliked here?"

The old Colonel, with both his hands on the railing, stared into the distant shore for a while. "Well," he began, "I wasn't here during his administration. I left with his predecessor, Hardinge. But we did get some disturbing reports in London of his activities."

"What sorts of reports?"

"To be fair, the fellow is only trying to do what he thinks is best for the East India Company and, naturally, Britain as well. He's virtually recreated the government here based on the British model. However, by doing so, he's stepped on many Company officials' toes and annoyed a number of influential natives as well. Although, we have to admit his numerous reforms are for the good of the people. You know, things like building schools and hospitals, like the one you are going to, as well as railways and canals; he brought in the telegraph; and, what's more, he also introduced a system of post offices like back home."

"Post offices!" I smiled. But, a bit confused, I asked, "Er … however, the locals don't like all these changes, do they?"

"Well, for one, he's made a lot of *zemindars* unhappy."

"You mean those tax-collecting landowners, like our squires and lairds? Why should they be unhappy with all those post offices and railways around them?"

"The money for all these expenditures has to come from somewhere!"

Just then, three Indian men—an older person, accompanied by two younger ones—dressed in flowing white robes and carrying small brass tumblers, came towards us. They were probably on their way to the washrooms for their morning ablutions, which I had learned was customary prior to their prayers. I had seen them earlier, but had not met them, for they kept pretty much to themselves. I was informed by another passenger that they were the emissaries of an Indian raja, and were on their way back, having gone to London to plead a case before the East India Company's Board. They put their palms together and bowed to us.

"Good morning, Mr. Bapurao. Sorry to hear that your petition was not accepted," Colonel Humphrey said, facing the eldest.

"What can poor people do, Colonel sahib?" he said with a sad face. "It's the *Sarkar's* wish. Our raja will have to give up his kingdom."

"Cannot be helped. The Dalhousie Doctrine of Lapse applies to all, you know," Colonel Humphrey said.

The three did not say anything, but looked at me inquisitively. In fact, one of the younger men, who sported a huge handlebar moustache, stared at me with his dark, piercing eyes.

Colonel Humphrey quickly introduced me. "This is Doctor Wallace, on her way from Crimea to work at a hospital in Delhi."

"Pleased to meet you," I said.

While Mr. Bapurao bowed to me, the younger man, who had been staring at me, remarked something in Hindustani to the other man, who snickered.

"What did you say?" Colonel Humphrey bellowed, and in a flash, like an expert boxer, with his right fist punched the man hard on the jaw. The man went flying across the bridge and hit his head on the bulkhead, then lay motionless. The Colonel also quickly drew his revolver and pointed it at the men. "Jackasses! You didn't think I understood Hindustani, did you?"

"Sorry ... Colonel ... sahib," Bapurao stammered. "He ... no say

... bad thing."

"Why, yes he did! Most disrespectful to this young lady." Colonel Humphrey waved his pistol. "Be off, you dogs, before I call the Captain and have you put in chains."

The two men quickly picked up the third and dragged him away.

All this time I had stood mesmerized. Finally regaining my composure, I asked, "What did the man say, Colonel?"

"Something about the Crimean widows. You needn't bother yourself." He holstered the revolver.

"No, I wish to hear. What about the widows?"

"If you must know, rumor has been going around that the British are sending the Crimean widows to India to convert the young men!"

"How thoughtless of them. Thank you, sir, for standing up for me," I said. Then, wishing to change the subject, I inquired, "And the Dalhousie's Doctrine of Lapse? What's that all about?"

"The Doctrine affects the raja, or the ruler of a state under the East India Company's influence, who dies without leaving a direct male lineal heir. Hence, as there is no monarch, the state is 'lapsed' and annexed by the Company."

"And what is the reason given for such a policy? Is the ruler not permitted to choose a successor?"

"No. Avoidance of possible mismanagement by the beneficiary is the main justification."

"How about adopted children? Are they not permitted to take over the throne?"

"No. They are not recognized as legal heirs. Although, from what I've read in some of the petitions, the Indians consider adoption a long-standing tradition, and claim it to be legitimate."

It sounded like a peculiar policy. More like a land grab, I thought but, mindful of the Colonel's rank, didn't express my view. I simply asked, "Has Lord Dalhousie applied this policy to many states?"

"Yes. And quite forcefully, too. In the last few years, at least five kingdoms were taken over. These men you just met were representatives of one such state. It's all for the good of the natives, you know," he replied solemnly. He took his cigar box from his jacket pocket, and turned towards me. "I say, would you mind? I need to have a smoke."

I shook my head. While the Colonel proceeded to light up, I

looked across the river to the bank, which in the increasing light had begun to show signs of life. A cool morning breeze blew over the waters and across the ship.

The events of that morning had distressed me. Wrapping my shawl about me, I faced the Colonel. "Would you excuse me, sir? I am a little tired and should return to my cabin."

"Why, yes, of course, Margaret. Do get some rest before breakfast. Are your parents coming to receive you?"

"I hope so, sir." I wished the Colonel a good day and, thanking him again for defending my honor, walked towards the companionway.

One deck below, I made a quick stop at the privy and proceeded to my cabin. I was happy to be sharing it with a non-commissioned officer's wife. I had travelled by ship from Crimea to Alexandria and then via train to Cairo, followed by a bumpy carriage ride to Suez. There the Captain of this vessel had asked me if I would mind travelling in the cabin with a sergeant's wife, for it was the only berth available. I assured the Captain that I had no qualms about it. It was either that or having to wait some weeks for another ship. I wished to be with my parents as soon as possible.

"Is that you, Margaret?" a sleepy voice from the far bunk asked when I entered the cabin. Then, upon seeing me, she said, "Aww … you've been up on deck already, have ya?"

"Yes, Mrs. Willoughby. I couldn't sleep," I replied while undressing.

"But in your condition? You ought to be more careful going up and down the stairs in the dark."

"I was careful, Mrs. Willoughby. It's getting light already."

"Are you all right? And the baby? It won't be long now, will it?"

"Yes. I'm well, and the baby too. Another five months to go, I believe."

"Aww … won't it be so nice to 'ave your mother at 'and. It's your fourth one, isn't it?"

"Third," I corrected her. I recalled having told her that a few times already, as I slipped into my bed.

"Two for me were enough. I'm glad I left 'em behind with me mum and dad. They'll get proper education there. But, you know what, I'm beginnin' to miss them already. Did you say you were goin' to bring your two over from Canada?"

I was starting to doze off, and the mention of my children brought a lump to my throat. I barely managed to reply, "They are with their grandma. I'll try to have them sent over, as soon as I've found decent accommodation and a school for them in Delhi."

"You'll have no difficulty, you being a doctor an' all. My Frank, 'e's only a sergeant, y'know. We can't afford to have the childa here on his pay, he tells me. But I say to him, the good Lord giveth and families ought to stay together. But you know, life is difficult here, amongst these strange people. Did you know they don't like to eat our food? Think it's polluted or somethin'. Will break their caste, they've told me. Fear they'll be reborn as a monkey or somethin' or the other. But I tell them …"

She kept talking on and on as I wiped more tears. Finally, when sleep was taking me away into a dream world, I was able to say, "Goodnight, Mrs. Willoughby."

"Goodnight, Margaret. Do rest up. You've a long journey ahead of ya. Is your father goin' to be at the dock?"

I believe I fell asleep before I could reply in the affirmative, possibly fearing that it might be a lie.

This time, it was the motion of the ship and sounds of shuffling feet on the deck above that woke me. It seemed as if I had slept barely five minutes, but judging from the bright sunlight shining through the porthole, it must have been longer. I noted Mrs. Willoughby had already left, and her trunk and other boxes looked packed and ready for disembarkation. I had crammed my sea chest earlier, but a few more things remained to go in there.

I went to the tiny washbasin in the corner. Mrs. Willoughby had thoughtfully left fresh water in the jug. I quickly washed myself and put on a clean blue dress. Running a comb lightly through my hair, I made sure the ringlets still held in place. I put on the straw bonnet—purchased at a bazaar in Alexandria—for it was already stifling hot in the cabin and likely hotter outside in the sun. Stuffing the remaining items into my sea chest, I locked it. I made certain I did not leave behind my dear Robert's service revolver, and placed it in the portmanteau. Reticule in hand, I strode out of the cabin. The aroma of brewing tea guided me towards the dining room, for I was hungry even for the watery soups, biscuits, salted pork or beef and dried fruits for dessert, served all during the voyage.

After a refreshing breakfast—or lunch, rather—I went up on deck to join the crowd at the railing. All were eager to get a first glimpse of Calcutta, while the ship gently maneuvered its way up the river. Slowly the scenery along the banks changed. The continuous rows of mud huts with thatched roofs gave way to sizeable buildings. Just as the Colonel had predicted, the waterway was swarming with vessels of all types. Finally, the buildings of Calcutta loomed ahead. Beyond the onion-shaped domes of mosques, pyramid-style temples, and stone structures of larger edifices were visible. They reminded me a bit of London's skyline, which I had seen when travelling up the Thames Estuary, from Canada with my dear Robert—a lifetime ago, it seemed.

A shrill sound, the likes of which I had never heard, startled me from my thoughts. I looked around at the other passengers' faces, wondering if they knew what the problem was. Had our vessel run aground? However, all seemed calm as ever, as if this was a common sound one heard regularly.

"It's nothing, Margaret," a familiar voice called out to me from behind. It was my mentor, Colonel Humphrey. "It's only the sound from a conch shell being blown by one of the priests in the temple, yonder. Listen, there it is again."

True enough, the strange shrieking noise came again. I peered in that direction and noticed a priest, wearing only a dhoti and white paint marks over his forehead and arms, standing at the embankment, a conch in hand. Behind him, the rose-colored temple loomed at the top of wide stone steps leading up from the water.

"Thank you, Colonel. With this welcome, I believe my introduction to India is now complete?"

"It never is. India is a fascinating country. It's full of different customs, religions and novelties. You will encounter something new every day." He withdrew his pocketbook and, opening it, said, "Margaret, in case I do not see you at the wharf, here's my card. Do call on me whenever you are in Calcutta."

"Thank you, sir ... er ... Colonel Humphrey. I will," I said, although I did feel a bit apprehensive at him paying so much attention to me.

The ship dropped anchor in midstream and the passengers were ferried across in tenders that plied from the ship to the quay. I tried to spot my parents among the throng of people lined up at the dock, waving at us. After a while, I gave up, for it seemed a futile attempt to locate them, and moved towards the line-up for the ferryboats.

There was a tap on my shoulder. It was the portly Mrs. Willoughby. "Margaret! I've been lookin' all over for you." She sounded out of breath. She handed me a slip of paper. "Here's our address in Delhi. We're in the Civil Lines. I know it will be a while before you get there, but as soon as you are there, do visit us. Frank and I will be delighted to see you."

I accepted her note and, opening my reticule, took out a paper and searched for a pencil. "Here, Mrs. Willoughby, let me give you my parents' address in Futtehgurh."

"Aww ... not to worry. I know exactly where they are. My Frank goes to the military station there ever so often."

"Good. Please do look in on us, whenever you are there."

"We surely will. Now let me find a porter. Do you want your luggage brought up too?"

"Yes, please. Here, let me pay you for him." I tried to fish for some coins in my reticule.

"Aww ... not to worry about that." She kissed me goodbye and hurried off.

Soon enough the tender, filled with anxious travelers, thumped the side of the wooden jetty. The small boat rocked as the passengers scrambled up the dock's steps. I climbed up slowly, holding the hem of my dress in one hand and the handrail with the other. Eventually I emerged onto the pier, followed by two red-turbaned porters who had carried up my sea chest and portmanteau. They placed the luggage at my feet and, putting their palms together, bowed and scampered back to the tender.

Just then, nausea and extreme tiredness overcame me. I cannot say whether it was due to the bright sun or not getting my land legs yet. The sea chest looked inviting enough and I tried to sit on it, but could not stay there and slipped down onto the ground. I recall hearing shouts and screams and the sound of feet running around me, but nothing else. I had passed out.

The next words I heard were someone calling my name. "Margaret, Margaret! Are you all right?" It was dear Papa. Squatting down beside me, he held me in one arm. What looked to be a bottle of smelling salts was in his other hand.

"Papa!" I cried and, putting my arms around him, sobbed.

A crowd had gathered. Seeing that I had been revived, they clapped and cheered.

A gentleman who looked to be in his early forties, dressed in a white suit and a pith hat, also knelt beside Papa. "I see your daughter seems to be all right, James. Shall we get her into the carriage?" he said in a slight Scottish accent.

Papa kissed me on the forehead and asked, "Are you well, Margaret? Can you get up?"

I nodded and both Papa and the other person helped me up. There was more clapping and cheering from the onlookers, as I trudged towards a waiting carriage. Helping me onto a seat, Papa sat next to me, while the gentleman took the opposite bench.

I put my head on the side of the padded, dark leather seat. Although I had regained full consciousness, overcome with too much emotion, I could not speak. Papa looked just the same. Despite the heat, he was still dressed in his dark suit and cravat, although he had put on a beige pith hat. His blonde moustache looked neatly trimmed on his square-jawed clean-shaven face.

We looked at each other for a while. I believe he was also speechless, likely from seeing his long-lost daughter faint before his eyes.

I finally said, "You look funny in that hat, Papa."

He laughed. "Your Mamma makes me wear it! Now are you certain you are fit to travel, Margaret? Shall we get you to a hospital?"

I shook my head. "I'm all right, Papa. It was only the sun." I must have smiled, for the heat was not the only reason.

The gentleman leaned forward and examined my eyes closely. "Hmm … yes. I think you are healthy enough. But, we will have to get you one of these." He touched his hat. "Although it is the cold weather season, the sun is still fierce."

Porters secured my baggage at the back of the landau and it rolled forward. As I looked out of the window, I was jolted to see the same three Indian men, one with a swollen jaw, standing on the side of the road. While Colonel Humphrey might have overreacted, showing off his boxing skills, I did feel that the young man had no right to make such a lewd remark about me. They glared as the carriage rolled by. I had a strange feeling that I would likely see them again.

"Of course, she could use a sun-hat. Can't have one of your staff fainting on you, Edward, can you?" I heard Papa say. "Margaret, meet Doctor Stewart."

"So pleased to meet you, Doctor Wallace." Doctor Stewart extended his hand.

"Likewise." I shook his hand, rather astonished. "Have you come all the way from Delhi, sir?"

"Oh, no, no. I'm here with the Calcutta Medical College. The new hospital in Delhi, which you have been recruited for, is under the Indian Medical Service. We are part of it. It's all due to the efforts of our GG, Lord Dalhousie, you know."

Papa asked, "Isn't he due to retire?"

"Yes, unfortunately, after doing so much good work here."

I remembered the not-so-good work the Earl had done, which Colonel Humphrey had mentioned. However, I bit my tongue and simply nodded.

Doctor Stewart continued, "I am not your supervisor, Doctor Wallace. You will meet him in Delhi. I am more like a liaison officer. When we heard of your arrival, we telegrammed your father. I know Reverend James is anxious to return to his work at the Mission, but my wife, Moira, and I would be delighted if both of you would spend some days with us. To help you recuperate from your long journey."

Papa smiled. "That's so kind of you."

"Doctor Wallace, may I offer my heartfelt condolences on the sad loss of your husband. We heard about his heroism in the Charge of the Light Brigade. Such a dreadful war in Crimea." He mopped his brow.

His kind words brought tears to my eyes, although I was certain he did not know of the treacherous way in which my Robert had died. I could barely whisper, "Thank you, sir. Please call me Margaret."

Papa squeezed my arm in a conciliatory gesture.

Feeling tired again, I rested my head on the side of the cushioned seat and looked out of the window. We were travelling in a southerly direction, on a road that wound its way along the riverbank. It felt like going back on the route the ship had travelled. The scenery looked familiar; only now, the masses of pedestrians in various clothing, the passing carriages and bullock carts all were real, not like dots I had seen from the ship.

We passed by a large fort, with thick, octagonal-shaped walls of brick and mortar. It seemed strong enough to repel even a combined armada of the French and Spanish fleets.

Doctor Stewart informed me, "It's Fort William—but the second one, mind, built in 1780."

"Really! What happened to the first one?" I asked.

"That one is in the city. It's a much older—1701, I believe—a mud structure. Most of it has crumbled by now. They are planning to replace it with a post office."

"Is the Black Hole still in there?" Papa asked in a solemn voice.

"Yes, a bit of the jailhouse, and some walls, are still standing. A monument erected by Lord Clive disappeared quite mysteriously. The native nationalist groups are all denying any involvement," he said with a smile. "Government House seems to be at a loss on deciding how to preserve the memory of those one hundred and twenty-three souls who perished there."

"That many people suffocated in there?" Papa asked.

"Yes, that was the number reported by Holwell, the fort's commander at that time. Although some dispute his count. I can take you there, if you wish."

"Yes, I would very much like to visit there, since so much has been written about it."

While they engaged in a philosophical discussion on the causes of that incident, I continued to look out of the window. It seemed we were approaching a more affluent part of the city. Rows of well-constructed, single-storied houses appeared, each having a wraparound porch like those in our southern states. Their manicured lawns and attractive gardens gave the neighborhood a distinct European look. Although smart carriages drove in and out from the homes, few persons walked in the streets.

Our landau turned sharply into the semicircular driveway of a pleasant-looking single-story house, and stopped at the front porch. Two persons dressed in native clothing—the loincloth and turban, but with shirts on—dashed from the house and opened the carriage doors. Doctor Stewart led the way and ushered us into a spacious drawing room.

Moira Stewart, wearing a green dress, came bustling out from what likely was the kitchen. Doctor Stewart introduced her. She was a young-looking woman with flaxen hair and deep blue eyes. She called for another servant, apparently the bearer, and asked him to fetch tea. The drawing room was cheerily decorated in a mixture of Western and Eastern furniture. Nevertheless, what intrigued me was the short wall hanging—a small tapestry—suspended in the middle of the room, strung over a bamboo pole from one end of the room to the other. I liked the cane sofas and chairs with their colorful cushions we sat on. In my heavy gown, I felt uncomfortable in the heat, and fanned myself with a magazine.

Moira must have noticed that and called to one of the servants, "*Punkha-walla ko lao.*" [call the fan man]

I wondered what that was all about, but thought no more of it as tea arrived. Being famished, I started to devour the delicious Indian snacks. However, soon enough the mystery of the *punkha-walla* was revealed. Through the bay window, I observed a small boy arrive on the veranda. Sitting in a cross-legged position, he pulled on a rope. Lo and behold, the tapestry hanging above us began to swing, much like a fan, to and fro. Just the slight motion of the air in the room made us comfortable and enabled making conversation much pleasanter.

We had arrived on a Friday, and although the Stewarts insisted that we stay longer, Papa informed them that two more days was about the most he could spare away from the Mission. Hence, it was planned that the next day we would just take a short trip across the river to Calcutta's renowned Botanical Gardens. The following day, being a Sunday, we would naturally start by attending the morning service at the church, and then take a leisurely drive about the city, visiting the famous landmarks. We intended to depart for Futtehgurh on Monday. Although a train service ran almost up to Allahabad, we would still have to take a day's coach ride from there on to Futtehgurh. Doctor Stewart, observing my advanced state, advised against the train and the coach travel. While it would take longer, it was decided that we should travel by sailboat, up the Ganges, all the way to Futtehgurh.

Tea being over, Moira led us to our rooms. Separate bedrooms were assigned to Papa and me. Though we protested and said we could share a room, the Stewarts would hear none of it. Their children being away at school in England, they had several bedrooms to spare. When we mentioned the extra cleaning and washing, Moira's response was, "What are servants for?"

My large and airy bedroom was charming. The furnishings were bright and colorful with Indian patterns, which looked comforting. It was most likely her daughter's room, for I saw some toys and picture books on the shelves. The furniture was made of the same cane that I had admired earlier. Large French doors opened out onto the veranda, which led to an inviting garden beyond.

Moira must have noticed that I looked tired and suggested that I take some rest, which I readily agreed to do. My sea chest and portmanteau had already been placed in a corner of the room.

As I drifted off in a fitful slumber, needless to say, I was overjoyed at Papa having come to receive me at Calcutta. Earlier, during a quiet moment when we were alone in the room, he had apologized for his past indifference towards me, which stemmed from my having married Robert. He offered his deepest sympathy on Robert's death. Was it my dear husband's demise that had brought my father back to me, I wondered.

The next day, thankfully, the Stewarts had not laid out an early start for the day of sightseeing, for I slept past sunup. Actually, I would have slept longer, if it had not been for the cooing, shrilling and squawking sounds of the numerous birds that flew about in the garden.

Pushing the mosquito netting aside, I got out of bed. Putting on my pink housecoat, I opened the French door to the veranda and the cool morning breeze blew in and brought with it the fragrances of the exotic flowers and fruits growing in the garden. I inhaled the fresh air. The sun was just rising above the trees and I noted several riders, already out for their morning jaunt, galloping along the river.

I ambled onto the veranda, and noticing a path running through the garden, I decided to follow it. The trail lay between fruit and other kind of flora. I was engrossed in trying to determine their type and names, when I found myself at the low boundary wall; beyond lay the road. I was returning to the bungalow when I noticed a rough looking young man, carrying a basket, run from one end of the garden, jump the wall and scamper away down the road. It looked as if he was stealing fruit, but I thought I recognized him to be one of the three Indian men from the boat. But I could not be certain, and hurried back to my room.

As it was getting late, I went to the corner of the room and, opening the sea chest, bent down to search for an appropriate dress for the day.

I heard a slight hissing and rustling sound from the top of the bed, a few feet away. I turned around and noticed the long, thick tail of a snake slithering on the silk bedcover. It must have spotted me, for it rose about a quarter of its length and displayed its ugly head through the parted mosquito net. It was a cobra.

I felt trapped. Being in the corner of the room, I could not have run out to either the garden or into the house. I dared not scream, for I knew it would then strike me instantly. There was only one thing left to do. The portmanteau lay on one side of the coffer. I gently slid my hand into it and, grasping the handle of the revolver, pulled it out. I stood up slowly; watching the cobra all along, I raised my arms, holding the revolver in both hands. The cobra teased its vile tongue in and out of its mouth. I knew I would get only one shot.

I took careful aim. With the cobra's fan-shaped mouth in the gun sight, I pulled the trigger. The revolver went off with a loud roar. I was thrown back onto the open sea chest. I looked up at the bed, but the snake was not on it. Thinking that I had missed and now the cobra was upon me, I fainted.

The sounds of rushing feet and everyone calling out my name brought me back to the world. I watched Doctor Stewart go to the other side of the bed and hold up the snake—its mouth shattered—by the tail.

"Where did you learn to shoot like that, Margaret?" he asked.

"Are you all right, Margaret?" Moira and Papa asked in unison.

I assured them that I was well and, although bewildered, was energized by the sight of the dead snake. The Stewarts mentioned that while they did not have snakes come into their home every day, it was not uncommon. However, they rarely bit anyone, and normally were scared away by the stamping of feet or sticks. That sounded strange to me, for this one seemed ready to pounce on me.

The excitement of the day over, after a hearty breakfast we piled into the waiting landau for our trip to the famous Botanical Gardens. During the carriage ride I told the Stewarts—what I had mentioned to Papa last night—about the altercation on the boat, with the three Indian men. I also remarked that I thought I had seen one of them in their garden that morning, but could not be certain.

"Oh, we have young men scurrying through our orchard, either taking a shortcut or helping themselves to the fruit, all the time," Moira said. "It probably wasn't that man from your boat, for how would he know you were staying here?" I agreed.

"Yes. The appearance of that cobra in your bedroom might be a bit of a coincidence, but I'll inform the *chaukidar* and keep my eyes open as well for those three scoundrels you've described," Doctor Stewart assured me.

It was very thoughtful of Moira to have lent me one of her pith hats—which she later asked me to keep—for the blazing sun that day was the fiercest I had ever experienced. The gardens were situated on the other side of the river, and we took a boat across. From the *ghat*, they were a short carriage ride away. While our carriage passed through some rather disagreeable-looking villages— a collection of mostly mud huts—the splendor of the Botanical Gardens made the journey worth the trouble of getting there. Doctor Stewart, refused the services of a guide, preferring to conduct the tour all by himself. No doubt, being a scientific person, he was intimately familiar with the abundant variety of plant life growing at the grounds.

The most imposing sight there was the Banyan tree. Being more than fifty years old and with its aerial roots spreading over twenty feet, it was the largest in the world, Papa and I were informed. Other notable sights were a large collection of palm trees from all over the world, clusters of bamboos with feathery flowers that swayed in the wind, and a very interesting display of ferns and cacti. Walking along the many ponds, we looked at various types of lilies and other aquatic plants.

One would have needed weeks or months to examine and admire each of the exotic flora, especially having such a well-informed guide as Doctor Stewart. He would pick up a leaf or hold a flower in his hand and go into a lengthy discourse on the characteristics of its variety over the other species, which I found interesting—having liked botany at college—but it made Papa's eyes gloss over; with a nod, he would move on to the next flower bed.

Due to the lateness of the afternoon, there was not enough time to look through the most exquisite collection, which was tendered in the orchid house. I must have seemed disappointed, and Moira invited me to return to Calcutta soon with a promise to bring me back there.

The next day, feeling still a bit tired from the sea voyage and yesterday's trip to the Botanical Gardens, I would have slept longer, if it had not been for a strange sound emanating intermittently from the veranda, as if a child was rolling a toy up and down the boards. I hurriedly put on my dressing gown and, drawing the curtain aside, peeked through the window. I saw an elderly native man, dressed in a white shirt and pajamas, sitting cross-legged before a sewing machine. He operated it by rolling its wheel with one hand and, while holding the material between the fingers of the other, fed the cloth through the bobbing sewing needle. Yards of colorful muslin lay around him and beside him was an open catalogue of color pictures of European dresses. I watched in amazement, as occasionally he would expertly hold the half-finished dress between the toes of one extended leg and the fingers of one hand to measure or align the material. How convenient, I thought, to have your dressmaker sitting at your very own doorstep.

I was almost dressed when Moira came bustling in. "Good morning, Margaret. I hope the noise of the sewing machine didn't wake you?"

I returned her greeting and said, "No, not at all. I should have been up ages ago. Is that your very own tailor?"

"No, he comes when called. I need to get some new dresses made and a gown for the GG's Spring Ball, coming up soon. Ordering clothes from home is so expensive."

"He can make European clothes, can he?"

"This man's a genius. Just give him the material, your measurements and a picture of the garb, and voila, he'll have it ready in no time." Then, looking at my dress, which fitted rather snugly around my belly, she said, "By the way, do you wish to have any of your clothes let out a bit?"

"Why, yes, of course. But I was thinking of doing it myself or getting Mamma to do it."

"Well, why don't we get this man to do it?"

"No, Moira. I wouldn't dream of imposing on you. Besides, wouldn't it delay your work?"

"Nonsense. It's no imposition at all. My stitching can wait. Get your dresses and let's go talk to him." She opened the door to the veranda and stepped out. I opened my trunk to pick out three of my frocks that were beginning to get really tight on me. I heard her say to the tailor, "*Darzi-ji aap ko eak our kaam hai …*" [tailor, one more job for you]

When I came out, clothes in hand, she said to the man, "Here is memsahib. Come from America. *Maloom?*"

The old man, putting his palms together, nodded to me. It seemed he knew where America was.

Moira continued and said, "Dress make big." She put her palms around her waist and extended them out. "You understand. *Bara karo.*"

The tailor nodded again and smiled knowingly. Getting up, he took off the measuring tape that hung around his neck. Very carefully, making sure not to touch me, he measured my waist and, moving the tape's end out a bit, looked at me as if to ask if I wished to let the dress out that much. I moved the end a bit more. He nodded again and made a note of the measurement. Moira handed him my dresses and impressed upon him, in her broken Hindustani, that I would be leaving tomorrow and needed the alteration done the same day. From his nodding and bowing, it appeared that he understood the urgency. Later, when I asked Moira the cost of the alteration and offered to pay for it, she did not wish to talk about it.

Moira and I got to the dining room and found Doctor Stewart and Papa already seated at the table. They greeted me, and with a quick "Morning, all," I slid into the chair held out for me by the bearer. Breakfast was a spicy omelet and leavened bread filled with potatoes, which I enjoyed. But I loved the selection of jams and comfitures, especially the guava jelly, which went wonderfully with bread and tea.

After breakfast, Moira showed Papa and me around her well-maintained garden, which extended from the back of the house down to the river having an abundant collection of oriental flowering shrubs and fruit trees. Papa remarked, "It looks to be a small piece carved out from the Botanical Gardens and transplanted here!" Moira smiled in appreciation.

We noted a carriage arriving at the front gate and Moira advised that it was time to go for the service.

It was another lovely day. A bit of cloud cover gave respite from the ever-present blazing sun. The carriage's top had been put down and the horses went clip-clopping on the road along the banks of the Hooghly River, where the tall masts of the moored ships were visible as far up the river as the eye could travel. From the familiar scenery, I deduced that we were travelling northwards towards the town.

"Which church are we going to?" Papa asked. "Is it St. John's or St. Andrew's?"

Doctor Stewart responded, "We usually attend St. John's. It's a larger church, a bit more airy in this heat, you know. It's also nearer, and after the service we can go for the usual stroll on the *Maidan*."

Moira tapped me on the wrist. "Margaret, a Sunday stroll on the *Maidan* is not to be missed. The whole gentry of Calcutta ought to be there. The perfect place to meet people." Then, observing me in my black dress, she immediately remarked, "Oh, sorry. I know you are in mourning. I didn't mean it that way."

"No offence taken, Moira," I said quickly. "I am getting used to being a widow."

Doctor Stewart quipped, "Ah, but don't tell the native princes that you have just arrived from Crimea."

"Oh, you mean, because of that rumor about the Crimean widows?" I asked.

"Ah, I see you've already heard that one!" Doctor Stewart exclaimed.

While Papa and I smiled, Moira shrieked with laughter. She then said, "Edward, why don't we go along the Chowringhee? Show our guests where the affluent live."

Doctor Stewart stood up in a stoop and, turning towards the landau's driver, said, "Chowringhee *chaloo*."

The driver nodded. At the next roundabout on the Garden Reach Road, he made a right turn and, after a short drive, turned left on to the Chowringhee Road. No wonder it was such a renowned thoroughfare. A façade of impressive European-style buildings lined either side of the boulevard, and we could easily have been driving along the streets of London, Paris or Rome. Moira seemed to be intimately familiar with the residences. As we passed them, she called out the names of the occupiers: Lord, Colonel or General so-and-so, including their high-ranking positions in the government. Some of the homes belonged to the heads of well-known business establishments. "Box-wallas," she called them. Sprinkled among them were some native mansions in which resided the raja or *nawab* of such-and-such state. They were no doubt the ones whose holdings had been taken over by the government, for one reason or the other, and were pensioned off.

The road led us straight into the heart of Calcutta and the coachman stopped the carriage before the entrance to St. John's Church.

As I was admiring its tall, fluted spire, Moira whispered, "Does it not remind you of London's St. Martin-in-the-Fields?"

I nodded. "Although my husband and I were in London for only a few weeks, Moira, many of the buildings here bring back fond memories."

The service, as expected, was attended by most of the Christian notables of Calcutta. The church was filled to capacity with the well-turned-out congregation, women in elegant gowns, officers in their colorful uniforms, and civilians in smart suits. The many native children, who peeked at us from the corners of the windows, must have found our faces, beet red due to the heat, amusing. Although a few *punkhas* swung to and fro, they barely moved the stifling air, and I found the closed, hot atmosphere excruciating—so much so that I could not concentrate and heard barely half of the sermon.

The service was mercifully short and we soon stepped out of the church, the ladies fanning themselves vigorously, and piled back into the waiting carriages. As we drove off, I heard some abuse in Hindustani being meted out to the driver of a neighboring coach by a well-dressed gentleman. Moira later explained that the expletives were being rained on one of the poor servants for he had not been at the carriage when the owners had returned. He had possibly wandered off for some tea.

As soon as we reached the *Maidan*, I realized the reason for it being called the "Lungs of Calcutta". It looked to be a huge park, comparable to New York's Central Park or London's St. James'. Refreshing air blew across the green turf, which extended from the banks of the river and Fort Williams on one side to the Chowringhee Road on the other. Just as Moira had said, the gentry of Calcutta, having attended the services at their respective churches, poured out of carriage after carriage and strode along the many walkways.

Moira had the carriage halted at the north end of the *Maidan*, for she wished to visit the Eden Park there, particularly to show us a recently built Burmese pagoda that had been acquired after the conquest of Burma. It indeed looked exquisite, between the ferns beside a pond, but was a stark reminder of the powers of the British Empire. Later we strolled by the impressive ramparts of Fort William. However, a look inside was postponed for a later time, as it would have taken some hours to see all the armaments on display there.

On our walk, we encountered many friends and acquaintances of the Stewarts, who kindly introduced Papa and me to them. All seemed happy to meet us and engaged us in pleasant discourse. Before parting, most presented us with their card with an invitation to call on them whenever we were next in the city.

As we turned back towards the carriage, for we still had some locales in the city left to visit, I heard a voice from behind call out my name. I turned around and a broad smile must have lit up my face when I saw it was the tall and erect Colonel Humphrey, smartly dressed in a blue uniform and hat, waving his swagger stick in the air.

He approached us and, after shaking his hand, I introduced him around.

Doctor Stewart seemed to remember him and said, "Welcome back, Colonel."

"Which regiment are you with, Colonel?" Papa asked.

"None as yet. I'm actually on Dal's staff."

I saw Moira's eyes light up. "Why, that's wonderful. Would you be attending the GG's Spring Ball?"

"I might," he said and then, turning to me, asked, "Why, Margaret, I thought you would be upcountry by now."

"I might have been, sir, if not for the kind hospitality of Moira and Doctor Stewart."

"I'll be on a tour up to old Delhi pretty soon."

I smiled at him. "Would that be on business or holiday?"

"A bit of both. Have to investigate some petitions from folks disputing their treatment. Nasty business, this annexation."

Doctor Stewart asked, "Are we annexing any more states?"

"Can't say what Dal or the new man, Canning, have in mind. This is some old stuff. Bithur and Jhansi."

"Is the Nana still not satisfied with the answers?"

"Apparently not. Has sent his man, what's the name … Azzi … or somebody, all the way to India House in London!"

"Well, Jhansi is not too far from us," Papa said. "Trust you'll stop by our humble Mission."

"Yes, I most certainly will. We've been hearing a lot about the good work you Americans are doing at Futtehgurh."

"Will you be meeting the Rani?" Moira asked.

"I'd like to, if she'll see me. But then again, may not actually *see* her. The old girl stays in *purdah*, you know," the Colonel said with a chuckle.

"What's happening in Delhi, Colonel?" Doctor Stewart asked, likely wishing for some insider information.

But the Colonel was not letting us in on anything. He simply replied, "Oh, have a chat with old Zafar. Make him feel like the Mughal Emperor he thinks he still is. We used to go on partridge hunts together. He's a damn good shot. Used to be able to hit a bird from horseback."

"Will your daughters be joining you here, Colonel?" Moira asked.

"Don't think so. They have their own lives. Children and husbands to look after … those sorts of things. I'll have to bach it here. But look, I've held you up long enough. I'm sure Margaret and Reverend James have lots more to see. You have my card, Margaret, don't you?"

I nodded. The Colonel left after bidding us good day and a safe journey.

It was past noon when we got back into the carriage. We drove for *tiffin* to the Grand Hotel, which was situated in a Victorian-style building. From its wide-stepped entrance and the hustle and bustle in the well-appointed lobby, I imagined it would have cost quite a bit to stay there. While the restaurant was charmingly decorated in an Eastern style, the cuisine was mostly British. It being Sunday, roast beef and Yorkshire pudding were the main features of the day. All the walking had made me very hungry and I enjoyed the four-course meal, served by polite Anglo-Indian staff.

After the fortifying lunch, it was time to visit the city. As we neared the center, the first imposing edifice Doctor Stewart pointed out was the Government House. Being the offices and residence of the Governor General, it was the seat of the East India Company, but more so the British power in India. I thought its central dome was what signified its importance. It was in there, Moira informed us, where all the magnificent balls were held.

We passed by many other prominent buildings, including the impressive structure of the Calcutta Medical College and Hospital where Doctor Stewart said he worked and I should visit on my next trip to Calcutta. After a round of the city streets, Doctor Stewart asked the carriage driver to stop at Tank Square, where we alighted. Around the tank, or pond rather, was where the original village had once stood; over time, it had become ringed by impressive European-style buildings.

We stood in front of a large, very Mediterranean-looking building.

Doctor Stewart said, "This is the Writers' Building, the offices of the East India Company."

"Why is it called that?" I asked.

He laughed. "Most likely because the many clerks, called 'writers', sit there writing business agreements, receipts and such."

"They'll be writing a lot more with all the expansion that's going on," Moira said.

"Really, like where?" Papa asked.

"I've heard Oudh's next," Moira said.

"Yes, I'm hearing rumors to that effect as well. Apparently the GG is not happy with the way the Nawab is managing his affairs," Doctor Stewart explained.

That puzzled me. "I don't see why the East India Company should meddle in his affairs."

Doctor Stewart merely shrugged. "Do you wish to see the old Fort Williams—what's left of it?"

I nodded and Papa said, "And, pray, could you take us by the Black Hole as well?"

Doctor Stewart looked inquiringly at Moira. "All right, Edward," she agreed. "I've finally got the courage to see and hear the death knell of all those unfortunate Europeans who were imprisoned there."

I wanted to see it as well. I was curious about that place, for I did not know the full story behind it. As Doctor Stewart led the way, I caught up to him and asked, "Why were the Europeans imprisoned?"

"It happened in 1756, Margaret. Until then, the East India Company and their staff, mostly British, had been permitted by the

Mughal Emperor to live in peace, for they were considered to be traders. I believe there was a treaty. They'd settled around Calcutta and built Fort Williams. It wasn't much of a fort, really. More like a warehouse, a safe place to secure their goods. A small garrison was also maintained there. However, the Nawab of Bengal, Siraj-ud-Daulah, likely being alarmed at the construction of the fort and the presence of soldiers, decided to capture it. Some say he also had other ideas: to expand his power base and annex a bigger chunk of the disintegrating Mughal Empire. The Company's small force that defended Fort William was no match for the Siraj's army. The fort was taken and the Europeans, who could not flee, were imprisoned there. The rest is history." He concluded the short chronicle with a grim expression.

We crossed a few streets and shortly came upon what looked to be the remains of an old mud building. It seemed that some construction had started at one end, and debris blocked the front of the structure. As entry was difficult, especially for European ladies dressed in voluminous frocks, Doctor Stewart knew of another entryway and waved at us to follow him. We walked behind him, round the crumbling walls, to the rear of the fort, where a small passageway was visible. While some of the people who passed by in the street gave us curious glances, we entered the semi-dark passage in single file.

The air smelled dank and musty, of animal excrement, and it made me wonder if it was a good idea to have gone in there. Sunlight filtered in where the roof had caved in at several spots.

After turning a corner, Doctor Stewart stopped before the doorway of a small room. A board barely hanging sideways on one nail, above the opening, read in faded letters: *Guard Room*. The door had collapsed and lay in small pieces inside the dusty cell.

Papa asked, "Is this it, Edward?"

Doctor Stewart nodded as he walked into the room and we followed.

Moira exclaimed, "Goodness, no windows at all. If it wasn't for those two small openings near the ceiling, it would indeed be a black hole."

My eyes were just beginning to get used to the dim light and I saw Papa pacing the room in measured steps.

"I make it about twenty feet by fifteen at the most. What do you say, Edward?" Papa's voice echoed in the small prison.

"You are about right, James."

"And one hundred and forty-five persons were crammed in here?"

"One hundred and forty-six was the reported number."

"That many? If they managed to squeeze all of them in, it's a miracle that even twenty-three survived that terrible night. Unbelievable," Papa shook his head.

"As I said, James, the count has been disputed," Doctor Stewart said in a calm voice.

"This place is beginning to give me the shivers," Moira said in a shaky voice. "If you all have seen enough, why don't we move on?"

I was starting to feel sick as well, and tears formed in my eyes. "Yes, I agree." I felt horrified, imagining the dead bodies of all those who had suffered and died here.

Papa said, "Before we go, let us pray for all those who died here that dreadful night."

We stood silently in a circle with our heads down and joined hands. Papa recited a prayer for the deceased.

Emerging from the fort into the bright sunlight was like returning into the real world, having travelled, as if in a time machine, into a bygone period. We slowly walked back towards the carriage. It was getting late and the setting sun cast an orangey glow in the clouds approaching from the Bay of Bengal. The numerous birds that had flown around chirping were beginning to take shelter in the trees, likely anticipating the heavy rain shower that was surely to follow.

When we reached the landau, the Stewarts asked if we wished to see some more of Calcutta. I was glad that all declined, for walking in the heat had made me quite weary.

On the drive back, while we sat in the clattering carriage, enjoying the cooler evening breeze and the landmarks, I was still absorbed in the past events at the fort. Wishing to learn some more about Calcutta's history, I turned to Doctor Stewart. "So when did the British retake the fort from that nawab—what was his name?"

"Siraj-ud-Daulah. As a matter of fact, it was in the very next year, 1757. Fortunately, in anticipation of a war with the French, the British had been accumulating a large armada at Madras. Have you heard of Robert Clive?"

I nodded.

"He was just a young man then, having grown up from a Company writer to a soldier. Since none of the senior officers thought that diverting a force towards Calcutta was a good idea, Clive was given command. He sailed with a small force. Would you believe he not only drove the Nawab's forces out of Calcutta, but also scared Siraj so much that he made peace? By February 1757, Fort Williams was back in British hands, and the Company's privileges were renewed and, moreover, extended to things like the permission to use their own money."

"But, Edward, wasn't there another battle at Plassey?" Moira interjected.

"Yes, dear. I was coming to that. It was hardly a *battle*, really."

"Then how did we drive Siraj out of Bengal?" Moira asked, looking perplexed.

"Intrigue, my dear. Intrigue!" Doctor Stewart said with a chuckle.

"Wasn't there a conspiracy of some kind?" Papa asked.

"Yes. Right you are, James. The poor Nawab was betrayed by his own General!"

"Oh, how awful," I said.

"Happens all the time, Margaret. In love as well as in war," he said with a smile.

I thought of something that had happened to me in Crimea, and said, "Yes. I know it only too well."

The others looked at me curiously, as if to ask what I implied. "I mean I've heard of such betrayals. So, did that General kill the Nawab in the battle?" I hastened to add.

"No. That might have meant him endangering his own life in a battle. That General, Mir Jafar—also a relative of the Nawab, by the way—ingeniously, simply kept his divisions out of the battlefield. The Nawab panicked and fled on a camel, leaving Clive to an easy victory over the whole of Bengal."

"What happened to the General?"

"Clive kept his promise all right. While he became the British Governor of Bengal, he appointed Mir Jafar as a nominal Nawab."

"That was Clive's first governorship, wasn't it?" Papa asked.

"Yes. During that term, he was involved in numerous intrigues and wars with the French and Dutch. I believe the earlier Danish settlement, at Serampore just north of us, was purchased. Hence, after restoring order in Bengal, Clive returned to England in 1760.

"Nevertheless, within a couple of years, things here fell apart again. There were mismanagements, corruption and gift-taking within the Company. These and other issues led to a serious crisis in 1764, when the whole Mughal army from Delhi, including the Nawab of Oudh, descended upon Bengal. However, using skillful maneuvers, the British managed to repulse the attackers. Clive was dispatched back to Calcutta, for a second governorship, in 1765."

"My wife's brothers served in the Company and, I dare say, profited greatly," Papa said. "But I've heard that later Clive himself got into hot waters with the British government. What was that all about?"

"Well, you know, Clive was a masterful negotiator. Using the defeat of the Mughal army in the 1764 battle, he negotiated a treaty with the Emperor. In a brilliant move, just for the return of some of the captured territory of Oudh, he had the Mughal Emperor declare the Company as his *Diwani*, the chief tax collector of Bengal. This virtually legalized the Company's power over Bengal but, nevertheless, opened the doors to widespread corruption. Unfortunately, Clive fell victim to that greed as well. Due to ill health, he returned to England in 1767 with a sizeable fortune. For a lad from Market Drayton to have amassed so much wealth was unacceptable in the eyes of the British public. He was tried and although exonerated, having been disgraced, he committed suicide in 1774."

"What a sad ending for a great person," Moira remarked.

"Yes, and a daredevil, I'd say. I heard that he used to scare the townsfolk by hanging upside down from the church's steeples!" Papa chuckled. "Does the Company still transfer, what's it called … the *Diwani* to the Mughal Emperor in Delhi?"

Doctor Stewart laughed. "No. Not anymore, James. Warren Hastings put an end to that a long time ago, although in Delhi, Shah Zafar is paid a large pension. But you know, soon enough …"

While Doctor Stewart and Papa engaged in a discourse on the British India politics, my mind wandered. Tears returned to my eyes as I thought again about the betrayal I had faced in Crimea, which had led to the death of my dear Robert. I wondered what had become of my tormenter, Albert, and if he had recovered enough to return to Canada. I was certain his wife, Nancy—who believed herself to be the prettiest woman in Grimsby—would not have wished to stay much longer at that hospital in Scutari, Turkey. Did she know what her husband had done? I thought not. But I was sure it was she who had enticed my husband, not the other way around, as Albert had claimed. Should I write to her? No—what would be the point? She would never believe me. Perhaps it would be better if I wrote to Robert's mother, Aunt Fiona. But then again, it would only distress her. She would be busy looking after her fruit preserves business and operating the shop on Grimsby's Main Street. A better person of whom to make some inquiries might be Cousin Heather. She was looking after my children, our children, Robert's and mine, the treasures he had left me. His parting gift had been this tiny one growing inside me. How much I missed my Bruce and Vika. I wondered if they were well and remembered their mother at all. Had it been less than a year since I had left them? Goodness, it seemed like a lifetime...

"Look, they have set up the tea table and chairs out in the garden, just as I told them," Moira exclaimed, as the carriage rounded the corner onto the driveway of their *Bengali-kothi*. Not being able to get my tongue around that name, I was glad that it was called a 'bungalow.'

I hurried to my bedroom to wash and change before tea, and was pleased to see the dresses the derzi had altered, neatly folded and left on top of the silk bedspread. I placed them in the sea chest, along with some of my other things in the room, for we were to sail for Futtehgurh the next day.

I had nearly finished changing when there was a knock on the door; at my "come in", Doctor Stewart entered.

"Ah, Margaret, I didn't wish to disturb you. Just want to leave this with you." He held out a white envelope.

I took it from him. "What is it, sir?"

"There is a letter from the Indian Medical Service, confirming your appointment to the Civil and Military Hospital in Delhi, and other information. You will be happy to know that," he glanced at my belly, "they have granted you medical leave. You will be on half-pay until you join them."

"Why, thank you, Doctor. It is so considerate of the IMS. Could you please pass on my appreciation to them?"

"I'll gladly do that. By the way, there is some advance pay in there and a receipt for it. Would you be good enough to sign it and give it to me? I shall deliver it to the IMS office tomorrow."

I scribbled my signature and handed the paper back to him. He must have thought of something and added, "Oh, yes. Your boat ticket, to Futtehgurh, has been purchased and is with your Papa. Please claim the balance of your travel expenses when you reach Delhi."

I said I would, and thanked the doctor again for all his kindness and hospitality.

He left after saying, "Do come out to the garden soon. Tea is ready. Moira had some of those Indian snacks prepared. You'll love the *gulab-jamuns*."

The next morning, it being a Monday, Doctor Stewart left early for the hospital, having wished a farewell to Papa and me the night before. Moira accompanied us in the carriage to the docks, from where we were to embark on a small sailboat for the journey up the Ganges.

There was the usual pandemonium on the pier. Travelers, mostly natives, hurried about, trying to find their vessels. The rich, dressed in colorful clothes, had coolies carrying their luggage, while the poorer ones carried their own, placing some of the trunks even on their heads. We found our boat and, having stowed our luggage in the tiny cabin, came back onto the dock to say goodbye to Moira.

Amid all the hustle and bustle, we found a quiet corner. Moira hugged me and said, "Margaret, dear, do send a telegram of your safe arrival at Futtehgurh. I will be so worried."

I said I would do that, and thanked her again for her wonderful hospitality and all the care and attention. Papa shook her hand and thanked her several times. We parted with her wishing me a safe delivery, and to return to Calcutta to show them the baby. We invited them to visit Futtehgurh soon.

As the yacht sailed away, we watched Moira standing on the pier in a red dress and matching bonnet. She kept waving her parasol until she was reduced to a dot; a rose amidst the sea of humanity.

While we had made many plans for the future, little did we know that the events that were about to unfold would alter our destiny.

Chapter Three

Journey up the Ganges River

1855, January: Ganges River, India

AS THE BOAT SAILED away and we stood watching Calcutta's receding skyline, a wonderful biblical inscription came back to my mind. In the Calcutta Cemetery we had visited, on the marble tablet headstone of Mrs. Louisa Lowrie, wife of one of our first American missionaries, I had read: *"She was lovely in life, and peaceful in death; and now she is blessed"*. I had heard that her husband was the founder of the first American Presbyterian Mission at Lodiana, in Northern India, but I did not know the details.

"How far is Lodiana from Futtehgurh?" I asked Papa.

"It's quite a ways up north of Delhi. A couple of hundred miles from Futtehgurh, I reckon."

"Did Reverend Lowrie also sail up the Ganges River?"

"Yes, part of the way, and it must have taken immense courage for him to do so. To make matters worse, his colleague, Reverend Reed, was also unwell and had sailed back to America. John had to travel alone all the way to Lodiana. He's written a memoir of his travels. A copy is in our Mission library. You may—"

"Hallo. Are you Americans?" a voice from behind us called out.

We turned around to see two other passengers—a European couple—standing behind us. They had just emerged from their cabin. Papa said that we were, and we shook hands with them. They introduced themselves as Patricia and Thomas Wainwright, who owned an indigo plantation near Lucknow. They were a young couple in their mid-thirties, neatly attired in a blue dress and khaki suit, respectively; they spoke in upper-class British accents. We told them where we were from and where we were sailing to. It was good to hear that they would be travelling with us up to Cawnpore. Their destination, Lucknow, was but a short carriage-ride inland, eastwards from there.

"What brought you to Calcutta?" Papa asked.

"A visit, and some business with the Company. My wife wanted to shop, as well," Mr. Wainwright said, and smiled.

"Just a few things. It's near impossible to find any decent garments up north," Mrs. Wainwright said.

Mr. Wainwright laughed. "Half the boxes in the baggage boat behind us are my wife's." He pointed to a smaller boat sailing behind us, laden with luggage and crowded with grinning members of the native crew.

"Why do we need so many people to operate a small sailboat?" I wondered aloud.

Mr. Wainwright smiled and said, "You'll see soon enough, Doctor Wallace."

It did not take long for me to realize that every member of the large group was essential for the journey. By mid-afternoon the wind died down, and made sailing virtually impossible. To remedy the situation, the boats drew closer to the sandy banks, and the teams of boatmen jumped down and pulled the vessels upstream by ropes. I pitied them, for it was definitely hard work, bent double, ankle deep in the sand, with the sun blazing on their backs. On occasion they had to wade or swim across side streams.

The boat's covered main deck consisted of the two tiny cabins and a small sitting area in the back, with cushioned bench seats and a dining table. Most of our daytime was spent there. The crew steered the craft and slept on the open upper deck.

By midday, the wind had picked up, and assisted sailing swiftly on the wide river, while we sat watching the flat farmlands, mostly rice fields—I recognized them from paintings I had seen earlier— that the boat passed by, on either shore. Papa and I conversed with the Wainwrights about our families and so on. Soon, I was getting hungry from the cooking smell that wafted from the kitchen at the front, and was delighted when a light lunch of fried fish and potato chips was served.

"Are you fully settled now on your plantation, Mrs. Wainwright?" I asked, cutting a piece of the fish.

She finished chewing. "Oh, call me Pat, please, we aren't so formal here. No, not quite settled yet. We've been there only a year. The estate belongs to Tom's family."

"And you should call me Margaret, please. We are not ceremonial either," I said.

"And call me Tom, please." He took a swallow from his beer mug. "Father and Mother were here for ages, but have returned home. We run the show now."

"Is indigo a difficult crop to grow?" Papa asked.

"Not really. The Indigofera plant grows quite freely in this climate."

"Is it a single-harvest-a-year crop?" Papa sipped his tea.

"Oh, no. We can collect the leaves up to three times a year. The plant lasts for about two to three years."

"How do you process the leaves?"

Tom smiled. "It's a bit like making wine! They are fermented in large, open-air tanks. Our native workers pedal large wheels to keep the water circulating. Once the dye settles to the bottom of the reservoirs, the water is drained and the sludge made into indigo cakes. But you know, you have to keep a close eye on the natives …"

While Tom continued telling Papa the details of the indigo-growing and processing business, my mind wandered. I must have been looking at a temple or something on the riverbank when I felt a tap on my wrist. It was Pat.

"When are you going to bring your children over, Margaret?"

"Soon, I expect, Pat. How about you?"

"I am hoping my two can come out this year, although Tom's parents are quite happy to keep them." She took a sip of her wine. "You mentioned your sister and brother are with your mother at the Mission. How many American families are there?"

"I don't really know." I turned towards Papa. "How many families are at Futtehgurh, Papa?"

"Well, there are several British officers and their kin, and four more American missionary families. Let me see—there are the Frasers, Camerons, Johnstons and Macleods." He counted on his fingers. "They all have young children. There'll be no shortage of playmates for you, Margaret," he said, looking at me with a smile. It seemed he still thought of me as his "little child"! This made me laugh.

"That's a fair number, Reverend James. Do you have any native priests?" Tom asked.

"Yes. There are four. Reverend Gopeechand is our longest-serving cleric."

"Really! So, how do the locals look upon your enterprise?" Pat asked.

"They've been reasonably accommodating, especially after we opened the orphans' asylum and schools. Donations have been coming in from several notables. There've been contributions from the Nawab of Furrukhabad, the Maharaja Duleep Singh, and even Colonel Wheeler."

Tom thought for a moment and said, "Duleep Singh. Hmm ... isn't he the last Sikh Maharaja? I thought he is in Lahore."

"Yes, he was there. But soon after the 1849 Sikh war, and the annexation of the Punjab, he was moved to a house in Futtehgurh, along with an English tutor. Mind you, he's only in his teens. I heard he's embraced the Lord, and is in England now. A favorite of the Queen, I understand."

I remembered hearing about the Maharaja when I was in England. "He should be favored, shouldn't he? After all, he gave up his family heirloom, the Koh-i-Noor diamond."

"Oh, I'm told it's an exquisite diamond. The largest one in the world, isn't it?" Pat said.

While we nodded, Tom asked, "Have you had many conversions, Reverend James?"

Papa smiled and replied, "Not as many as we would like. But you know, we have a whole Christian village named Issapur. 'Issa' being the name of our Savior in Hindustani."

I had heard about the village, but Pat and Tom looked inquiringly at Papa.

Papa hastened to explain, "The hamlet has simply grown out of the orphans' asylum we built after the 1837–38 famine. The children grew up, married and settled in the Christian colony."

"Where do all the Christian villagers work? Surely not everyone can be employed in the schools and the church?" Tom asked.

"Yes, you may well ask. Their support and employment was a major issue. Due to religion and caste barriers, it was difficult for them to find work in the neighboring towns and farms. Hence, with some financial help, we initiated two ventures. One, a wool carpet-weaving enterprise, and the other, a tent-manufacturing factory."

"How are those businesses doing?" Pat asked.

"Very well. The tent department has performed beyond expectations. That, of course, is due to the increase in the army garrisons around us and their need for marquees."

Pat had likely consumed too much wine, for she asked after a slight laugh, "Now why didn't your red Indians think of this business, Reverend James?"

Papa smiled, keeping his composure. "I'm not certain, Pat. It seems they preferred hunting, fur trading and other—"

Just then, the *manji* appeared and, while collecting the empty dishes, asked in broken English whether we needed anything else. I felt like another cup of tea and the others thought they would have some more drinks as well. From where I sat, I had a view of the kitchen at the other end of the boat, and saw some of the crew preparing what looked to be a number of different dishes. I thought the fish was delicious, and wondered why they didn't wish to eat it.

"Don't you like fish?" I asked the *manji*.

He shook his head. "No, memsaab. I no eat fish. Only rice, vegetables and dhal."

"What are the other boatmen eating?" I asked.

"Everyone eat different food." He bowed and left.

I noted the Wainwrights were smiling. Looking towards Pat, I asked, "I know I've been in India less than a week, but isn't it strange that not all will eat the same food?"

She patted my arm. "It's a religious thing, dear. Each caste must cook and eat their own food."

"This reminds me of an incident Reverend Olson, of our mission at Allahabad, mentioned when I stopped there on my way down to Calcutta," Papa said. "He told me the story of a native Christian lad, from their orphan asylum, whom Brother Olson had employed at the printing press. But the boy, being something of a slow learner, was relegated to the duties of fetching drinking water from the well. The youngster used to bring it in the usual goatskin bag. It came as a surprise to Brother Olson when, despite the intense heat, some of the workers refused to drink the water brought in, and preferred to go themselves to the well. It seemed they considered the water fetched by a Christian water carrier unclean!"

While everyone had a good chuckle at that anecdote, it dawned upon me that I had a lot more to learn about Indian culture, just as Colonel Humphrey had mentioned.

That evening, the boat docked at Serampore for the night. In the twilight the riverbanks looked picturesque, dotted with trees and green fields. However, from the poor condition of the houses, with their crumbling walls and broken windows, evidently the famous former Dutch colonial town had fallen into disrepair. This was probably from the time of the takeover by the British, in 1845. William Carey, the first English Baptist missionary to arrive in India in 1793, had made the town famous. Carey and his team were renowned for having translated the Bible into several Indian languages and also for having set up schools and colleges. Papa wanted to take a tour of the town to see the Serampore College building and visit Carey's grave but, feeling tired, I declined. Papa and Tom hired a carriage and went for a jaunt about the settlement, while Pat and I retired to our cabins.

I liked Papa's and my cabin; although sparsely furnished, with two bunk beds and a dresser, it was clean and functional. When I slipped into the lower bunk, after saying my prayers, I realized it was many years ago, as a child, that I had last slept in the same room with Papa. I was most happy to note, but dared not mention it to him, that he had changed considerably from his earlier strict disciplinarian ways. Could it be that life in India was mellowing him?

The next morning, I awoke to find we were already underway. The boat must have weighed anchor well before sunrise. I realized this was another feature of travelling in India. In order to utilize the cooler part of the day, journeys began very early. Indeed, a riverboat voyage was by far a more pleasurable journey than it would have been by either carriage or the other most peculiar form, being carried on a palanquin. The latter seemed to be a fairly popular mode of travel. On the roads along the river, we spotted many groups trudging along in that fashion: four bare-chested natives carrying on their shoulders what looked to be a four-poster bed covered with bright material, and the prone occupants.

When not dining or conversing, we spent our time reading, writing or simply watching the scenery on the banks. The countryside through most of Bengal was quite monotonous, in the form of flat farmlands and numerous streams that branched from the main rivers to form the delta. The Ganges is not unlike our

Mississippi River, which traversing the length of the country, forms the delta in Louisiana. Later, as we left Bengal and entered the lands of Central India, the panorama changed, and ranges of mountains could be seen in the background, although the views on the banks were nearly the same. The mud houses of village after village lined the embankments, each having their collection of pyramid-shaped temples and the onion-shaped domes of mosques, peeking behind trees. Every once in a while, it was a change to see some European-looking dwellings with barn-like structures, which Tom informed us, belonged to indigo plantations.

When the boat anchored at some of the smaller villages to pick up provisions, Papa usually took the opportunity to visit the rural community to distribute tracts—translated into several native languages—which he carried in a canvas bag. Sometimes I accompanied him on these walks. As we trudged up the path into the village, ignoring the curious glances and some stares from the natives, soon enough, we usually collected a following of children. At first the little ones would keep their distance, each one shouting a *nameste*, but by and by, having overcome their shyness, they would come closer and even hold my hand.

We thus arrived at the center of the hamlet with Papa leading, much like the Pied Piper of Hamelin, with the urchins and me following behind. The village square was usually dotted with large, shady trees; at the foot of each, village elders clad in turbans sat on *charpoys* smoking *hookas*. Papa would approach them and, after the customary exchange of *namestes*, explain in his smattering of Hindustani that he wished to deliver the words of our Lord to them and would they care to listen? Invariably there were nods all around; the seniors more than likely had heard similar orations before. It being usually past noon, the younger men, having come in from working in the fields, would also begin to congregate in the square, possibly due to the quick-spreading news that a "padre-sahib" was in the village. In a fairly short time, the square would be packed with young and old.

In English, speckled with words of Hindustani, Papa would narrate the Story of Creation. He waved his arms around and with loud noises and pointing towards Heaven and to the ground, indicated how God had created Earth. Using animation, he would go through each of the days of Creation: the placing of land, water and plants separately; the making of the fish and birds; and up to the sixth day, the creation of animals and humans. After counting up to the seventh day on his fingers, he would sit down on the ground, indicating the Sabbath day. From the nodding, it seemed he was generally successful in getting the message across.

Later, with much dynamism, he related the story of Adam and Eve. After sliding his lips on an apple—he carried in his pocket—as if munching it, he would cover his genitals with some leaves in his hands. It usually gave rise to much laughter all around, indicating that they understood the message. However, when Papa showed pictures of our Savior and tried to explain, by stretching his arms on an imaginary cross, how He was crucified for our sins, from the blank faces, I am not sure if the villagers comprehended.

I was not able to help Papa, for I had not learned enough Hindustani by then. Nevertheless, he would save the day by distributing the tracts. As he handed them out, he would stab a finger at the pamphlet saying, "*Kahani*, in here. Read, *purho*." Although the men accepted the leaflets, I am not sure if they were able to read them, for I was to learn later that the literacy rate among them was very low. By then women would appear, their heads covered by the ends of their colorful saris, carrying trays with brass tumblers of tea and plates of sweetmeats. Being thirsty and hungry by then, I loved those snacks.

Pat and Tom, having as a rule gone on a side shopping venture or something, would turn up and wave at us to hurry up, for it was time to board the boat.

One afternoon we reached—at roughly the halfway point of our journey—the fabled city of Benares. Although earlier the *manji*, while clearing away the lunch plates, had informed us of the approaching city where we were to spend the night, its first sight was a wonderful surprise.

Since the city is built on a bend in the riverbank, in a crescent shape, the whole metropolis came suddenly into view. I must admit that having not seen some of the similar European cities, like Venice, it was a thrilling experience to observe the houses built so close to the water's edge. The wide steps of numerous *ghats* led up to colorful temples, behind which stood multi storied dwellings, some up to six levels.

As the boat approached a dock, numerous persons—including women wearing saris—could be seen on the steps of the *ghats*, dipping themselves into the water as if taking a bath. While the boat was being secured to a dock, and we prepared to disembark, I noted the bathers seemed to be washing in a ritualistic fashion. They dipped their cupped hands into the water, mouthed a prayer, and sprayed the water onto themselves and back into the river.

I tugged at Papa's sleeve and asked, "What are they doing?"

"They are worshipping their goddess, Ganga."

"You mean the Ganges River?"

"Yes, but perhaps not exactly. I understand they believe that bathing in it is a form of atonement for their sins, and prepares their soul for its final journey."

"So how did the goddess Ganga become a river?" I asked, puzzled.

"I am not too certain, Margaret. But one text I read said that they believe the sacred water in god Brahma's vessel turned into a maiden. Later, in answer to prayers from some kings on Earth, who wished their soul to be cleansed, Brahma sent Ganga down to Earth. But she fell on god Shiva's head and he, having trapped her in his hair, let her out in streams. Thus she created this river."

Pat, who had been listening to Papa's explanation, said, "Yes, but, Reverend James, didn't she create streams in their other two worlds as well?"

Papa looked baffled. "I'm not aware of that. But I know there are several different versions of her legend. I'll have to read some more."

It seemed to me that the rationalization of the formation of River Ganges by the goddess Ganga was likely as puzzling to some as the story of the Creation.

When we had walked up the *ghat* steps to the dock, the *manji* addressed us: "Please look around the city carefully. Come back to boat early for dinner. Then you go watch the *Agni Pooja* at nearby temple. They make wonderful fire there. You must see." He concluded with the usual *nameste* and a bow.

Climbing up another steep set of stairs, we found ourselves at the entrance to the narrowest street I had ever seen.

Tom eyed the scene. "Reverend James, I fully agree now with what you said earlier. Benares and Babylon indeed existed at the same time, but it would seem Benares has survived intact!"

Papa smiled. "I understand Buddha gave his first sermon, in 528 B.C., a few miles from here. I've heard the temple still exists. But perhaps it is a bit too far to travel there this afternoon."

Pat agreed. "Yes, why don't we leave it for another time? I'm more interested in looking in some of those fabulous silk shops they have here."

"Haven't you bought enough silk in Calcutta, dear?" Tom asked.

But Pat had already started to walk into the crowded street and we followed her. In addition to the throng of people streaming through the narrow street, one had to watch out for the numerous white humpbacked Brahma bulls, which ambled in the streets like emperors. I happened to pass rather close to one of those, and all of a sudden he swung his head at my back, trying to gouge me with his horn. Fortunately, he missed gashing me by a hair's breadth. Passers-by noted it, and shooed him away. Most thought it was unusual for a bull to attack a person, for they are rather well behaved. One lady believed it was likely due to the red shawl—she tugged at it—that I had wrapped around me. "The red make bull angry," she said.

Thankfully, during our stroll about the city streets and bazaars that afternoon, there were no other unpleasant incidents. The usual collection of beggars and street children followed us, and we soon learned not to give them any alms, for the distribution of even a few *paisas* to only one or two would be spotted and brought a horde upon us. They would eventually leave, but only when ignored or sternly ordered to scurry away. We passed numerous saffron-robed priests and devotees with white-painted foreheads, making offerings of flowers, fruit and sweetmeats at shrines dotted along the alleyways. The whole city was full of aged pilgrims desirous of freeing their souls after one final dip in the Ganges and praying in the temples of the holy city. In order to accommodate their wishes, there seemed to be not only enough *ghats,* but also numerous places of worship.

Walking along the narrow, twisting streets lined with diverse shops, we came upon the Kashi Vishwanath Temple, the city's most important. It is dedicated to the god Shiva, known to the Hindus as the "Lord of the Universe". We gazed at the temple's walls, admiring the interesting carvings with floral designs that adorned its exterior, and the gold-topped spires.

Papa knew it was not appropriate for persons of another faith to enter a Hindu temple. Hence, we stood outside and watched the throng of worshippers, each clanging the bell hanging above the gate, to announce their arrival to the god, as they entered the temple. Beside the temple was an ancient well that, we were informed, contained the *linga* from the original temple, which was destroyed by the allegedly cruelest of Mughal emperors, Aurangzeb, in 1669.

Not too far away stood the typical three marbled onion domes and two very tall minarets—which reminded me of Constantinople—of the mosque. Musselmans, some with flowing beards, dressed in white shirts and pajamas and a round cap, strode into the mosque. One of them, upon seeing us standing outside gazing at the edifice, advised us in broken English that it would be all right for us to go in, provided we took off our shoes. Since it was getting late, we declined the offer.

Although Papa wished to see the British military and European part of the city, and also the Baptist missionary's house—where they had converted a room into a chapel—remembering the *manji's* evening arrangement, we decided to head back towards our boat's berth. However, at Pat's insistence, we stopped at some of the shops selling silken materials and other wares, where she wanted "just a few things for the house". Papa and I only admired the soft silk fabrics with lovely patterns, rubbing them between our fingers, and glanced at the rows of display cases filled with intricate pieces of jewelry sets with glittering stones. Their price tags confirmed that they were beyond the reaches of Papa's pastoral wages and my salary as a junior medical doctor at a hospital on an outpost of the Empire.

After dinner, our *manji* took us to experience the *Agni Pooja* at the steps of a nearby *ghat*. We were delighted to observe the place decorated with garlands of colorful flowers and illuminated by hundreds of small oil lamps, which created a festive atmosphere. Priests sat cross-legged on several separate large platforms at the edge of the water. They wore the traditional red-and-yellow-striped robes, and had in front of them a number of brass pots with intriguing powders, rice, grains and other condiments. A smoldering charcoal brazier lay to their side. The peculiar smell of burning incense wafted in the air. A crowd of men, women and children was already seated on the *ghat* steps.

I wondered if there was room for us, when the *manji* led us up the stairs of an adjacent building—possibly a hotel—to a wide balcony that had above its entrance a sign saying *Reserved for European Visitors Only,* and guided us to a table with four empty chairs. He departed with his customary bow, and saying he would see us back at the boat. There were other Europeans at adjacent tables, and we exchanged greetings. A native bearer arrived to take our orders. Papa and I requested tea. Pat and Tom asked for their usual wine and brandy, and frowned when the bearer informed them that only non-alcoholic drinks were available. They settled for limewater.

The terrace provided a clear view of the proceedings. The gathering below grew by the moment and soon people were sitting or standing there shoulder to shoulder at the steps of the *ghat.* Finally the priests, after ringing bells, started a chant. It was the commencement of the ceremony.

"Do you know what this service is all about?" I asked Pat.

"Darned if I know, my dear. My first time here." She sipped her limewater, and then turned towards her husband. "Tom, do you know?"

"My headman mentioned something. I understand they make some sort of offerings here to their deities."

Papa said, "Well, I know *ag* means fire. Perhaps that container of fire there has something to do with it?"

"But what's this *pooja* all about?" I asked.

Since no one answered, an elderly British lady sitting near me at the adjacent table, having heard our dilemma, turned to me and said, "Excuse me, dear, are you an American?"

"Yes, ma'am," I replied, making a mental note to try speaking more in a British accent.

She smiled. "I can see you haven't been here very long, have you?"

"No. Hardly a month. I must admit this ceremony has us all baffled."

"Yes, I thought so too, when we first saw it. My husband's stationed here and we come to this *ghat* every now and then." She nodded towards a gentleman who, dressed in a white suit, sat very rigidly across from her. He nodded as well, but kept silent. He reminded me of Colonel Humphrey.

The priests, having finished their hymn-singing, threw handfuls of rice and other grains, likely mixed with oil, onto the braziers, which burst into flames. The priests lifted the vessels like torches and the thick fragrant smoke blew over the *ghat* steps and reached up to our terrace.

"Why did he do that?" I asked the lady.

"Well, that is the *pooja*. The offering to their gods, Shiva, Ganga, Surya, Agni and the whole universe, I understand."

"But why use the fire? Couldn't the gods simply come down to the *ghat* and pick up the offerings?" Papa, who had been listening intently, asked.

The lady, noticing Papa's white collar, said, "Yes, Father, the deities supposedly visit their houses. They have a *pooja* corner in each home. But here, I understand, *Agni*, the fire god, acts as a messenger to their other gods."

"That's one way to get the gods' attention! How very interesting. Thank you, ma'am," Papa said.

The priests continued the *pooja* ceremony by alternating the hymn-singing with bells ringing and burning the offerings on the braziers. The smoke hung like clouds over the *ghat*. This process was repeated for quite some time, until eventually, all the offerings having been burnt, the service ended. People got up from the *ghat's* steps and started to leave, converging on the narrow stairs and paths that led up into the city. We stayed a bit longer on the terrace and conversed with our newfound acquaintances.

Eventually, the crowd dissipated somewhat, and it was time for us to depart. We exchanged directions and, thanking our new friends, proceeded down the terrace steps towards our boat's dock.

Since I had become "a bit heavy", I lagged behind the others. As I walked along the *ghat*, I noticed one of the priests standing there, holding what looked like a tray in his hand, and people were going up to him. In the dim light I could not see clearly what he was doing; I walked up to him. Peering curiously into the tray, I noted it held a small cotton-wick oil lamp, glowing incense sticks stuck in a jar, some cups that contained a red paste, sweetmeats, sugar, nuts and other items, as well as some money on one side. On seeing me standing there, the priest dabbed his right thumb in the red paste and applied it to my forehead in the shape of a dot. I was stunned. But there were murmurs of happiness from those around me. Noting the money, I quickly opened my reticule and, taking out a rupee coin, threw it onto the tray.

After a quick *nameste* to the priest, I retreated hastily towards the others, who waited impatiently for me at some distance. As soon as I joined them, Papa was the first to notice the red dot, but he did not say anything. Pat and Tom did have a good chortle and made some fancy remarks, which I care not to remember.

On reaching the boat, I wobbled down the gangplank onto the deck, and the *manji,* standing on one side, bowed and bid me a *nameste.* But when he saw the *bindi* on my forehead, he said in an excited voice, "Memsaab, you do *pooja,* yes?"

"Yes, *manji.*"

"It bring you very, very good luck."

I thanked him and walked towards my cabin, wondering what "very, very good" fortune I should ask the gods for. That night, before going to bed, I added in my prayer that what the *manji* had said might come true, and the visit to the *Agni Pooja* ceremony might bring prosperity and happiness not only to me, but also to my unborn child and my two others in Canada.

The boat departed, customarily, close to sunrise the next morning. Having walked a considerable distance the previous day, I was particularly tired and slept in. It seemed Pat did the same, since we came for breakfast at nearly the same time, to join the others. Papa and Tom informed us that we had missed a central sight of Benares. When I asked what it was, Papa told me of having observed several early morning cremations. He had seen bodies laid upon layers of logs and set alight; the ashes and any remaining bones were then deposited into the Ganges. I asked if he had seen any evidence of the ritual of *sati*—where widows were coerced or occasionally voluntarily immolated themselves—but Papa reminded me that the British had outlawed that custom. I was glad to hear that it was no longer being practiced.

Pat shuddered. "I wouldn't watch a cremation, even if they paid me for it."

I agreed with her.

One morning, the boatman announced that we would soon approach another one of the holy cities in India, Allahabad, located at the sacred junction of the Ganges and the Jamuna Rivers. Actually, the *manji* told us that in fact three rivers link here, but the mythical Saraswati is supposedly underground and hence invisible. Papa and I stood on the boat's bow and watched the approaching peninsula formed by the confluence of the two revered rivers.

As the massive ramparts of Fort Allahabad, flying the British and Company flags, came into view, Papa pointed in that direction. "That location reminds me of the Forks of the Ohio River, where it meets with the Allegheny and Monongahela Rivers."

I had visited Pittsburgh during a school trip. "Yes. Isn't there a fort there as well, Papa?"

"Indeed. That would be Fort Pitt, built during the French and Indian Wars, I believe."

I pointed towards the looming fort and asked, "When was that one built?"

"I am not sure," Papa said. He turned towards the boatman. "*Manji*, who built that fort?"

"Badshah Akbar make it, sahib."

Papa said, "So it was Akbar. Then it must have been … let's see … sometime in the late 1500s."

The boat drew closer to the shore, and what I had thought from the distance to be a flock of ducks turned out to be the bobbing heads of hundreds of people bathing in the confluence waters. There also seemed to be some kind of a fair or festival going on at the banks.

I asked the *manji*, "Why are so many people bathing there?"

"It is *Kumbh Mela*, memsaab."

"What's *mela?*"

"It is the place where Vishnu dropped sacred nectar from heaven. People think, take bath wash away sins. You like take bath, memsaab?"

"Oh, no, thank you." I laughed. "I don't believe I have any sins to wash away."

"But we must visit the American Mission and the Printing Press," Papa said. "I have to pick up some more tracts and booklets. Would you like to come, Margaret?"

"Yes, I'd be interested, and abscond from this cramped boat for a while, at least." I proceeded to my cabin to get ready for the call on our American missionaries. Papa had also invited Pat and Tom to accompany us, but they declined, saying that they still had some more shopping left to do, and would not have much time at the next stop, Cawnpore, their port of disembarkation. But they would share the carriage with us into the city.

The boat secured to a pier, the four of us walked up the steps to the dock and into the bedlam of the *mela*. Families dressed in colorful native garb—women in their usual multicolored saris and men in *dhotis* and shirts, some bare-chested—walked about, chatting excitedly. From the constant shouting, it seemed the children wished to do some other thing, or go somewhere else than what their parents wished them to do.

Walking along the embankment, I found the crowd quite friendly and they gently gave way to the group of European memsahibs and sahibs, except for the little children and *fakirs* who followed us with raised palms. They were ignored, for we had been told that giving a coin even to one would have an army of them descend upon us. Carts of numerous vendors of jewelry and other odds and ends lined the street. It was best to walk by without even a glance at their wares, for an exhibition of the slightest interest would have the peddler following you, with the item in hand, and offering it at an ever-reducing price.

Nauseating smells of deep-frying victuals wafted from the pushcarts of food hawkers, each shouting, at the top of their voices, the goodness of their delicacy.

Thankfully we reached the carriages' station in good time and, hiring one, were on our way. I dreaded that from the heat and the overcrowding, I might have a repeat of the fainting incident I had experienced at the Calcutta docks. I also kept a watchful eye out for any of those impudent men I had encountered on the voyage to Calcutta, that Colonel Humphrey had dealt with so heavy-handedly. I was also certain that it was one of them who had set that cobra in my room, and might try a similar ploy again. However, not having spied any of that group, I believed I had seen the last of them. I did press my reticule to feel the revolver.

As the carriage clattered towards town, a refreshing breeze blew in the window. I looked out and saw a sea of pitched tents on either side of the road. "Papa, who is living in those tents?"

Papa didn't seem to know and he looked towards Tom, who sat beside him.

Tom said, "This is a tent-city set up temporarily for all the visitors to the festival. I'm sure the operators charge a pretty penny to rent one of those."

Papa said, "Ah, yes. I remember now. Brother Olson told me they usually rent a tent and do some preaching and distribute pamphlets and tracts here."

Pat sat next to me, looking out of the window on her side. "Allahabad certainly looks like a good place to spread the Gospel. How did the Presbyterian Church happen to set up a mission here?"

"It was a situation of 'man proposes but God disposes'," Papa said with a smile. "As I mentioned earlier, in 1834 our Reverend Lowrie established a mission up the Ganges, past Delhi, at Lodiana. A few years later, another group of missionaries were bringing a printing press in a boat that unfortunately toppled nearby here. A box containing some parts for the press was lost. It was Brother McEwan, I believe, who while purchasing parts for the press, here in Allahabad, met some Baptist missionaries. They asked him to conduct a service at their church. He impressed the European congregation so much that they earnestly requested him to settle in Allahabad. He did, and subsequently built a Presbyterian Church. The hand of Providence led us here."

Tom grinned. "Pat, I hope your shopping in our luggage-boat does not meet the same fate as those missionaries' printing press!"

"Well, Tom, if it does," Pat responded, "you will just have to serve as a missionary here, to recuperate the loss. Is there any room in your church, Reverend James?"

Papa smiled. "Oh, I'm sure some accommodation can be made. In return for samples of indigo, I trust?"

While we laughed, the carriage passed by a huge tree. I noticed a man, nearly naked except for a loincloth, with long hair and painted body, his arms and legs tied by ropes to a branch, swinging slowly from the tree.

"Would you look at him, Papa. What is he doing?"

Papa watched the man. "Yes, I've seen that before. He's performing a *tapasya*, a form of meditation."

"Really!" I said. "It must require good balance to hang like that."

"I understand the objective is to dissolve the negative energies and strengthen devotion to their god," Papa explained. "It's also a form of penance."

Pat said, "Tom, you should try that some time at the end of the day, when you feel all frazzled out."

Tom laughed. "I'll take a brandy and water over that any day."

We passed through several villages with rows of mud houses along the road. These subsequently changed to buildings of brick and mortar, indicating that we had reached the outskirts of the city. The carriage stopped before a brick building with a fence around the front garden, which had colorful flowerbeds and shady trees. A sign over the entrance announced it was the Presbyterian Press. Papa and I alighted here and wished Pat and Tom well on their shopping venture into the city.

As we walked up to the building, a short gentleman with close-cropped, greying hair came out of the door and walked hurriedly towards us.

"Brother James, so good to see you again," he said in a broad Yankee accent, and extended his hand. "And this must be your lovely daughter."

Papa shook his hand and introduced me to Reverend Joseph Olson. He took us inside, where we met another priest, Reverend Lawrence Harris, who was in charge of the operation of the press.

While Papa went to the storage room to pick up the tracts and booklets, Reverend Harris took me around the shop where, with much clattering sounds, the printing machinery was being operated mostly by native men, and some women as well. The whole operation impressed me and I looked through the stacks of religious books, pamphlets and tracts already printed. They were in several Indian languages. In addition to those, a number of forms and brochures lay in stacks. It seemed the local government was a good source of revenue for the Mission.

The reverends wanted us to see the church, the orphanage and schools that were situated in the city, and they also invited us to their homes, to meet their wives and families. Unfortunately, due to shortage of time, and a long journey still ahead of us, we declined their kind invitation. It was late afternoon, but we did stay a while to join them and their staff for some coffee.

Papa having filled his canvas bag with the publications, we bade goodbye to everyone with promises to return soon, and for them to visit us in Futtehgurh. We did not have to stand too long by the roadside, before Papa hailed an empty carriage. It took us speedily back to the dock. Although I found the visit to Allahabad and the printing house absorbing, I was tired from the journey and was glad to be back in my cabin. While Papa perused some of the books, and before Pat and Tom returned, I slipped into my bunk bed and enjoyed a nap before dinner.

It did not take long to sail from Allahabad to Cawnpore, and one afternoon, the boat docked at the infamous Sati Chaura Ghat. My hands tremble as I recall the sight of the approaching *ghat*, for we did not know then, that just a few years later, it was to be the site of that terrible event. That incident was to become one of those historic episodes that are rarely forgotten, and their causes are endlessly debated. However, on that day the riverbank looked like any other peaceful and tranquil sight that existed all along the Ganges.

The Sati Chaura Ghat at Cawnpore was not as dramatic as the ones at Benares, where rows of houses were tethered at the embankment. While there were some of the usual homes located along the waterway, only one large building stood to one side of the *ghat's* steps. A pink-stone temple with the customary cone-shaped dome rose above a wide platform. The bottom floor had an unusual array of pillared arches, forming a colonnade that supported the platform. Rows of worshippers entered and left the temple, each newcomer ringing the bell. Others sat under the inviting shadows of the tall trees, no doubt seeking shelter from the blistering sun.

I wondered if there was enough time, for I wanted to ask Papa if we could explore the temple. I longed to sit for a while in a shady spot on the temple's terrace and adore the peaceful vista of the flowing river and the green banks. However, there was never enough time to relish such tranquil moments.

Pat and Tom were to disembark at the *ghat* and take a carriage to their plantation. It was located on the eastern side of the river, close to the city of Lucknow. As they collected their handbags, we bade them a fond farewell.

Pat hugged me dearly and wished me well. She gently patted my ballooning belly and whispered in my ear, "I just can't wait to see your little one."

We exchanged directions with promises to visit each other as soon as possible. As they walked away from the dock, having hired a number of coolies to carry their numerous boxes, Papa and I waved to them from the boat. They turned and waved back, looking happy to be going home, but oblivious to the calamity that would befall them before long. While standing there, I wondered when or if I would see them again.

I felt a bit unhappy at seeing our friends depart and not having their company for the remainder of the journey.

Papa put his arm around my shoulder. "Futtehgurh is not too far off, Puppet. After all, we have reached the jurisdiction of the American Presbyterian Synod of Northern India."

True enough. It wasn't long until one evening, after dinner, the *manji* informed us that we would dock in Futtehgurh the next day.

Chapter Four

Futtehgurh, at last!

1855, February: Futtehgurh, India

AS THE BOAT SAILED lazily up the Ganges, its waters glittering in the mid-morning hot sun, the first sight of Futtehgurh, still embedded in my mind, was of the high riverbanks and a grey mud fort looming in the distance on the western embankment. Tall, shady trees drooped over the slopes and birds swooped down for either a sip of water or a morsel of fish. Rows of thatched houses towards the west, indicated the area was inhabited mostly on that side of the river. The eastern region was left to farming, and there lay the open country of the kingdom of Oudh. On my usual question, Papa informed me the fort was built much earlier by a Mughal emperor and was taken over by the Company soon after the occupation of Bengal and its neighboring states. However, Futtehgurh had lost its strategic importance as a northern outpost of the Empire. Although a regiment was maintained there, the British, having conquered the province of Sindh and wrestled the Punjab from the Sikhs, did not believe there was any possibility of an invasion, either from the north, or the west, or from the much-weakened Oudh to the east.

"Those houses look nice," I said, pointing to a row of neat, whitewashed buildings that appeared next to the docks.

"They belong to army officers and merchants. The natives live in the nearby city of Furrukhabad," Papa said, as we collected our hand baggage and prepared to disembark. He held me by one hand, going up the steep steps of the *ghat.*

Our luggage was hauled out by the *manji* and his crew from the smaller boat, and carried up to be loaded onto a small one-horse trap waiting on the street. Futtehgurh seemed like a sleepy cantonment town, nothing like the bustling communities we had passed through. Some persons walking on the street, soldiers and others, recognized Papa and waved to him. The boatmen waited in a line beside the carriage. Papa tipped them and from their smiles, it seemed they were satisfied by their gratuities.

I opened my reticule and gave the *manji* another ten-rupee note, as a special baksheesh for all his extra care and attention during the voyage. The young man was truly elated, and thanked me by joining his hands together and bowing several times. We boarded the two-wheeled *ekka*, finding seats amidst all our baggage, and were off on the road towards Furrukhabad.

"How far is our Mission, Papa?"

"Not far. It's close to the next village, called Rukha, formerly the parade ground. Our orphans' asylum, the tent and carpet-weaving factories are also there. Did I mention we are considering building a new church? The present premises are getting rather congested for the growing congregation."

"No, you hadn't. But how are you going to pay for it? Can the Mission afford it?"

"Hoping to raise funds by subscriptions and donations. Perhaps Maharaja Duleep Singh and possibly the Nawab of Furrukhabad will contribute."

"The Nawab? Who is he?"

"Tafazzul Hussain Khan. He's the last remaining figurehead of this principality. I believe he hails from a Pathan family that settled in this area much earlier, and for service during the wars were titled by a Mughal emperor. One of his predecessors ceded this territory to the Company, in exchange for an allowance. The Nawab lives in a palace outside Furrukhabad."

"If he's lost his lands, how does he support himself?"

"He still receives a fairly sizable pension. Earlier he'd made a large donation to our Mission and has contributed to our schools, but now we're not certain of his help."

"Why's that?"

"From what I've heard, lately he's given in to much soft living and debauchery."

"Debauchery!"

"Oh, he holds lavish parties, which I haven't attended, of course. Some of the British from the cantonment have. There are talks of him squandering away his wealth on dancing girls and other excesses."

"Isn't he married?"

"Yes, I believe so. Interestingly, he's expressed an interest in learning English and conversing with the Europeans. I hope he might go on to read some of our scriptures and tracts. God willing, with a little help from us, his spirit might still be salvageable from all the immorality he's succumbed to."

"I wish you success, Papa," I said and laughed, wondering whether anyone's spirit is redeemable. Just then we passed a house with a well-appointed garden, nicer-looking than the ones around it. "Whose house is that?" I nodded towards it.

"That's the station commander, Colonel Smith's, residence. Duleep Singh lived there, prior to his departure for England."

We passed by the fort. It looked to be a bleak structure set on a treeless plain. A mud wall joined numerous bastions. A large, dry moat lay in front of the walls. In one corner, the flywheel of a huge steam engine revolved, and steam billowed with hissing sounds from a funnel. There were no cannons on the ramparts and I saw several civilians going in and coming out of the main gate.

"What's going on in the fort?"

"It's not really a fort now. A gun carriage factory and some warehouses are located in there."

Soon, the trap turned off the road onto a small avenue lined by shady trees, which led to a large, flat area that indeed looked to be a former parade ground. Neat rows of single-story houses, having either flat or thatched roofs, stood on either side of a laneway. Picturesque gardens with hedges and flowering bushes lay before the small verandas of each bungalow.

"Stop at that last house in the row," Papa said, pointing to a bungalow.

The driver pulled on the reins and arrested the *ekka* before a thatched-roof cottage. The spire of a small church peeked in the distance behind a larger building that looked to be the schoolhouse. Children, dressed in blue uniforms, filed in and out of the rooms. Other structures lay farther along towards the river.

Papa and I alighted amid the dust cloud kicked up by the horse and the carriage's wheels. I did not mind it at all, for I was so excited to be home at last. With tears in my eyes, I hugged Papa.

While Papa helped the coachman unload our luggage, I ran up the front path, anxious to meet Mamma. But halfway along I slowed down, realizing that it was mid-afternoon and she would still be teaching at the school. My brother and sister would not be home either. I entered the house and immediately felt relieved to be out of the sun and in the coolness of the bungalow. Walking along the hallway, I passed the front parlor and three bedrooms, and entered the kitchen with a small dining area in the back. I saw a young Indian woman wearing an old beige dress bending over some pots on a fire. The aroma of spices and cooking made me realize that I was hungry.

I might have startled her, for she spun around, but upon seeing me, a broad smile broke on her dark face. "Good afternoon, memsahib. Did you have a good journey?" she said in a reasonably good English accent, and bowed.

Papa came in behind me. "Margaret, meet Elgin Fernandez. She's been helping your mother, and quite frankly, we wouldn't know what to do without her."

I shook her hand and, replying that the journey was pleasant, asked her to continue her task. While Papa instructed the coachman to place my sea chest and portmanteau in one of the bedrooms, I walked through the small dining room out to the backyard.

Hedges and tall mango trees enclosed a small garden. The outhouse stood at one end. After visiting the privy and washing my hands and face with cups of water drawn from a hand-pump, I noted some chairs and a table set up in a shady spot, and sat down there.

It being late afternoon, the fiery sun was preparing to set, and the hot air that had blown all day seemed to be cooling off. While chirruping birds flew about and a few crows squawked, it was most serene in the garden. All the noise of the booming cannons in the Crimean valleys, and the tiring ocean voyage were now behind me. While I still ached deep in my heart for my dear Robert, I felt relieved to be finally at home.

As if she had read my thoughts, Elgin brought out a tray of tea and biscuits, and put it on the table. Papa, having placed our bags in the rooms, joined me there. I poured him a cup of tea. He seemed to enjoy it and the biscuits as much as I did.

While Papa sat reading some of the mail he had brought out, I must have dozed off, but when I opened my eyes, I noticed an envelope lying on the table in front of me. It had a red Canadian stamp—with the Queen's portrait in an oval frame—and was addressed to me in Cousin Heather's familiar hand.

Picking it up, I hurriedly took out the letter, from the already opened envelope. It indeed was from Heather and read:

Dearest Margaret,

We are all extremely grieved to learn of our dear brother, your beloved husband, Robert's heartbreaking death on the battlefield of Crimea. Our heartfelt condolences go out to you. Mother has been despondent in her usual quiet way, not speaking or eating much, but she seems to be coming around of late. Just a few days ago she inquired of Colonel Mitchell whether it would be possible to travel up to Balaclava to visit dear Robert's grave. He said that he would look into whether arrangements for such a trip could be made.

Your lovely children, Vika and Bruce, are well and happy. Bruce has learned to read and write a bit. Poor Vika tries to imitate him. They haven't been told yet about the loss of their father. Perhaps I will do so, at an opportune moment. I know you had written that you would like to have them sent over to you, and I mentioned that to Mother. However, she is noncommittal. It seems she doesn't wish to part with them, not just so soon, anyway. I understand how you feel and will try and get her to consent.

By the way, you might have some more company in India. Colonel Mitchell mentioned that Albert has put in for a transfer to a regiment for service in Delhi! So Nancy and he might come knocking on your door …

I could not read any further, for I was unable to hold the paper in my hand, and put it down on the table. The mention of Albert's name, and now learning of him trying to follow me over here, made me tremble. Papa looked quizzically at me, and asked if anything was the matter. Too distraught to speak, I just stared past him at some rosebushes in the distance. Fortunately, I was saved from Papa's cross-questioning by the appearance of Mamma, followed by my sister and brother, at the back door.

Mamma rushed along the garden path, her arms raised. I flew up to her and we embraced. Tears welled in my eyes and I sobbed on her shoulder.

She ran her fingers over my hair, in her usual way, and said,

"Now, now. There is no need to cry, Puppet. You are home now, dear." She then put her hand on my belly and whispered, "How's the baby?"

"Fine," I murmured.

I then hugged Elizabeth and David in turn. They had grown up much since the last time I saw them, and were almost as tall as me. We returned to the table and sat down. There wasn't much tea left in the pot and Mamma asked Elizabeth to put some hot water in it. Watching her go to the kitchen, her fair locks flowing from her bonnet, I was amazed to see she had blossomed from a scrawny child into a young woman. But after all, at twenty-three, she was only two years younger than me.

Mamma looked well. It seemed the Indian climate agreed with her. The sun had bleached her blonde hair to a lighter shade and tanned her face to a healthy glow. David, at twenty-one, looked like a strapping lad with muscular arms and shoulders, whom a sergeant would be proud to have in his platoon.

I smiled at David. "What have you been doing? Not thinking of joining the army, I hope."

"No. I'm not the fighting type. I like to build things. I'm working at the tent factory."

Mamma looked proudly at David. "He's a foreman there, you know."

"David might be going to the Thomason College of Engineering at Roorkee, north of here," Papa said.

"If I can pass their entrance exams, in June."

"Oh, I'm sure you will, David. From what I remember, you were always breaking and restoring your toys," I said.

Elizabeth arrived with the teapot and asked if I would like some more.

"Yes, I would." I handed her my cup. "And what have you been doing, young lady?"

"Nothing much," she said. "Just helping Mamma at the Mission School. I teach English, History and Geography."

"Have you been going to many dances?"

She blushed. "No. Not many."

"Oh, that reminds me," Mamma said. "You have arrived in time. Colonel and Mrs. Smith have invited us all to the Winter Ball at the Officers' Mess this Saturday."

I felt apprehensive, for I did not wish to face all the inquisitive eyes and answer personal questions from the regimental ladies. "I don't think I'll be able to go, Mamma."

"Ah, but you must, dear. It's their annual event. All the officers, and the plantation owners and their families will be there."

"Let's see how I am feeling that day," I said, not wishing to disappoint her.

Papa then told them about Patricia and Thomas, the indigo farmers we had met, and started to narrate our journey from Calcutta. I felt really joyful sitting there in the shady spot under the mango tree.

Hearing voices from the neighboring houses, I looked around and observed that people were starting to come home, and tables and chairs were being set up in backyards. Life in India is mostly lived outdoors, I realized.

At some distance, behind our row of bungalows, I noted a large area of village-styled houses built of mud walls and thatched roofs. As the familiar dung-fire smoke, which I had smelled all along the Ganges, spiraled skywards from their cooking fires, and little children played in the compound in front of their houses, I realized it was the native Christian village Papa had talked about. I recalled the time when, as a little girl, I had attended a lecture at our church given by a visiting missionary from India. The priest had spoken about the children who were orphaned during the famine and the asylum that was organized for their care. It occurred to me that it was then I had expressed a desire to my parents, to their great indignation, to go to India to care for the young ones. Now, I felt contented because I had reached my destination and realized at least a portion of my dream.

Papa was still recounting in detail our journey from Calcutta, to which the others listened with some interest; I felt a bit tired and, getting up, excused myself, saying that I had better go and unpack. Mamma stood as well, telling me she would show me where everything was.

We walked up the garden path and into the kitchen. Elgin was still busy there and I saw her flattening small balls of dough with a rolling pin. After she rolled one into a thin round crepe, she lifted it with the palm of one hand and dropped it on top of a curved metallic plate, placed over the fire.

"What is she making?" I whispered to Mamma.

"Those are the Indian chapattis, dear. Haven't you had any yet?"

"Oh, yes. I had them all during the boat journey. So that's how they are cooked."

"Elgin makes the best ones, crisp and fluffy."

"I cannot wait to have some."

Elgin looked over and smiled at us.

"Where do you live, Elgin?"

"In the village, memsahib." She pointed a flour-covered hand towards the back of the house.

"Are you married?"

She shook her head shyly and, bending down, started to roll another chapatti.

Mamma went into the hallway. "Let me show you your room, Puppet."

I followed her, and she turned into a bedroom. It looked to have been cleared recently, and I could tell it was Elizabeth's, for some of her dresses and dolls were in the open closet. The bed had the usual mosquito netting on the four posts, which rested in water-filled cups on the floor.

Mamma saw me staring at the single bed. "You will sleep there alone. We have moved Elizabeth into David's room. They don't mind sharing for the few months you will be with us."

Knowing they were quarrelsome, I was about to say that she need not have, when she led me towards a corner. "And look what we have here." It was a lovely crib made of Indian wood I had not seen before. It looked like mahogany, but a bit lighter. I walked up to it and ran my fingers over the ornamental carvings along the edges. Looking at the small empty cot with white cotton sheets and trimmings, tears again welled in my eyes.

I embraced Mamma, and she led me to the four-poster. Pushing the mosquito net aside, we sat down. Still sobbing, I laid my head on her shoulder.

She ran her fingers again through my hair. "Now what happened in Crimea, child? I want you to tell me all about it."

I told her as much as I could of poor Robert's death, taking care to avoid any mention of Albert's involvement. It was as if she knew I was holding back something, for she asked, "Couldn't Albert or any of the others have helped him? Brought him back to camp, I mean."

"No, Mamma. No one could have aided him. He was shot in the chest. I tried desperately to save him. I got there too late!" All those memories brought out a flood of tears, which dripped down my cheeks. I hugged Mamma, and again putting my head on her shoulder, wept bitterly.

Mamma held me and comforted me by running her hand over my back. "Now, now, child. No need to cry so much. It is all over. You are safe here and Robert is in Heaven. You have the baby to think of. We are all here to help you." Then, as if remembering something, she added, "Have you read Heather's letter? You will have some company in Delhi. Nancy and Albert will be there soon!"

Although I felt like screaming an obscenity on hearing Albert's name, I simply nodded.

I felt relieved after the good cry and Mamma's soothing words, and dried my eyes and blew my nose in a handkerchief Mamma handed me.

"I'll let you rest here for a while. I must go and see what Elgin has prepared for supper. Do come out when you are refreshed." She got up and left the room, but I noticed tears in her eyes as well.

I slid my boots off and lay down on the bed, but could not sleep. Thoughts of seeing Nancy and Albert again, and how I should treat them, kept churning in my mind. Finally, with a heavy heart, I got up and emptied out my sea chest and put away some things on the dressing table and on the limited shelving in the room. I hid the revolver behind some books and squeezed my few gowns and petticoats into the closet next to Elizabeth's clothes.

Thankfully, due to the house's thatched roof, it was not too hot in the room, but I was in a sweat by the time I finished. I had a wash from the basin that stood on a stand in one corner, and changed into a loose, comfortable dress that Moira's *derzi* had altered in Calcutta.

Soon there was a tap on the door and Elgin opened it ajar. "Dinner ready, memsahib. You need fresh water and towel?"

I told her they were here, and I would be out shortly. Being waited on felt good, but I wondered how we would survive in India without servants.

With the few gifts in hand that I had managed to purchase on my meagre salary, I walked to the kitchen and found the others seated at the corner dining table. I presented Mamma with a Turkish pashmina-wool shawl, printed in red and blue, which she liked very much. She hugged me, then immediately put the shawl around her shoulders and turned herself around, for our approval. I handed Papa a box containing a matching set of silver cufflinks and a tiepin with a cross. He was thrilled to receive it and, kissing me on the cheek, said he would wear it while delivering the sermon next Sunday. For Elizabeth I had a set of hairbrush and comb made of silver and ebony; she smiled and, thanking me, said she needed a good one like that. I gave David a polished leather belt with a brass buckle. He held it with both hands and exclaimed a "wow". He thanked me and said that he had been wishing for a good new belt, just like that, for all his old ones were too worn out to wear at a dance.

I sat down and Elgin served us dinner. For the first course we had an exquisite tasting soup made from lentils. There was curried chicken next, and while I had tried it before, it was her special blend of spices and just the right amount of chilies that made eating it with the fluffy chapattis a real delight. While most of us ate in the European way, with knife and fork and breaking the bread with our left hand, I noticed David ate by holding a small slice of chapatti and a piece of chicken between his fingers, dipping the morsel in the curry sauce, and taking it to his mouth! Much like the Mexicans eat their tacos. When I looked at him oddly, he informed me that it was the native Indian way of eating he had picked up from workers at the tent factory.

Elizabeth frowned. "I've told him not to eat like that, especially in front of my friends, but he keeps on doing it."

"You should try it, Sister," David said, between mouthfuls. "Makes the food taste better. Besides, I don't care what those military officers you go out with think."

Elizabeth glared at him. "I'll never eat like that. And I can choose who I wish to go out with. What about the girl *you* are seeing?"

It seemed Elizabeth was about to say something else, when Mamma intervened. "Children, behave yourselves, especially now that Margaret is home."

I laughed. "Listening to you two going on at each other, and eating home cooking, makes me feel good to be part of our family unit again."

"You'll be dining out a lot in the next weeks," Mamma said. "The missionary and military families have invited you for suppers. You are quite a celebrity, my dear."

"Oh, Mamma, I'm not sure if I should attend too many parties. Can't you see I have gained so much weight? I must get some exercise." Looking at Papa, I added, "I wish you had a horse I could ride." But from the look on Papa's face, I regretted having said that, for I should have known that he could ill afford to keep a mount.

Papa sighed. "Yes, child. I'll see about getting you a pony."

The next morning, after breakfast and the others having already left for work, I walked to the church and school buildings. Although constructed in the local style of whitewashed mud walls and thatched roofs, they looked pleasant enough. I peeked into the church. It seemed too small for the large group seated there, crowded on plain wooden benches, for the morning service Papa was organizing. I walked towards the schoolrooms, a few yards away. As I approached, I heard children's voices repeating their lessons after their teachers' words. Mamma taught one class, while Elizabeth and another missionary lady instructed two other groups.

Mamma must have seen me through the window and came out of the classroom. "Ah, Margaret. Good that you came over. Mrs. Johnston wishes to meet you." She led me into the other classroom.

We walked to the front of the class and Mrs. Johnston stopped writing on the blackboard and came over to us. She was a slim young woman with bright blue eyes and short dark hair parted in the middle. She wore a blue dress with a high-necked, frilled collar. Her stern features reminded me of one of my schoolteachers.

She shook my hand. "Margaret! You are here, finally. I've heard so much about you."

We exchanged pleasantries. She informed me that she was originally from Pittsburgh and I told her that I had been to college in Philadelphia, which she seemed to know.

She introduced me to her class of dark-faced children, seated on bench seats at long tables. "Good morning, Doctor Margaret," they all repeated, in unison, after her.

After some small talk, Mrs. Johnston said, "Margaret, I know you've just arrived and will be going on to Delhi," she glanced at my belly, "but while you are here … before the baby arrives, I mean … I was wondering if you could help me on Sundays, at the bazaar schools?"

"The bazaar schools, Mrs. Johnston?"

"Oh, yes, my dear. I should have explained." She touched my arm. "They are small gatherings we hold in the villages for tutoring native girls, and women, who cannot attend this school or the one in Furrukhabad run by my husband. We usually rent a small room in a vacant shop or a house."

"Sounds interesting. I'll be happy to assist in any way I can."

"Good. I'm sure with your education, you'll have no difficulty at all. But let me warn you, some of the girls hardly speak any English. You may have to start with the very basics."

"I'll do the best I can. Are you holding one this Sunday?"

"This Sunday may not be convenient for you, Margaret," Mamma quickly interjected. "There is the ball this Saturday evening."

Mrs. Johnston agreed and we arranged to go out the following Sunday. I left the ladies to their teaching and walked back to the bungalow. Not wanting to disappoint Mamma, I searched my meagre wardrobe for something suitable to wear at the ball. I found a dark blue taffeta gown with full sleeves and a decent high neck, for Mamma would never have allowed me to wear a low-cut one. I had worn it to officers' balls in Canada and received admiring glances from the other attendees. I tried it on and it seemed the Calcutta *derzi* had done a wonderful job of letting it out; it fitted me perfectly, both around my enlarged breasts and waistline. Although it was a bit creased, it did not need washing. I added a clean tucker with frills around it and a silver brooch with blue stones in it to hold the tucker in place.

I asked Elgin if there was a flat iron in the house. She said there was, and she would press my gown that evening, using the leftover coals from the fire. I felt satisfied that, despite my matronly condition, I would look proper for the evening.

I spent the next few days getting familiar with the Mission. Not having a horse, I could not walk too far in the heat, although people kept reminding me that it was the "cold season" and all the memsahibs were back in Futtehgurh, having spent the "hot season" in the hills. I passed by the Christian village and waved at the women squatting outside their huts beside their outdoor kitchens, preparing grains and vegetables for their meals, or doing other chores. None of the men folk seemed to be around; they were likely at work.

Some of the children, playing in the alleyways, came to me and stood shyly at a distance.

When I extended my hand, one of them held it and tugged at it, pointing to his hut. I let him lead me there. His mother sat on a mat, slicing vegetables for their meal; she stood up. She was a small, dark-complexioned woman, clad in a red sari. She bid me a good morning, which I returned.

"Where did you learn to speak English?"

"School," she replied, pointing towards it. "Memsahib like come inside, for tea?"

"No, thank you, I've just had tea. But I would like to take a peek inside your home."

She led me into the shack. Entering, from the bright sunlight, it took my eyes a while to adjust to the darkness. There was just one room, and it seemed all their worldly belongings were in it. Cotton sheets covered the floor and there was no furniture, except for some rolled-up mattresses and boxes lying along the sides. Two other children slept in one corner. On the center support pole of the thatched roof, I noted a cross and a picture of our Lord, pinned to the wood.

"Do you go to church?" I asked.

She nodded. "Memsahib come from Amrika?"

"Yes. How did you know?"

She smiled. "My husband working for you brother."

I laughed and said something about news travelling quickly in a small village. We chatted for a while and she told me more about the village life and that they all were very happy there. I was glad to hear it, and as I left the hut, I gave a rupee coin to the little boy who waited patiently outside. While at first his mother objected, but on my insistence, she let him keep it. I could tell from the smile on his face that he was thrilled.

On the way back to the bungalow, I admired the tenacity of these people, who seemed to be content living their simple lives. However, I did wonder if they had dreams and ambition and what they planned to do to improve their lives and well-being. I made a mental note to talk to some of them about it.

On another lovely sunny morning, for a change, I wanted to walk in the other direction from the village, towards the cantonment. Since my parents had advised me against going out alone from the village, I asked Elgin if she would accompany me. The poor girl put the broom aside and, putting on her slippers, was ready instantly to walk with me. We passed by the well-laid-out bungalows of the British officers. They were similar in construction to those of our missionary families, but looked better maintained, with more picturesque gardens, manicured lawns and expertly pruned trees and shrubs. Elgin pointed out that they had much more help available, in the form of native orderlies and servants. I noted some of them scurrying in and out of the homes, carrying items under the supervision of the officers' wives.

Having walked far enough, we turned and started back towards home. We were about halfway to Rukha when a well-appointed carriage, with a dark polished exterior, shiny brass lamps and spiffily harnessed horses, came towards us. The native coachman, wearing colorful garb, pulled on the reins and stopped the landau beside Elgin and me. An Indian gentleman, dressed in a gold-threaded jacket and a bejeweled turban, leaned his head out of the window and said something in Hindustani to the coachman.

The coachman addressed me: "Nawab-sahib asking if memsaab like to take carriage to home?"

I noted Elgin shaking her head. "No, thank you, we are just out for a walk," I said. Then, not wishing to sound rude to the Nawab, I added, "You are most kind, sir. But I am not far from home." The Nawab looked up at the coachman, who translated my words to him.

The Nawab turned to me, and smiled. "Thank you." He then motioned to the coachman and the landau started to pull away.

As it passed by, I managed to get a glimpse of its other occupants. Two European women sat on the seat in front of the Nawab. One was an elderly lady and the other, much younger—a pretty thing—who looked to be the daughter. While from their dresses the ladies seemed to be British, I was at a loss as to why they had not spoken to me. They probably were not British, then, I consoled myself, and we walked back to the bungalow.

Later that evening, at the dinner table, I related the incident to my parents and siblings. Their reaction was another surprise for me. While Mamma and Papa looked away, as if trying to concoct an explanation, Elizabeth and David burst out laughing.

"What is it? Have I done something wrong?" I asked, bewildered.

"No, no, dear, you haven't done anything out of the ordinary," Mamma said quickly. "It was the Nawab of Furrukhabad you saw in the carriage."

"Oh, Papa has told me about him. But who were the two women?"

"Possibly, Mrs. De Fountain and her daughter, Bonny. Captain De Fountain passed away some time ago. The Nawab has been kind to her. Takes them out now and then," Mamma said.

Elizabeth squealed: "Oh, yes. He's really *kind* to Bonny." And in between giggles, she added, "Too bad, Sister, you did not take up his offer for a ride home! You might be wearing some jewels now." She shook her shoulders.

"Elizabeth! Mind your manners," Papa said sternly.

"What is the problem? Are we not supposed to be friendly to the natives, especially the head of state? Papa, did you not say that we are looking for charitable donations from him?" I asked.

Papa frowned. "Yes. Being sociable is one thing, but when they start making advances towards our women, it is another matter."

I frowned back at him. "But, surely, Papa, isn't it up to the women to decide whether or not to accept the attention?"

Mamma put down her knife and fork. "Yes, Margaret. But you know one thing leads to another. Why, some years ago, the brother of the very Nawab absconded with an English girl and has allegedly married her! She is his wife number two, we believe. What's her name, Jim?"

Papa thought for a moment. "Harriet Birch."

"Didn't her father or the authorities do anything?"

"They tried, but what could they do? She was of age, and testified that she had gone of her free will."

"So, where is she now?"

"Still in that palace, full of concubines. She's even changed her name to Begum something or the other."

While Elizabeth and David tittered again, I still wondered what the fuss was all about. What a double standard, I thought. While we are expected to be kind to the indigenous people, marrying them was something not "made in Heaven".

The Saturday of the Station Commander's Ball arrived with great fanfare. Mamma had asked Elgin to bring her brother to help us get ready. A metallic bathtub was placed in one room and filled, emptied and refilled with hot water by Elgin and her brother, under Mamma's supervision. We each took turns going into the room for a bath. Later, Elgin helped me arrange my hair in a chignon. To my amazement, she reached inside a basket and produced a corsage of lovely colorful flowers. She pinned it to my bosom, and tied a matching wreath around the chignon. She had similar ones for Mamma and Elizabeth as well. I thanked her for her kindness and consideration. She must have spent much time collecting the flowers from our garden and making the arrangements. I walked out from my bedroom and found the others, all elegantly dressed, waiting on the veranda. I admired Mamma and Elizabeth's blue and pink gowns and told them they looked lovely. I noted that Mamma had my gift, the pashmina shawl, around her shoulders. Papa was dressed in his usual dark suit, which fitted him well. Smoking a cigar, he resembled a country parson, which he was. David, dressed in a beige suit, looked reasonably presentable; while I mentally questioned his choice of color for a ball, I did not mention it for fear of upsetting him.

A carriage had been ordered, and it arrived close to five o'clock; the ball was to start at six. I suppose the early start was to permit the safe arrival of the numerous guests during daylight hours. We climbed into the landau and it clattered towards the cantonment. David preferred to sit up with the coachman for, being a big man now, he was no longer able to squeeze inside the cab with Papa and three women and their voluminous skirts.

The sun was beginning to set over the Ganges River and its rays filtered through trees that lined a laneway, onto which the carriage turned from the main road. It slowed down to join a line of buggies. The vehicles drove slowly past a wide *maidan*, the new parade ground. Cricket and hockey fields lay on the other side and led up to a large building by the river's embankment, the Officers' Mess. It was a two-story structure with a wide, colonial-style veranda supported on archways at the front.

Chinese lanterns, hanging on posts and tree branches, illuminated the surroundings. Smartly dressed footmen, in long white jackets with red sashes and turbans, opened the carriage doors and helped us alight.

While the dining room was downstairs, we were directed to rooms upstairs to deposit our cloaks and visit the powder room to tidy up. We then proceeded downstairs to join the line-up to meet our hosts standing at the entrance to the reception room. The line slowly crept up to the dignitaries. Papa introduced us to them and their wives: the Station Commander, Colonel Smith; the Collector, Mr. Probyn; the District Judge, Mr. Thornhill; and the Joint Magistrate, Mr. Lowis.

After shaking hands and exchanging a few quick words with the hosts, I was glad to be in the large reception room, which buzzed with conversation from the considerable crowd already gathered there. Thankfully, swinging *punkhas* moved the cool evening breezes from the river, making mingling with the other ball-gowned ladies, uniformed officers and sprinkling of dark-suited gentlemen bearable.

A large Union Jack hung on one wall and regimental colors, various armaments, war memorabilia and stuffed heads of stags, bears and other hunt prizes were mounted on others. Vibrant flower arrangements stood on the sideboards. Were it not for the Indian bearers, who moved expertly around with trays of drinks and hors d'oeuvres in between the groups, I could have been in any one of the British military officers' mess in the several countries I had visited. When offered, I picked up a glass of sherry and quickly ate a couple of pieces of patties, for I was beginning to feel hungry.

On spying me, Mrs. Joyce Johnston came over excitedly. She kissed me on the cheek and I wished her a good evening. She said she was glad to see me and asked how I was feeling. I told her I was well. She then took me around to introduce me to her husband and some of the other missionaries and their wives and children.

Reverend Johnston, who was in charge of the schools, was dressed in a dark suit and white collar. "Ah, Margaret, welcome to Futtehgurh. I have been wanting to talk to you."

"Thank you, Reverend Johnston. Can I be of any service?"

"Yes, you certainly can help us. I understand you will be assisting Joyce at the bazaar school, but we have received a teaching request from an important individual."

"Why cannot that person attend the Mission or the bazaar schools?"

"Oh, no. He's much too eminent to attend a regular class. He wishes to engage a private tutor for English lessons. In fact, he's the Nawab of this principality."

On hearing that, I must have broken into a slight smile, and when the Reverend gave me a puzzled look, I hastened to explain, "I believe I've heard of the Nawab—in fact, I saw him just the other day." I narrated the incident.

The Reverend, on hearing of my refusal of the Nawab's offer for the carriage ride, smiled. "What a coincidence! You are acquainted with the gentleman already. So, are you agreeable to taking on this assignment? You see, we are looking for a ... er ... mature teacher, and you seem to be well suited for this task. At least for the few months you are here, before your departure for your *real* job in Delhi."

Although I was not pleased on being pressed into this assignment, I remembered Papa telling me the need for funding from the Nawab for the new church, and not wishing to disappoint my parents—who stood by listening to the conversation earnestly— I told the Reverend, "I would be happy to assist."

"Good," Reverend Johnston said, relieved. "Of course you will need the services of an interpreter. The Nawab doesn't speak much English, and has agreed to pay for a helper as well."

Mamma interjected and said, "Brother Johnston, we know just the right person for the interpreter's job. Our Eurasian servant, Elgin, will be more than happy to assist Margaret."

From the look on the Reverend's face, it seemed he probably had someone else in mind. However, he quickly responded, "Why, that would be a suitable arrangement, Mrs. Wallace. Margaret and Elgin could travel together to the Nawab's *haveli*. He'll send his carriage over. I'll finalize the arrangements with him and let you know."

Mamma nodded her agreement. "Margaret, you would pick up some Hindustani too, which you have been wanting to. Couldn't you, dear?"

While I nodded, Reverend Johnston spoke, "It is Urdu the Nawab speaks. Margaret will find it very useful in Delhi."

"Do not hurry, we have some time before the *namaz*," Nawabsahib said.

"But we really must go. Also, don't you have to do your wash before the prayers?" I asked.

He nodded.

I impressed upon them again to practice their English lesson, using the booklet. They seemed to comprehend its importance and nodded their agreement once more. Elgin and I collected our belongings and followed the others towards the palace entrance and the waiting carriage. I lingered behind with Nur and we exchanged a few words. I asked her to visit me at the Mission and bring her daughter as well. She was hesitant at first, but agreed when I mentioned that Mamma and Papa would like to meet her.

The Begum and the Nawab thanked me numerous times for the lesson and implored me to return the next week. I said we would. There were goodbyes and salaams all round. Elgin and I boarded the landau and it clattered off on the road towards Furrukhabad.

I was happy that Karim, having to go for prayers and upon my assurance that it was all right, had not accompanied us back. We unrolled the leather shades over the carriage's windows and settled down for a quiet ride. Despite the heat and dust, we were able to rest and nodded off a bit during the journey.

I did wonder for a while why the Rani had asked the Nawab to see her. But Nawabsahib's explanation had sounded reasonable. It seemed proper that anyone in the Rani's predicament would wish to consult with as many ex-rulers as feasible. My eyes closed and I did not think any more of it, but that one remark by the Begum: "… She will not let her lands be taken away so easily …" lingered in my mind. Later I realized it was to have a grave impact on our future life in India.

It was almost evening when the carriage arrived before our cottage's front gate. I spotted Mamma and Papa, as usual, seated on the wicker chairs on the veranda. I went up and hugged them. The coachman helped Elgin unload the boxes of our teaching materials. I tipped him a five-rupee coin. The poor fellow was most elated and salaamed me his "thank you" a few times.

After a quick wash and freshening-up, I walked out to the back yard to join my parents in the sitting area in the shady spot under

The dinner gong sounded and everyone proceeded to the dining room, where we sat at long tables. Futtehgurh being a smaller outpost, the dining was not as elegant as some of the larger military stations I had been to. However, their staff had done their best. After a prayer, delivered by the military chaplain, and the toast to the Queen, dinner was served. The food—roast beef, chicken, mildly curried vegetables and other items—was agreeable and the service pleasant enough. I was seated next to Reverend and Mrs. MacLeod. They were originally from Philadelphia and engaged me in amiable conversation about the city when they learned I had attended medical college there.

After dinner, we lingered over more drinks and tea outside on the lawns, where chairs and tables were set up. The dining area was cleared and prepared for dancing. The military band arrived. It consisted mostly of native Indian soldiers, and I was amazed to see them play the European tunes, by ear, without a scrap of sheet music!

While I tapped my feet to the melodies, I did not wish to dance. I did not even carry a program, but Elizabeth's dance card was nearly full even before the dancing started! Although several officers came over and asked me, I declined. In my expectant state, I was in no condition to dance. I hoped I did not sound rude, but was glad that after a glance at my belly, they understood the reason and excused themselves.

Elizabeth had a string of requests and was on the floor for virtually every dance. There were one or two young men she seemed to dance with more than a few times. I expected she would bring them over and introduce them, but she did not. I made a mental note to ask her about the officers. I sat at a table in the cool night air in the pleasing garden with Mamma and other ladies, enjoying the music and chatting with them.

Colonel and Mrs. George Smith were doing the rounds, meeting the guests, and came over to our table. Papa stood up and while the Colonel talked with him, Mrs. Smith sat down next to me on the chair just vacated by Mamma—she had gone to the powder room. We exchanged pleasantries. Mrs. Smith asked about my experiences in the Crimea, which I narrated. She, in turn, told me about their travels all over India, where they had resided for quite some time.

"How long have you been in Futtehgurh?" I asked.

"Oh, not long. The regiment returned from Burma only last year. I hope we can stay here for a while. George is about to retire and we are looking forward to a peaceful life back home."

Remembering what Colonel Humphrey had told me in Calcutta, I asked, "How is the sepoys' morale? I heard in Calcutta there is some discontent in the ranks."

"Oh, no. Not in our regiment. The sepoys revere George and their officers. Will do anything for them. Despite being called in the bazaars 'the Christian Regiment'."

"The Christian Regiment?" I must have had a puzzled look on my face.

"Yes. That's what the *paan* sellers jeer at them for having crossed the 'black water' to serve in Burma."

I had heard something about the Brahmins not wanting to sail across an ocean. "You mean they believe they broke their caste by going overseas?"

"Exactly. But what has displeased George and me is that Calcutta has yet to show some appreciation for all their good work in Burma."

I thought the sepoys had reason to be distraught, at having been ignored. But before I could say anything, Mamma returned. Mrs. Smith got up and, after exchanging a few words with Mamma and wishing us a pleasant evening, left us.

Later, I noted that while Papa danced with Mamma and some of the other ladies, David was nowhere to be seen.

When Mamma returned to the chair beside me, I whispered to her, "Where is David?"

"Oh, he's probably gone over to the Christian village," she said calmly.

"But why? Doesn't he wish to dance?"

"He's probably gone to see Amari, or Mari, as we call her."

"Who is she?"

"An Indian girl. Her father works with David at the tent factory."

At first I could not believe that David would have started going out with an Indian girl! However, it slowly dawned on me that he had come here as a young boy and it was so natural and entirely possible.

"How long has he been seeing her? Does Papa know?"

"About a year, I believe. I'm sure your father knows."

Having noted that some of the younger officers had invited their lady friends—they looked to be daughters of the nearby European plantation owners—I asked, "Why didn't David bring her here?"

Mamma put her hand on my arm and whispered, "You wouldn't know this yet. But Indian persons are not permitted to attend these parties."

I was shocked to hear that and was going to ask more questions, but Reverend Johnston came over and asked Mamma to dance. She gladly walked with him to the dance floor.

It was a wonderfully cool night, and the party carried on into the wee hours. Finally, all rose for the playing of "God Save the Queen" and guests began departing one by one.

Yonder, from the *maidan*—where the carriages were parked—I heard shouts and abuses in Hindustani, hurled by the bearers dispatched to fetch the vehicles, at the sleeping coachmen. Our carriage appeared before long and, after giving our thanks to the hosts and wishing friends goodnight, we boarded it and headed for home. I was certain Papa knew that David had left early, for he did not ask about him.

The drive home was rather quiet, each one of us engrossed in their thoughts. I reflected on how my life had changed in the last year, which seemed to have slipped by so quickly. Even in the few short weeks after my arrival in India, adjustments to my existence were gradually taking place. There were many new ideas and events I was experiencing. However, at that time, little did I know that the past proceedings were insignificant compared to the ordeals that lay ahead.

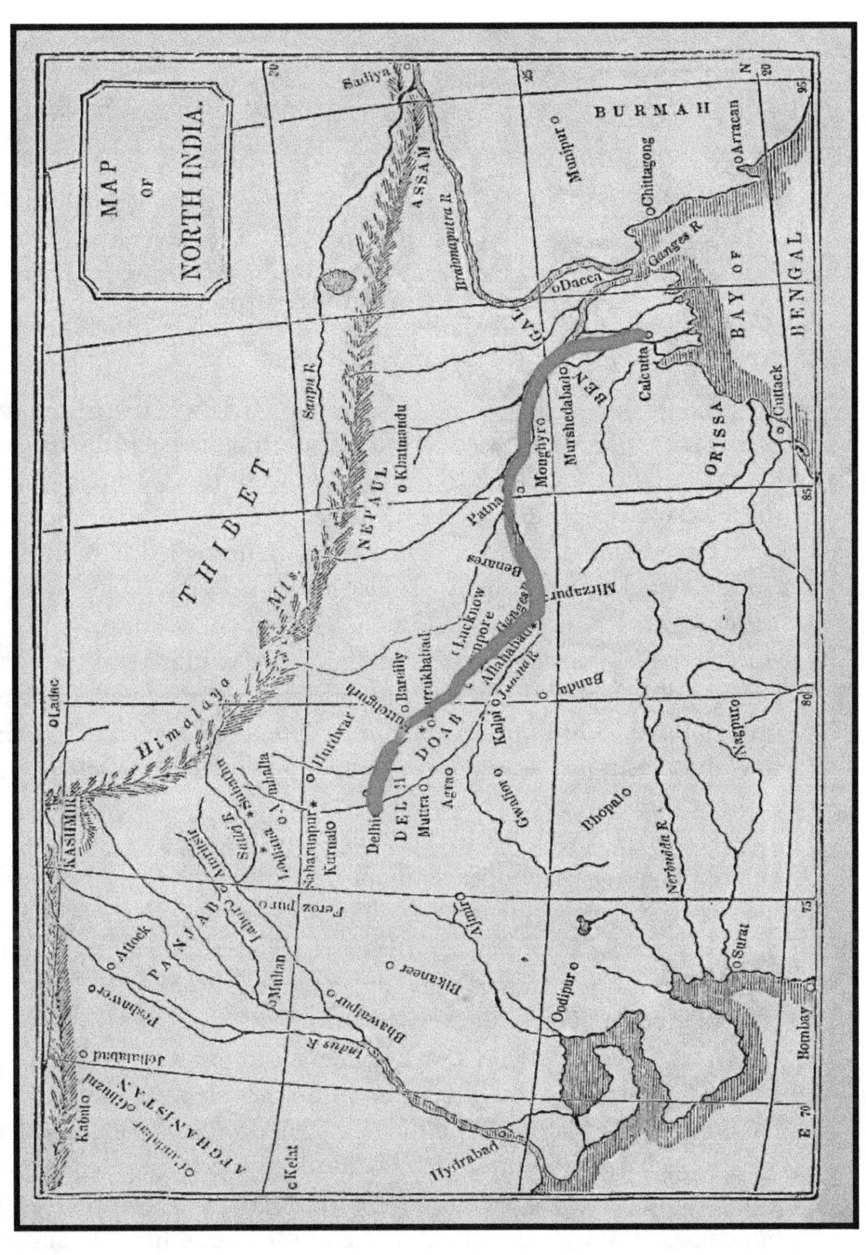

MAP: Margaret's route from Calcutta to Delhi

Chapter Five

Life at Futtehgurh

1855, March: Futtehgurh, India

THE FOLLOWING SUNDAY morning, Elgin and I waited on the veranda for Joyce Johnston. We were to accompany her to the bazaar school, in a nearby village. A carriage soon appeared, clattering down the street, and its chauffeur reined it before our garden's picket-fence gate. While Joyce waved at us from the window, a native middle-aged Indian gentleman, wearing a Christian priest's beige-cotton frock, alighted from within and held the carriage door open. When I reached the vehicle, the gentleman held out his hand. "Good morning. I'm Reverend Gopechand." He had fine dark features, a thin nose and lips, and his coal-black hair showed signs of grey.

"Hallo." I shook his hand. "I've heard so much about you." I entered the carriage and, exchanging greetings with Joyce, sat beside her. I noted that Elgin, after passing our bags and water-bottles up to the driver, was stepping on the carriage wheel to climb up to the bench-seat. "Elgin, come inside the carriage," I said.

"Memsahib, I sit with the *tongawalla*."

"You will sit inside. I don't want you to get sunstroke," I said sternly. She wore an old blue dress with short sleeves, likely a hand-me-down from Mamma, and did not have even a hat or a bonnet.

Gopechand motioned with his head for her to get in. The poor girl scampered inside the carriage and moved to one corner of the opposite seat. Gopechand entered and sat beside her. He shouted to the driver, "*Chaloo*." And we were off.

The carriage turned onto a badly rutted side-road that ran between farmlands of green, yellow and purple crops. Fields stretching for acres on either side were occasionally dotted with clumps of trees. While hanging onto the leather straps, to avoid being thrown about in the coach—as it bounced over potholes—I observed the scantily clad farm-workers busy at their chores, hoeing or planting. Irrigation ditches crisscrossed the plantings. To give the crops moisture, the workers simply shoveled a portion of earth away from the channel and let the water in. At a few shallow ponds, nude children splashed water onto the backs of cows and buffalos, and waved to us.

Finally the road improved, for we were likely approaching the village, and I was able to converse with Joyce. "How long have you been holding this school?"

"Not for long. The attendance is growing every week and soon might be too large for Gopechand and me to manage. Hence I requested your assistance."

"And I'm happy to help. How did you choose this particular village?"

"The headman is a former pupil of our Mission School. He speaks some English and now his son is enrolled there. I spoke to him about bringing the village girls there. While he did not like the suggestion, he agreed to have *us* come and teach the girls in the village."

"I see. That gives us a foot in the village, so to speak. How about the older women? Don't they wish to be at the school?"

Reverend Gopechand interjected, "Oh, no. The men wouldn't want their wives to learn English. Might make them too independent, you see."

We laughed.

Joyce said, "Well, I've pleaded with the headman to let the wives attend, along with their daughters. But he wouldn't hear of it, and even remarked that the women are poor learners; it might be easier for me to teach parrots!"

"Oh! How unkind of him," I observed.

"Yes. And I told him so. I've asked him numerous times to at least give the poor women a chance to be taught," Joyce said.

From the sounds of dogs barking, smoke and cooking smells, we knew we had arrived at the hamlet. The landau entered the street that wound through the houses and came to a stop at what looked to be the central square.

We descended and were greeted with *namestes* from a small crowd. We returned their greetings. The headman came forward and led us to one corner of the square where, under a huge tree, a bamboo hut had been erected. It had rows of wooden benches and a couple of chairs at the front.

Little girls swarmed around us, but were told sternly by the chieftain to go and sit in the school. There were about a dozen of them, dressed daintily in red or blue skirts, colorful shirts and even some bangles on their tiny wrists. They ran into the hut with shouts of joy.

Gopechand and Elgin unloaded our bags from the carriage and brought them into the hut. Joyce set up the blackboard on an easel at the front of the class. Elgin and I helped Gopechand take out the books, small slates and chalks from the boxes and handed them to each wide-eyed child seated on the benches.

I heard Joyce, who was talking to the headman, call out, "Margaret, can you come here, please?"

I went up to them.

"Meet Mr. Suresh Tyagi, the headman of this village."

He again bid me a *nameste* and I did the same. He wore a grey blanket around his shoulders and was likely a Brahmin, for he had the sacred red thread tied around his wrist and a red streak of *pooja* paint was visible on his forehead, below the turban.

Joyce turned to me and said, with a smile, "Do you remember me talking about 'teaching parrots'?"

On hearing that, Mr. Tyagi immediately put his hands together and, shaking his head, said, "Memsahib, me very very sorry for saying 'parrots'."

"It's all right, Mr. Tyagi. So now you want us to teach the women?" Joyce asked.

Tyagi rotated his head. "Yes. They waiting in my house. Can you please come?"

"It might be difficult for me to go. I've prepared some special lessons for today's class," Joyce said. She then turned to me and asked, "Margaret, I was wondering if you would be kind enough to visit Mr. Tyagi's house? You may take Elgin with you."

"Yes. I'll do that," I said, and called out to Elgin to join us.

Carrying a few slates and books in our hands, Elgin and I walked behind Mr. Tyagi. He led us through narrow winding streets, asking us to be mindful of the open sewer channels on the sides. The stench at first was appalling, but we soon got used to it. We finally reached his single-story house, which looked to be somewhat bigger than those around.

He opened the front door and led us into a courtyard that had a veranda and rooms around its four sides. There was a water well, in the middle of the square. Several elderly people and children either sat or slept on *charpoys* in the shade of the veranda outside their rooms. Smoke and cooking smells wafted from one corner of the quadrangle, which was likely the kitchen. At one end, under the shade of a mango tree, a group of half-dozen women sat on *charpoys*. On seeing Mr. Tyagi approach, they covered their heads quickly, with the loose ends of their saris.

Mr. Tyagi spoke to them in Hindi and then, turning to me, said, "Memsahib, I go for work. I come back in two, three hours. My wife here," he pointed to her, "help you. She speaking very very good English." Laughing a bit at his last remark, he *namested* and left us.

A plump lady with a *bindi* on her forehead, and dressed in an expensive-looking blue silk sari with a gold border—obviously Mrs. Tyagi—got up. She said, "Good morning." As she *namested*, the numerous gold and silver bangles around her wrists slid down to her elbows. She led me to the other ladies, who were similarly dressed in fine clothes and jewelry. All looked to be high-caste women from rich families.

Mrs. Tyagi nodded to me. "You *chai?*"

I understood, she meant tea, and nodded back.

Mrs. Tyagi pressed my shoulder and motioned towards a *charpoy*. I sat down there. The other ladies hovered around me and, holding my hand, looked at it closely and ran their palms over my wrists. They then felt my dress sleeves. It seemed I was the first European woman they had seen up close!

They chatted excitedly among themselves and said something to me. Elgin translated: "They ask if you are very poor."

"Please ask them, why they think so."

"They say that, because you aren't wearing any jewelry!"

"Tell them, I have only two silver bracelets and I don't wear them when I am working, for I'm afraid I might break them."

"They are asking why your husband doesn't give you more. Their husbands do."

"Please tell them, I am a widow."

On hearing that, the ladies, putting their hands on their heads, sighed and moaned. They said things like: "Oh, the poor woman … so young … that is why she is having to work … hope she'll find a husband soon …"

While feeling moved by their concern, I was saved from further grief and tears by the arrival of the maid with a tea tray. She placed it on a *charpoy* and rushed to fetch another tray of snacks.

Having gobbled the tasty nibbles and washing them down by the aromatic *chai*, it was time for the English lessons to begin. I made them rearrange the *charpoys*, which were set about haphazardly, in a semi-circular fashion. I handed out a slate and chalk to each of the ladies, which they gingerly accepted, likely never having seen one before. I had Elgin stand beside me, at the front of the class, to translate the instructions.

This was to be English Lesson One but, since this class was unexpected, I did not have enough copies of the lesson booklet— printed at our Allahabad press—that we normally handed out to the pupils. I held up the one book of the English alphabet that had, on each page, the letters of the alphabet and a picture, starting with A and a painting of an apple, B with an image of a ball, and so on. Turning the pages, I had them write the letter on the slate and repeat after me its name.

As expected, they had some difficulty writing with the chalk for the first time, but soon mastered it. However, the major problem was with the pronunciation of the letters. Except perhaps for Mrs. Tyagi, it seemed the poor ladies had not even *heard* a word of English before! They pronounced, for instance, A as "ah" and C as "she". After many repetitions by me, and much coaxing by Elgin, they seemed to be enunciating the letters a bit closer to what they should sound like.

From the sounds and not many reiterations, it seemed the lesson was going well. Soon we were up to Z and I called a break. The ladies looked exhausted from the exertion of repeating and writing the alphabet, and reached for some more tea.

I had another cup and spoke to them. Each told me about their families.

It was past noon. The front door opened and Mr. Tyagi and his son walked in. It looked they had been out working in the fields. The son bid me a quick "good morning" and went towards one of the rooms.

"I see, memsahib, you and my wife good friends. You having good school?" Mr. Tyagi asked.

"Yes, Mr. Tyagi. The lesson went well. And your wife does speak good English," I said, and asked her, "Where did you learn?"

"The District Magistrate wife, good friend," she replied.

"Very good. We have food now. Yes?" Mr. Tyagi asked, for I imagined he must have been rather hungry.

I reluctantly agreed, for I feared the dishes might be too spicy, but I was getting peckish and besides, it would have been bad manners to refuse their hospitality. I was not certain how they would accommodate Elgin and me who were not of their caste. But I let them worry about it. Mrs. Tyagi shouted at the servants to get lunch ready.

Elgin and I were led towards their dining room. More servants appeared, with pitchers of water, soap and towels for us to wash our hands. Dining was to be in the oriental style—seated on the floor— for there was no furniture in the room. A long tablecloth was spread on the rug, and the Tyagi family and Elgin and I placed ourselves around it.

Maids brought in food on individual platters for each diner. The circular brass plates, called *thalis*, had several small bowls of different food items. Large helpings of rice and *chapattis* were placed in the center of the tray. The aroma of the cuisine was intoxicating and I was anxious to start, but waited for the cutlery to be handed out. It soon dawned on me that there was none available! I noted the others began using their fingers the way, I recalled, David ate. I must admit that just the effort of making the morsel made the food tastier.

Mrs. Tyagi was concerned that the vegetarian food might be too spicy for me, and kept asking if it was all right and instructed the maid to keep refilling my water tumbler. Although the curries were indeed piquant, I managed by making sure that I ate plenty of bread or rice with each mouthful.

"The DC's wife never eat in my house," she confided to me. "Next week I make chicken curry, especially for you," she assured me.

I again wondered how that would be possible in her Brahmin kitchen. But I noticed that Elgin and my *thalis* and bowls were a bit different from the others'. It then dawned on me that they likely used different crockery for their guests of another caste.

Elgin and I washed our hands again, and took leave from the Tyagis. The whole family gathered in the courtyard to bid us goodbye. I thanked them for their hospitality and they in return expressed gratitude for my having visited their abode, partaken in their food and tried to teach them some English.

I was curious how the other ladies had felt about the session. Hence I asked Mrs. Tyagi, slowly, "Did … your … friends … like … the … lesson?"

She nodded. "Yes. Yes. They like. One thing good."

That puzzled me. "What was the 'one good thing'?"

She tried to formulate the sentence, but evidently could not. She turned towards Elgin and said something to her in Hindustani.

Elgin said, "Mrs. Tyagi is saying that the ladies were most happy to see that you did not teach them from the Bible, and try to convert them."

This concern did not surprise me, for I had heard of similar complaints expressed to some of our missionaries when they had possibly tried to make the pupils read the Bible.

"Oh, no. Please tell them that my intention is to teach them only English. If they wish to read the Bible, then it would be up to them."

Elgin translated and Mrs. Tyagi nodded her head and said, "Good. Good. Come on Sunday?"

I was glad to hear that she wanted me to return, and replied, "Yes, of course. Not only to teach but also for the chicken curry you've promised!"

Mr. Tyagi led us back through the laneways, the way we had come, towards the village square. We arrived at the bamboo hut. The school was over, as none of the children were around and Joyce and Reverend Gopechand, seated on the chairs, were finishing their sandwich lunch.

"Hallo, Margaret, there you are. I was wondering what kept you. Would you like some sandwiches?" Joyce asked.

"No, thank you. We've had lunch. But I'll have some water."

"You didn't eat there, did you?" she exclaimed.

"Yes, I did. It was a nice change from roast beef and potatoes!"

Joyce looked a bit astonished. "Well, you are the doctor. You should know better."

"The food was delicious. I am sure it was harmless. I've been eating curries all the way from Calcutta!"

"One cannot be too sure with their food," she said, nodding towards Mr. Tyagi. "I would suggest we stop at the cantonment dispensary and get the surgeon to give you some medicine."

"I'll be fine, Joyce. Not to worry. I'll see the surgeon if I need to."

We bid Mr. Tyagi goodbye and assured him we would be there next Sunday. He left with a bit of a sad face. He had stood by patiently listening to our discourse. I felt sorry that he must have understood Joyce's remarks about their food. I wondered if these were the kind of little comments about their cuisine and culture that made the Indians unhappy with us.

On the way back, in the carriage, Joyce seemed to have settled down and asked me about my first day of teaching, and that to a group of Indian women! I gave her a detailed account of the proceedings. She seemed happy to hear the women had enjoyed their first lesson.

"Ah! That reminds me to confirm with you. Are you going to teach our Nawab?"

"Yes," I said and noted Reverend Gopechand raising his eyebrows.

"Well, I clean forgot to tell you. My husband received word, just yesterday, from the Nawab. He will be expecting you on Wednesday. He'll send his landau over. Would you be able to go?"

"Yes. Wednesday would be all right. I should have recovered from today's journey by then." I looked at Elgin, "Are you all right for Wednesday?"

She nodded.

It did not take long for the carriage to reach the Rukha village missionary homes' laneway and stop in front of our bungalow. Elgin and I alighted, and were greeted by Mamma and Papa; they were all questions about the trip. We retired to the sitting area under the trees, in the cooler back yard, where Elizabeth and David also joined us. While Elgin fetched fresh tea, I narrated my experiences of the day.

Next Wednesday morning I spotted, through the partings in the curtains of my bedroom window, the Nawab's landau appearing before the front gate. As it had arrived a bit ahead of time, I was not quite ready. A gentleman came to the door and Elgin asked him to wait, while I saw her taking the books, slates and other educational material up to the carriage. I hurriedly finished dressing and, putting on my bonnet and straightening the tresses that hung loose, walked out onto the veranda.

The gentleman, wearing a fine silk shirt over baggy trousers and a colorful short waistcoat, greeted me. I was ready to bid him a *nameste* but he said, "Salaam, memsahib," and, bending from the waist, brought the tips of his right hand to his forehead. I recalled this was the Muslim salutation.

"Good morning," I said.

"Me, Karim Khan, *munshi* of Nawabsahib."

I was glad that he spoke *some* English and followed him down the front path. As we approached the carriage, the coachman probably recognized me and salaamed as well. Entering the coach, Elgin and I sat on one bench and Karim Khan on the opposite one.

"What does a *munshi* do?" I asked as the coach rolled on.

"Writing letters, memsahib. Only Persian, Urdu and Hindi. No English."

"Then, who does the Nawab's correspondence in English?"

"I bring to man in bazaar. Too many rupees. Nawabsahib no like. He want to learn English."

"Isn't there anyone at the palace who speaks good English, and could teach him?"

"No. Only Nur Jehan Begum, wife of Nawabsahib brother. She no like to teach Nawabsahib."

That must be the Harriet Birch, Mamma had mentioned, I thought. "I see. Is the Nawab married?"

"Yes. Wife name, Bilqis Begum. She very bad."

"How do you mean 'bad'?"

"She make servant do lot of work," he said, waving his arm to emphasize his point.

The carriage drove through a somewhat arid area, devoid of much vegetation, likely due to the rocky terrain situated away from the river. Some trees and shrubs dotted the barren landscape, and dustbowls could be seen swirling up in the wind.

Having heard much about the robbers of India who waylaid carriages, I asked Karim, "Are there any dacoits around here?"

"Oh, no, memsahib. All thugs dead now. *Sirkar* no like

thuggees."

I was relieved to hear that. As the carriage approached the gates of Furrukhabad, the Nawab's palace loomed on a small hill, above the town's houses. A huge, grey stone wall encircled the settlement, like a python, and the landau drove in through one of the gates.

"What is the population of Furrukhabad?" I asked Karim.

"One lakh peoples living here."

I looked inquiringly towards Elgin, who quickly explained, "He means, one hundred thousand persons."

That sounded a sizeable number, which was later confirmed, for inside the town seemed to be in a state of bedlam. All types of vehicles lumbered through the bazaar and people scampered about, carrying bundles of provisions. The coachman shouted and cracked his whip over their heads to clear the way. Shops lined the street. Each sold various items, from grains and spices that were displayed like tiny pyramids, to rolls of cloth. Smoke and cooking smells wafted from the eating establishments. Elgin pointed out to me a white-stuccoed building of the school where some of our missionaries taught.

Eventually, we reached the road that wound its way up the hill towards the palace, which was enclosed by another thick stone wall with a number of guardhouses having small, domed roofs. Large, onion-shaped tops of several edifices peeked above the ramparts.

"Who lives in those?" I asked Karim.

"Brother, sister of Nawab." He pointed to the highest building. "Nawabsahib live there." He then motioned towards another marble domed structure, with four large minarets. "Mosque."

Several mini palaces were clustered around the commons. On one side were sheds that housed a number of elephants; as the coach went by, they rocked on their chained feet as if in a dance. Some even raised their trunks and trumpeted. The carriage drove up to the portico of the main palace and two servants ran down the marbled steps to open the landau's doors.

Karim Khan shouted to one of them, "*Nur Jehan Begum ko bulao. Jaldysay.*" [call, Nur Jehan Begum, quickly]

The servant ran inside, obviously to fetch someone.

The other servant picked up the teaching material bags, and Elgin and I followed Karim up the short steps to the terrace that led into the palace. The first somewhat disturbing sight was of the wilting plantings in an unkempt garden located in the building's quadrangle. In the center stood a marble fountain, but from the soil and algae on it, it looked as if water had not spewed out of it for ages.

We were led along a dusty corridor of marbled pillared archways—adorned with flowery engravings—towards the right side of the courtyard. Walking past a central hall, we reached what looked to be a private chamber. The room was decorated in the usual oriental style, with dark red carpets and divans on which lay bolsters covered with silken material whose colors were beginning to fade.

A middle-aged lady, attired in a colorful shawl and a long white silken shirt over a wide blue skirt, entered from the left doorway. Likely upon seeing the men, she drew the shawl over her head. At first, from her attire, I thought she was the wife of the Nawab, for she had dark hair and a fair complexion, but when she drew closer I noted her distinct European features, a thin nose and lips.

"Good morning. I am Nur Jehan," she said, with just a slight hint of an Anglo-Indian accent, and extended her hand.

I caught a whiff of her fine perfume, a mixture of jasmine and roses. We shook hands and she led me towards a cushioned divan. While Elgin and the other servant busied themselves arranging the blackboard on the easel, Nur and I sat down. "So, you must be Harriet Birch?" I asked.

She looked at me with her large brown eyes and replied, "That was my maiden name. I am married to the Nawabsahib's brother, Sarbaland Khan."

I had expected a sigh or sadness in her voice, but there was none. "How long have you been married?"

"About twenty years. And you?"

Before I could respond, there was a commotion at the door and the Nawab entered. Several ladies followed him, some with trays in their hands. Nur got up, and so did I.

"Thank you," the Nawab said with a bow to me and motioned with his hand for us to be seated. While he was close enough for me to get a hint of his light perfume, he did not shake my hand. He was a young man of about thirty years, with fine, handsome features and a light complexion, typical of the Pathans of Northern India. He wore the same gold-threaded beige jacket—which extended to his knees over loose pantaloons—and the turban I had seen him in, that time in the carriage.

While the younger women—likely the maids—put down the trays of tea and snacks on the small stools, a well-attired lady came towards me. She was dressed similarly to Nur, but was laden with much jewelry, and her strong eastern perfume preceded her.

"Bilqis Begum," the lady said, pointing first to herself and then towards the Nawab; he grinned. She then put her palms on my temples and mumbled what sounded like a prayer in Arabic.

I looked towards Elgin, who explained, "Begum is praying to keep you safe from the evil eyes."

I smiled and thanked the Begum.

The Begum, bidding me to sit, gave sharp instructions in Urdu to the maids. They came hurriedly to me and handed me a china cup and saucer of tea and placed plates containing a selection of appetizers beside me. It was still a bit early in the morning and, having had a full breakfast, I was not particularly hungry. However, since all eyes were upon me, I made an effort to take some bites of the snacks. They were either too spicy or too sweet, but I expressed my pleasure by "ooh-ing" and nodding my head.

The aromatic tea—which I asked to be changed to a non-sugared cup—was laced with cardamoms and tasted lovely, but I was sorry to see the patterns on the fine bone china service had faded and edges of the plates were chipped. The silver spoons needed a good polish.

While consuming the refreshments, I conversed with the Nawab and the Begum through Elgin and was assisted by Nur, when Elgin could not translate. They gave a brief history of their Pathan families who had migrated to these parts, during the famines or wars, from the northern regions closer to Afghanistan. Being industrious and good warriors, they had cultivated the lands and served in the armies of the Mughal Emperors.

I inquired of the Nawab his reason for wishing to learn English. He replied that now with the decline of the Mughal armies, and high taxes on the farmers, there was much unemployment among his people. It was his desire that they become educated and learn other trades and be able to do business with the Europeans. But, noting some reluctance among the populace, he wished to serve as an example. By himself learning English, he hoped others would follow suit.

I mentioned that those were noble intentions, then suggested we get started. The maids took the crockery away. Nur also left, saying she would look in on me later and show me the palace. I told her I would like that.

Both the Nawab and the Begum settled down comfortably, slates and chalks in their hands, and arms on bolsters on the divan. I moved the blackboard in front of them. It seemed the Begum was somewhat interested in learning English, but watching her reach for the *paan*-tray and the silver spittoon constantly, I felt she was there more out of curiosity. However, the Nawab looked genuinely enthusiastic about learning the new language and eagerly awaited my instructions. Their *munshi*, Karim, also grabbed a slate and sat cross-legged on the rug.

I commenced the lesson in pretty much the same way I had taught the village ladies. I distributed the Lesson One booklets and asked them to repeat after me, and write the letters of the alphabet on their slates. I enunciated and scribed the letters on the blackboard as well.

The lesson progressed at a fair pace. There were the usual difficulties in their pronunciations of certain letters and I went over them again and again, until they had grasped them, spoken and written, reasonably well.

I saw Nur return and take a seat on a divan. The early morning breakfast, the tea and nibbles were having their effect on me. I requested Elgin to continue the lesson and went to Nur. "Is there a ladies' room nearby?" I asked.

"Yes. Let me take you there." She got up and led me out of the door.

I followed her along the corridors towards the left side of the palace. Noticing only women going about their business and children playing there, I believed that part was the females' residence, the *zenana*. The washroom I was ushered into was moderately clean, although I thought the marbled floor and walls needed a good scrub with soap and water. The toilet—built into the floor in typical eastern fashion—drained out to an open sewer channel that stank like a cattle manure hovel.

Emerging out of the washroom onto the courtyard, I saw Nur and a maid waiting for me with a pitcher of water, soap and towels.

I washed my hands beside a bed of banana plants and thought the poor wilting trees would be happy to receive a trickle of water.

Nur led me up a side stairway to the upper floors. "Please come. Let me show you my home."

"Doesn't anyone look after this garden?" I asked, as we walked up the stairs.

"We used to have many *maalis*. Now the Nawabsahib cannot afford to keep even one. The coachman will water and weed the plants once in a while."

"It's a shame to let this fine palace run down," I said as we came up to the landing of the second floor and walked along the corridor.

"It is. But what can we do? Nawabsahib's pension is hardly enough, and everything is getting so expensive. Look," she pointed to the tiled floor whose patterns were smudged with dirt, "I have asked the cleaning woman to sweep my floor days ago. But she is too busy doing other jobs. At my father's plantation, she would have been dismissed long ago. Nawabsahib is too kind to his staff."

It would not hurt you to pick up a broom once a while, I felt like telling her. We had reached the end of the corridor that obviously was her part of the palace's wing. The hallway's outside wall was lined with marble-latticed windows. We stood by one, to catch our breath on the cool fresh air that filtered through. The casements offered a good view of the palace grounds and ramshackle buildings of the town. The faint blue line of the Ganges River was visible in the distance.

"Where is your parents' farm?"

She pointed in the southerly direction. "Close to Futtehgurh, yonder, by the river. It's an indigo plantation." Then she moved abruptly away, as if she did not wish to talk about it. "Come, let me show you my flat." She unlocked the latch of a door and led me inside.

Just as I had expected, the rooms were decorated in the oriental style. Low divans had multi-colored silk coverings and bolsters. The floors were carpeted with expensive-looking rugs. Silk tapestries with eye-catching patterns hung on the walls. The tables and wardrobes were constructed of wood that looked like oak, with ivory inlays. There were three rooms in the apartment: one a general sitting room, one her daughter's and the other their bedroom.

Seeing that I was perhaps getting a bit fatigued from all the walking in the heat, she asked me to sit on a settee. She fetched me a glass of water and sat adjacent to me.

"Where's your husband?" I asked, taking a sip of the cool water.

"Out to work. He manages what little of the farmlands are left. But now in his old age, he has much work to do. You know, Margaret, I am so glad that you have come to teach the Nawabsahib some English. It will help us greatly."

"Why do you think so?"

"I am hopeful my husband, Sarbaland, will follow his brother's example and learn as well. Then he could open a business of his own, and not have to depend on the Nawabsahib so much."

"What would he do?"

"Perhaps start a factory or open a shop. But one has to know English to trade with the East India Company officials. If one deals through interpreters, they'll steal you blind."

"I heard you speaking Urdu. Did your husband teach you?"

She laughed. "Oh, no! I could speak it much before I met Sarbaland. I was born here, you know."

"How did you meet him?"

"He was one of Father's business associates. Used to visit our plantation often."

"Did your parents approve of him marrying you?"

I realized that I had touched a soft corner in her heart, for she grew silent and grave. She looked at the wall for a while and, spying the clock on the mantelpiece, said, "My! Look at the time. It's nearly noon. Begumsahiba will be wondering what happened to us. Shouldn't we be getting back?" She stood up.

"Yes," I said and, putting the glass of water on the table, followed her out of the door. I did not press my question further, for her silence answered it fairly well.

While we walked along the corridor, I asked, "Tell me, does the Begum know of the Nawabsahib visiting the De Fountains in Futtehgurh?"

She smiled. "Of course she does. She doesn't mind, really. For it's Mrs. De Fountain who's sending him chits asking to come and see her."

"What does she wish to see him about?"

"I'm not certain. But it seems she wishes to start some kind of a business with Nawabsahib. She's a widow, you know, and her husband's pension is hardly sufficient to support her. Nawabsahib is of course interested, and that's why he wants to learn English."

"What about her young daughter, Bonny? Some people in town think it inappropriate for the Nawab to see them."

"Margaret, you likely know how it is. People will start gossiping at the slightest opportunity. I'm certain the Nawabsahib was never alone with her. She's so young, after all."

"So you don't believe there is anything improper?"

"I don't think so. You don't know our Nawabsahib. He's such a kind-hearted person. He cannot refuse help to anyone."

I was satisfied with Nur's explanation and left it at that.

We returned downstairs to the sitting room. I noted the lesson had gone well and Elgin had taken them through to nearly the end of the alphabet. The Begum cast an irate look at Nur, but continued writing on the slate.

Nawabsahib looked at me and said, "Thank you."

I smiled and said, "You are very welcome, Nawabsahib. But you must learn more than 'thank you'."

He looked confusedly at Karim and, when he translated, the Nawab's face lit up in a broad smile.

Upon reaching the end of the alphabet, I went over some of the letters they had difficulty with, which Elgin had written at one end of the blackboard. It seemed they had attained a reasonable grasp of the alphabet. I impressed upon them to study the booklets and master the letters, before we could proceed to the next lesson. There were nods all around.

The lesson being over, I started to collect my things and prepared to take their leave. Upon seeing that, Bilqis Begum said something in Urdu to Elgin. She translated: "Begumsahiba is saying that she would like us to stay for lunch."

"Please thank her and tell her that we should be going, as it is a long carriage ride back to Futtehgurh."

But the Begum would hear none of it and said in a loud voice to Nur, "Ayee Nuri, *khana lagwao!*" [put dinner on the table]

The poor girl scampered out of the room, likely in the direction of the kitchen. The Nawab gestured with his hand for us to follow him.

It was a pleasant surprise to see the dining room we were ushered into. It seemed the whole contents of the room, furniture, draperies and all, were transported from a castle in the British Isles. However, from the poor conditions of the furniture and the unmatched pieces, it was obvious they were likely purchased at sales or gifted by departing British families.

The oak dining table was chipped on some sides and the assortment of eight chairs around it, were in no better shape. The sideboards were in a lighter-color wood and had deep scratches on the top and along the sides. The ancient-looking chandelier had lost several glass pendants. There were sections of window panes missing as well in a couple of curio cabinets in the corners, and the assortment of silver and gold ornamental pieces inside them looked as if they hadn't been cleaned since they were placed there.

It appeared the room was not used much, and from the likely hurried sweeping—spots of dust were still visible—it looked that it was opened just for that occasion. The silver, china and the crystal glasses, set neatly on the table, looked clean, though, for they must have been brought out and washed just for that lunch.

Nawabsahib went up to the head-chair, at the end of the table and, pulling it out, motioned for me to sit there.

"No, Nawabsahib, this chair is for you. If you wish, as your guest, I could sit at your right side," I said. While Elgin translated, I pulled that chair out and sat down. Nawabsahib looked confused for a moment then smiling, sat down on the head-chair. Bilqis Begum came hurriedly and sat on the chair to the left of Nawab. The others took their seats and the maids started serving the food.

As I had expected, there was no alcohol served, and only water was poured in the crystal wine glasses. There was a rose-colored sherbet also available, but I declined it, for it likely would have been too sugary.

The other surprise for me was that they had likely gone to great lengths to prepare a fully British-style meal, just for me! The first serving was a lovely-tasting chicken soup that had been spiced up a bit to enhance its flavor. The second course was fillet of fish which, although slightly overdone, tasted fine to me. I noted the Nawab and the Begum adding liberal doses of chili pepper to it. The main course, I had guessed correctly, was roast beef and Yorkshire pudding. While it was cooked to well-done, the spicy marinade and grilling over the charcoals had added a special flavor to the meat that I enjoyed very much.

The final pièce de résistance of the lunch was the multi-colored trifle of fruits and cream. It was brought, filled in a large bowl, by the chef himself. He looked to be an older Englishman. After serving it, he bowed to me and asked, "Was everything to your satisfaction, madam?"

"Yes, thank you. The meal was most delicious," I replied. He bowed again and left.

While the maids served the aromatic tea, I asked Nawabsahib, Elgin translating as usual, "Is he your regular cook?"

"Oh, no. He's a retired army man. Married to an Indian woman. They live in town. We call him for special occasions, such as this one, in your honor," he replied and smiled.

I thanked him for their thoughtfulness.

In between sips of tea, Bilqis Begum joined in. "Previously, we used to have several chefs. One for each type of national cuisine. Now we can hardly afford to keep one cook."

"But your Indian cooking is so delicious," I said, trying to appease her. "You don't need many cooks."

"Of course, we can get by without any cook, if only our *bhawajs* would help!" she said, looking towards Nur. The poor woman just stared down at her plate, with a straight face. But I felt that as soon as I was gone, there would be a verbal barrage between them.

During the meal we had talked a bit about the neighboring kingdoms. I took this opportunity to change the subject and asked about one of those states. "Nawabsahib, you mentioned the state of Jhansi was annexed some years ago. Is it really ruled by a woman?"

"Yes. Rani Lakshmibai. But she's now a rani in name only. I've heard that Lord Dalhousie has turned down her appeal to recognize her son as the heir to the throne."

"Really! Why did he do that?"

"He's an adopted child, you see. In the *Latsahib*'s mind, an adoptee is not a direct descendant and hence has no right to the kingdom! Therefore, his Lapse policy applied."

"Didn't the Rani have any children of her own, perhaps a daughter?"

"A son was born about four years ago. But unfortunately he died just three months later."

"Oh, how sad. So, what's the Rani doing now?"

"She lives on a pension, confined to her palace with her son. She still likes to go riding every morning, from what I've heard."

The Begum interjected, "But she hasn't given up, you know. She's engaged this British lawyer. What's his name, husband?"

"Lang sahib. I believe he hails from Australia. He's quite popular here, for he's won a few cases on behalf of some Indian clients against the Company."

"So, what's he doing for the Rani?" I asked.

"I understand he's helping her to appeal the Governor General's decision. Rumor has it that he might take the case right up to the Court of Directors in London, and possibly even to Queen Victoria herself!"

"It's remarkable that the Rani is going through all this trouble and expense to recover her rightful kingdom through legal means. But what else can she do?" I said, somewhat philosophically.

I wasn't really expecting an answer to my rhetorical question and, while sipping tea, my mind was still engrossed with the Rani's predicament, when suddenly I heard the Begum blurt loudly, "Oh, yes, she can. She will not let her lands be taken away so easily. Husband, didn't she send word to see you?" No sooner had she said this, she must have realized her recklessness, for she covered her face with the end of her shawl and wiped tears from her eyes.

The Nawab was silent for a while. He finally said, "Yes, Begum. Lakshmi wants to see me and I will visit her." Then, turning towards me, added, "It's likely nothing. Lakshmi probably wishes to discuss her situation and perhaps ask for our help. But what can we do? We are at the mercy of the Company ourselves."

"I understand," I said. "I am sure Mr. Lang will be able to do something for the Rani, even if he has to go all the way to London to plead her case."

We deliberated the Rani's and the other states' former rulers' situation a bit more. But it was getting late and, finishing my dessert and tea, I requested leave of the Begum and Nawab. Although they insisted I stay longer, I declined and thanked them for their kind hospitality. I was also helped in my wish to depart by a melodious sound, like a song in Arabic, that filtered in from outside through the latticed windows. It was similar to the murmurs I had heard in Turkey and was amazed at the similarity of the singing. It was the call for the afternoon prayer by the *moazzen* from the neighboring mosque.

the mango tree. Elizabeth and David had not returned home yet. Elgin, having made tea, was already scurrying about in the kitchen, getting dinner ready.

"How did the lesson go?" Papa asked even before I had taken a seat.

"Very well," I said, reaching for a cup of tea. "It seems the Nawab is really keen on learning English."

"Why do you think that might be, dear?" Mamma asked.

"Since they don't have any lands left, they wish to get into business and start trading with the East India Company. At least, that's what Nur told me."

"Nur, who?" Mamma said.

"Nur Jehan, or Harriet, as she was called before."

"Oh, you met her! What is she like?" Mamma inquired.

"Quite normal, really. A pretty lady. Looks like she's become one of their household. She speaks fluent Urdu, but she told me she did that even before she married the Nawab's brother. She was born here, you know."

"She *married* him!" Mamma exclaimed.

"Who got married?" Elizabeth said as she came to the table. She gave me a peck on the cheek and, pouring herself a cup of tea, sat down.

"Nur … I mean Harriet. You can ask her yourself. I have invited her to visit us," I said.

"You did not!" Mamma exclaimed. "Can you imagine, what will the neighbors say?"

"Let them say what they think. Why cannot we invite whom we please? The Nawab visits the De Fountains."

"Humph …" Papa started to say something, but stopped himself. He picked up a newspaper and started to glance through it.

I was perplexed. I looked from Mamma to Elizabeth. "What?"

Elizabeth, reaching for a shortbread biscuit, said, "Haven't you heard?"

"Heard what?"

She nibbled on the biscuit and replied, "They've shipped Bonny off to boarding school in Calcutta. Now who will the Nawab visit?"

"It is not how you imagine it to be," I said emphatically.

Chapter Six

A visitor and a gift-horse

1855, March: Futtehgurh, India

THE WARM AND WONDERFUL spring days at Futtehgurh passed by lazily. I occupied myself by continuing to teach the women at the village, and the Begum and Nawab at their palace. Although I had set realistic goals, and did not expect them to be reading or writing complete English sentences anytime soon, nevertheless I was impressed with the progress they made.

One Wednesday morning, during a lesson, the Nawab looked up while holding the slate and chalk in his hands, and asked—interpreted by Elgin, as usual—"Mrs. Margaret, do you like to ride horses?"

I must have been busy thinking of the lesson and replied offhandedly, "Yes, of course. I used to have my own mare in Crimea. But here, not even a pony!"

"Hmm ..." he said, and went back to scribbling on the slate. I continued on with the lesson.

The next Sunday, after spending another tiring day at the village schools, I returned home in the coach with Joyce and others, as usual chatting with them about the events of the day. When it turned into my street, through the window I spotted a carriage with the Futtehgurh regimental crest on its door and two red-coated *sepoys* standing by the garden gate. I thought it was likely the station commandant, Colonel George Smith, and his wife, Anna, come for a visit.

I bid a hasty goodbye to Joyce and Reverend Gopechand and hurried into the house; Elgin followed behind, carrying the teaching aids.

I quickly freshened up in my bedroom and walked out into the back garden. To my surprise, the visitor, sitting there with Mamma and Papa, was my seafaring fellow traveler, Colonel Humphrey!

Upon seeing me, he immediately got up and came towards me, both his hands outstretched. I must admit he looked dashing in the colorful uniform on his lean and erect frame.

"Hallo, Margaret! So good to see you."

I must have blushed a bit and wondered if I should let him kiss me on the cheek, which he evidently wished to do. But I thought better of it, and did a small curtsey and shook his hand. He led me to the table.

"What brings you here, Colonel Humphrey?" I asked, sitting down.

"I'm on a tour. Just visited Lucknow, in Oudh, you know. Being so close to Futtehgurh, thought I should pass by and see my old chum, George. We've spent some good times together. Anna and he have been kind enough to put me up for a few days. Then, remembering that you and Reverend James are also in this cantonment, here I am."

"I'm so glad you thought of us, and have come by," I said, reaching for a teacup.

"So, Colonel, was it all business in Lucknow?" Papa asked.

"Oh, yes, yes. Mostly official stuff. Delivered a few messages from the GG to Nawab Wajid Ali. But did manage to find some time to take in a *shikar* with William."

"That would be William Sleeman, I believe?" Papa asked.

"Yes. Yes, our Resident, you know. Poor fellow has run into a bit of conflict with the GG."

"I see," Papa said.

I wondered if Papa really understood. It was clear that for the Governor General to have a message delivered personally by one of his senior aides did not bode well for the kingdom of Oudh. Also the mention of a conflict with the Resident was strange. The rumors of Oudh's annexation were likely true, I mused.

"Did you bag a tiger?" Papa asked.

"No such luck. My daughters, in London, have been clamoring for tiger-skin rugs. I might end up having to buy some!"

"How many children do you have, Colonel?" Mamma asked.

"Three daughters. Their husbands are all box-wallas. Spend their time buying and selling God knows what." We laughed at the connotation.

"Any chance of them returning here?" Mamma asked.

"Oh, no. They are all comfortably settled in London. Have their children and families to look after, you know. They were here during their childhood, of course, but have tasted their last curries, I'm afraid. Come to think of it, they weren't particularly fond of it, as I recall."

"London can be an interesting place to live, as I discovered from the little time I spent there," I said, perhaps not realizing that I was sounding pretentious.

"Yes, I dare say, they likely spend their time attending all the balls and parties, particularly during the season."

"Ah, the London season!" Mamma said, as if she had attended one, which I knew she had not.

The Colonel turned towards me. "So, tell me, Margaret, how have you been spending your time?"

"Teaching mostly, Colonel," I replied. "At the village and in the Furrukhabad Palace." I gave him a brief account of my impromptu schools.

"The Nawab's learning English! Really?"

"Yes. Seems to be very interested. Says he wishes to set an example to his people."

"Is that so? How many are in your class?"

"Just him, the Begum and their *munshi*."

"Is that all?"

"Yes. Oh, and, Nur … err … Harriet, sits in now and then. Just to listen in, of course. Do you know her?"

"Yes. I've heard of her. Are you certain there is no one else? Perhaps sitting in an adjoining room?"

I laughed. "No. I don't believe so. There are the servants, but they are busy in their chores."

"How interesting. Hmm …" He stared into the distance contemplatively, while I sought Mamma and Papa's eyes.

They looked just as perplexed, as I must have. I wondered why he had asked that, but I put it down to his inquisitive nature.

Finally, after some more small talk, the Colonel took his gold pocket-watch out and opened it. "Goodness, look at the time. Anna and George must be wondering if I was kidnapped by a thuggee! I must take your leave."

"Must you go, Colonel? Wouldn't you stay for dinner?" Mamma asked.

"Thank you. But I'm afraid I must, Mrs. Wallace. It being Sunday, there is the formal dinner at the Mess that I have to attend. I should be away by Wednesday, and have some matters to discuss with George. But before I go, I would like to come by again, if I may?"

"Yes, please do, Colonel. We will be most pleased to see you again," Papa said.

The Colonel got up and prepared to leave. We followed him to the front door. Before exiting, he turned around, as if he had remembered something, and said, "Margaret, I understand from Reverend James that you like to go riding?"

"Yes, I do, Colonel."

"May I take you out? The syce tells me there is the gentlest mare in the stables that would be most suitable for you. In your condition, I mean," he said with a smile.

Mamma must have looked confounded. "Oh! Just the two of you?"

He turned towards her. "You need not worry, Mrs. Wallace. We'll have a full escort."

"Oh, I wasn't thinking about chaperones, rather about those ruffians you met on the ship."

"I believe they were from a state much further away. But even if they are here, they daren't make a move against us. We will be fully armed."

"I am relieved to hear that," Mamma said, and Papa nodded.

I did not comprehend the fuss Mamma was making and said, "Why, thank you, Colonel, for thinking of me. I should very much like to go riding. I could do with more exercise."

"Good, then. How about tomorrow, about six o'clock? Early morning is the best time here."

"That would be wonderful. I'll be ready," I replied.

He again extended his hands, as if attempting to embrace and kiss me, but I quickly stepped back and, grasping his hand, shook it.

We followed him up to the garden gate. He entered the carriage and departed with a final wave from the window, and reminding me about the riding on Monday morning.

I saw Mamma and Papa were all smiles, and Papa put his arm

around Mamma's waist.

"Is it all right for me to go riding with the Colonel?" I asked.

"Of course it is, dear," Mamma replied. "I cannot see what's wrong in it. After all, he's a widower, not to mention what you told us about how he took care of you during the voyage to Calcutta. And, how he protected your honor from those Indian nationalists."

"Yes, I am much grateful to him for that."

"But mind, you be very careful in your condition, Margaret. No galloping, jumping fences or anything of that sort," Papa warned.

"Yes, of course, I'll take care. I've just started my third trimester. I'll be cautious." I felt elated and, turning to Mamma, hugged her.

That night, before going to bed, I prayed to our Lord. I thanked Him for all the blessings he had bestowed upon me, and for having delivered me safely into the loving arms of my parents. I thanked Him particularly for opening all the doors that would lead me to future contentment.

As I lay in bed and before I could drift away into much-needed sleep, my mind wandered. I felt happy that someone of the Colonel's status and position in the English society was taking so much interest in me. In Calcutta, Moira had told me that he was a younger son of an earl, and while his elder brother, Lord Humphrey, had inherited the title and the estate, the Colonel had considerable wealth behind him as well. "You would do very well, if he was to wed you", she had whispered to me, and I had likely blushed. Not that it was my main reason for being attracted to him, but I admired him for his integrity and candor. As for looks, he was rather handsome, although much older. "Fifty isn't that old", Moira's words rang in my head, and he certainly did not look his age. However, despite all his captivating charisma, there was something about him that I could not grasp in my mind. It was as if distant bells rang faintly, warning me to be cautious. I wondered what it could be. Was it the quick-tempered way he had reacted against that Indian separatist, over the native's dim-witted remark? Well, most military officers are volatile. What was so unusual about that? Yet, there was that little voice in the back of my head that cautioned me to be wary of him.

It was getting late. I put those thoughts out of mind and drifted off to sleep.

I was up before sunrise the next morning. After a quick breakfast of toast and tea, I was ready and waited, with Mamma and Papa, for the Colonel out on the veranda. I was happy that I could still fit into the riding-habit I had acquired in Crimea. It was in an older high-waist pattern with an ample flowing skirt that accommodated my bulging belly and "looks presentable", as Mamma had put it, while making tea. She had wanted to ask Elgin to come early and accompany me. But I had prevented her. "Mamma, there is no need for that. She was out with me all day yesterday. Besides, the poor girl has plenty to do, with making breakfast for her whole family, prior to coming to work for us."

We sat on the wicker chairs, watching the pre-dawn rising up above the treetops, and birds flying around, chirruping. At the appointed hour, a group of scarlet-coated riders turned into our street and cantered towards the house. Colonel Humphrey rode up front and was followed by three red-turbaned Indian *sowars*. One held the reins of a rider-less grey. They stopped at the front gate.

I bid Mamma and Papa a hasty farewell and walked out to meet the group. The Colonel dismounted. He was dressed impeccably in a spotless uniform with shiny brass buttons, and had his usual revolver in the holster. One of the *sowars* brought the mare to me. She indeed looked to be a gentle creature and bobbed her head as I approached her. I rubbed her mane. She was fitted with a customary side-saddle and the syce cupped his palms for my foothold.

The Colonel and I exchanged pleasantries. He came behind me and, saying, "Let me help you," held me by the waist and assisted me up onto the mare. He might have held my waist just a little longer than necessary, but I supposed he was making sure that I did not slip. It was nice to be up in a saddle again after many months. The Colonel took off his blue forage cap, raised it to my parents and mounted his stallion. I waved to them and, heeling the mare, guided her to follow the Colonel's charger.

"Shall we ride by the river?" Colonel Humphrey asked when I got alongside him. "George mentioned a picturesque trail goes through the woods there."

"That would be wonderful. It should be much cooler by the water."

"Yes. The sun will be high up soon. I'm glad you have your solar hat on."

We followed the street down to the river and turned onto a trail that meandered along the bank of the Ganges, which flowed serenely towards Calcutta and the ocean. The tide being low, there was room enough for the Colonel's and my horse to walk side by side. The sepoys followed behind us at a respectable distance. The tall trees further up on the embankment, with their drooping branches, protected us from the hot rays of the rising sun, which made riding in the cool morning breeze that much more enjoyable.

The Colonel engaged me in pleasant conversation. He inquired about my past life in New Jersey, and how I had become interested in medicine, and managed to attend a medical college, and enter a profession so much restricted to women at that time. He was careful not to dwell too much on my former marriage, and my husband's death, for that would surely have brought on tears and plunged me into a depressed state. I asked him about his family. He spoke at length about them, his daughters, and his wife, who had passed away a few years earlier.

Soon we had travelled through the cantonment area and entered a wooded knoll. I looked up the bank and saw up on the small hill the white domes of a building peeking through the tree tops. Upon getting closer, it looked to be an old mansion, in a ramshackle condition.

"Colonel, what would that dwelling be?" I pointed towards it.

"I don't know." He turned in the saddle and spoke in Urdu to one of the soldiers, who—for I had picked up some of the language—advised that it was an abandoned *haveli*.

"Would you like to look in there?" the Colonel asked.

Being interested in exploring old buildings, I nodded. He said something more in Urdu to the *sowars* that I could not comprehend, and turned his horse towards the hill. I guided my mare to follow him on the narrow path that led up to the mansion. The three soldiers stayed behind, and I saw them dismount and take their horses to the water for a drink. While I had expected them to follow, I thought better than to make a fuss.

Having climbed up the hill, we reached the front yard of the house. It was an old brick and mortar structure, perched on a ledge, with a large stone patio overlooking the river. While its walls looked to be in disrepair, the house still stood in one piece.

We dismounted and tethered the horses to the branches of some overgrown trees that hung over the neglected garden. The front wooden door was padlocked; we walked on the path to the rear of the house and climbed the short steps up to the stone patio. A semi-circular, knee-high stone wall ran around the patio, and we strolled up to it. A breath-taking vista of the river and the country lay before us. Beyond the trees on the riverbanks, green and yellow fields extended for miles, interspaced by mud huts of the farm villages.

The Colonel took out his handkerchief and dusted the wide stone wall ledge to clean a spot for us. I was happy to sit down, for I was getting a bit tired in the heat of the sun, which had risen quite high. He took a spot beside me and, fishing out his cigar box, asked if I minded his smoking. I replied in the negative.

Colonel Humphrey lit up and gazed out into the distance for a while, then, carefully blowing the cigar smoke away, turned towards me and asked, "So tell me, Margaret, how are the Nawab and family keeping?"

"Well, as far as I could see."

"How are they progressing with the English lessons?"

"Seem to be coming along nicely. Have learned the alphabet, and some of the basic words so far."

"I see. And as you mentioned, they wish to start a business?"

"Yes. It would appear so. Looks like their pension isn't sufficient."

"Well, it never is," he laughed, "especially to continue leading the life of opulence they were used to. But, tell me, apart from their financial situation, how are they mentally coping with the political situation?"

"Seem to be handling it well. It would appear they wish to live peacefully alongside the Europeans."

"Are they not agitated by some of the states' annexations taking place around them?"

I should have thought about my response, but perhaps in the heat, I did not deliberate enough, and said, "Yes, I recall the Begum does seem disturbed by the situation of the Rani of Jhansi. Is she really going to lose her kingdom?"

"I'm afraid so. The GG has turned down her lawyer, Mr. Lang's, appeal."

"Yes, the Nawab mentioned that. So, what is Mr. Lang going to do?"

"He is welcome to take it up with the East India Company's directors in London. But, tell me, how did the Nawab hear of it?"

"He said he heard it from the Rani."

"Really! And ...?"

The Colonel's curiosity did intrigue me a bit, but I put it down to his inquisitive nature and responded, "He said she had asked him to see her."

"Is that so! Has he visited her?"

"Not yet. At least, I don't think so. He said he might go and meet her. But what can the poor fellow do? He doesn't have much money. As it is, his own palace could use some more servants. It looks to be quite run down."

"I've never been there. But, having seen similar palaces, I can imagine the condition. Most of them are in a dilapidated state. Such as this one, for instance." He looked towards the house. "It looks like the back door is cracked. It might be open. Shall we look inside?" He got up.

Sitting out in the sun, I was getting a bit hot and sweaty in the riding habit, and a peek inside the mansion was inviting. I looked down towards the river and noted the sepoys there, squatting under a shady tree. I smiled to myself, as I followed the Colonel, realizing that he had told the soldiers to stay down there. He tried the back door, it unfastened with a screech, and he held it open for me. We went in to what looked to be the parlor.

It was indeed pleasant inside the *haveli,* for its marbled floors and columns still retained some of the night's coolness. We strolled through the different rooms, leaving our footprints on the dusty floors. The Colonel opened some of the windows and we looked out at the different views of the river and the gardens they offered. It seemed the place had been owned by a rich landowner, for although it was devoid of any furniture, the intricate moldings on the white columns and the intriguing patterns on the marble floors were indicative of its once prosperous ownership.

"Hmm ... seems the place was likely owned by a prince," the Colonel murmured.

"Who might possess it now?"

"The Company, I should think. Might be allocated to an officer to be stationed in this part of the country."

Having seen enough, I started back towards the parlor. It was then the Colonel came up to me and, holding me with one hand on my shoulder gently turned me around to him. He looked at me with his piercing blue eyes. "Margaret, good that we are alone. For I've been meaning to tell you something."

"Yes, Colonel? What is it?" I said, trying to retain my composure, and dreading what he might do next.

"Oh, please call me William. You know, I am getting very fond of you."

"Why ... I had no idea ... Colonel," I stammered and must have blushed crimson.

"William, please. My dear Margaret. I haven't been able to stop thinking about you."

"Why ... Col ... William. I am most flattered ..."

He then put his arms around me and drew me to him. While one side of my brain told me to resist and push him back, I could not. Likely due to the ecstasy of the moment, which seemed to have put me in a trance. I succumbed to his advances. He held me in a warm embrace. I felt tears of happiness in my eyes and, putting my arms around him, felt his muscular chest pressing on my breasts. He was taller than me, and I looked up at him. He bent his head down and gently kissed me on the lips. It was a tender kiss, not a passionate one that lovers might share. It was an exquisite feeling nonetheless.

He held me in the kiss for a while until I moved my head back and whispered, "Shouldn't we be getting back?"

He immediately let go of me. "Oh, Margaret, my dear. I'm so sorry for getting carried away. I know you are still in mourning. I have no right to act this way."

It was the first time anyone had kissed me since my Robert's death. It brought tears to my eyes. I wiped them quickly with a kerchief I carried in the fold of my dress's sleeve. "It's ... all right ... Col ... William."

He drew me to him, once again. "Hush now. I know the memories of your husband must still be fresh. But there's no need to torment yourself, my dear. You are young. You have your whole life ahead of you."

At his comforting words, I put my head on his chest, but tears still trickled down my cheeks. He held me tightly and ran his hand on my back. "Margaret, my dear, my dear." He held me close for a long time. Mixed feelings of elation and caution went through me, when I heard him say, "Margaret, my dear, may I see you when you are in Delhi? I go there often on business."

I simply nodded, unable to speak, as bewildering thoughts raced through my mind. Did the Colonel really love me? Why me, from all the high-society women he could have the pick of? Why did he wish to visit me in Delhi? Was it a proposal?

The Colonel finally released me. "Are you all right, Margaret?"

Wiping my tears and blowing my nose, I again nodded. "Sorry for being so emotional, William," I managed to whisper.

"It's all right. I understand." He closed the mansion's windows he had opened, and held out his elbow to me.

I held his forearm and followed him out into the bright sunshine. We retraced our steps to the horses and, mounting them, rode down the mountain path to the riverbank. The languishing sepoys jumped to attention and scrambling onto their mounts, followed us.

"Have you a place to stay in Delhi?" he asked.

"The chaplain, Jennings, has offered to put me up. But I should find a place of my own, once my children are here from Canada."

"Yes, of course. But I believe you would be most comfortable with the Commissioner, Simon Fraser, in his huge Gothic mansion, the Ludlow Castle."

"Really, a castle in the center of Delhi!"

"Imagine that! I know Simon. I'll arrange for you to stay there."

"Thank you. But only for a while. I am anxious to bring my children over."

"I understand."

We chatted amiably at some length and soon reached my parents' cottage. The Colonel helped me dismount, and led me into the house. No one was around, for they were at work or school. Elgin had likely gone to the market.

"Would you like some tea, William?" I led him to the small dining table in the kitchen.

"Don't mind if I do." He sat down on a chair, and took off his cap.

I put the kettle on and, placing some biscuits on a plate, brought them to the table. I sat down beside him. He held my hand and looked lovingly into my eyes. While it felt good to be once again desired by a fetching man, and of the Colonel's standing, still, tiny warning bells rang in my head.

"Margaret, I am so happy to have made your acquaintance."

"Likewise, William. You have been so kind to me. I just cannot believe that you would be interested in me, a widow with children!"

"Yes, my dear, I am very fascinated by you. And don't forget I'm a widower too, with much grownup children."

He looked into my eyes for a while, and then, putting his arm around me, drew me to him, and kissed me once again. The whistling of the kettle drew us apart and I hurried to the stove.

While we had tea, we conversed affably about his family and mine, and also my children. He again asked me more questions about my teaching the Nawab and the Begum at their palace.

The time passed quickly and, it nearing noon, he got up. "Well, Margaret, reluctantly, I should be getting back to the cantonment. But I trust this is not goodbye. I hope to see you before I depart, and of course soon in Delhi."

"It will be my pleasure, William."

He kissed me again. "Do look after yourself, my dear, and I trust you will not have a too laborious time." He glanced at my belly.

I must have blushed. "Thank you. I'll take care."

"I'm looking forward to seeing the little one." He kissed me again, a lingering one this time, and strode out of the house to his waiting escorts.

The next morning, while I relaxed and breakfasted alone—other family members having gone to their respective jobs—there was a knock on the front door. Elgin had just finished frying one of her delicious spicy omelets and, putting it before me, hurried to the door. While I nibbled on the omelet, together with a piece of chapatti, I heard her talking in Urdu to a man and their voices trailed off, for it seemed they went into the front garden. I heard her footsteps as she returned swiftly into the kitchen.

"Memsahib, you not believe this," she said in an excited voice.

"Who is it, Elgin?"

"It's Karim the *munshi*. Nawabsahib send a present for you!"

"Really!" I quickly donned my pink housecoat, which hung on a chair's back, straightened out my hair, and followed her to the front door and onto the veranda.

Karim stood there and I spotted the coachman waiting by the

garden gate, holding on to the reins of their horses. Upon seeing me, both Karim and the coachman salaamed. I had expected to see a parcel of some kind in their hands, which I thought would likely be jewelry, and I had a good mind to refuse it, but there was none. "Yes, Mr. Karim. Is something the matter?"

"No, no, memsahib. All well. No problem. Nawabsahib give you that *ghuri*." He pointed to a young and exquisite-looking grey mare by the fence.

"Oh, no, I cannot accept it," I said, with a lump forming in my throat.

"Please, memsahib. Come take a look." He walked towards the horse and motioned at me to follow.

Being fond of horses, I thought that at least I should go and pat her, and walked up to the mare. She indeed was a fine-looking creature, with shiny ivory-like skin, and a golden mane. She perked up her ears, bobbed her head, and whinnied softly on seeing me approach. I gently rubbed her nose and neck. The coachman produced a small apple and presented it to me in his palm. I took it and brought it to the mare's mouth. She gingerly accepted it and chewed away happily, bobbing her head. I noted a new tan leather side-saddle over a colorful checkered blanket on her back. The Nawab had considered everything, I mused. My heart said to keep her, but my mind said no.

"She's indeed a lovely horse. What do you call her?" I asked Karim.

"Her name, Sultana. Meaning 'princess'."

"It's a fitting name. But really, Mr. Karim, much as I like her, I cannot agree to this gift. Please take her back and thank the Nawabsahib for his kindness."

"Oh, no, memsahib. He no like me take *ghuri* back. He say leave here. He going to be very angry with me."

"Honestly, Mr. Karim. Why should he be upset at you? Besides, it is too expensive a gift."

"No, no. No very expensive. Nawabsahib has many, many horses." Karim waved his hands to emphasize his point.

On hearing that, my heart softened a bit. I knew Papa, although he had said he might, would never be able to afford to buy me a mare as fine as that one. On the other hand, not only did I love to ride, but we could have used a horse for those household errands that needed to be done. My parents were forever requesting our neighbors for assistance, it being far too expensive to hire coaches.

I turned towards Elgin for her opinion. "What do you think, Elgin? Should I accept it?"

"Well, memsahib, you may know it is considered bad manners in their culture to refuse a gift. Also, the Nawabsahib can afford it. He give away horses, cows and many animals as gifts all the time."

"Is that so? But where are we going to keep her? We have no room here in our tiny bungalow."

"My father look after her. There is space in shed for one more horse. He and my brothers will be happy to keep her, and groom her as well."

I was glad to hear the mare could be suitably looked after and, not wishing to cause a rift between us missionaries and the Nawab, I decided to accept. I turned towards the two Indian gentlemen, who stood by patiently. "Let me try her out first."

They nodded. Karim helped me mount Sultana and, while they all watched, I took the mare up and down the street in a walk and then in a slow canter. She was a gentle animal, seemed to be well trained and responded appropriately to my instructions.

Returning and alighting, I said, "All right, Mr. Karim, since Nawabsahib has a large stable, I will keep the *ghuri*. Please thank him from all of us. But there is one condition." They looked at me with a confused expression. "I have to get my father's permission. If he refuses, Sultana is going back."

They both nodded. Karim said, "Yes, yes. If padre-sahib no like, we take *ghuri* back."

Satisfied that I was happy with the animal, Karim and the coachman salaamed in their customary fashion and reminded me that they would be over with the carriage tomorrow morning to pick me up for the lessons at the palace. Then, mounting their stallions they galloped away, likely pleased at having accomplished their mission.

That evening there was, what seemed to be, a barrage of questions from Papa and Mamma on my having received the gift-horse. It felt just like the times when as a little girl I used to bring home a stray cat or a puppy. At first both were vehemently opposed to my keeping the mare, and Papa was particularly livid at my having accepted it without his consent, but calmed down a bit when I mentioned that it was conditional upon his approval.

Their major objections were related to the gift's appropriateness and the muttering it might create in town. I tried my best to dispel their fears. There were also the usual questions of housing the horse and the cost of its feed and care. Although it seemed my assurance had some effect when I mentioned that she would be cared for by Elgin's father and I would pay for all of Sultana's maintenance expenses, I noted from Papa and Mamma's stern faces that they were still not satisfied. Fortunately my savior arrived, in the form of my brother.

"Hallo, whose lovely mare is that I see tethered to our fence?" he said, taking a seat at our table in the back garden. While he cut a thick slice of the chocolate cake, Mamma poured a cup of tea for him.

"Mine," I said.

"Yours? Have you been promoted already, without having amputated a single limb yet?"

"No, and I haven't received a pay increase, either. The horse is a gift from Nawabsahib."

"For all those English lessons?"

"Exactly. At least he has the decency to show some appreciation for my efforts."

"And I am advising Margaret to return the animal. We shall receive all the gratitude from our good Lord, for our labors in educating the heathens," Papa said in his solemn voice.

"But why, Papa? Why shouldn't we accept some gratitude from the people here on Earth?" David's words were like music to my ears.

"Not if it comes with some conditions," Papa replied.

"What conditions? I didn't hear any. Are there some, Sister?"

"None that I know of," I said.

"Margaret, you are being too naive. There might be some encumbrances later. One can never tell how the mind of these natives works," Papa said.

"Papa, you are being too cynical. I work in their community. They give and share without any ulterior motives. I would say, let Margaret keep the horse. The Nawab has a large enough stable. May I ride her sometimes, Sister?"

"Yes, you certainly may, David."

"All right, children. If you so badly want the horse, you may have it," Papa finally relented.

David, having finished his tea and cake, got up and left us, saying, "All right, I'll be the first to take the mare out for a ride."

I imagined he would have ridden over straight to his Indian girlfriend's house to show her our new acquisition, and that from the Nawab of Furrukhabad!

I had hoped that it was the end of the discussion about the gift-horse, but I should have known that it was bound to surface again.

The next morning, it being Wednesday, and knowing William had mentioned something about coming over, early, to say goodbye, I was expecting him. But when he did not show up, thinking he was likely too busy, I wasn't too concerned.

Later, Elgin and I waited as usual out on the veranda for the Nawabsahib's carriage. It had surprised me that it was not there at the appointed hour, for they were invariably early and had to wait for me.

I spotted Papa walking up the driveway, and when he reached me, I stared inquisitively at him. He looked weary. I wondered if he, or someone we knew, was ill.

"Margaret, can you come inside, please?"

I followed him and we sat down at the dining table, in the kitchen. Elgin hurried to pour him a cup of tea. "What is the matter, Papa?"

"The Nawab's carriage will not be coming. Reverend Johnston just came to see me. Sorry, Margaret, he has decided to cancel your teaching at the Nawabsahib's palace."

That information stunned me. I was silent for a while. Upon recovering from the shock, I asked, "But why, Papa? Was it something I said or did?"

"No. It has nothing to do with you, child. It was his decision."

Remembering how Reverend Johnston and his wife had implored me to teach at the palace, I asked again, "But why? And when did he reach this decision?"

"It was yesterday afternoon. He sent a message over to the Nawab last night."

"Did someone else provoke him? Papa, why aren't you telling me everything?"

"All right. He had a visit from Colonel Smith. Apparently he does not think it appropriate for you to be teaching the Nawab and his family."

"But, why not? What's wrong with teaching them simple English?"

"Aww ... I don't really know. Something to do with the Nawab getting involved in politics. I didn't press for details."

I realized that if it was politics, there could be only one source for this ruling. "Did Colonel Humphrey have a say in this?"

Papa nodded, and sipped his tea. "Probably. He was with Colonel Smith when they visited Reverend Johnston. Listen, Margaret, sorry to be abrupt. I have to get back to the Church. There is a meeting going on and I am expected back. I came to inform you, as soon as I heard."

"What about the mare the Nawab gifted me?"

"Oh, yes. They would like you to return the horse as well."

This was the second shock of the morning, and I was speechless once again. Papa came to me and hugged me. "I'm sorry, Margaret. But do take heart. It is their choice. Nothing to do with you, or your performance. Besides, you shouldn't be teaching anymore, in your condition, I mean."

"It's not that, Papa. I was going to stop travelling to the palace soon, anyway. It's just the way they have handled this issue." I had tears in my eyes.

"Incidentally, they want to commend you for the teaching. Brother Johnston will be speaking to you, at a gathering, soon. Look, I really must go." It seemed he said that likely to cheer me up. He gulped the remaining tea in the cup, and left the house. Elgin, who had been listening, stared at me in disbelief. I did not say anything to her. I got up and went to my room and lay down on the bed. I felt very tired.

Chapter Seven

A birth and plans for Delhi

1855, May: Futtehgurh, India

AFTER THE ABRUPT CANCELLATION of my classes at the Furrukhabad Palace, and although I continued to teach the women in the village at the headman's home, my heart was not in presenting the lessons anymore.

Joyce did not go into details of the cessation, apart from a brief mention: "Oh, I hope the Nawab is not disappointed at the termination of the classes." I was glad she did not elaborate, for I could not have discussed the circumstances with her. I smiled at her calling it a "termination", for it was really an "abandonment" I thought. I felt disgusted at recalling how quickly her husband, Reverend Johnston, had succumbed to the wishes of the cantonment commander.

No doubt Colonel Humphrey had had a hand in it. I was certain, for it was evident by the way he had departed so speedily. Despite confessing all his fervor for me, he had not come by even to say goodbye.

Joyce must have noticed my lack of enthusiasm, but more so that I had begun having some difficulty walking. Due to the additional weight of the baby and the heat—it was getting increasingly sweltering by the day—my ankles had begun to swell. Hence, with my approaching delivery date, it was only natural that I would discontinue teaching altogether.

There was also the matter of returning the gift-horse to the Nawab. David had ridden up to the Palace one Sunday morning. While he was met cordially, the Nawab had steadfastly refused to take back the mare. Hence, David was happily riding all over Futtehgurh and the surrounding area, sometimes with his petite girlfriend, Mari, at the back of the saddle, her arms tightly around his chest. I was in no condition to ride much, but looked forward to the day when I could go galloping.

On that fateful day, I had started to feel uneasy since noon. Although I was experiencing the familiar contractions and pains for some time, but could not be definite when the actual delivery day would be. During dinner, Mamma sensed my apprehension and inquired a few times if I was all right. I responded that I was fine.

Later that night, it being the monsoon season, a fierce storm descended upon our town. Heavy rain broke through the dark clouds that were gathering all day and pelted the thatched roof of the bungalow with ferocity. I was getting ready for bed and had just finished my toilet when there was a piercing pain in my abdomen, and I noticed some telltale blood on the washcloth. It was when the water broke, and when I felt it drip down my thighs, I knew it was the start of the labor.

I tiptoed to my parents' bedroom and knocked on their door. Upon her inquiry, I said, "Mamma, I think it's time. Perhaps you should send David to fetch Elgin and the *dai*?" They lived in the Christian village, behind our house. Mamma asked me to lie down and hurried towards David's room.

After all, it was my third baby, and not having had much difficulty with the two earlier births, I thought it would be a much easier delivery. The *dai*—a diminutive and very dark Indian woman—had come to see me a few times earlier. While she thought the baby seemed rather big, but knowing the European children usually were, she did not believe there would be any complication. Also, it being late at night, I did not think it was necessary to bother the station surgeon, Doctor Flemings. Little did I know how wrong I was.

I lay down for a while but, feeling nauseous, I got up and walked about in the hallway, having covered myself with a shawl for warmth from the wind that howled outside and blew in through the window cracks. I watched, through the windowpanes, the trees swaying in the garden and rain falling like a sheet of water. When the contractions started to come regularly, and lasted longer, I lay down again.

Mamma came in with extra pillows to support my back, and informed me that David had gone to fetch the women and they should not be too long. She examined me, and being knowledgeable in these matters, informed me that my cervix was dilating nicely. I found that breathing deeply and exhaling helped to ease the periodic pains that had increased in their sharpness. Subsequently, I felt the intense ache and throbbing that was due to the stretching of the cervix, which prepared for the baby to descend into the birth canal. All was well up to that point. The problems were to commence from thereon in.

Dai—I cannot recall her name—and Elgin finally arrived. Mamma told Elgin to put water to boil and Dai came hurriedly into my room. She went to the washstand and, after washing her hands, pulled the bed sheet up to my waist; she spread my thighs apart and examined me carefully. She was at it for a while. Mamma also came in and looked inquiringly at her.

Finally, Dai withdrew her fingers from my vagina and, after rewashing her hands, said, "Me say before. Baby too big."

Hearing that bewildered me; all kinds of birthing complications swam in my head.

"What do you mean, Dai?" Mamma asked, looking perplexed.

"I say baby head too big. I feel head with fingers. No come out." Then, looking towards me and with a hand gesture, she added, "Memsahib, no push. No push. Understand?"

I nodded. What she said seemed to be true, for the pain was increasing in intensity by the minute. Despite the urge, I heeded Dai's advice, and refrained from pushing. It was, however, comforting to know that at least it was not the situation of a breech birth.

"Really! Is there anything we can do?" Mamma asked. "How do you feel, Margaret?"

"I'm in terrible pain, Mamma." By then I had tears in my eyes.

"I try massage," Dai said. She opened a small bundle she carried, and took out some vials containing oils of different colors. Selecting one, she rubbed it on her palms and fingers and, getting between my spread thighs, started to give me a perineal massage.

While the rubdown and kneading by her gentle fingers felt good, it did little to help relax the muscles. It seemed the baby was just not able to descend down. She then made me get into a squatting position and, when it did not help, onto all fours.

Going through these maneuvers did little to nudge the baby. I felt exhausted and as the pain intensified, I slumped down again on my back. I sobbed and prayed silently to our Lord to let my baby live, for it was not the baby's fault for being born, and if He wished, to take my life instead.

Mamma went to the door and said excitedly to Papa, who stood in the hallway, "We'll probably need forceps. I don't believe Dai has any. We must send for Doctor Flemings."

David was also in the hallway, and I heard him say: "I'll go right away. I had Sultana saddled and brought over, just in case." Putting on his rain jacket and hat, he dashed out of the front door.

Nausea and waves of intense pain, emanating from my abdomen, travelled through my body. I writhed in discomfort, while Mamma, Dai and Elizabeth in turn tried to restrain me. I had images of David galloping away on the grey mare, in the intense rain and windstorm towards the cantonment, and on reaching the good doctor's house, hammering on his door.

The possibility of the use of forceps had alarmed me, for I had heard of its snags and seen the bruising it can do to the baby's head and face. I was, however, comforted by the thought that Doctor Flemings would arrive soon. I believed him to be a competent surgeon, and one who would make the best decision.

Dai, turning me over on my side, gave me a back rub and administered other techniques they used to assist women in labor. These procedures helped for a while only, and the throbbing aches returned.

I drifted off in a daze, and it felt like hours that David had gone, when I was transported back from my stupor by the sound of the opening of the front door and shuffling of boots in the hallway. I heard Papa and Mamma greet Doctor Flemings and, in whispered conversation, they informed him of my condition. I heard him say a few times, "Hmm ... I see ... is that so ... I see."

Finally Doctor Flemings strode into my room. He was a tall man in his fifties, with a dark greying beard. It looked that he had dressed hurriedly and thrown on his dark coat over grey trousers. His white shirt was creased and cravat-less. He put his medical leather bag on a table and went to the washstand. While washing his hands, he turned towards me and said, "Hallo Margaret. Looks like you got yourself in a pickle!"

That bit of humor helped to elevate my spirit somewhat. "I'm afraid so, Doctor Flemings. But I'm so glad to see you. Thank you for coming directly."

"No problem at all. How are you feeling now?" He approached the bed, wiping his hands.

"In terrible pain."

"I see." He reached over and rolled the bed-sheet up to my chest. "Let's have a look." He took his time and examined me carefully. Also, he took some measurements using various instruments from his medical bag, and wrote notes on a pad.

Mamma stood at the head of the bed and mopped my forehead with a damp cloth. Papa and others stood outside the room in the hallway, and peeked in occasionally.

"Do you believe forceps will be necessary, Doctor?" I had to ask.

"No. In this situation, I would not use them." He proceeded to make some more notes and, from his bag, took out a folder containing some papers; he glanced through them.

While I was relieved to hear that, I was still confounded and dreaded the thoughts of him using some of the other alternatives I had heard about. "So, what would you suggest, Doctor?"

"It seems the baby's head is lodged a bit high and due to the tightness, possibly from the dryness of your vagina, is having difficulty moving down. I don't think forceps would help, but a bit of surgery might. I'll need your consent, of course."

"Oh, no, Doctor. I do not want my daughter to die!" Mamma exclaimed. She knew that the mother's survival in those types of operations was very rare.

"No, Mrs. Wallace, I am not suggesting cutting Margaret in the belly; rather, a small incision in the perineum. You know, the area between the vagina and the lower opening."

While I tried to think back if I had heard of this procedure before, Mamma said, "Why, this seems most unusual. My darling cut like that! Have you undertaken it before, Doctor Flemings?"

"No, I have not, Mrs. Wallace. I have only recently become aware of it. It has been tried successfully in your country. The United States, I mean. The cut can be sutured and heals well." He turned to me. "Would you agree to my using this procedure, Margaret?"

What he had described seemed simple enough. Doctor Flemings looked intently at me.

"Fine, Doctor Flemings. Please go ahead. Do what you have to do. The way I feel right now, I would not mind if you cut my belly open to bring my poor child into this world." Tears welled in my eyes.

"All right, Margaret. I'll proceed immediately. I'll apply a topical anesthetic, but the cut will smart, mind."

I nodded.

He took out several instruments and, after dipping them a few times in a freshly brought hot-water basin, laid them on a clean towel on the table. He asked Mamma if she would kindly hand him the tools he asked for. He then got between my thighs and asked Dai and Elgin to hold them apart, as wide as possible. With a long, sharp looking surgical scalpel in his right hand, he inserted two fingers of his left hand into my vagina opening and pulled the wall out. "I think I will go with a mediolateral incision, that way ..."

I did not hear the rest of his sentence, for when he proceeded with the cut, I felt the most excruciating pain of my life, and passed out.

I was brought back to life, literally, by the familiar, pungent aroma of smelling salts the doctor applied close to my nose.

"Are you all right, Margaret?" he asked.

I nodded.

"I think it's time, and you may push gently now. I can see the baby's head crowning."

I did as told, and with my mind in a daze, heard the monsoon rain spatter and winds howling outside, while waves of pain shot through my body.

"One more push, dearest. The baby is nearly out," I heard Mamma whisper in my ear.

With that final effort, I felt as if a large weight had been lifted from my body. It was an exquisite feeling, a most relaxing sensation that pulled me into a dream world, a meadow of colorful flowers, and I lay among them peacefully.

The crying of a baby woke me. "Are you awake, Margaret?" I heard Mamma say and opened my eyes to look at her. "You have a lovely baby boy, my darling." She brought a screaming red-faced baby, wrapped in a clean towel, close to my cheek. She laid him gently by my side.

Despite the intense pain at the bottom of my belly, I turned around to face my child, while he still kept whimpering. With a finger, I caressed his wrinkled cheeks, which felt like the smooth underbelly of a bird. Intense sensations of relief and happiness returned to me. I thanked the Lord for having answered my earlier prayers, and having brought my child safely into the world, and having spared me my life in the process … I thought of my dear Robert, who was likely watching from above in Heaven. He said he was delighted to see his son, and wished me and our child much happiness … My mind wandered until I drifted off again into a deep slumber.

Later that night, Mamma brought my baby back to me. She nudged me gently. "Your child is hungry, Margaret. Aren't you going to nurse him, dear?"

In my trance, I had forgotten all about that. Mamma gently undid the top buttons of my blouse and uncovered my breast. She then moved the baby's head towards it. As soon the child felt my breast—which had engorged with milk—he moved his mouth to find the nipple, clamped his lips on them and instinctively began sucking on it. While I had nursed my two children earlier, it is always a delightful sensation and waves of nerve tingling feelings passed from the breast into my body.

I named my child Jan. In Hindustani, it means life, for he indeed was a miracle baby. I have often wondered if it had not been for the Nawab's gift-horse, David might not have been able to ride out in the thunderstorm to fetch Doctor Flemings, who performed the timely episiotomy to give life to my son. God only knows what might have transpired if the good doctor had not arrived in time. More than likely, my child and I would be in Heaven by now.

The news of Jan's birth reached afar, and congratulatory telegrams and letters arrived almost daily. The very first one was from Moira and Doctor Stewart from Calcutta; followed by our Ganges sailboat friends, Patricia and Thomas Wainwright, the Oudh Indigo Plantation owners; and several others, even one from my sea-voyage cabin companion, Mrs. Willoughby from Delhi. She had added that she was most anxious to see me in Delhi and kindly offered to have me stay in their "humble quarters in the Civil Lines." A rather tardy congratulatory telegram did arrive from Aunt Fiona.

There was, of course, a rather lengthy telegram—sent using the free government service, no doubt—from Colonel Humphrey. After the usual congratulations in flowery language, he had added:

"Have been in contact with Delhi Commissioner Fraser. Agrees to put you up. He will contact you. Looking forward to renewing our conviviality in Delhi. With much love and fondness. Yours. William."

Mamma and Papa were all smiles when they glanced at the telegram I held in my hands. "It's William now, is it?" Mamma said in a cheery voice.

"Oh, I don't know, Mamma. I just can't bring myself to call him that."

"Why not, child? See the great length he's gone to find you a place at Mr. Fraser's. I know Mr. Fraser is a widower, but there will be plenty of room in the Residency, and no end of servants," she said.

"I'll grant the Colonel that. And he's done it of his own accord," I said. "But I'm wondering about the kind of 'conviviality' he has in mind for us in Delhi."

"Don't be silly, Margaret. He is a colonel and a gentleman. But you know we have the offer from Reverend Jennings," Papa interjected. "You are welcome to stay with the Delhi chaplain. His daughter, Miss Jennings, is also there and would be good company for you."

"I'm not certain if they will have the room for Margaret and her child, and an *ayah*," Mamma said. "I've heard they live in a small flat, and that too they share with Captain Douglas and his wife. And I understand another friend of Miss Jennings, a Miss Clifford, is also there with them."

I had heard that Reverend Jennings had gained prominence not only in Delhi, but in the Christian community all over India, from his successes in converting a few Indians. He had also opened a school, named after St. Stephen, last year.

"It's most kind of Reverend and Annie Jennings," I said, "but I would prefer to find a place of my own. May I take Elgin with me? I'll need an *ayah* for Jan."

"Of course you may, dear. She adores Jan, and will go to no end to look after him," Mamma said.

"I am expecting to have Bruce and Vika over from Canada, soon."

"You will need to hire a governess as well, then. Have you heard from Fiona?" Papa asked.

"No, apart from her telegram. I imagine I should have a letter soon."

A dispatch did arrive shortly. We were sitting at the breakfast table, when Elgin had answered the door knock and brought the missive to me. It bore the familiar red Canadian stamp, embossed with Queen Victoria's solemn face. I opened it hurriedly. It contained a two-page epistle from Heather. While I longed for correspondence from my best friend and cousin, it was a disappointment to not have received even a simple note from Aunt Fiona.

Heather wrote in her usual long and detailed manner. She offered her congratulations again on the birth of her nephew. She then described all the recent happenings in Grimsby, her current romances and so on, which I raced through, wishing to learn of my dear children. Finally, towards the end, I spotted their names. She mentioned that they were both healthy, attending school regularly and taking part in music lessons, sports and so on. In closing, she wrote:

> *... Dearest, as I had written earlier, I have approached Mother at opportune moments on your wish to have Vika and Bruce repatriated to you in India. But she still is noncommittal. Don't take it to heart, precious; I'm certain she will come around. It's just that it's not even been a year since our beloved Robert's death, and she cannot bear the thought of separating herself from her only grandchildren. Listen, I have an idea. As you know, we all are anxious to visit Robert's grave in the Crimea. Mother has been talking to Colonel Mitchell, who informed her that since the war there is now over, he will look into making our travel arrangements. As Mother wishes to take Vika and Bruce along, I will persuade her to extend our trip to India. Wouldn't it be lovely, dearest, to see you again? And your adorable children will be with you as well ...*

While Heather's plan seemed plausible, her kind words did little to pacify the ache in my heart for my precious children. However, it was her very next sentence that plunged my mind into turmoil:

... And you will be pleased to hear that just last week, Nancy and Albert finally set sail for India. They might even be in Delhi before your arrival! I can imagine the delightful looks on your faces when the three of you convene, possibly in one of the numerous picturesque gardens I have read about and seen paintings of ...

This bit of news, of having to see Albert's menacing face again, opened the floodgate of emotions that had been accumulating. I could not read any more, for tears blurred my eyes and dripped down onto the letter. Mamma, who was sitting beside me, turned to me and put her arm around me. I rested my head on her shoulder and wept bitterly.

"Now, now, darling. What is it? What have they written?" She gently took the paper from my hand.

"Aunt Fiona ... she will not let ... my children ... come to me," I managed to blurt out between sobs. Mamma glanced through the letter, while the others around the table looked on, bewildered.

"Why that ... that ... Irish woman!" Mamma exclaimed. "Hasn't she caused enough problems for you? And now this. Why, she must have a heart of stone!"

"Now, let's not get too upset over it. Let me see. What has she written?" Papa picked up the letter and read through it. "Well, look. Heather writes that they all might be coming here. Now isn't that encouraging news?"

"Not very likely, if Fiona has her way. She'll find some other excuses. You'll see," Mamma said in an angry voice.

Just then I heard Jan cry from my bedroom, for it was his feeding time and he needed changing. I got up, dried my tears, and hurried to his cot.

A week or so later, I had an amiable visitor from the Palace. It was Harriet, or Nur Jehan. Good thing she had arrived in the middle of the day. Mamma and Papa were at work; otherwise they might have made a fuss over her call. She was accompanied by the *munshi* Karim, and two of her maids, clad in colorful garb, carrying silver trays covered with gold-threaded red silk cloths. "Gifts from the Nawabsahib, and us, on the birth of your dear son," she said.

While Karim preferred to squat on the veranda, I led the ladies to the kitchen. They placed the trays on the dining table and removed the silk coverings. To my surprise and delight, one tray contained an assortment of aromatic and delicious Indian sweetmeats—which Nur knew I loved—and on the second one, there were several suits of baby clothes and a red velvet box in the center, which no doubt contained jewelry. I picked up the baby outfits and examined them. While I had received from the cantonment ladies a number of clothes for Jan—the standard ones in the usual cotton or wool—these were of a far superior quality. Each was stitched in a silken material with interlaced gold and silver threads, which gave them a shiny appearance. All seemed fit for a little prince. I could not thank Nur enough for the gifts.

I asked Elgin to get tea ready and invited the ladies to our back garden patio, under the shady mango tree, which served as our parlor. Only Nur accompanied me outside. The two maids preferred to remain in the kitchen, saying they would help Elgin prepare tea. Our neighboring military-wives were out in their gardens, and I waved a good morning to them. They waved back their hallos but gave Nur hardly a second glance. They would have seen the Nawab's carriage and the coachmen at the front gate and probably guessed who my visitor was.

Nur had thoughtfully dressed in the European style, rather than in the oriental fashion she preferred. She had put on a purple high-waist Regency skirt that, although a bit out of date, looked wonderful on her slim figure. She had let her ringleted, raven hair flow down to her ample bosom. I complemented her on the attire and told her she looked like a heroine out of a Jane Austen novel. She blushed and her blue eyes sparkled when she thanked me, saying I was being "too kind".

We sat down at the table in the shady spot, on chairs side by side. Nur spoke at some length about the happenings at the Palace and inquired about our life at the Mission and in the cantonment. Elgin and the maids brought out the tea and snacks. I asked them to join us, but they declined, saying they would have theirs at the kitchen table. No doubt they wished to gossip, as I had learned by then that servants in India usually did, and that was one way to learn of the goings on in other families.

I asked Elgin to bring out Jan. She did so with him wrapped in a blue blanket. Although he was asleep, he looked adorable, and moved his head with the golden hair, which was beginning to grow, from side to side. I held him for a while and presented him to Nur. She held him in the crook of her arms and rocked him. He woke up and looked at her with his pretty blue eyes. She baby talked to him, but he started to whimper. I took him back, but it looked that he needed changing and Elgin took him back into the house.

While I ate a couple of the delicious Indian sweets, I offhandedly asked Nur, "Has Nawabsahib been to see the Rani?"

Although she seemed taken aback by the question, she replied matter-of-factly, "Yes. The Begum and he were there a few weeks ago."

"What did the Rani wish to see him about?"

"I'm not sure. Perhaps something to do with the recognition of her adopted son as the heir to the Jhansi throne. You know the Governor General has turned down her appeal, don't you?"

I nodded. "So, what is she going to do now?"

"She probably wants Lang sahib to take her case to London. But she'll need lots of guineas for that."

It then dawned on me. "Oh, so she has asked Nawabsahib for financial help?"

"I think so. But Margaret, what can the poor Nawab do? We hardly have enough money to support ourselves."

I knew that the Nawab and his household were having to survive on the meagre pension, yet I was impressed by the respectable manner in which they wished to lead their lives. Hence, the meeting intrigued me. "I suppose the Rani knows the Nawab's financial situation very well. So why, do you think, she asked to see him?"

"I imagine, to get as much support as she can muster from other states," she said without any forethought.

"*Support* for what?"

Nur took a sip of her tea and gazed into the distance, reflectively. It seemed she had said something she should not have. Finally, after looking around to see if any of the neighbors were within earshot, she responded in a whisper, "Margaret, this is for your ears only." I nodded, and she continued, "I don't really know. But there are some goings on I have observed."

"What sorts of *goings on*?" I whispered.

"I can't say for sure what it is, but there seem to be a number of persons coming to the Palace to see Nawabsahib."

"What's so unusual about that? Couldn't they be visiting him for various reasons; air out their grievances and so on?"

"No. It couldn't be that, for they come at odd hours and are more than the number of visitors he used to have."

"Who are these persons?"

"Appear to be emissaries from the neighboring kingdoms."

"Have you overheard any of the conversations?"

"Not much. They usually speak in low tones and always become silent or change the topic if I happen to pass by within earshot."

"Interesting," I observed, thinking about the nationalists I had encountered on the ship. "They are not plotting a revolution, are they?"

Nur looked worried. "Oh, I hope not. How will they fight the British forces with just their *talwars?* They do not have the latest cannons and rifles."

Just then, an image flashed through my mind. It was of the Indian gentleman I had seen in the Crimea, at the Russian camp where I had been taken as a prisoner. I tried to remember his name. It had sounded like "Azzi" or some such name. "Couldn't they buy arms from another country? Russia, perhaps?"

"I don't know, Margaret. I hope not. I hate to see murders and killings. The innocent civilians, women and children suffer the most. I fear for the lives of my family." She looked at her pocket watch. "Goodness, look at the time! The afternoon is nearly gone, and I have to visit my parents at the plantation as well." She finished her tea and got up. "I hope you will drop in on us at the Palace, before you leave for Delhi? And do bring Jan. Everyone there is longing to see him."

"Yes, I certainly will," I said and led her to the front door.

A few days later, true to his word, Papa received a nice letter from the Delhi Commissioner, Mr. Simon Fraser. He wrote that he had heard both from his good friend, Colonel Humphrey, and Padre Jennings of my posting at the new Civil and Military Hospital in Delhi, and would be more than happy to accommodate me at the Residency. He scribed:

… Altho' upon the unbearable loss of my beloved wife, I have not remarried, I am certain Doctor Wallace will be most comfortable here. She will have the company of many respectable ladies in the cantonment, including Miss Jennings and her delightful companion, Miss Clifford. The Residency has many spare

rooms and I shall endeavor to make a whole wing available for her, her child and her maid's accommodation. The services of all my staff will be at her disposal. If I may be so bold as to suggest that Doctor Wallace will be a most valuable addition to our small church choir, if she would care to join the little group we have set up. Through the good efforts of our churchgoing community, I am able to bring people together here at the Residency, every fortnight, for a musical evening ... If it is agreeable to Doctor Wallace, I could make arrangements for her to travel to Delhi in the dak carriage on a date suitable to her ...

Mamma looked thrilled after having read the letter. "How kind of the Resident to offer to put you up. And he will even arrange for your transportation to Delhi!" she said gleefully. "Isn't it very thoughtful of Colonel Humphrey to have made all this possible for you, dear?"

I caught her drift, but kept silent. While I was happy that Jan and I would have a reasonably comfortable journey to Delhi, and we would be well received, there still was a nagging voice in the back of my head that warned me about Colonel Humphrey's involvement in these arrangements. As it turned out, my premonitions proved to be correct.

Chapter Eight

Futtehgurh to the *dak bungalow*

1855, September: Futtehgurh to dak bungalow, India
THE DAY OF MY DEPARTURE for Delhi finally arrived. Dressed in a grey gown, solar hat in hand, I waited in the late-night darkness on the front veranda for the *dak* carriage. These coaches, carrying mail and officials, travelled between the British Residencies in the towns all the way from Calcutta to Delhi and also provided a convenient mode of travel for others, if permitted by the Company. I considered myself fortunate to have secured a passage on this conveyance, and wondered—for Mr. Fraser had not mentioned it— if Colonel Humphrey had a hand in having it offered to me.

Oil lanterns, hanging from the porch-pillars, shone dimly into the garden, where trees cast giant shadows and crickets competed with other insects to bleat their presence. Mamma and Papa sat next to me on cane chairs and Elizabeth, her legs curled up, catnapped on one. David sat cross-legged at one side on the wooden floor in a meditative pose, which he had no doubt learned from Amari. Elgin, dressed in an old, worn-out blue frock, sat on the steps cradling Jan, rocking him gently. Bundled up in a blanket, he slept peacefully after his late-night feeding from me.

Mamma, with occasional inputs from Papa, kept up a constant stream of advice of do's and don'ts on how I was to live and behave while in Delhi. Since I had heard much of it several times earlier, I listened and acknowledged it with nods and whispers, "Yes, Mamma … I know that … I will, Mamma …", while putting it away in the back of my mind.

My sea chest, a portmanteau with Jan's clothes, Elgin's battered suitcase and her holdall—something that looked like a rolled-up sleeping bag with clothing and other knick-knacks in it—lay beside the front gate. Papa was going to send along Jan's crib and later bring over other items, when Mamma and he were to visit me during the

Mission School's Christmas break.

Just past midnight, there were sounds of carriage wheels, jangling of bridles and horses' hooves, which grew louder, and finally the coach appeared out of the misty gloom in front of our garden-gate. Soldiers on horseback—the escort—followed behind, with spare horses in tow. The sergeant barked an order in Hindustani and two *sowars* jumped off their mounts and began to hoist and secure my luggage onto the carriage's roof.

I bid a tearful farewell to my siblings and parents, and with Mamma's parting words, "Now, you be very careful, Margaret," ringing in my ears, followed Elgin towards the landau. An officer alighted from the carriage and held the door open for me. The brass buttons on his red jacket shone in the dim light from the carriage-lamps.

"Good morning, Doctor Wallace," he said, removing his forage cap. "I'm Captain Jack Herford," and, raising his hand towards the carriage, "my wife, Catherine."

A very white-faced lady poked her head out of the window. I exchanged greetings with her and, climbing into the landau, sat on the bench opposite hers. Elgin passed the bundled Jan to me.

Captain Herford entered the carriage, slumped beside his wife, and started to close the door.

Since there was plenty of room on my seat, I said, "Oh, would you mind, sir, if my *ayah* sat next to me?"

Captain Herford looked down at Elgin and then turned his head towards me. "I'm sure she'll be quite comfortable up with the coachman. Don't you think, Doctor Wallace?"

I looked inquiringly at Elgin. She immediately scrambled up to the driver's bench. Herford shut the door and we were off. I leaned out of the carriage window and looked at my family, who stood by the garden fence, waving, until they disappeared into the night shadows.

"We heard about you in Calcutta. How wonderful to finally have a lady doctor in Delhi," Catherine said, looking towards me.

"Thank you. I'm glad to be here."

"The surgeons here do not have a clue about female ailments." She frowned.

"Yes, my dear. Now you won't have to travel to London for treatment." Herford put his arm around Catherine's shoulders. He turned towards me. "My wife's just returned from home. I met her ship in Calcutta and we are on our way to Delhi. I dare say, she'll likely be your first patient!"

"I'll be happy to assist in any way I can," I said. "Although I have yet to learn much about the tropical diseases."

"I'm sure that would be no problem for you. I understand you are an American?" Catherine asked.

"Yes," I said, and proceeded to give them a brief sketch of how I came to be in India.

They told me a bit about themselves. They both were from London, and from their accents, seemed to be well educated and from affluent families. Captain Herford had been stationed in India for a while. Catherine had come out to join him, but it seemed she had caught some mysterious illness that still affected her. She spoke about it at some length, but her symptoms did not sound familiar to me and I said I would look into her situation.

Captain Herford stretched out his legs. "Have you been to Delhi yet, Doctor Wallace?"

"This is my first visit. What's the city like?"

"Somewhat less appealing than Calcutta. But it's still a magnificent place," Herford said. "It used to be the capital of the Mughals, you know. But with them no longer in power, many of the fine buildings are crumbling away."

"Isn't a Mughal emperor still there?" I asked.

"Good old Zafar, you mean!" Herford chuckled. "He's more like the sheriff of Delhi. His authority extends to no more than the city walls. Besides he's quite old, really. Over eighty, we believe."

"He looked really frail, the last time I saw him at one of the *durbars*," Catherine said.

"If he's that old, why doesn't he hand over to his heir?" I asked.

"Yes ... well, he has a designated crown prince; the son of one of his older wives. But it seems a younger wife wishes her son to succeed," Herford started to explain. "Also, the poor King is under the control of the Company. Most of his decisions have to be approved by the Governor General, you know."

"Oh! When did the Company take over Delhi?" I asked.

"In 1803, when General Lord Lake defeated the Marathas and restored the Mughal Emperor, Shah Alam, back on the Delhi throne. But he was in reality a puppet king, you know. He'd been blinded by an Afghan war-lord who'd stormed Delhi earlier. But, actually, the Mughals' downfall had started much before that, in 1765, I believe, when they granted the *Diwani* rights to Lord Clive," Herford said and chuckled.

"I've heard about the *Diwani,* but I'm not sure what's it all about?" I likely had a puzzled look.

"Yes. Shah Alam gave the Company the rights to collect taxes in Bengal, Bihar and Orissa."

"Oh! And why did he do that? Did he get something in return?"

"In exchange for his life, really. He was also awarded an annual pension of about 2.6 million pounds and a portion of Oudh, around Allahabad."

"Really! He received the city of Allahabad in exchange for the Company to collect taxes from those three large provinces! How did it all come about?" I must have looked really silly. "Sorry for all these questions, Captain Herford. I did not study Indian History in College."

"I understand. You must have had enough medical books to peruse. I'll be happy to narrate an account of the decline of the Mughal Empire, but it could take some time. Wouldn't you rather rest? It's quite late."

"No, not at all. I'm not tired, really. I had some repose earlier," I said eagerly, for the events he had spoken of intrigued me.

"Go ahead, dear," Catherine interjected. "I've heard you recount the twilight of the Mughals so many times at the after-dinner parties that I too know it quite well. I am sure Doctor Wallace would be interested in hearing it." She turned towards me, "Jack read history at Oxford, you know." And then leaned her head on the side leather cushion of the carriage's seat and closed her eyes.

"Yes, I would very much like to listen to it. And, please call me Margaret," I said.

As the carriage bumped along on the uneven road in the dark night, and sinister images of tall trees like *jinns* whizzed by the windows, the Captain narrated the incredible account of the last days of the Mughal Empire.

Captain Herford cleared his throat. "The Mughal Empire began to disintegrate in 1739 with the invasion of the Persian King, Nadir Shah, and his carrying away Delhi's Peacock Throne. The Mughal's were much weakened, and civil war broke out between their differing factions. On the other hand, the Marathas, taking advantage of the disorganized Mughals, occupied parts of northern India up to the Punjab."

"Didn't the Afghans also intervene?" I asked, for I had heard of their incursion into India as well.

"Yes. The Afghans entered into the foray in 1756, when Ahmad Shah Abdali invaded India. However, it is said, Abdali was unable to withstand the Indian heat, and returned to Afghanistan a year later. There was turmoil again in Delhi and, afraid for his life, the Mughal crown prince, Ali Gauhar—later Shah Alam II—escaped from Delhi and took shelter with the Nawab of Oudh in Allahabad. The Afghans returned to India. And with a combined force of Rohillas and the Nawab of Oudh, they routed the Marathas at the third battle of Paniput. Again after much plundering of northern India, they returned to Afghanistan. However, before leaving, Abdali recognized Shah Alam II as the Mughal Emperor, who was still in Allahabad, and 'ruled' from there."

"Then what happened?" I was curious.

"For the next few years, while the Marathas had retreated southwards, at least temporarily, two new warring powers in the form of the Sikhs and the Jhats emerged to challenge the Mughals. The Mughal Empire remained in a floundering state."

The carriage clattered on in the darkness, passing innumerable villages dimly lit by oil lamps, and through smoke from the dung fires; while Jan slept peacefully at my side, I gazed out of the window and wondered about the amazing turn of events that had led to the fall of the Mughal Empire. Nevertheless, how the British came to be in Delhi was still unclear to me.

I asked, "So, how did we—the British, I mean—take over Delhi? Were they not still ensconced in Calcutta?"

"Yes, we were, and this was your original question that started this conversation! Sorry for the rather long-winded answer, but I am happy to complete the story for you."

"Yes, please," I said eagerly.

"Back in Bengal, disagreement over taxation led to clashes between the Nawab Qasim's forces and those of the Company's. Qasim was defeated and he escaped to Oudh. There he took refuge with the Mughal Emperor-in-absentia, Shah Alam II. There was another battle, the Mughals were defeated and Shah Alam was exiled in Allahabad."

"Oh, so that's what started the conflict between the British and the Mughals." The situation was starting to get clearer to me.

"Exactly. From 1766 to 1771, while the Mughal Emperor Shah Alam lived the life of a pensioner in Allahabad, things were not going so well in the Delhi area. The Maratha leader, Sindhia, occupied Delhi. But he needed an ally to hold Delhi. Therefore, in a strange strategic arrangement, he offered to restore the Mughal Emperor-in-exile, Shah Alam, back to Delhi! And, despite the displeasure expressed by the Company, in January 1772, Alam agreed to the Maratha proposal and under their escort, marched triumphantly back into Delhi. As a consequence, the Governor General, Hastings, immediately cancelled the stipend the Company had been paying Alam!"

"I suppose Hastings believed that Alam had contravened the treaty, and Alam thought that having regained his kingdom, he didn't need the pension anyway?" I conjectured.

"Quite so. To his credit, for the next ten years, Shah Alam ruled admirably from Delhi. Nevertheless, in 1788, the sworn enemy of the Mughals, the Rohilla, Ghulam Qadir, attacked Delhi. He committed the most heinous crime of blinding the Emperor Shah Alam. Upon receiving the news, Sindhia came to Alam's rescue, and chased and caught the fleeing Rohillas. Shah Alam, albeit blind, was restored again as the nominal 'Emperor'."

"How interesting. Shah Alam got his Delhi kingdom back a second time!" It sounded very thrilling to me.

"But not for long, on account of other world events. Earlier, in 1774, France had declared war on England, and hence, in India the British captured the French colonial seaside towns of Chandernagore and Pondicherry in 1794. In 1798 Napoleon sailed into Egypt and it was strongly believed that he was intent on proceeding towards India. Although Lord Nelson stopped Napoleon's advance by destroying the French fleet in the battle of the Nile, the Company, fearful of the Sultanate of Mysore making alliances with the French, attacked Tippu Sultan in 1799. The British force, led by General Sir Arthur Wellesley, won the battle, killed Tippu Sultan and captured Mysore."

"Oh, that was the battle with the famous Tippu Sultan of Mysore, in the south of India. But then how did that event affect

Delhi?"

"It had a profound effect. For in 1803, a British force under General Lord Lake was dispatched to break the Marathas' power and dislodge them from Delhi. This was the start of the second Anglo-Maratha war. The Battle of Delhi took place on 14 September 1803, on the left bank of the Jamuna River. The Maratha forces, under the command of a Frenchman, General Louis Bourguin, were routed, and the British army, crossing the river, entered Delhi. Lord Lake was escorted by a Mughal prince into the palace, where he met the aged and blind Emperor Shah Alam. Since the Company was not yet strong enough in India to rule from Delhi, and preferring to remain in Calcutta, they took Shah Alam under their protection, and restored him once again as a nominal 'Emperor' in Delhi!"

"Goodness! Shah Alam was put back on the throne for the third time!" I shrieked, for the story seemed so incredible.

"Yes, but 'Emperor' in name only, mind. Similarly, for his successors, Akbar Shah and the present Bhadur Shah Zafar." Captain Herford smiled.

"Oh! Now it's all perfectly clear to me. Thank you so much, Captain Herford." I felt like I had attended a whole year of lectures on Indian history.

My exclamations had awakened Catherine. She opened her eyes and looked towards her husband. "I heard you mention Zafar, so I imagine you have reached the end of your narration, darling?"

"Yes, I have, my dear. Oh, look," he said, pointing to the horizon out of the window, where a faint red glow over some hills could be seen. "The sun's about to come up."

"And with it the heat," Catherine remarked. "How far is it to the *dak* bungalow?"

The Captain leaned out of the carriage's window and conversed in Hindustani with the driver. He then slid back onto the seat and announced, "The rest house isn't far. We should be there within the hour. I'm ready for the *choti-hazri* and a nap. Are you both, as well?"

"Yes, I am," I said. "Thanks to your interesting conversation, the time has passed quickly."

"I had a good slumber." Catherine yawned. "I wouldn't mind the *dak*'s spicy omelet for breakfast, but I do hope they'll have something other than curry chicken for lunch *and* dinner!"

"Not likely, my dear," Herford remarked. "We should let

Doctor Margaret know that in these *dak* bungalows, all we are likely going to get for meals will be curry chicken, chapattis and rice."

"I've been enjoying the Indian vegetable curries," I said. "Perhaps we could ask them to prepare some okra-curry for us?" There was no response from either of them; they simply looked out of the windows.

Finally, the carriage slowed and turned into a badly potholed side road. After a short bumpy drive, the coach entered through the boundary wall gates into a large courtyard. A set of low-level buildings loomed ahead in the darkness. Barking of dogs welcomed our arrival at the *dak* bungalow.

The carriage entered the *dak* bungalow's courtyard. In the oil lamps' dim light, several mud-walled low thatch-roofed buildings appeared, each with small verandas. I peered out through the window and saw another carriage stationed to one side. It had a military insignia on its door, which I recalled having seen before, but could not place just then.

Our carriage stopped before the main building. On its veranda, some blanketed figures, the *chaukidars*, could be seen sleeping. If the barking of the dogs and the clattering of the horses' hooves did not awaken them, it was the escort sergeant's swearing in Hindustani— which even I understood—that made them jump up and run to open the doors of our carriage.

A Eurasian gentleman emerged from a hut on one side of the bungalows, and hurried to meet us. He had thrown a dark coat over his night pajamas and held a bunch of keys in his hand, like a housekeeper. Upon Captain Herford's inquiry, he informed us that two rooms were available and a colonel-sahib occupied the remaining third one.

The manager led Elgin and me to a room, and I was relieved to see it had a reasonably clean floor and whitewashed walls. There was a small bed, and on one side a washstand and an *almirah* with a mirror at the back of its door, which the manager, with a smile, opened to show me. On seeing Jan in Elgin's arms, he shouted an order to one of the servants to fetch a cot.

"And, sir, can you please have another bed brought here for my *ayah*?" I asked the manager.

"No, memsahib, she sleep in the servants' quarters over there." He pointed towards the back of the bungalows.

Elgin nodded her agreement to this arrangement and I was too tired to argue. When the cot arrived, Elgin laid Jan in it. He slept on peacefully. The manager departed after wishing me a pleasant stay and advising that breakfast would be served at eight o'clock in the main dining room. He left the key in the door.

Elgin opened the door at the back of the room; it revealed a small water closet room with a commode. From there, another door led to the rear of the bungalow and to a smaller courtyard with a well. Elgin fetched a pitcher of water for me and poured it into the washbasin. She wanted to stay and help me wash and change, but she looked tired and I let her go to her hut to rest. She said she would be back later, to take care of Jan when I went for breakfast.

A chorus of the birds, flying back and forth between the large mango trees in the courtyard, and the bright sunshine greeted me, as I walked down from the veranda towards the dining room. Although my nap was brief, I felt rested and looked forward to the breakfast. Walking across the courtyard, a stray dog ran towards me, but was chased away by a servant.

I entered the dining room and noted the other guests were already at the table. Captain Herford and another person, smartly dressed in scarlet jackets, immediately rose and bid me a good morning. I returned their greeting and nodded to Catherine, who sat beside Herford. I then recognized the other grey-whiskered officer to be my admirer, Colonel Humphrey! He pulled out a chair beside him and motioned for me to sit.

I sat down. Although I felt he had betrayed me in Futtehgurh, due to the presence of the Herfords, I decided to be civil to him. "Colonel Humphrey, what a surprise to see you. What brings you here?"

"I happened to finish my meeting early with Wajid Ali, in Oudh, and now am on my way to Delhi to see old Zafar. I dare say, I am very pleased to see you, Margaret. Congratulations and how are you and the baby?" The Colonel beamed at me.

"We are both well. Thank you for asking, and your telegram, earlier."

A bearer poured tea and putting down a plate of toast, asked if I would like an omelet or boiled eggs. I chose the former, with spices in it.

"How *is* Nawab Wajid Ali?" Catherine asked the Colonel.

"He looked well enough. Arranged a sumptuous banquet for me."

"What's he been doing these days?" Herford asked.

"Instead of looking after Oudh, I imagine he's busy with his poetry, singing, theater, and other frivolous activities. There was a wonderful song and *nautch* show after dinner." The Colonel chuckled. "I don't think the Begum's happy, though."

"Oh! How so?" Catherine asked.

"She looked miserable. Sat very quiet, next to the Nawab. Did not say a word. She's probably got wind of what's coming to them," the Colonel said rather casually.

While I, churned that bit of information in my mind, Herford asked tactfully, "And your meeting with the Nawab, didn't take too long?"

"No, it wasn't a lengthy affair. Just delivered a letter from the Governor General and some personal messages," Humphrey replied matter-of-factly, and turned towards me. "So, *Doctor Margaret*, are you looking forward to your duties in Delhi?"

"Indeed, I am, sir. And thank you so much for arranging my accommodation at the Residency."

"It was no problem at all. Commissioner Fraser is an old friend. I trust he will put up with me as well, for the few days I will be there."

So he was going to stay at the Residency also; and this meeting here, was it all prearranged, I wondered? My omelet arrived and I enjoyed every mouthful, although, to overcome the spiciness, I had to follow with buttered toast and gulps of tea.

"Is this your first time back in Delhi since your return from England, Colonel?" Catherine inquired, sipping at a cup of tea.

Now why was she asking that? Was not the information about Oudh enough, I thought?

"Yes. And I believe we met the last time I was there, did we not?" the Colonel said.

"Wasn't it at Prince Jawan Bukht's wedding?" Catherine asked.

"So it was. In April 1852."

"Wasn't it a magnificent affair? I recall we watched, from the Delhi Bank building's balcony, the long procession of all those painted and decorated elephants and carriages followed by marching bands and soldiers. They must have travelled a long way from the Fort through the Chandni Chowk streets to the bride's home. Wasn't it to Walidad Khan's *haveli*?" Catherine asked.

"Yes, indeed. But that entire spectacle was for an eleven-year-old boy and his ten-year-old bride!" The Colonel guffawed. "Zafar very nearly went bankrupt from the expense of it. But we know he did it at the behest of his favorite wife, Zinat."

"Didn't you ride in the *howdah* on an elephant, Colonel?" I asked, for I had seen a painting in a London arts gallery of that procession.

"No. Although invited, I did not. But weren't you in the parade, Captain?" he asked, looking at Herford.

"Yes. I was in Captain Douglas's Palace Guards group. But we rode only partway along the procession route. It was just a nominal appearance of our Company's troops."

"I was there merely as an observer. The Resident, Mr. Metcalf, advised us not to participate," the Colonel said.

"Why not?" I asked.

"That lavish affair was not sanctioned by the Company. It was merely an attempt by Queen Zinat to elevate the prestige of her young son, Jawan, over the other older princes."

"So, is Prince Jawan to be the next heir?" Catherine asked.

I then realized that was what Catherine wanted to know.

"No. We still believe the King's eldest son, Prince Mirza Fakhruddin, is the rightful heir," the Colonel said, rather cogently.

Herford smiled. "And you will likely remind King Zafar of our preference, will you, Colonel?"

The Colonel finished a mouthful of his breakfast. "I might very well do that. And I trust Zinat will also listen."

The conversation at the table changed to other topics, but my mind stayed on what the Colonel had said about not recognizing Prince Jawan as the heir-apparent, and the Company's preference for Prince Fakhruddin. I wondered why there was so much interference in the affairs of Delhi. Especially since the primogeniture policy was a British practice, one that was not widely applied in Indian states. Moreover, with the Muslims' acceptance of polygyny, it would be rather difficult to determine the "first male-born" of any of the wives as the inheritor, when each of the wives were supposed to be treated equally. Surely the King had the right to select his successor? Hence, it occurred to me that the Company likely had an ulterior motive in supporting Prince Fakhruddin. Whatever it was, I was not able to resolve it at that moment and concentrated on finishing my omelet.

Finally, with the breakfast over, and while the bearers cleared the table, Colonel Humphrey turned towards me. "Margaret, I believe there's a lovely path nearby that runs along the riverbank. Would you care to join me for a walk? And after that, if I may be permitted, I should like to take a peek at your lovely boy."

"Yes, Colonel Humphrey, a walk would be lovely. It's been rather cramped travelling in the carriage." I looked at Catherine and Herford, expecting them to join us, but they both, realizing the Colonel wished to talk to me alone, made some excuse of having to catch up on their correspondences and left the dining room.

The Colonel led me to the door and, upon seeing him, two of his sepoys jumped to attention. He told them in Urdu to follow us. They did so, but stayed respectfully behind, out of earshot. We took a footpath that led out of a small gate at the back of the *dak* bungalow's perimeter stone-wall and meandered through a light forest of tall trees towards the river. I was glad to be in the shade, for although I had my solar hat on, the sun had risen high and beat down fiercely.

We walked in silence for a while, mindful of the tree roots and brush that littered the path, enjoying the fresh morning air and the scents of the forest and the nearby river. A family of monkeys followed us, jumping from one tree branch to another, chattering excitedly. Initially we talked about general subjects. The Colonel inquired about my family, and me his, and so on, then finally he came to what was on his mind.

"I am glad to be alone with you again, Margaret. Do you recall the last time we went riding together at Futtehgurh?"

"Yes, I do, Colonel Humphrey."

"Ah, as I requested earlier, call me William. Please."

I did remember him asking me to call him that and kissing me as well, but after he had the Mission School cancel my teaching the Nawab, was most infuriating. "Do you think we could still be on first-name basis, after what you've done?"

"And, pray, what have I done?" He frowned.

"You had my teaching at the Nawab of Furrukhabad's palace terminated."

He stopped walking and turned towards me, with an irate look in his steely blue eyes. For a moment, I believed he was going to deny having anything to do with my dismissal, but he perhaps thought there was no use refuting it, for I must have known about his and Colonel Smith's visit to Reverend Johnson. "My dear Margaret, I am very surprised to see you so distressed. My suggestion for you to stop travelling to Furrukhabad was for your own good. In your condition, at that time, I mean."

"Colonel Humphrey, my condition is my own worry. Was your concern for my good, or for the benefit of the Company?" The anger rising in me would have shown on my face.

"Come now, Margaret. Pray do not be so disturbed." He came closer to me and tried to put his hands on my shoulders.

I backed away. "Disturbed! What bothers me is that your thoughts are only for political aims and not for me or my family's welfare."

"Ah, no, Margaret. It's not true. What predisposed motives could I have?"

"To keep the natives uneducated and ignorant, thus enabling the Company to control them better."

"Oh, no, Margaret. This simply is not the case. The natives have full freedom of education. Consider the number of schools we are running."

"Yes, but those are for the children. What about their parents and other people, such as the kings and nawabs?"

"They are free to learn whatever they wish."

"So why not let the Nawab of Furrukhabad learn English?"

"Ah, Margaret, that is another matter, between him and the British residents of that area. Something to do with him seeing an English lady, and his brother having married an Englishwoman. I don't know the details."

"So you had my teaching position ended!"

"Oh, no, Margaret. It was not my suggestion. Colonel Smith had brought it up in the meeting with Reverend Johnson. As I said, I merely agreed, out of consideration for your situation. Now that you know the details, are you satisfied?"

He tried to put his arms around me again, but I stepped further back.

While the Colonel's explanations sounded plausible, there was still something that did not sound right. Initially, Reverend Johnson had almost pleaded with me to take the teaching post, and I knew that the Mission needed the Nawab's financial support. It seemed the Colonel's justification was a smoke-screen for some other objective. I did not wish to argue the point further.

"No, not entirely," I said. "Did you not think how it would affect my parents? Not only losing some income, but having to return the Nawab's gift-horse? You know they need a mode of travel. My father cannot afford to purchase one." Tears welled in my eyes.

"My dear Margaret." He put his arms around me and held me in an embrace, as tears flowed down my cheeks. "Please forgive me. I did not foresee this situation." He drew a clean handkerchief from his jacket pocket and handed it to me.

"It's all right. They'll manage. Please don't worry about it." I wiped away my tears, while he still held me close to him. His embrace felt comforting.

"No. It's not all right. Tell you what I'll do. I'll send a message to Colonel Smith, that under this circumstance, since we asked you to terminate your teaching and return the horse, you have a right for compensation. I'm sure he will agree and allocate your father a horse from the regimental stables. Will that be satisfactory to you, my dear?"

"Oh, no. Please don't. You don't have to write to Colonel Smith."

"Yes, I must. And if he doesn't deliver a horse to your father, I'll purchase one and take it over to him myself, on my return from Delhi."

"Oh, you are very kind, William," I said, overwhelmed by his generosity.

He hugged me closer, and if it had not been for the two soldiers squatting in the shade of a tree at some distance, he might have kissed me.

"Perhaps we should be getting back?" I suggested. I felt not only tired from the lack of sleep, but it was getting much hotter even in the shaded forest.

"Indeed we must, before Captain Herford sends out a search party." He released me. I laughed with him.

I held on to William's arm as we ambled back to the *dak*

bungalow. When we passed by the Herford's cottage, I spotted Catherine watching us from the window. From the conversation over breakfast, it was apparent that she had known William before his return to England and perhaps in London as well. I made a mental note to ask her about him. Although, I must admit I found him alluring, the one thing that still puzzled me was, being such an eligible widower, why had he not remarried yet? Did he have someone waiting in London, and I merely a prospective mistress in India?

Since he wished to see Jan, we walked over to my cottage. Upon entering the room, to my surprise, I saw it was empty. William followed me in, and I heard the door close and a click of the key turning in the lock.

"Oh, I believe Elgin must have taken Jan out for a stroll," I said.

"Yes, the child needs some fresh air." William said, taking his cap off and placing it on top of the wardrobe. I was speechless when, looking me in the eye, he came closer and embraced me again. "My dear, Margaret," he whispered, and took off my solar hat.

My fair locks tumbled down on to my shoulders.

"Er … William … please, I …" I stuttered, and tried to step back.

He continued his advances and hugged me tightly. Running his fingers through my hair, he held the back of my head and brought his lips down on mine. As our lips met, a shiver ran through my body. It was a pleasant feeling. I could not help but put my arms around him. He continued the kiss and, gently parting my lips with his tongue, inserted it into my mouth and ran it over my tongue. The sensation was delightful. It had been a long time since anyone had kissed me like that, and I likely hummed in my throat.

"Oh, my darling, Margaret. It's delightful to kiss you," he said, sliding his lips over my cheeks on to my neck. "I have been looking forward to this moment with you for some time. I trust I am not offending you?"

"No, Col … William. A kiss is fine, but … perhaps … we should stop? Elgin will be here any moment."

"She'll be a while. Let's enjoy our time together." He slid his hands down my sides and over my breasts. His thumbs circled the nipples. It sent further quivers down my spine. My legs felt weak and he gently pushed me down to sit with him on the nearby bed.

Still holding me tightly, he started to kiss me again while we sat on the edge of the bed.

However, this time the kiss was not as pleasant. The feel of his tongue and the bitter taste of saliva mingled with tobacco brought me back to my senses. I began to feel uneasy about what he was doing and that he likely wanted more. I wished he would stop. When he tried to force me sideways, to lie on the bed, alarm bells rang in my head. I tore my lips away and, putting my hands on his strong shoulders, tried to push him back. But he held on to me.

"Please, William … please, stop … kindly let go of me." I was furious.

"Oh, my dear Margaret. I adore you. Don't you have any feelings for me?"

"Yes, William. I do have a high regard for you. But I think we should stop. Let's go outside. The Herfords are waiting for us." Nevertheless, despite my protests, he continued to hold me and crush my breasts against his chest.

"No one is waiting. Let's stay here for a while," he implored. He loosened his grip and began to rub my neck and back.

I pushed hard against his shoulders and managed to extricate myself by shoving him backwards. Jumping up from the bed, wishing to run outside, I moved to the front door. After twisting and rattling the doorknob a few times, I realized it was locked. When I searched for the key, to my dismay I found it missing from the lock. There was only one person who would have removed it.

I turned towards the Colonel, still sitting on the bed. Stretching my hand to him, I asked, "Can I have the key, please?"

"Why are you leaving, Margaret? Do come back." He caught my arm and pulled me on top of him onto the bed.

As I lay over him, he held me forcefully around the waist.

"Please let me go," I said loudly, thrashing my arms and legs about. I must admit the feel of his bulging manhood on my belly was most embarrassing. He would not release me and began to whisper sweet nothings into my ear. I was afraid to shout for help, for it would have created an alarm and resulted in a scandal that would surely have sullied my reputation. He would probably have gotten away with just a few laughs and snickers from other officers, for in such instances it was invariably considered to be "the fault of the woman for leading the man on" and "why did she bring him in her room, in the first place?". I felt like a trapped bird. I knew I had to get away, somehow, from the room.

He ran his hands over my buttocks, squeezing them, and slid his fingers between my legs. I kept struggling, telling him to stop. Then, when he moved his hands to bring them up to hold my face, to try and kiss me again, there was an opportunity. Putting my hands on the sides of the bed, I leaped out, and ran to the back door. I flung it open, and entered the water closet. I struggled to unfasten the sliding latch of the outside-door and managing it, shoved it open. I stumbled out into the back courtyard.

It was nearly noon. The blazing sun's rays radiated down onto the square. I was glad it was deserted. Shielding my eyes with the palm of my hand, I saw, and smelled, cooking-fire smoke rising from the servants' quarters at the back. Still breathing heavily from exertion, and in a rage at what the Colonel had tried to do, I calmed myself, straightened my dress and ran fingers through my hair to untangle it. I felt secure, knowing that he would not dare chase me outside, not in his aroused condition anyway.

Thinking myself lucky to have escaped, yet fuming at his having dared to try to seduce me, and considering what actions I could take, I walked steadily across the quadrangle towards the huts.

Elgin spotted me and, holding Jan in her arms, came out of the door of a hut. "Sorry, memsahib. I not know you come back soon from walk."

"It's all right, Elgin. It's too hot. We returned early. How is my dear boy?" I took Jan in my arm and, cradling him, rocked him to and fro. He opened his eyes, kicked his feet and smiled at me. That pleased me so much that it very nearly took away all the mental anguish I had experienced moments ago. I kissed his rosy cheek.

"You like lunch, memsahib? We cook vegetable curry and chapattis." Elgin knew that I loved the spicy Indian food.

"Yes, but just half a chapatti, please," I said, not wanting to impose on their food, and also knowing that I would be lunching later. I entered the hut and the servant and his wife, who squatted by the back door before a makeshift three-stone cooking fire, stood up. Putting their palms together, they mumbled a "gooding morning" to me. I returned their greeting and at their bidding, sat down on one of the two *charpoys*.

While Elgin scurried about getting my snack, I played with Jan on my lap. Elgin served me a dollop of steaming-hot vegetable curry on a slice of chapatti, placed on a clean piece of banana leaf. I took it from her hands and she collected Jan away from me.

The servant and his wife watched me, amused that a mem would eat curry with her hands. I blew on the food to cool it, and bit off a mouthful. The combination of the brown-bread and spicy vegetables tasted heavenly. With the morsel still in my mouth, I nodded at the others and saw wide smiles break out on their faces. I finished the half-chapatti and, thanking them, smacked my lips in the Indian custom, to show appreciation for the food. At that, their wide smiles grew into broad grins. But, despite their insistence, I declined to eat more and asked them to have their lunch.

I took the cup of tea Elgin handed me, and while they ate I conversed with them, mostly about their families and the life around that area. It was interesting to listen to their anecdotes and the happenings in the nearby village, where they were from. They did not ask me many questions, for I believe Elgin would have enlightened them about me.

Having finished his meal, the man stood up and prepared to leave, saying that he had to go and help set the dining room for the midday meal. Before departing, he *namested*, but as he stepped out of the door, remembering something, he turned to me. "Memsaab, be very very careful on the road to Delhi. We hear many dacoits are robbing people."

"Thank you for the warning. But I believe we have a good escort to protect us," I said, and he left, *namesteing* me again.

I realized I should return to my room to wash and get ready for lunch. I left Jan with Elgin and instructed her to not linger in the servants' quarters for long, as we were to depart from the *dak* bungalow in the afternoon.

"Yes, I come quickly and pack up," she said.

Relieved to see that the Colonel was nowhere in the chamber, after a quick wash and, combing my long hair, I changed into my dark blue travelling gown with a matching bonnet. Stepping out onto the veranda and squinting in the bright sunlight, I was surprised to see only our coach standing in the main courtyard. Colonel Humphrey's carriage, along with his sepoys, was gone. Probably they were sent on an errand, I thought, as I entered the dining room. Only Captain Herford and Catherine were seated at the table, glasses of what looked like gin-and-tonic before them. Taking a chair next to her, I exchanged greetings with them and glanced at their faces, but could not discern any unusual expression. I felt relieved that they were unaware of Colonel Humphrey's antics.

"How was the walk?" Catherine asked, coyly.

"Good, thank you. We didn't go too far, on account of the heat," I said. "So, where is Colonel Humphrey? Isn't he lunching with us?"

"He took a picnic lunch and left early. Wished to make a head start," Herford replied with a surprised look. "Didn't he tell you?"

"Oh, yes. He did mention something about leaving ahead of us," I lied. "So difficult to remember things in this heat." It seemed my cover-up worked, for they did not comment and continued to sip their drinks. I was glad he had left hastily, for I was dreading the thought of him travelling with us all the way to Delhi. But what if he again tried to snare me there? How should I react? I tried pushing those thoughts out of my mind.

"Drink, memsaab?" A bearer approached me.

"Yes. A gin-sling, please." I needed one to calm my nerves.

Later that evening, our carriage rolled out of the *dak* bungalow's gates, the escort leading and following on horseback. The sun began to set and the stifling air that had blown all afternoon was beginning to cool. Following the bland lunch of badly baked chicken, potatoes and mushy peas, I had managed to catch a few winks in my room and felt rested.

Catherine and Captain Herford sat on the leather couch opposite mine, books in hand, and Jan lay bundled in a blanket beside me. Thankfully, the rocking of the carriage had put him to sleep, as he had howled earlier until I nursed him. Occasionally I heard Elgin, who sat up on the driving bench, chatting away in Hindustani with the coachman.

I had my journal on my lap and tried to bring it up to date, but could not concentrate on the writing. I closed it, with the pencil in it, and looked outside the window. The road turned away from the banks of the Ganges, which we had travelled along so far, and traversed northwards towards the Jamuna River; Delhi lay along its shores. Having passed through flat lands with numerous green fields, and farming villages, the carriage clattered along slightly rocky ground towards a range of hills that loomed in the distance. Those would be the start of the Himalayas, I thought, for I knew Delhi lay not far from those mountains.

While large boulders jutted out from the uneven surface on the sides of the road, it itself was remarkably smooth. I remembered someone had mentioned that this was the Grand Trunk Road that the Mughals had built, from Kabul to Calcutta, to transport their armies swiftly from the north to the south of India. Surely, it must have taken them considerable labor to construct this highway; however, with their empire shrunk to within the Delhi city walls, they did not need it anymore, I mused. I recalled what the Colonel had said that morning over breakfast, about Oudh, and realized I was still intrigued by his remarks.

Glancing at the Captain, I noted he was also looking out of the window. His book lay closed on his lap.

"Er ... Captain Herford," I said. When he looked at me, I asked, "Why do you think the British ... I mean, the Company, are not in agreement with King Zafar's choice for his successor?"

"Well, it's really his wife, Zinat's, preference for *her* son, Prince Jawan, and Zafar is simply abiding with her wishes." He smiled. "But really, the Company's choice of Prince Fakhruddin was made much earlier, upon the advice of the former Resident, Mr. Metcalfe."

"Oh! But why did Mr. Metcalf make that recommendation?" I must have had a puzzled look.

Herford did not answer and turned his head, reflectively, to look outside the window at the setting sun. However, Catherine, who seemed to be resting with her eyes closed, sat up and, looking at Herford, said, "Go on, dear, tell Doctor Margaret. She should know the reason."

Herford finally looked in my direction. "Ah, well. It's probably not a secret anymore. Some years ago, there was a confidential agreement between Sir Thomas Metcalf, the Delhi Resident at that time, and Prince Fakhruddin, that the Prince is officially recognized as the heir-apparent and upon King Zafar's death would inherit the throne."

I was puzzled. "It still doesn't make sense to me. Why would the Company make this agreement? In return for what?"

"Well, there is always something one has to give up, doesn't one?" Herford smiled. "In return, the Prince would move his court to a small house out in a suburb of Delhi, and hand over the Red

Fort to the Company."

I felt flabbergasted. "Give up the Red Fort! Why, the Mughals have ruled from there for more than two-hundred years."

"Yes, they have. But, sadly, it's now pretty much the end of their empire."

"You said this agreement is common knowledge, so King Zafar knows about it?"

"Yes, we believe he does, and particularly Begum Zinat, because—"

"Because, on account of it, she had Sir Thomas poisoned!" Catherine interjected.

I gasped. "Poisoned! How awful. Do you know this for certain?"

"Yes, it was definitely poison. His daughter, Emily, confirmed it in her letters," Catherine said.

"What about Prince Fakhruddin? Is he still alive?" I asked.

"Yes, he is. But we can't say for how long. He might meet a similar fa—" Herford stopped in mid-sentence, as there were sounds of musket fire in the distance.

The carriage stopped with a jolt, and the escorting soldiers from the rear galloped forward. We peered out of the windows and saw, a few yards up ahead, a carriage lying on its side. I recognized it as Colonel Humphrey's. One of its horses lay dead and the other one had bolted. It looked as if there had been an ambush, for some of his red-coated soldiers could be seen crouching behind trees or boulders and firing at the attackers up front.

Our escort sergeant came riding back and opened the door of our carriage. "Bloody thugs are attacking us. Please come out. Take shelter over there." He pointed to a rocky ridge at the side of the road and galloped forward again.

We moved speedily out of the carriage. I noted Elgin climbing down and, in a moment of quick thought, shouted at her, "Elgin, could you please bring down my medical bag." I recognized I would need it, not only for attending to any wounded, but I also had my revolver in there. Elgin extracted the bag from amongst the luggage and handed it down to me. She took Jan from my arms and we ran to Catherine and Herford, sheltering behind a rock at the side. The coachman, taking hold of the horses' bridle, turned them and the coach around. He then trotted them away to a safe distance in the back, to hide behind a clump of trees. Ahead of us, the gunshots grew in intensity.

Captain Herford took out his revolver from the holster. "I'll go up and see what's going on." Crouching low, he moved forward, taking cover from tree to tree.

"Be very careful, darling," Catherine stared over our rock and shouted to him. Then she turned to me and exclaimed, "Oh my God!"

"What is it?" I asked.

"Look over there." She pointed towards another boulder ahead of us.

I stared at it and, in the fading light, discerned the bodies of two soldiers lying there. One of them, a native sepoy, seemed to be dead, from the way he lay in a pool of blood. The other, a ruddy-faced one, in an officer's uniform, looked to be alive. Holding his right arm with his left hand, moved his legs as if signaling for help.

Recognizing him, I turned towards Catherine. "That's Colonel Humphrey, isn't it?"

"Yes, it is," she said, her face drained of color.

"I must go and help him." I collected my medical bag.

"No, don't. You'll get shot." She tried to hold my arm. "Wait for help."

"I must go to him. Waiting might be too late." I turned to Elgin. "Please take care of Jan." Then in a crouch, bag in hand, I ran towards the boulder where the soldiers lay.

A bullet whizzed by me—someone must have spotted me. I reached the prone bodies. From the look on the poor sepoy's face, I realized he was dead.

I moved towards Colonel Humphrey. He lay cupping his right arm.

"Ah, Margaret. So good of you to have come."

"Are you all right?" I knelt beside him.

"Bloody savages. Got me in the arm. Hurts like Hell. Pardon the language. Poor Jemadar Abdul there came to help. Got shot in the belly." He sighed.

I examined his arm. There was a bullet wound in the muscular part and blood oozed out of it. "Can you move your shoulder?"

He moved it gently. "Yes, barely."

"It looks like the bullet is lodged in the muscle. I'll try to take it out. It might hurt a bit."

"Please go ahead. I'm in your heavenly hands, darling doctor."

Ignoring his amorous remark, I opened the medical bag and searched for the bullet-pulling forceps.

"Margaret! Look out!" I heard Catherine shout.

I spun around and saw a big, muscular native, scantily clad in white robes and a turban, emerge from a clump of trees a few yards away. He ran in my direction, waving a large *talwar* in one hand and a knife in the other.

"Dammit. I lost my pistol when I got shot. Do you see it, Margaret?"

I looked around, but could not locate it. There was a musket lying beside the sepoy, but it was probably unloaded.

"Run, Margaret, run!" Catherine screamed again at me.

Chapter Nine

Dak bungalow to Delhi

1855, September: Dak bungalow to Delhi, India

AT THE SIGHT OF the devilish-looking brute charging towards me, *talwar* raised in the air, I froze to the ground. My hand was still in the medical bag, searching for the forceps.

"Oh, no," Colonel Humphrey muttered. He rolled over to the nearby dead sepoy's body, and yanked out the bayonet from his belt. Humphrey then jumped up in a crouching position, bayonet in his good left hand, and pointed it at the advancing rebel. "Come on, you bastard," he said loudly, and in the next breath shouted, "Captain Herfoooord!"

"Jaaaack! Over here!" Catherine screamed again.

I frantically looked around, but could not spot the Captain. With the Colonel holding the small bayonet and the attacker lunging forward with the huge, gleaming sword, it looked to be a hopeless match. I believed, in horror, he would have the Colonel's head at any moment.

Just then, my hand, in the medical bag, touched the cold steel barrel of my Robert's service revolver. I grabbed its butt, pulled it out, and pointed it at the fiend.

"*Rookoo*," I yelled at him to stop.

The rascal, upon seeing the revolver in my hand, stopped in his tracks and, lowering his hands, dropped the *talwar* and knife to the ground. To my amazement, I recognized him to be the same man who had made that improper remark about me on the ship, which had led to Colonel Humphrey knocking him down. However, I could not do more than shout to him, "*Bhag jaoo.*" I waved the revolver sideways, hoping he would run away. I simply did not have the heart to pull the trigger. He turned and started to scamper back to the grove.

"*Rookoo*. Stop!" someone behind me shouted. It was Herford approaching us in a stoop, his revolver in hand, pointing at the rebel.

The native looked back, but did not stop and continued to sprint. Captain Herford fired. The rebel tumbled forward onto the ground.

"Good shot, Herford!" Colonel Humphrey yelled.

Herford ran over to the Colonel and me, to take shelter alongside us, behind the boulder. The fallen man did not move. "It seems you got him in the heart, Captain." Humphrey looked admiringly at Herford, as if congratulating a fellow hunter.

"Thank you, sir. You all right?" Herford beamed at the Colonel.

"Ah, just a flesh wound. Nothing our Margaret can't fix. And thanks to her, I did not have to fight a duel with the devil! Was he not the same swine we met on the boat, Margaret?"

I simply nodded. A shiver ran through my body. I could not believe that having killed a man, they took it so sportingly. "Did you have to shoot him, Captain?"

Herford took a deep breath. "You should not have let the scoundrel get away, Margaret. He'd have returned to attack us another day. But it was his choice: death or prison."

"He would have hung, anyway," Humphrey remarked.

While the gun battle continued around us, bullets striking the boulder occasionally, I attended to the Colonel. Cutting his shirtsleeve off and using the forceps, I pulled the bullet out carefully, making sure not to graze the bone. After cleaning the wound with tincture-of-iodine and putting a tight bandage around it, I put his right arm in a sling around his neck. He expressed, a few times, his gratitude and thanks for saving his life. I put his earlier abominable behavior out of my mind, as my concern for the injured patient was foremost. However, I consoled myself that I would deal with his conduct later.

Suddenly, there was silence. All the firing ceased, indicating that the attackers either were all dead or had scuttled away. The sergeant came trotting over on his horse and waved at us to come forward. "The situation's under control. You may come out of the shelter." He then hollered at the coachman holding the carriage at some distance, to bring it over. The soldiers started to return from their entrenched positions.

While Catherine came out from behind the boulder and

embraced her husband, I scurried over to Elgin, who sat holding Jan in her lap. I heard him whimper. "Is Jan all right?"

"Yes, he good boy. Wake up from the noise and cry. Now he need changing."

I took him in my arms and coddled him. From the smell about him, it was obvious that he needed a change. "Could you please fetch the baby's bag?" I asked Elgin. She hurried out to the coach which had arrived nearby. Elgin spread a blanket on the grass and we cleaned and changed my baby. He looked happy and started smiling again. We were soon ready to board our *dakgharry*.

Colonel Humphrey's carriage was righted, and its poor dead horse pulled away from the road. While fresh horses were available, the carriage needed the broken wheel replaced. It was to be a while before they could get going. The Colonel still sat on the ground, his back supported by the stone ledge. I went to him and upon my inquiry, he moved his shoulder and mentioned there was some pain. From the medical bag, I took out a bottle of Belladonna and, mixing a few drops in a tin can of water, gave him the sedative to drink. He swallowed it and said, smiling, he already felt much better. The Herfords offered to give their seat to Colonel Humphrey in our *dakgharry* saying they would wait, for his carriage to be repaired. When I heard of this proposal, I was horrified at the thought of travelling with the Colonel in the same coach. But it was a relief when I heard him decline the offer, indicating that he was not badly injured, and preferred to wait and remain with his troops.

I left the Belladonna bottle with him, cautioning him not to drink too much of it at one time.

He agreed with a nod. "Thank you, dear Margaret. What would I have done without you?"

I did not answer. Putting his endearment out of mind and, medical bag in hand, walked back to my carriage.

We settled in our *dakgharry* and, still with worried looks, were on our way. With the darkness settling in around, I put my head back on the leather headrest and noted the Herfords did the same. No doubt they were just as glad as I was to have come out of the dreadful ordeal unscathed. Closing my eyes, I said a little prayer to our Lord. I thanked him for having saved me from the clutches of, first the evil Colonel, and then that Satan-like attacker. I also prayed that He would continue to grant me all the bounties He was bestowing upon me, and for those I was truly thankful … I continued to pray for the welfare of my son and his siblings in Canada, my parents and my sister and brother and others I could think of, until I drifted off into a deep slumber.

We continued our northward journey, and apart from a few minor sandstorms, which required taking shelter in abandoned buildings and once in a cave, the travel was uneventful, and stops at *dak*-bungalows bearable. It seemed Colonel Humphrey's party was delayed, for they would have not only made repairs but buried the dead as well, and I was happy that he did not catch up to us. The countryside changed once again to pastures and green fields of various crops, some I recognized were corn. It looked that we were again passing through fertile land, crisscrossed by irrigation channels.

"Are we approaching the Jamuna River?" I asked Captain Herford, who also gazed at the farmlands.

"Er … no. Not yet. We have to cross the Hindan River first. Thankfully, it has a suspension bridge. Thereafter, when we are on a bridge of boats, it'll be the Jamuna."

"And you'll get the first sight of Delhi from there," Catherine said, opening her eyes, but still resting her head on the seat cushion.

"Is the Jamuna too wide for a regular bridge?" I asked.

"Yes. At that location, it has several branches. One runs along the city wall," Herford said.

"The city's well protected, then?"

"Very well, I'd say," Hereford replied. "The high wall surrounds the town and the palace inside has its own keep."

"It seems Shah Jahan built an impregnable capital for his Empire," I remarked.

"He certainly chose a strategic location. A ridge runs to the north-west of the city. It, together with the river to the east, offers natural protection from any invader." Herford also added, "They even built a canal to bring water into the city."

"Is the Chandni Chowk's channel, still dry, dear?" Catherine asked.

"Yes, afraid so. Its water-tank doesn't shimmer in the moonlight anymore. So we shouldn't call it a '*chandni*' any longer." He chuckled. "The upstream farmers are using all the water for irrigation."

"Where is this 'moonlit courtyard' situated?" I asked.

"It's the city's main market square, just west of the palace wall's Lahore Gate. The main thoroughfare runs through it. There are some excellent shops and the Delhi Bank is situated there as well. Catherine will take you out shopping. Won't you, my dear?"

"I'd be delighted to," Catherine said.

I believe their suggestion was in consideration of the drab blue gown I had worn all along the journey. My spirits lifted at the thought of purchasing some of those delicate native silks, but they soon subsided when the sight of my empty reticule, except for a few coins, came before my eyes. I wondered how I was to support myself—maintain a home with servants and an *ayah* for Jan, and for my two to join me soon from Canada—on my meagre salary as a junior medical officer. Although I was qualified and had proved my worth at the military hospitals in the Crimea, I had the nagging suspicion that I would have to work harder to gain the confidence of my superiors, and it would be some time before I could expect an increase in remuneration.

I simply nodded at Catherine's offer and, to change the topic, asked, "I imagine the military cantonment is outside the city?"

"Yes. It's just beyond the Ridge. However, the Residency, the Ludlow Castle, where you'll be staying, is just below the Ridge, close to the city wall's Cashmir Gate."

"Oh, so that gate faces towards Cashmir, does it?" I asked.

"Yes, that's how those gates were named—"

"But wouldn't Doctor Margaret be working at the hospital in Daryaganj?" Catherine interrupted. "Why, that's at the other end of the city. My coachman has much difficulty getting through the narrow streets, whenever I go there."

"Yes, it's on the southern side, outside the palace's Delhi Gate," Herford explained. "You may wish to find accommodation in Daryaganj. Most of the city's Europeans and native elites live there. There are charming mansions and pleasant bungalows along the river. The river-market should be most convenient."

"Yes, I should live closer to the hospital. I shan't be staying too long at the Residency."

"Will you be working for the Assistant Surgeon, Doctor Chaman Lal?" Catherine asked.

"I've heard of the doctor," I said, remembering reading that he had converted to Christianity not long ago. "But I'm not certain. I have to report to the Civil Surgeon, Doctor Balfour."

"I think Doctor Lal is the best of the lot at the hospital. I haven't seen Doctor Balfour, for I've been away. But I trust he is unlike his predecessor, Doctor Ross," Catherine remarked, with a snigger. I must have looked puzzled, and she explained, "Doctor Ross was well known for his customary treatment."

"Oh, and what was it?"

"For the slightest ache or pain he would hand you a jar of leeches to be applied to the spot."

"Did they help?"

"Hardly," she said, smirking. "They made me weaker, and much sicker. I used to have them thrown out into the Najaf Canal, behind our bungalow."

"Well, we've had some real interesting doctors here," Herford joined in. "Have you heard about Doctor Sprenger?" I shook my head, and he continued. "Rumor had it that in the evenings, his wife used to hide his good trousers to prevent him from going out and leaving her alone!"

We all had a good laugh at that piece of intelligence, and the clamor woke Jan. He began to whimper in the manner he did when he was hungry. I took him in my arms and rocked him gently. Herford, reading my thoughts, looked out of the window and said, "Shan't be too long to the next *dak*-bungalow. I imagine we should be in Delhi by tomorrow morning."

"Oh! That would be a most welcome relief," Catherine remarked.

I awoke from either the change in the motion of the carriage— from the usual rocking to a smooth ride—or the early morning sun's rays, which shone in from the windows. I glanced out and observed the vast expanse of a river and, looking down, noticed bows of boats tied together to form a bridge we travelled over. Turning my head towards the shore up ahead, an Italian saying, I had read in a travel-book, came to my mind: "*Vedi Napoli e poi mori*". But, at the first sight of the sun shining on the fort's red walls and the city beyond, I made a mental note to write in my journal: *See Naples, as well as Delhi, before you die*. As the carriage drew nearer the embankment, a fortress with circular bastions appeared. It was situated on a small island and joined to the main fort with another arched bridge.

The Herfords had also awakened and looked out of the windows as well.

"Is that the Red Fort?" I asked, pointing towards the grey fortress.

"Er, no," Herford replied. "That's the older Salimgarh Fort, erected in early 1500, by Salim Suri. It's part of the Shahjahanabad complex that lies beyond, built in the 1630s."

The red sandstone walls, running along the river and curving into the city and the palace, came into view. Behind it emerged, lit by the early morning sun's rays, the domes and minarets of the mosques, and the city's mansions and houses. It was a picturesque sight of the metropolis indeed, and its numerous paintings, which I had seen in London's arts galleries, hardly did justice to its grandeur.

Emerging from the bridge-of-boats, the *dakgharry* clattered right through a gate in the city's ramparts. The native sentries at the checkpoint, upon recognizing the Company's coach and the uniformed Captain Herford, snapped to attention and saluted. He pointed to the marble walled palace. "There's King Shah Zafar's residence. He's probably awake now and saying his morning prayers at the Pearl Mosque, over there."

The carriage traversing through some narrow streets, drove by a church that had a huge pink dome with a large copper ball and a cross. Imposing porticoed porches, with Grecian triangular fronts on white pillars, stood at the sides.

"Is that the St. James' Church?" I asked, for Papa had mentioned it often enough.

"Yes. Built by Colonel James Skinner, in 1836. He lies buried in a marble crypt below the altar," Herford said. "And, if you look quickly on the opposite side, you will see the mosque he also built for one of his Muslim wives!"

I turned my head to see the typical three onion domes and arches of a small mosque, cheery looking in pleasant red and white colors.

It seemed the chauffeur knew the way to the Residency by heart. We crisscrossed the constricted lanes, through districts with congenial two or three storied houses with wooden balconies. Some had colorful cotton awnings over the large windows. Minarets of the famous, grandiose Jami Masjid were visible above the buildings.

It being early morning, the streets were not crowded, except for two distinct groups of pedestrians. One faction, of only males, heeding the prayer calls from the minarets, made their way to the mosques. They mostly wore *topis* or skull-caps, and long cotton shirts over tight-bottomed pajamas. All had beards, usually trimmed but some rather long. Another group, with painted foreheads, wearing baggy, colorful robes—women in saris—seemed to be heading for the river *ghats*, for early morning pujas and bathing rituals.

Being in the northern region, the citizens' complexions were from light to olive skinned, but they had dark, piercing eyes that looked up questioningly at us, as they stepped aside to the edge of the street's drainage channels or into the houses' doorways, to let the carriage pass by.

The *gharry* jangled through another exquisitely arched gateway, and we were again outside the city, in an open field on a road that led up gradually to a ridge. Shortly the turrets and the towers of a miniature citadel, more like a French chateau, loomed ahead. On my questioning look, Herford remarked, "Yes, there's Ludlow Castle." As we drew nearer, the grand, Gothic-styled edifice's two-storied battlements came into view.

The carriage drove up and stopped outside the pillared portico. One of the two sentries, who had likely been napping, ran up and, opening the carriage door, pulled down its steps.

"I'll go in and see if Simon is up," Herford said. He alighted and hobbled into the mansion. He soon emerged, followed by an elderly, rather rotund gentleman dressed in a red silk robe.

"Welcome, welcome! Doctor Margaret." He came up to the carriage and offered me his hand to help me down. "I'm Simon Fraser, at your service, ma'am."

We shook hands and exchanged pleasantries. I apologized for having inconvenienced him by arriving too early, to which he said, "Oh, no. It is no bother at all. I am an early riser. Moreover, I, and I should add, all the British residents of Delhi have been expecting you, and are most anxious to make your acquaintance."

He greeted Catherine and asked the Herfords if they would stay for breakfast? They declined saying they should go directly to their bungalow for it has been a long journey. I thanked them for their pleasant company that made the travel bearable. They also thanked me in return, and saying they will see me soon, drove away towards the Civil Lines.

Mr. Fraser escorted Elgin and me into the castle, saying, "No doubt you must be tired and famished from your long journey. Do join me for some tea. Breakfast should be ready shortly." At the look of hesitation on Elgin's face, I nodded at her to come in with me, and she followed with Jan in her arms. An English butler appeared and ushered us into the drawing room, while Mr. Fraser hurried along the corridor to his rooms to get dressed.

After the arduous journey, and the unpleasant stops in the *dak*-bungalows, the Residency seemed heavenly. The large, lofty room, well furnished with woolen carpets, cushioned chairs and sofas, looked so inviting that Elgin and I made ourselves comfortable on a settee immediately, Jan in-between us. The *punkah* in the room's center started swinging to provide some relief from the heat that, although it was still early, was starting to build up. While I admired the paintings hanging on the walls, a body of native servants arrived with trays of tea and refreshments in hand.

Mr. Fraser reappeared, all dressed in a dark coat and tie, his fair hair brushed back tidily. We conversed about the long journey from Futtehgurh, particularly the attack on Colonel Humphrey. He had already heard about that incident.

After tea, he asked the butler to show me to my room. "The whole of the second floor's east wing is unoccupied. The corner bedroom is particularly delightful. You'll enjoy the lovely views of the Jamuna and the city. Your *ayah* may stay in the adjoining room, if she wishes."

"Yes, she would like that. You are most kind, sir."

The rooms, as Mr. Fraser had indicated, were tastefully decorated, with snug-looking beds, and I spotted a cot in a corner of the bedroom. The butler left, mentioning that breakfast would be served in the dining room in about an hour. After a visit to the water closet and a quick wash, I nursed Jan, who drank hungrily. I then changed into a fresh grey gown, and Elgin helped me tidy up my hair. She said she would breakfast later, after settling in her room next door. Jan, by then, was sleeping peacefully in the cot.

I walked along the corridor in the bright sunlight that shone through the numerous windows. I stopped for a moment to gaze at the scenic views of the Jamuna, the Red Fort, the Jami Masjid, and other parts of Delhi. I said a silent prayer of thanks to the Lord. The blissful atmosphere elated my heart, as I walked down the oak staircase towards the dining room. Approaching it, I heard murmurs of conversation. I was expecting to see only Mr. Fraser but another person was also present.

Upon seeing me at the door, they stood. The other person, bowing a bit, said, "Good morning, Margaret." My heart sank, and all the euphoria that I was feeling left me, when I saw the speaker was my adversary, my tormenter, Colonel Humphrey.

Although the sight of the despot arrested me at the door, I recovered my composure quickly and, murmuring a good morning, entered the dining room. The butler pulled out a chair. I sat down and, ignoring Humphrey, ordered my usual breakfast, toast and spicy omelet. One of the native servants poured me a cup of tea.

I noticed the Colonel did not have his arm in the sling, but the bandage showed under the short shirtsleeve. It must have been the doctor in me, for I asked, "How is the arm, Colonel Humphrey?"

"Ah! Very well, thank you. I can now raise it up to here." He attempted to move his elbow horizontally, but stopped about halfway and grimaced a bit.

"I don't think you'd be able to go partridge hunting with Zafar, yet!" Commissioner Fraser remarked, sipping tea.

"It's only a flesh wound. I should be able to ride and fire a rifle soon," the Colonel said, massaging his upper arm.

"Does the King still ride?" I asked, sipping a cup of tea.

"Don't think so. The old fellow uses palanquins and elephants now," Fraser responded, and motioned to the butler for another helping of bacon and eggs from the platter on the sideboard. "When are you going to see him, Colonel?"

"Likely tomorrow. Could you please let Captain Douglas know of my arrival?" After Fraser nodded, the Colonel turned towards me. "Would you like to join me, Margaret? While I am with the King, you could visit the *zenana*. Afterward, I'll take you around and show you a bit of the city?"

"Er ... no thank you, Colonel," I replied quickly, rather taken aback at his suggestion to drive around in the carriage with him. "I must report at the Civil and Military Hospital. Doctor Balfour might be wondering whatever happened to me." I sipped at the cup of tea to hide my embarrassment. Although, intrigued with the idea of visiting the *zenana*, putting the cup down, I added, "But I should like to go and see the *zenana* another day, if I may?"

"Certainly. I'll mention it to Zafar," the Colonel responded.

"I'll be seeing Doctor Balfour today, on some official matter … something about opening another clinic in Chandni Chowk. I'll advise him of your arrival," Commissioner Fraser said, looking towards me. "Shall I have a carriage take you to the CMH, tomorrow morning?"

"Thank you, sir. You are most kind." My breakfast arrived, and while Fraser and Humphrey continued in their general conversation, engaging me now and then, I busied myself buttering the hot toast and eating the delicious omelet.

Finishing my breakfast, I felt weary, and not wanting any more dialogue with Colonel Humphrey, also knowing that Elgin had not eaten yet, I gulped my remaining tea, quickly. I then excused myself and, after thanking the Commissioner again for his hospitality, and wishing Humphrey a good day, left the dining room.

******

The sound of a cannon-shot roused me from a pleasant slumber. I sat up in bed, wondering what was going on. Were the rebels attacking the Residency now? Then, remembering what Catherine had told me about the firing of the cannon, thrice daily, from the Flagstaff Tower on the Ridge, I slumped back down onto the pillow. However, at the thought of it being my first day at the hospital, I jumped out of the bed.

When I opened the drapes over the windows, the red ball of the rising sun just above the glimmering waters of river came into view; the city dwellings lay spread along the riverbanks. I unbolted the window to open it ajar. It let in not only a cool breeze, but also the Arabic sounds of the call for morning prayers from the minarets of the mosques visible in the distance. I looked at Jan's crib and saw him still sleeping peacefully, like a golden-haired doll.

The clatter of my bustling about the room, to get washed and appropriately dressed, must have alerted Elgin in the adjoining room. She gently tapped on the door and entered with a tray in hand. "Good morning, memsahib. I bring you tea. You like breakfast?"

"Thank you, Elgin." Too excited to eat much, my stomach in

knots, I said, "No, not a big breakfast. Just some toast and jam, please."

Putting the tray down on a side-table, she rushed to the kitchen downstairs. I heard Jan awaken and, going to the crib, picked him up. He opened his eyes and smiled at me, as if to say *he* was ready for a big breakfast. I sat down at the edge of the bed, unbuttoned my blouse and, cradling him in my arms, gave him his morning feed; he drank with relish.

Elgin arrived carrying a tray of tea and chapattis with butter and guava-jam, for she knew that I preferred those to white bread. While she took care of Jan, I finished dressing in a dark blue gown and a matching bonnet.

I asked Elgin if the Residency's carriage was available. She peeked out of the window and informed me that indeed it was waiting downstairs. I finished dressing and, after a quick peck on Jan's cheek, strode downstairs, a parasol in hand. At the landing, I met Mr. Fraser. He bid me a pleasant day and said he was off to the *kutchery*, located in the west wing of the building.

The red-liveried coachman opened the carriage door and let the stairs down to help me climb in. "Go to CMH, memsaab?" he asked. I responded in the affirmative.

As the carriage rolled out of the Residency's compound, I noticed a number of coaches waiting at the far wing of the edifice, and people bustling in and out of the offices. The peons held the bamboo curtains over the doors for the visitors. I imagined Commissioner Fraser having to face another busy day at work, administering the affairs of Delhi. This place is virtually like the White House, I thought.

The coach traversed through many of the same streets we had travelled on the previous day. But, it being a bit later in the morning, the traffic was much heavier and the carriage had to stop a number of times for other vehicles, and frequently to let some of the white Brahma bulls majestically cross the street. After crisscrossing through a number of narrow lanes, in the older part of the town, we clattered on a road that ran along the banks of the river that lay on the other side of the city wall. Along the riverfront, there were several well-maintained cottages and buildings, indicative of a prosperous section of the city.

Finally, the carriage stopped at a two-story brick building that looked more like a nawab's *haveli* than a hospital. There was a large courtyard in a picturesque garden, surrounded by a stone boundary wall having steel gates with two sentries standing on either side. A number of sickly-looking persons had already lined up outside.

The coachman stepped down and told me through the window, "CMH here, memsaab. Please sit. I go and find orderly."

I waited, and finally a native gentleman, dressed in a white shirt and pajamas with a matching *topi*, came over and opened the carriage door. He salaamed and said, "Welcome, Doctor memsahiba. Good see you. We waiting for you for long time. Doctor Balfour in office. Please come."

"I wait here for you, memsaab?" the coachman asked.

I handed him a rupee. "No. You may go. I'll hire another carriage for my return." He salaamed me several times, obviously happy for the tip.

I followed the orderly past the iron gates and up the garden path. Several gardeners working the beds of unfamiliar flowers stopped to look at me curiously. Turning around a large central marble fountain spewing streams of water, I observed 'CIVIL & MILITARY HOSPITAL' written in black paint in a semicircle on the white wall of the entrance archway. We entered the hospital through two large, ornamentally carved wooden doors. He led me along familiar antiseptic-smelling corridors and up the stairs to the second floor. Some of the staff, who passed us, stopped and *namested*. The hospital looked remarkably hygienic, and it appeared there was no shortage of cleaners, for a number of them were busy sweeping or mopping the floors.

We finally arrived at a polished mahogany door, having a brass plate that read: *Doctor Balfour - Civil Surgeon*. The orderly knocked on the door and, opening it, motioned for me to enter. I went inside what looked more to be a waiting room, with chairs and a nurse sitting behind a screen at a small desk. On one side was another door that led to the Civil Surgeon's office.

The dark-complexioned and raven-haired Eurasian nurse, dressed in a brown frock, stood up and came towards me, her arm extended. "Good morning, Doctor Wallace. Everyone has been looking forward to your arrival, most anxiously." We shook hands. "I'm Pamela. I look after Doctor Balfour's affairs. I believe he is free and will see you right away." She knocked on the doctor's door and, opening it, announced my arrival and ushered me in.

Doctor Balfour sat at a desk on one side of the room, working on some papers. Upon seeing me, he immediately got up and came towards me. He was an elderly gentleman, grey haired and sporting a heavy beard; he looked to be close to sixty years of age. He wore a dark suit and his bearing reminded me of the head surgeons I had met in various hospitals.

"Welcome. We have been expecting you." We shook hands. He then turned towards Pamela. "Can you please ask Doctor Lal to come in? And yes, please order some tea. Thank you." He motioned to a chair in front of his desk.

I sat down. We exchanged pleasantries. He asked about my journey, my parents, the American Mission in Futtehgurh, and so on.

He finally came to the matter that seemed to be on his mind. "Doctor Wallace, there is something I wish to discuss with you, before we go over the medical matters at the hospital." After I nodded, he proceeded. "As you know, you will be our very first lady doctor in Delhi. I note you have an excellent service record in Crimea, particularly during the war. What's more, you come highly recommended to us. Hence, I don't believe working here will be a problem for you. However, I have just one concern. If I may clear it up with you?"

"Yes, Doctor Balfour. What is it?" I asked, feeling a bit confused.

"You see, Doctor Margaret … If I may call you that?" I nodded. "While this hospital has been in existence for many years, and we've had a number of doctors from the British Isles serving here, but, mindful of the situation, we have a policy of encouraging native people to join us in the medical profession. In that regard, we've had a good response and I'm happy to say that one of my assistants, Doctor Chaman Lal, whom you will meet shortly, is a most competent professional. We are very satisfied with his performance and have been happy to promote him to Assistant Surgeon." He paused a bit, wondering if I was comprehending his rambling speech. I nodded for him to continue. "As his department is in charge of the medical health of the female members of our district, your services would be best utilized in his section. Hence, Doctor Margaret, may I ask you if you would have any objections to working for a native head of department?"

"Oh, no, Doctor Balfour. I would have no qualms in working for an Indian doctor," I responded immediately. "And far from it, I feel it would be advantageous for me to have him guide me in my work here, especially when it would involve treating the female population. After all, who else would know more of the locals' problems than a native person?"

"I am so glad to hear that. Thank you for your understanding." Doctor Balfour looked relieved. "By the way, I should also mention that Doctor Lal converted to Christianity a few years ago!"

"Yes, I'd heard that. My father read about him in the *Delhi Gazette*. It seems he's quite a celebrity!"

Doctor Balfour smiled at the inference.

There was a knock on the door, and Pamela stuck her head in. "Doctor Lal is here."

She opened the door wider and the doctor entered. He was a short, somewhat corpulent person, with a dark complexion and black wavy hair. He wore a white jacket over a blue shirt and dark trousers, in the European-style.

Doctor Balfour introduced us and we shook hands.

"Pleased to meet you. So kind of you to have come all the way from America to join us," he said, sitting down on the chair beside me.

"I am happy to be here. My parents came earlier to Futtehgurh, and I followed them from Crimea."

A bearer arrived with trays of tea and snacks. Over the refreshments, we entered into a small discourse about me. I brought them up to date on my family situation, my experiences in the Crimea and my impressions of India, so far. In turn, they informed me of the state of affairs at the hospital and a bit of the history of the area, some of which I had learned already. Doctor Balfour asked if I was happy with the accommodation at the Residency. I informed him that while it was most comfortable, it being at some distance, I wished to seek suitable housing closer to the hospital. Doctor Lal said he knew of some bungalows along the river road that might be available and he would inquire and let me know. I thanked him.

Doctor Balfour looked as if he remembered something and, putting his teacup down, said, "Doctor Lal, is there anything more on that inquiry from the Missionary Society on opening a new clinic for women?"

"Yes, they are very keen on it. As you know, they had earlier requested Miss Florence Nightingale to come to Delhi. It seems she is busy, setting up the hospital in Turkey, so Doctor Wallace is here in her place," Doctor Lal responded, looking towards me with a smile.

"I met Commissioner Fraser yesterday, and he is receptive to the Missionary Society's suggestion. Do they have any ideas where this clinic could be located?" Doctor Balfour asked.

"I believe they are considering some locations in Chandni Chowk," Doctor Lal said. Then, turning towards me, asked, "Would you be interested in assisting in this new venture?"

"Yes, certainly. I'd be delighted to help in any way I can."

"Good," Doctor Balfour said. "Doctor Lal, perhaps you could show Doctor Margaret her office and around the hospital, a bit?"

We stood, and I followed Doctor Lal out of the office. We went down the stairs to the ground floor and walked along the corridors towards the back of the building, where the Women's Ward was located. We passed by the General Ward, where numerous beds were laid out side by side. The overcrowding and the painful look on the patients' faces reminded me of the hospitals that I had worked in, particularly in Crimea.

Doctor Lal pointed out to me a few rooms that were reserved for private patients, and the delivery and operating theatres at the end of the corridor. He stopped at one office, which had his name on the door. He opened it and, asking me to come in, introduced me to his nurse, Gita. She was an Indian lady, a young woman dressed in a blue-bordered white sari, and a red dot on her forehead. She came forward and bid me a *nameste*, with a smile.

Doctor Lal then took me to a vacant room farther along the corridor, which was to be my office. It was a small room, barely large enough for the desk and a filing and medicine cabinets in there. He asked if the office was satisfactory. I answered in the affirmative. He said he would let me settle in and would be back later to discuss my duties. In the meanwhile, he would send Gita to introduce me to my nurse. She would show me around the rest of the hospital. I thanked him, before he left the room.

I took off my bonnet and hung it, together with my parasol, on a hook on the wooden clothes-stand that stood in a corner of the room. I sat down on the oak chair, which thankfully had a wool-cushion that felt comfortable enough. I looked at the polished oak desk and surveyed the small room. A feeling of intense joy and pleasure passed through me. This was my very first office, which I had strived for, and longed for. It had been a long journey. It was indeed a wonderful feeling to have finally achieved this desire. Closing my eyes, I said a little prayer to the good Lord, and thanked him for once again showering me with his benevolence and kindness.

A knock on the door brought me back to the present. Gita came in, followed by a young English woman, carrying an armload of writing papers, journals, pencils, pens and an ink bottle.

"Hallo, Doctor Wallace. Please meet Betty, she will be your nurse," Gita said.

I shook hands with Nurse Betty, "Pleased to meet you."

"Welcome Doctor Wallace. Are you settling in all right?" She placed the supplies on my desk. "May I show you around?"

"I am. Thank you, Betty." I stood up. "Yes, please lead the way. I am anxious to see the rest of the hospital, particularly where the ladies' room is!"

I followed her out of the office and along the corridor. She pointed out the women's washroom and asked if I wanted to go there. I told her, I felt comfortable for the moment. She showed me where the cafeteria was, but cautioned me, with a smile, against eating there too often. I nodded, and told her that I would normally bring my own sandwiches for the lunches. She then took me to the nursery, where I noted several children playing around under the watchful eyes of their *ayahs*. Upon my question, Betty answered that, yes, it was possible to arrange to have a child and a nurse placed there for the day care. I was happy to hear that, and relieved to see the nursery, for I was worried about leaving Jan alone with Elgin for the whole day.

After visiting other areas of the hospital, Betty brought me back to my office, and I thanked her for the tour. We chatted a bit. She told me that her husband was a sergeant, and they were from the South of England. She departed saying that her desk was in the adjoining room, and Doctor Lal would come in to see me shortly. I went for a quick visit to the washroom, to be ready for my supervisor's visit and my first cases.

Doctor Lal arrived shortly, a stack of files under one arm. Placing them on my desk, he sat down on the chair opposite mine. At first, he went through the general operating procedures at the hospital. The working hours were from seven a.m. to twelve noon, followed by a two-hour lunch break. Normally, I would see patients in the morning and attend to any deliveries or surgery as needed. Thereafter, he mentioned, due to the intense heat in the afternoons—and it was beginning to get stifling hot already—the doctors did not normally see many patients nor perform major surgeries, later in the day, unless it was an emergency. He indicated that there were two other senior doctors, whom I would meet later, in our gynecology and obstetrics department, and I would be required to assist them as needed. I nodded.

He was kind to offer that during the first few months of starting my work at the hospital, he would not expect me to work during the afternoons, unless required, and I could go home at noon. I thanked him for his generosity. He did mention that from time to time, there was a request for a lady doctor to visit the home of a patient, because the woman was either too sick or reluctant to come to the hospital. I said I would be happy to visit the female patients in their homes. Doctor Lal asked if I had been learning Hindustani. I responded that I had picked a bit of it. He said that he would arrange for an appropriate nurse or a translator to accompany me.

Next, he went briefly through the files of the patients he had brought. Most were cases with minor ailments that he felt I could handle without much difficulty. But, not that very day, for these were outpatients whom he had been treating. He suggested I look over the files and examine the sick with him on their next visit. He stood up, and again said that he was very pleased to have me help him at the hospital, for he badly needed a lady doctor assistant to treat the many cases that were being referred to him. I thanked him for his kindness. He left repeating that I would not be needed that afternoon and was free to go home at lunchtime.

I fetched a cup of tea from the cafeteria, and, putting it on my desk, got busy perusing the files. As Doctor Lal had indicated, these cases—mostly European ladies—were either normal pregnancies or minor ailments that could be treated adequately. I made notes and jotted down the dates when these patients were to visit the hospital again. Soon it approached lunchtime, or *tiffin* as they called it there, and, putting on my bonnet, I walked out of the office.

As I strode out of the hospital's doors, I needed to put up my parasol, for protection against the blazing sun's rays. A line of *tongas*—a small carriage on two wheels, where the passengers sat on a seat behind the driver—waited in the lane outside the hospital.

The *tongawalla* of the first one shouted excitedly to me, "Memsaab, memsaab, come. Where you go?"

I told him, and ascended, with some difficulty, on the high seat. The *tongawalla* drove with maddening speed through the crowded lanes, narrowly missing many pedestrians while shouting at them to move away, and cracking his whip at the horse every now and then. I hung on for dear life.

When we got out of the city's Cashmir Gate and onto the open road, he increased the cart's speed even faster, as if we were in a Roman chariot race. It seemed the horse did not mind the whip-cracking, for the creature seemed to enjoy the gallop and in no time he raced in through the Residency's gates, and at the pull of the reins, come to a sliding halt in a cloud of dust outside the portico. It was the most thrilling ride I had ever had! In addition to the fare, I tipped him an extra rupee.

I spotted Elgin sitting, cross-legged, on the marble floor of the veranda, with Jan on her lap, talking to one of the other servant girls. She looked thrilled to see me return so early, and, getting up, came at a trot to me. I took Jan from her and after kissing him, rocked him in my arms and tickled his belly. He squealed with delight.

"You like lunch, memsahib?"

"Yes, I am very hungry. Is there any curry chicken and rice on the menu?"

"I go see. Come to dining room." She scampered off towards the kitchen.

I met the butler on the way to the dining room. He asked if I wanted a drink. I requested a gin and tonic, for I felt like celebrating. After all, I had just finished my first day at work at a hospital in India! My drink arrived and Elgin brought me a steaming plate of hot curry chicken, and chapattis in a breadbasket. I took a large gulp of the tasty gin and relished forkfuls of the curry chicken. Elgin sat on a chair beside me, Jan in her arms. She was all questions about my first day at the hospital.

While I was talking to her, the butler returned with two

envelopes in hand, which he placed on the table beside me. "Your post, ma'am. Just came in this morning."

I thanked him and glanced at the direction on the envelopes. One was from Mamma, in her typical slanting handwriting. I opened it. It was a short note, simply inquiring if I had arrived safely in Delhi. And there was not much to write about, as all was well, as usual, at the Mission. The other one—I could not recall the handwriting on its direction—it was addressed to me at Futtehgurh, and Mamma had redirected it to me. I opened it, wondering who it could be from. To my surprise, it was a two-page letter from Nancy Miller, and had a Calcutta hotel return address, in the top corner. It read, in part:

> *Dearest Margaret,*
>
> *This may be a surprise for you, but I just could not wait to write to you to tell you that, would you believe, we have finally arrived in Calcutta! The journey from Crimea was most tiring, but I am sure you would know all about that. Albert is well, and sends you his best wishes. We are both looking forward to joining you in Delhi, as he has been posted to a regiment stationed there. How nice it will be to see you again …*

She had written more about their experiences during the journey and the places they had visited in Calcutta. But, I could not read any further, and put the letter aside. Just the mention of Albert's name, and the thought of them hounding me now here in Delhi, saddened my heart. Was not Albert's despicable behavior towards me and dear Robert, in Canada and on the voyage, and then again in Crimea, enough?

All the euphoria I had been feeling, after my very first day at work, evaporated. I pushed my lunch plate away, for I could not eat any more. My ravenous appetite had also suddenly vanished. Putting my elbows on the table, I massaged my temple with my fingers, for I was beginning to get a headache. Tears welled in my eyes, and rolled down my cheeks.

"What is it, memsahib? Bad news from Futtehgurh?" Elgin had a worried look on her face.

I pulled out my handkerchief and, dabbing my eyes, blew my nose. "No, not bad news from Futtehgurh. But some people, I detest, are coming to torment me here." I got up from the chair. "I am very tired. I think I will go and lie down for a bit. Please take care of Jan." I turned, and walked to the stairs and up to my bedroom.

Chapter Ten

Delhi life

1855, October: Delhi, India

THE LATE EVENING sun's rays, sloping in through the windows and shining over my eyes, woke me. Although I had slumbered well, I still felt tired from the day's events. However, mindful that I had slept through dinner the previous day, and not wanting to be impolite, I slid out of bed and made my way wearily to the washbasin. Although knowing that it was the custom in Delhi for the gentry to get dressed in the evenings and go about in their carriages or stroll around in the city's parks, I did not feel in the mood for it. I clad modestly, in the same dark blue gown I had worn in the morning.

I went downstairs and made my way towards the drawing room. In the hallway, I met the butler. "Would you care for some tea, or a drink, ma'am?"

"I would love some tea, please. Is Elgin around?"

"I believe she's sitting in a hammock out in the garden, with the baby. I will send her in."

I sat down on the couch, and soon Elgin arrived with Jan in her arms. I took him from her and, squeezing him to my breast, kissed him. He smiled, displaying his pleasure. My tea tray arrived and Elgin proceeded to pour me a cup. Hearing footsteps out in the hallway and someone asking for a whiskey, I looked up at the door.

"Margaret, there you are, and your handsome boy!" Colonel Humphrey, dressed in the British-red military uniform, strode into the room and sat down on a wing chair. "So, tell me, how was your first day at the hospital? Performed any amputations yet?" he asked with a chuckle. The butler brought him a whisky.

"I had a good day, thank you. Amputations! Hardly, sir. I don't believe any of the female patients assigned to me are in need of that."

"Ah, yes. I daresay you will be spending more time in the delivery rooms."

"Possibly. Although I may be visiting the sick women in their homes as well. How is your arm, sir?"

The Colonel moved his arm. "Tolerably good. Thank you. Not much pain now." Seeing that Elgin had taken the baby from me and left the room, he moved his chair a bit closer to me. "By the way, dear Margaret, why so formal again? Were we not on first-name basis? Pray continue to call me William," he said in a whisper, leaning towards me.

"Not after what you tried to do to me at the *dak*-bungalow! Have you forgotten that?" I responded in a stern voice.

"Oh, dearest Margaret. Please forgive me for that. It is just your beauty that carried me away. I beg your exoneration for my despicable conduct. I humbly request your pardon. Will you grant me that?"

Upon hearing those words, instead of tenderness, a feeling of rage swept through me. "Hardly, sir! Your actions were most ungentlemanly, and unbecoming of a military officer. I am considering reporting that incident to the authorities."

"Oh, no, Margaret. Please don't do that. For one thing, they'll never believe you. Besides, what good would come of it?" he murmured.

I seethed with fury and nearly shouted, "It certainly will make you grasp what a—" I heard footsteps and voices in the hallway.

"Hallo, Doctor Wallace. How was your day? Is Doctor Balfour treating you well?" Commissioner Fraser entered, a glass of whisky in hand, and slumped on a chair.

"Yes. Very well. Thank you, sir," I replied, composing myself. The Commissioner asked more questions and in response I gave him a full discourse of my first day at the hospital.

"Ah, yes. Doctor Lal is a most competent physician. I have heard only good reports about him. I am certain you will enjoy your work in his unit. Also, visiting the patients' homes should be interesting. Don't you think?"

"Yes, I should like that. But I don't know many families in the city, yet."

"Ah! Speaking of that, there is a choir practice after dinner, at the church. Would you be interested in attending it? There'll be some citizenry there."

"Yes. I would like to listen to the choir."

"That reminds me." Colonel Humphrey shifted in his chair. "I have arranged with Zafar for you to visit the *zenana* in the palace, next Sunday, after the church service."

"Thank you, sir. Most kind of you."

"Good, my carriage will be at your service. But now, may I take you for a drive through the city to get you familiar with the streets?"

"No, thank you, sir. I have already had two carriage rides through the city today. I finished my cup of tea and got up. "I should see to my child."

The two gentlemen also arose and bowed as I left the room.

After dinner, having changed into a decent-looking grey dress—one of the few I owned—I joined Commissioner Fraser and Colonel Humphrey in the carriage for the ride to the Saint James' Church. As we drove out of the Residency, on the road at the foot of the Ridge towards the city, they pointed out to me the various landmarks. The most notable one was a Palladian residence that loomed in the distance, on the west bank of the river. From the carriage, in the fading dusk, it looked like an enormous European-style palace. I admired the double-storied bastion, with a stone veranda around it, having a bowed mid portion. Impressive Grecian-style double columns of marble pillars supported the second floor. An attractive façade decorated a low parapet on the upper story. The building was surrounded by well-manicured gardens dotted with pathways that meandered through cypress trees and orange groves. The whole estate must have comprised at least a few hundred acres.

"That is a lovely mansion. When was it built?" I asked.

"It's the Metcalf House, built in the thirties, I believe. Sir Thomas, the former Commissioner, acquired the land from the Gujjars. I daresay they are still fuming at being evicted from their village homes and croplands," Mr. Fraser responded.

"Who lives there now?" I asked, remembering that Sir Thomas Metcalf was alleged to have been poisoned.

"His son, Sir Theophilus. Our Joint Magistrate and Deputy Collector," Mr. Fraser informed me.

"He is much more sociable than his father was," Colonel

Humphrey remarked.

"That he is. He will likely have the first ball of the winter season, fairly soon. You will enjoy that," Mr. Fraser said, looking towards me, but noting my dark attire, quickly corrected himself. "I'm sorry. The Battle of Balaclava was only late last year. You are still in mourning, are you not?"

"It's all right, sir. It's almost a year since my husband died." At the thought of Robert, as he lay dying on the battlefield, tears welled in my eyes. I quickly looked out of the window and dabbed my eyes with a handkerchief.

"My deepest condolence," Mr. Fraser said.

"And mine too," I heard the Colonel murmur. "If it's any consolation, I've heard that we have captured Sebastopol. The whole of Crimea should be in our hands fairly soon."

"Thank you, sir," I said. "I am glad to know that my husband's death was not in vain." Then, remembering the treacherous way he was killed, brought fresh tears to my eyes. I continued to stare out of the window, wondering how I was going to deal with Albert when he arrived in Delhi.

My mind was brought back to the present by the jolting and slowing down of the carriage, as it approached the Cashmir Gate, for many vehicles were trying to get in and out of the city. We finally got through, and the coach turned leftwards on a smaller laneway towards the river. Another fine-looking building with a long colonnade, a large lawn and gardens in front of it, appeared on the left. Groups of young men and women, dressed in either Western or Eastern style and carrying books, streamed out of the main gate.

While I looked at them, Colonel Humphrey said, "It's the Delhi College, another first-rate institution being supported by the Company. Knowing you are an excellent teacher as well, I am certain they could use your help."

Noting that he was attempting to be supportive, I responded civilly, "How interesting, to have a college nearby. I'll be happy to assist. Do they teach in English?" The thought of teaching there was tempting, not only for the prospect of earning some additional income, but also for the opportunity to meet some of the local students.

"Actually, it is in both mediums. They have an Oriental and an English section," Mr. Fraser responded. "Where have you taught before, Margaret?"

"The Colonel is most kind. It was only at the Mission School in a village near Futtehgurh. I gave English lessons to the native women."

"And don't forget your teaching the Nawab and his wife at their palace," the Colonel added.

Yes, and you had me removed from that job; I fumed at the thought of it. But bit my tongue.

"Well, that is most interesting. The principal of the college, Mr. Taylor, will likely be at the church tonight. I will introduce you to him."

"Thank you, sir."

"This is the old Residency building, is it not?" Colonel Humphrey said.

Mr. Fraser nodded. "Yes. It was originally the library of Shah Jahan's son, Dara Shikoh, but by 1803 had fallen into much disrepair. When we took Delhi, the King presented it to us, and our first British Resident, Sir David Ochterlony, restored it. You'll notice the European front and the Mughal architecture at the back."

I had already noted that odd mixture, as if one civilization had ended and another continued in front of it.

"Good thing you don't live in there, Simon," Colonel Humphrey remarked.

"I wouldn't think of it. I fear the ghosts of Sir David's thirteen wives would visit me, one every night!"

The Colonel guffawed. "And not to mention Sir David and his wives parading by the gates, on thirteen elephants every evening."

Although I found the banter distasteful, I smiled, to appear to enjoy their crude merriment. I had heard that Sir David had caused quite a stir within the British establishment at having "gone native", by dressing in local costumes, eating Indian food, smoking hookahs, and holding *nautch* parties.

The carriage rolled along the street and soon I spotted the familiar Italian-style dome of St. James' Church loom up ahead over the treetops. The carriage turned into its semi-circular driveway and stopped at the front portico. The coachman jumped down and opened the door. Colonel Humphrey alighted first and helped me down. We proceeded into the church through its enormous entrance, and heard the familiar sounds of a piano's warm-up bars.

A number of people sat in the pews and, there not being a choir gallery, the members of the choir stood at the front. We slid into the dark wooden bench of a vacant pew; I sat between Mr. Fraser and the Colonel. Catherine and Captain Herford arrived right behind us, wearing their best evening attire. Nodding good evenings, they took their seats on the same pew. Both looked much refreshed and relaxed after our long journey and the harrowing experience in the forest with those revolutionaries.

While we waited for other visitors to arrive and take their places, and the choir to assemble, I looked around to admire the high ceiling, the arches and the stained-glass windows. Papa had informed me that the late Colonel Skinner—the son of a Scottish officer and a Rajput princess—had built the church in 1836, but when I spotted the columns supporting the dome, a smile crossed my face. I recalled reading in Mrs. Fanny Parkes' travelogue through India, of her visit to the same church, some years earlier. She had written that she found the support bars to be "a most unsightly affair". I must admit that while they seemed a bit odd, situated in the middle of the hall, they did not appear quite so "unsightly," for they had been covered with carved wooden moldings, and connecting arches, to make them look presentable.

Soon the hall was filled to capacity, and the choir began practicing the hymns. An attractive young woman, dressed in a charming pink gown and matching bonnet, directed the group, waving her right hand and holding the songbook in the other. Blonde ringlets dropped down her swan-like neck. Next to her stood the padre in a dark suit and white collar, and from the strong facial resemblance, he definitely looked to be her father. The choir did not need much prompting or correcting, for it seemed they were well rehearsed, and sang admirably in unison.

After an enjoyable session of singing the lovely hymns, particularly the "Amazing Grace," which the audience and even myself joined in, we retired to a smaller room where some of the volunteer ladies served tea and biscuits. The attendees, teacups in hand, walked around greeting each other or stood around in groups, talking. It seemed the main purpose of the evening was to meet and catch up on the news.

While I stood with Mr. Fraser and the Colonel, they introduced me to a number of the European elite of Delhi, as they passed by, and I shook their hands. All seemed pleased that I was there, and wished me the best in my new position. The chaplain, Reverend Jennings, and his charming daughter, Miss Annie, came over to our group specially to meet me. We spoke at some length. Reverend Jennings had heard of my father and inquired about him. Miss Annie introduced me to her friend standing by her, a Miss Clifford, another striking Englishwoman, who was visiting the Jennings.

A handsome young gentleman had followed Annie and stood shyly behind her. She introduced him as Lieutenant Thomason, whom I recognized as one of the basses in the choir having a clear voice. They left with Reverend Jennings, who reminded me to, "Please do bring Brother Wallace to meet us, when he visits Delhi. We are not hard to find; we're sharing accommodations with Captain Douglas at the Lahore Gate." I told him that we would definitely come by.

Commissioner Fraser brought over a middle-aged gentleman, whom he introduced as Mr. Taylor, the Principal of Delhi College.

"Pleased to meet you." Mr. Taylor shook my hand. "I hear you are not only a fine doctor, but an experienced teacher and know Urdu as well!"

"Mr. Fraser is too kind." I smiled. "I've taught a bit and have picked up a smattering of the native language."

"I'm certain you are too modest, Doctor Wallace. I know you are busy during the days at the hospital, but would you consider teaching a class or two on some evenings? We have an evening program as well."

"If I can arrange my hospital duties accordingly, I would be delighted to."

"Good. Here's my card." He handed me a card. "Please come and see me. I am certain you can help us in our efforts to educate the native population." He then left, bidding us a good night.

Catherine and Herford came over, both with flushed faces, not only from the heat but also from the bustling about to meet as many people as they could, particularly the important ones. "Margaret, there you are. Haven't had a moment to talk to you. How are you getting along at the CMH?" Catherine asked.

I brought her up to date.

Captain Herford said, "By the way, do you know Lieutenant Albert Miller?"

"Only too well. But, a Lieutenant? The last time I saw him in the Crimea, he was a Captain. What happened?"

"I'm not certain. It seems he was keen on serving here, so much that he either opted or was demoted to a lower rank, and was transferred. We certainly can utilize junior staff with war experience. He will be in my unit."

I was dumbfounded to hear that, thinking he was definitely demoted for his antics. But kept my composure. "I've heard from Nancy, his wife. They are on their way here. When are they due to arrive?"

"Possibly next week."

The Herfords then left, wishing us a good night.

This new information swam in my head as I followed Commissioner Fraser and Colonel Humphrey out to the carriage. Albert being demoted and following me here, did confirm my suspicion of a psychological problem within him. It seemed that when such people had set their mind on doing something, they would stop at nothing to achieve their objective. Even if it meant murder. I shuddered at the thought. But how was I to deal with his improper conduct?

"So, Margaret, are you happy now that you will have a teaching position, to educate all those natives?" Colonel Humphrey asked in a raised voice, above the clattering of the carriage wheels and the horses' hooves.

"Yes, I am pleased. But all the natives? Hardly, sir. There is just one college for the whole of Delhi. And, actually, I was wondering about the objective behind us teaching only a handful of the population. Surely, there is dire need for more similar educational institutions."

Mr. Fraser, who had been listening intently, responded: "Well, we wish to create, to quote from Thomas Macaulay's famous 'Minute,' 'a class of persons Indian in blood and color, but English in tastes, in opinions, in morals, and intellect ....' A most noble endeavor, don't you think?"

"Educate a few, to what purpose, if I may ask, sir?"

"By creating this class of persons we trust, they will be interpreters between us and the millions of people and help us govern them as well."

Colonel Humphrey leaned forward, to be heard clearer.

"Margaret, it's not just one person we are educating. It's his whole family behind him. Think of it. He would be able to transfer the knowledge to far more people around him. Would you not agree?"

"Sir, this would be true if that person's family were to stand behind him. But, if they do not, by creating this elite class, isn't there a danger of alienating a whole generation of Indians?"

"Not really. There isn't any evidence of it. Is there?" Colonel Humphrey responded.

"I believe there is." I leaned forward, as well. "For instance, I recall reading in the *Delhi Gazette* that the conversions of Mr. Ramchandra and Doctor Chaman Lal caused quite a 'stir' within their families and other religious factions of the city. Possibly leading to their alienation. Also, aren't there widespread rumors that we are out to make them all pious Christians?"

Both the gentleman laughed, politely.

"No, not really," Mr. Fraser responded. "Those reports in the *Gazette* were somewhat exaggerated. True, there was some mild dissension, but it was soon over. Some children were indeed taken out of Delhi College, their parents fearful of Master Ramchandra's teachings. But, the enrolment is up now. Also, as you would have noticed first-hand at the CMH, Doctor Lal has an endless list of patients, and for that we had to call you up here to assist."

I was still not fully convinced, by the Commissioner's assurances. "But the fact remains, sir, that we haven't had many more conversions, and also not produced the large number of Indian doctors and nurses they need."

"We are working on it," was his calm response.

We had reached the Residency and the Colonel, gallant as ever, helped me down. They bid me a good night, and I wished them the same.

As I went up the steps towards my room, the Colonel reminded me, "Don't forget, Margaret, you have an appointment to visit Queen Zinat, next Sunday, after Church."

"I thank you for arranging it, sir."

Chapter Eleven

A visit to the Palace *Zenana*

1855, November: Delhi, India

THE FOLLOWING SUNDAY, I awoke early, even prior to the firing of the cannon on the Ridge, for the visit to meet Queen Zinat was very much on my mind. Peeking at my baby's cot and finding him sleeping peacefully, I proceeded to the adjoining water closet for my toilet. After a good cleanse—having had a hot bath and washed my hair the night before—I was back in the bedroom and looking through the clothes hanging in the *almirah* to pick out a suitable gown when, following a tap on the door, Elgin entered.

She put down the tea tray, on the side table. "Good morning, memsahib. Look at this!" From the tray, she picked up a tiny pouch by its drawstrings.

"What is it?" I asked. She approached me, and placed the item in my palm. It was made of blue velvet, and looked like a small money bag. "Where did you get it?"

"*Bura-sahib*'s *chaprassie* ask me to give you."

My inkling was confirmed when, loosening its golden thread strings, I opened it and drew out with my thumb and forefinger a shiny gold coin. On one side, it depicted the bust of King William IV and the date "1835" was engraved. The reverse had an embossed lion under a palm tree, and "East India Company Two Mohur" was scrolled around the circumference; cool and heavy in my palm, it was an exquisite coin.

"Is there a note?"

"Yes." She held up a small silver plate with a folded piece of paper on it.

I opened the note. It read:
For your presentation to Queen Zinat.
Simon Fraser.

"How thoughtful of him!" I immediately put the pouch into my reticule, lest I forgot it.

"The man said to take the tray also." Elgin handed me the little sparkling silver tray.

"Oh, yes. One can't just put a money bag in a queen's hand!" I laughed at my silliness.

Elgin giggled. Our noises woke up Jan and, while taking sips from a cup of tea, I nursed him. Elgin proceeded to tidy up the room.

I selected a reasonably pretty silver-grey gown. It was taffeta and not real silk, but it was the best one I possessed. I certainly needed some new clothes if I was to attend these sophisticated events. I made a mental note to take up Catherine's offer to go shopping with her to Chandni Chowk. However, considering my meagre salary, it could not be for some time.

With Elgin's able assistance, I put up my fair hair and let a few ringlets dangle. I normally did not use rouge—pinching my cheeks made them fairly rosy—but that day I put some on, and applied a bit of beeswax on the lips. Elgin picked up the silver bottle of kohl and rotated its handle with the needle inside the bottle, wanting to apply some to my eyelashes. I shook my head, thinking it would not be appropriate for that occasion. Taking a final look in the mirror, I felt I was sensibly attired for meeting the Queen.

After giving a hug to my baby, I handed him to Elgin, who was to give him his morning wash and change of clothes. It was nearly time for breakfast, and I stepped down the stairs towards the dining room. Commissioner Fraser and Colonel Humphrey were already at the table, their faces buried in newspapers. They made an effort to get up, with murmurs of "good morning".

I quickly took my seat, returning their greetings. "Thank you, Mr. Fraser. So kind of you, for the lovely gift for Queen Zinat."

"It's a small token. The custom here, you know: offer a *nazr*," Mr. Fraser said.

"Yes, I've heard of it. But *two* gold mohurs, sir! I recall reading in Mrs. Parkes' journals that she presented only one gold mohur when she visited the palace."

"Well, we will have to do better than Fanny, won't we?" Fraser smiled.

"Of course. I remember Mrs. Parkes only visited a princess, not the Queen," I said.

"But I would caution against accepting a large gift in return," Colonel Humphrey said, putting the newspaper away.

"Why is that, sir?"

"We have been discouraging these rulers from lavishing expensive gifts on their subjects. Furthermore, she might use that to win some favors, you know," the Colonel said with a smile.

"Oh, I do not think she would offer anything substantial, in return. They are in dire straits as it is. But if she does, you may just touch it, and not actually take it. That is acceptable," the Commissioner enlightened me.

Although I was not looking for any endowment from the Queen, I did think their instructions were rather peculiar. "Thank you, sir. I will bear that in mind," I said, and ordered my breakfast from the butler, who had waited patiently by my chair.

The breakfast soon arrived and I busied myself enjoying it, while continuing to make small talk with the two gentlemen.

Following breakfast, I went briefly to my room to freshen up, and after hugging my child and bidding Elgin farewell, proceeded downstairs to join the Commissioner and the Colonel in the carriage. We were soon on the road towards the town, and St. James.

This time I sat in the coach on the side of the bench, facing the Ridge, which loomed in the distance. I noticed the two buildings at the top, which although I had seen before, I did not know much about. One, was a small octagonal castellated tower that flew the Union Jack, and beside which stood the cannon—the source of my morning wake-up calls—and the second, a fine-looking mansion, another Palladian villa, somewhat similar to the Metcalf House situated by the river.

"Mr. Fraser, who lives there?" I pointing towards the building.

"Ah! That's a house owned by Hindu Rao, a Maratha nobleman. Once it belonged to a kinsman of mine, William Fraser, a former Resident."

"Where is Mr. Fraser now?"

"Unfortunately, he was murdered and is buried in the St. James' Cemetery."

"Oh, how awful! When did it happen?"

"It was some time ago, in 1835. It seemed William got into a dispute with a nawab of a neighboring district, who had him shot."

"And did they determine who did it?"

"Yes. I was the magistrate here at that time. I helped Sir Thomas and Mr. Lawrence in the investigation. The culprits were apprehended and hanged."

Colonel Humphrey, while looking out of the window, had been listening. He turned towards the Commissioner. "That was quite a stroke of good luck, was it not, Simon?" He guffawed slightly. "You and Mr. Lawrence, noticing the Nawab's servant's horse."

Mr. Fraser laughed a bit, as well. "Indeed, Will, it was. We had gone over to a *haveli* of a friend of the Nawab, only to make some inquiries. Mr. Lawrence just happened to look at the horse and noticed its shoes had been reversed! And they matched the pattern at the scene of the crime."

"What a coincidence!" I remarked.

"Yes. But not only that, we found pieces of an incriminating letter written by the Nawab to his lackey," Mr. Fraser added.

"William was quite a colorful person, was he not?" Colonel Humphrey said.

"Aye, that he was. Might have picked up some of the traits from his superior, Sir David Ochterlony. They were like two peas in a pod."

The Colonel smiled, shifting slightly, and bending his head towards the Commissioner, asked in a low tone, "Now, how many *bibis* did William have?"

"Well, I don't rightly know, but I believe there were at least six or seven. A number of children too, I understand, and each took up the religion of their respective mothers ..."

While the two continued to gossip about the former Residents and their wives and concubines, my mind wandered. I gazed out of the window at the passing landscape, and wondered in amazement how those Europeans who had first arrived in Delhi adored and respected the Indian ways of life so much so that they had adopted the customs and the dress of the land. There had been not only intermarriages, but also a mingling of cultures and ideas. I had heard they had even given up eating beef and pork out of respect for the religious feelings of the inhabitants. But the situation was much different now. Why had it changed? Was it due to the arrivals of the Evangelicals and the number of British women coming in search of husbands—the "fishing fleet"?

Soon the carriage clattered through the entrance of St. James' Church and, rounding its curved path through a picturesque garden, came to a stop in front of its imposing portico. We descended, and entering the main hall, took our seats in a pew. I noticed most of Delhi's European residents were there and already seated, all dressed in their Sunday best. Reverend Jennings stood at the lectern and the service began. The padre delivered a lengthy sermon, which he was renowned for. If I recall, he dwelt—among other issues—particularly on the unexpected changes one might face in life, and implored us not to delay atonement, for the future was most uncertain. Indeed, I thought the future, particularly in that part of the world, was definitely unpredictable.

During the sermon I had noted a lady, sitting a couple of rows to the front and to the right, turn and look at me a number of times. She did seem familiar and I searched my brain to recall who she could be. Then it abruptly came to me that she was Mrs. Willoughby, my cabin companion on the voyage to Calcutta!

As soon as the service was over, she got up and came hurriedly towards me, a red-coated soldier following her.

"Aww … Margaret, there you are. I'd been wondering when you would be in Delhi," she said, taking my hand. "My neighbor, Nurse Betty, told me you'd arrived."

We exchanged greetings and she introduced me to her husband, Sergeant Frank. We spoke at some length, and I brought her up to date.

"Well, Margaret, you had better be going, if you wish to keep your appointment with Queen Zinat," Colonel Humphrey said loudly, having stood somewhat impatiently next to me, ignoring the sergeant.

"Aww … Margaret, I had better let you go. But do come and visit us. We are in the Civil Lines, you know."

"Yes, I certainly will."

I said goodbye to them, and followed Colonel Humphrey out of the church. His carriage, with the East India Company crest on its door, was waiting outside, and he helped me into it. He got in as well, and sat beside me. I did not mind him doing that, for he was being so kind and it would have been inappropriate for me to object. The carriage rolled forward.

"I think I should take you up to the palace gate, to make sure you are received properly."

"That is most kind of you, sir."

"No problem at all. But dearest, will you not call me William, as you used to?"

I stiffened. "That was before your despicable behavior towards me at that *dak*-bungalow."

"My dear Margaret, will you not forgive me?" He tried to hold my hand.

I quickly moved my palm aside. "Please, sir! I don't think I can accept that nothing has happened between us. I am sorry."

"Margaret, Margaret, do not be so cross with me. I am willing to make amends." His pleading sounded a bit forced.

I did not respond, and simply looked out the window at the fort's tall red wall and its towers with the onion domes, which the carriage rolled by.

After some moments, he apparently sobered. "It's good that you are visiting the Queen," he began, "but there's something I have been meaning to tell you."

"Yes, what is it?"

"You might have heard our former Commissioner, Sir Thomas, is believed to have been poisoned?"

"Yes. Captain Herford mentioned it."

"He probably did not say, but we strongly suspect it was Queen Zinat's doing."

"Really, sir," I said, horrified. "The Queen! And what about the King? Did he invite Sir Thomas for dinner?"

"No, we don't believe Sir Thomas had a meal there. I know Zafar fairly well. He would never stoop to such malice. But we understand Zinat has a network of henchmen, headed by the chief eunuch of the *zenana*, Mahbub Ali Khan. He gets things done for her."

"Why do you think she had Sir Thomas murdered?"

"It wasn't only Sir Thomas. There were two other officials. The three Company officers had opposed the petition to have her son, Jawan, recognized as the heir apparent. All of them died at about the same time, with similar symptoms of food poisoning."

"Really! How terrible. And has the Company uncovered any proof of the murders?"

"Not yet. But the case is still open. Margaret, could you please let me know if you see or hear anything?"

"Yes. I will," I said, rather automatically. But then it occurred to me: was I being used as a pawn? A spy or an informant? However, I put that thought out of my mind. For at that time I did not really believe a Mughal Queen would resort to such contemptible tactics. What had she to gain from all those murders? I continued to stare out of the window.

From the church, it was just a short drive to the Lahore Gate, the main entrance into the fort. The carriage soon stopped in front of the imposing red sandstone archway. It looked wide and high enough for a large elephant to pass through. There were two large towers on either side of the gate. I noted several windows above that I thought were the apartments of the Jennings and Captain Douglas.

One of the sentries at the gate, recognizing the coach, hurried to open its door. Colonel Humphrey alighted and, while helping me down, spoke in Hindustani to the sentry. It seemed I was expected, for a palanquin with four bearers stood at one side. A bearded young soldier, smartly dressed in the native force's uniform—white trousers; green knee-length jacket; a *talwar* thrust through a golden sash around the waist; and a white-silk turban with an emblem—approached the Colonel and saluted smartly.

"Gooden morning, sir! I Sepoy Sharif Khan, of his Majesty's palace guards. I taking Doctor sahiba to the Queen," he said loudly.

The Colonel eyed the sepoy and then, with a smile, turned towards me. "Looks like you are in good hands, Margaret. The fellow speaks English! I will return to the Residency and send the carriage back for you." He re-entered the carriage and departed.

I followed the sepoy—he looked hardly twenty-years-old, but was a tall and muscular chap—to the palanquin.

The sepoy gestured towards the litter. "Madam, please sit. We take you to the Rang Mahal. Queen Zinat living there."

A bearer parted the lace curtain of the palanquin and, crouching inside, I reclined on its white-silk cushion. To get more comfortable, I rested one elbow on the red-and-blue-striped balustrade. The bearers lifted the palanquin and we bumped along, on a short bridge over the dry moat, and through the Lahore Gate, to inside the fort's walls. It was my first time on a palanquin, and while the motion seemed strange at first—as if sailing on a small boat—I soon got used to it.

Sepoy Sharif Khan walked beside, and I was able to converse with him.

"Madam, you come first time in the fort?"

"Yes, it looks very pleasant." I glanced around at the numerous lovely buildings, constructed in white marble with intricate patterns and carvings on the walls. Each edifice had several archways that led to a veranda in front of the rooms. Wonderful gardens surrounded the buildings, with watercourses and fountains that gave the place a peaceful atmosphere. Several people milled about. From their attire, one could discern if they were workers or part of the royal family. One wore cotton, and the other silken clothes.

We arrived before a small, rectangular building, where a group sat on the veranda cross-legged on a red carpet. The bearers put the palanquin down in front of the terrace.

"This the Naubat Khana, the drum house. We play welcome music for you," Sharif Khan said, and shouted an order at the musicians.

The instrumentalists immediately began to play a delightful tune. While I had seen some of the Indian musical instruments elsewhere, hearing them played in unison was entertaining. They performed for a while and then, standing up, salaamed me. I thanked them, and being long enough in the country to know the customs, opened my reticule and took out a couple of rupees and gave them to Sharif Khan, who passed them on to the bandleader. Each musician grinned broadly, and salaamed me again several times. I was delighted at the musical welcome, for I did not remember reading if Fanny Parkes had been accorded this honor.

The dolly was lifted up, and I was taken farther into the palace grounds. We passed by a large open hall, its roof supported on numerous marble pillars and engrailed arches. Sharif told me that it was the Diwan-i-Am—the hall of public audience—where the Emperor addressed his subjects and received petitions. The Emperor's marble throne was visible through one of the arches.

We went around this pavilion, on a garden path, and then along a dry water-channel that led into a square courtyard with a water tank and a fountain, but through which hardly any water flowed.

"Mr. Khan, why is there no running water in the channels?"

"Madam, please call me Sharif, thank you. No water, because not coming from the river anymore."

"And you may call me Doctor Margaret, Sharif. Why has this happened?"

"Long time ago, the Jamuna River flow very good. Water come in to fort at the Shahi Burj tower, over there." He pointed to an octagonal tower at roughly the north-east corner of the complex.

"A water channel runs all the way from there?"

"Yes. There are *hammams* over there." He pointed to a set of white marble buildings. "Also water going through the Khas Mahal, the Emperor living there; the Rang Mahal of the Queen; and Mumtaz Mahal for the *zenana* ladies." He waved his arm out to the three palace buildings situated in a row in the distance, along the bank of the river.

"How interesting! These ancient palaces had their own water supply."

Passing through gardens of lovely flowering plants and fruit trees, the bearers halted in front of an imposing palace, and set the palanquin down before the steps leading to its terrace. A group of ladies dressed in colorful attire were waiting on the veranda, and came hurriedly down the steps.

"Welcome to Rang Mahal, Doctor Margaret," Sharif announced. "The women look after you now. I return when you go back to Lahore Gate. Yes?"

"Yes, thank you, Sharif. You have been most helpful."

While Sharif and the bearers departed, one of the ladies extended her arm through the curtain to help me out. I was glad to be standing up but, it being almost noon, the hot sun's rays beat down on me. Also, having neither my solar hat nor the benefit of the light tunics and head silk coverings that the other ladies wore, I was beginning to feel uncomfortable in my heavy gown. I was glad when the pretty lady salaamed and beckoned me to follow her into the *mahal,* while the others stood shyly at one side.

Entering the marbled entrance hall of the palace was a relief. Although in the center of the room, there was a small fountain with an exquisitely carved lotus-shaped base, but no water sprayed out. Now that would have cooled the place a lot more, I thought.

Just then, a short, plump fellow in native dress came waddling down the hall towards us. He was rather dark complexioned, had large black eyes, and no facial hair, although it did not look as if he had shaved. He bowed low and salaamed me.

"Doctor sahiba, this is Mahbub Ali. He take you to the Queen," the lady told me.

"Welcome, madam. Please follow me," he said in a slightly high-pitched voice.

Walking behind the little giant along the corridor, I was impressed by the marble walls and high ceiling with intricate colorful mosaics, which no doubt gave the *mahal* its name, Rang, meaning "color". This palace looked to be much cleaner than the one Fanny Parkes had written about. The water channel that ran through the building was dry, and did not have the *"offensive black water, as if from the drains of the cook rooms,"* which Fanny had written. They might have cleaned up for my visit, I mused.

Mahbub Ali stopped before a door in an exquisitely carved oak panel that spanned an archway. He took his shoes off, and opened the door for me. Following his cue, I slipped my shoes off as well, and entered the Queen's apartment. He followed me inside, announced my arrival, and moved to one side.

The room was sparsely furnished. A number of ladies sat on the floor, some reclining on bolsters along the walls. In the center, a white cloth covered the red carpet on the marble floor and the Queen sat on a low divan at the back of the room.

I approached her and, bending from the waist, salaamed in the manner I had seen others do. She did not get up, but salaamed in return and gestured to me to approach. From my reticule, I retrieved the silver tray and the pouch with the gold coin. I went up to her and presented the tray with both hands. A broad smile broke on her fair-skinned, slightly oval face, and her large, dark eyes sparkled as she accepted the tray. She was a young woman of about thirty. Her raven hair was parted in the middle, and flowed down a long, swan-like neck. While I admired the numerous exquisite pieces of gold and precious-stoned jewelry she wore, her natural beauty impressed me more. It was evident that she was King Zafar's favorite wife.

She beckoned at two ladies who stood to one side. One carried a tray on which seemed to be a bouquet of flowers but turned out to be a lovely garland of jasmine and roses, which the other woman picked up and put over my head. I inhaled the wonderful aroma and thanked the Queen. At another gesture from her, a lady brought a chair from the side of the room and placed it by the divan, close to the Queen.

Seeing the other women seated on the floor, I protested. "Your Majesty, I can sit on the floor."

"No. No, you sit on chair," the Queen said, motioning me to be seated.

I sat, grateful, for reclining on a hard floor usually produced cramps in my legs.

Immediately, several maids entered the room through a side door, carrying trays of grilled and curried dishes, chapattis, fruits, sweetmeats and drinks. The aroma of spicy cooking wafted through the open door. It being past noon, I was beginning to feel peckish. The ladies presented the trays to me and, putting Colonel Humphrey's worries aside, I was glad to partake in the delicacies and the cool sherbet. The other women did the same. While I had begun to enjoy Indian cooking, these dishes were the best I had tasted so far. For no doubt I was being entertained by a Mughal queen, and likely would not get any better cuisine elsewhere.

The Queen ate sparingly, while conversing with me. I was happy to note that she spoke some English. It seemed she might have been taking lessons. She inquired about my background and my parents and my children. She also had the usual questions of how was it that I chose to become a doctor, and more so, come to India.

I was captivated by her charming personality, and it seemed unlikely to me that she could have arranged the murder of those three Company officials, as Colonel Humphrey suspected. I asked her about her family and about the King and her children.

"I only one son. You meet. He take you see *zenana*. Yes?" Queen Zinat asked.

"I should like that very much."

As soon as we had finished our lunch, she motioned at Mahbub Ali. It was her cue to fetch the Prince, for he arrived presently. It seemed he was waiting in an adjoining room for the summons.

Prince Jawan Bukht was a pleasant-looking young man of about fourteen. He wore beige silky trousers under a long shirt, and a red waistcoat with golden-threaded patterns. His cap had matching designs. He had inherited all the good features of his mother, including the light complexion.

He came up to me and salaamed, which I returned.

After the introductions and brief conversation, the Queen asked him, "*Beta*, can you take Doctor Margaret to *zenana*?" Then, turning to me, "When you come back, we drink *chai* in the *tehkhana*."

I told her I would like that, for I had heard much about those *tehkhanas*—the underground rooms used by the Mughals, which provided much relief from the heat—and I had wanted to see one of those.

The Prince waved to me, and I followed him. Mahbub Ali came behind us. We descended a flight of steps into an underground passage.

"We go in tunnel to the Mumtaz Mahal. No need to walk in sun," the Prince said.

"Where is King Zafar?" I asked.

"He living in Khas Mahal. Sleeping now in the *burj*." The Prince pointed in the opposite direction.

How interesting, I thought, that people could walk between the *zenana* and the *mahals*, not only out of the sunlight, but unseen by others.

Soon we were in the Mumtaz Mahal and climbed the stairs to the main floor. This building was in a state no better than the dreadful conditions Fanny Parkes had described in her journal. Although her account was quite different from the opulence and grandiose environment Francois Bernier—a French physician who had visited the same *zenana* in the 1660s—had noted. However, since then, it looked that the state of affairs had greatly deteriorated.

Shabbily attired women and children of all ages milled around in the corridor, or sat on those Indian string-beds, *charpoys*. Some peered out through the lattice windows, either towards the river or at the gardens. Young boys and girls ran about, shouting and screaming, playing games that I could not comprehend.

The Prince introduced me to some of the ladies by name. Some were the King's wives, or other relations. While the younger ones were in reasonably good health, the older women were thin and fragile in appearance. In general, most looked malnourished with decaying teeth. It was difficult for me to remember all their names. However, they seemed pleased and touched my forehead as their mark of respect for me.

Discarded pieces of clothing, broken furniture, toys, torn books, and other miscellany were strewn all over the place. The floors looked as if they had not been swept for ages.

The Prince saw me glancing around. "Madam, please excuse bad appearance."

"Why is the place so dirty?" I asked.

"Because no servants to clean. King has very little money."

It was evident that the King was having difficulties surviving on his pension. But, I wondered, why did he have to have so many wives? Then again, I reminded myself that it was the custom of the land, and a king, more so an emperor, was expected to have a large *zenana*. The measure of a man's status was judged by the size of his harem.

It did not take long to go around the *zenana,* and I suggested to the Prince that we return. Retracing the route, we arrived back at the Rang Mahal, and the Prince led me into the *tehkhana*. Indeed, being underground, it was much cooler. I shivered, and it felt as if the cool weather had suddenly arrived. It being dark in the room, it took a bit of time for my eyes to get used to the dim light. The walls were lined with white marble, and a tank also lined with marble, like a bath tub, was situated in the middle the room. Although there was water in the tank, its purpose was clearly not for bathing, but for cooling the room. At one end of the room, on a raised platform, the Queen, along with some of her ladies-in-waiting, sat on a divan. I went up there, and the same chair was brought for me and placed beside the Queen.

"Come, Doctor Margaret, come. You like *zenana*, yes?" She motioned for me to sit.

Out of politeness, I said: "Yes, the ladies are nice," then dropped my voice to add, "but, Your Majesty, the *mahal* could use some cleaning."

"Yes, yes. I saying all time to Zafar. They need more servants. But he no listen."

"Ammi, how can he. Abbu's pension is so little," Prince Jawan interjected.

"Yes. He asking the Company all the time. Write so many letters. But no reply." The Queen waved her arms to demonstrate her frustration.

Tea was served, and while I sipped from my cup, the Queen must have made a discreet, possibly an eyes-gesture to the other ladies, who left the room one by one. Shortly the Prince left as well, and I was sitting alone with the Queen while Mahbub Ali stood, respectfully, at some distance.

"Doctor Margaret, what you think about my son, Jawan?" she asked.

"He is a very nice boy."

"Do you think he can be next king?"

"Not for me to decide, Your Majesty. I believe it is something King Zafar should discuss with the Governor General."

"Oh, he has been trying lots of time. Make many petitions. But the Company want that lazy boy Fakhruddin to be the *waliahad*."

"Yes, I've have heard that, Your Majesty. It would appear the Company favors Prince Fakhruddin."

"Margaret, can you help, please? Change Company mind. You good friend of Commissioner Sahib and Colonel Humphrey. No?"

"Your Majesty, they are good to me. But I am not sure if I can tell them how to conduct their official business."

"Margaret that is the same answer I hear from men. You are a woman. You can think different of the situation. It is the wish of me, the Queen, and my husband, the Emperor, the refuge of the word, for our son. Why should the Company interfere in our business? Do you not think?"

"Your Majesty, as a mother, yes, I would want the best for my children. But I don't know enough to be able to judge the situation in Delhi. I have been at the hospital here for only a few weeks."

At my stubborn response, she seemed to change her tack. "Yes, I understand, my dear. Perhaps in time, you appreciate our circumstances better. So how your work at the hospital? I hear you working for Doctor Chaman Lal?"

"Yes, my work is going well. Thank you. Doctor Lal is a good man."

"Although he Christian, he also physician of my husband. You know Zafar kind to all religions?"

"Yes, he told me that. Do you need a lady doctor for your *zenana*?"

"Certainly. We need lady doctor badly. Good you here now. I like you. Be my personal physician. Yes?"

"Of course, Your Majesty. I will be honored to treat you for any ailments you might have."

"Oh, I have so many problems. Perhaps you come some other day and bring me strong medicine. Pills. Yes?"

At that time, not comprehending what she might be driving at,

I had simply responded: "Yes, of course, Your Majesty." After taking a peek at my watch, I added, "It is getting late. Perhaps I should be getting back?"

She agreed, and instructed Mahbub to have the palanquin brought for me. While the Queen and I talked about some general topics, he returned to say the palanquin was outside the *mahal*. I thanked the Queen again for a wonderful visit. She in return thanked me and wished that she would see me again very soon.

Just as I was leaving, the ladies with the tray of garlands appeared again, and added a few more strings of the fragrant flowers around my neck. They showered rose petals over my head as well, as I walked towards the exit. Having received such royal treatment, I felt like a queen myself. I wished my parents, and particularly my dearly departed husband, Robert, could have seen me then. The thought brought tears to my eyes.

Soon I was in the palanquin and the bearers were jogging along, carrying it towards the Lahore Gate. The faithful sepoy, Sharif, strode beside to see me safely to the carriage.

"Doctor Margaret, how was your visit?" he asked.

"Very good. Thank you, Sharif. I saw the Rang Mahal, the *zenana* ladies. And the Queen has asked me to come back and treat her."

"Good, we see you here again. But I want to ask you if you could please see my wife?"

"Yes, of course. Is your wife sick?"

"No. No, she not sick … only … with child," he said, a bit sheepishly.

"Certainly, I will see your wife. Can you bring her to the hospital? Where do you live?"

"In Daryaganj, close to CMH."

"That is convenient. Why don't you come tomorrow, and make an appointment with my nurse?"

"Thank you. I will make appointment. I am happy you see her, because she no like to see a man doctor."

Perhaps without much thought I said, "Good that you live in Daryaganj, for I am looking for renting an apartment there. If you know of a good house, could you please let me know?"

He contemplated for a moment, and nodded.

The palanquin soon arrived at the Lahore Gate and, going over the moat's bridge, they set me down in front of the carriage. It had been waiting there for me, likely for some time.

I thanked Sharif and the litter bearers. In appreciation, I gave the bearers a rupee each. This delighted them and, bowing low, they salaamed me a few times.

Soon I was in the carriage, which clattered on the road towards the Residency. I leaned back on the cushions and closed my eyes. I felt happy and satisfied that I had had a good day: visited inside the Red Fort, met the Queen, and seen the *zenana*. Apart from the Queen, the miserable state of the other women was a surprise; although I had read of such conditions in Fanny Parkes' journals, somehow I had foolhardily expected to see the luxurious settings Francois Bernier had described. I was amazed at how the state of affairs could have changed so drastically for the "great" Mughals. No wonder they despised the Company officials, and possibly dreamed of happier days. Now why had the Queen asked me to bring her some strong pills? I wondered.

My mind wandered and I must have dozed off, due to the heat. The opening of the carriage door, by the coachman, woke me. But when I looked out of the window, I did not wish to get down, for I saw the loathsome faces of Albert Miller and Nancy, standing on the veranda at the entrance to the Residency.

When they waved at me, I felt like telling the coachman to drive me back into the city.

Chapter Twelve

Nancy and Albert Arrive in Delhi, and an Apartment in Daryaganj

1855, November: Delhi, India

THE COACHMAN held the door open, and waited patiently for me to alight. It took me a few moments to regain my composure, having lost it at the sight of Albert. I finally clambered down and thanking the coachman, handed him a rupee. He bowed low, salaaming his appreciation; I made my way up the steps to the Residency's veranda to face Nancy and Albert standing at the entrance.

Nancy looked the same, tall and pretty, dressed in a pink silk dress and a matching bonnet over her golden hair. She came swiftly to me. "Hallo Margaret! We thought we would surprise you, and we have some good news to tell you, as well." She hugged and kissed me on the cheek.

Good news for me? I was certain, coming from her, it would be rather upsetting. "No, you did not catch me unawares. I've been expecting you. Do come in and tell me all the news."

Albert's dark mustachioed puffy face was beet red, probably more from alcohol than the heat. He looked portly in a lieutenant's uniform. Bowing, he wished me a good afternoon. I returned his greeting, and we proceeded into the Residency's hallway. The butler opened the door to the drawing room, and we went inside. I asked if we could please have some tea; he nodded.

Albert plumped on a chair, and Nancy sat on the couch beside me; she touched my arm. "So, Margaret, how is your baby? We heard you had a boy, congratulations! May we see him? And guess what? Father is arranging for your children to join you here!" she said, without pausing to take a breath.

"Yes, I'd heard that in a letter from Cousin Heather. Oh, I don't see Jan's *ayah* about. I think he's having his afternoon nap. Perhaps you'll see him later," I replied brusquely, for I had no intention of putting my baby immediately in her arms. But then, realizing they were my deceased husband's friends from his Canadian hometown, Grimsby, and considering Nancy's father's involvement in arrangements for my children's passage, I resolved to show them some semblance of politeness. Hence, feeling magnanimous, I turned towards Albert. "How is your head wound, Albert?"

Albert took his cap off, showing a full head of dark hair. "Fully recovered now. Thank you." He patted the portion of his skull above the right ear, where he had the sword slash, inflicted by the Cossack. "Ah, that reminds me. Did you hear that Lieutenant, Captain now, Alexander Dunn was awarded a Victoria Cross?"

"No, I haven't. I am sure he deserves it. After all, he fought so courageously in those horrible battles."

"I'm sure Robert would have received one too. If only he was ...." Nancy broke into tears. She got her handkerchief out and dabbed her eyes.

"It's all right, Nancy. The war is over now. Robert is in another happy place." I rubbed her shoulder, wondering if she too had loved him dearly, and still thought of him.

"Oh, I'm so sorry for your loss, Margaret." She put her arms around me and resting her head on my shoulder, wept. I rubbed her back and looked towards Albert. He had turned his head, and stared out of the window. Yes, I thought, he is too ashamed to look me in the eye. Rage built up in me. How dare he sit there so calmly, after what he had done? For an instant, I felt like telling Nancy all about how my dear Robert had died. I had been meaning to do that, but the moment did not seem right. The idea of further upsetting the poor woman, crying on my shoulder, calmed me. What good would come of it? It would only torture the pitiable soul and make her life miserable in this strange land, some thousands of miles away from her home. Hence, I kept quiet.

At the sound of the door opening, Nancy straightened and wiped her tears. Two bearers brought in trays of refreshments. Over tea and biscuits, we talked of various matters and brought each other up to date on our affairs. Upon my inquiry, Nancy mentioned that her parents were in good health, and had written that they had visited Robert's mother at Wallace Hall, and both my dear children,

Bruce and Vika, were well. Aunt Fiona was planning to visit my Robert's grave in Crimea, and might travel to India thereafter, and also bring my little ones to me. Nancy's father, Colonel Mitchell was helping in making the travel arrangements. I was relieved to hear that, and felt it was the least thing Colonel Mitchell could do, for he was instrumental in having Robert assigned to serve in the Crimean war.

The butler brought in my post and placed it at a side stand beside me. The top envelope was an official looking one and had the mark of the City Magistrate. Thinking it might be something urgent, relating to the CMH, I picked it up and opened it. It was from Sir Theo Metcalfe. On a large folded card, printed in a flourishing script, was an invitation to the Delhi Christmas Ball, to be held on December twenty-fourth, at Metcalfe House. I showed the card to Nancy. "Look, I've been invited to the Christmas Ball! But I'm not sure I can attend."

"Why ever not?" she exclaimed.

"I don't believe I have an appropriate gown for the occasion."

"Oh, but you must go to the ball. I've heard it's such a grand affair. My trunks are expected to arrive any day now. I have many gowns I purchased when we were in London. Don't you remember? I can easily provide you one. Do say yes, Margaret?"

"It's very kind of you, Nancy. Let me think about it." I stuffed the card back in its envelope.

She turned towards Albert. "Darling, do let's go home and see if we have an invitation, as well. I know you are only a Lieutenant now, and in case we haven't received one, you must go right-away to the magistrate's office and get one. Won't you dear?"

Albert got up. "Yes, I will. And I think we should be going. Let Margaret take some rest." He looked sheepishly at me. "We have a bungalow in the cantonment. It's nothing like our Grimsby home, but it's comfortable. Please visit us soon."

I stood and followed them to the door. "I will," I said, although I had no intention of doing so. We said good bye and they were gone.

As I trudged up the stairs to my room, I thought it was true then that he was actually demotion from a Captain to a Lieutenant. I wondered for what reason, and reflected it was more than likely for making amorous advances on another officer's wife. Also, why did he transfer here? Was it just to see India, or did he have some other ulterior motives?

Later that evening I joined Commissioner Fraser and Colonel Humphrey for dinner. A pretty dusk was settling in, with a hint in the air of the arrival of the short Indian Winter. When I descended the staircase, the butler ushered me towards the back garden. A dining table was set up on the lawn, and liveried servants waited for their instructions. The setting sun, over the Ganges in the distance, threw a bright orange glow on the sky. I wrapped my pashmina shawl about my shoulders, feeling glad I had put on a warm dark woolen gown, I walked on the soft grass past multi-colored flower beds to the table.

The duo were already seated, dressed in dark suits and cravats, with drinks in hand. From their loud bantering, it was obvious they were enjoying themselves. Upon seeing me, they stood and mumbled greetings. I returned their good evenings. A waiter hurried to pull a chair for me. He asked if I wanted anything to drink, and I requested white wine, which he poured for me directly. Spicy aroma, from the trays on the table, of Indian hors d'oeuveres wafted, and I put some on the side plate.

Colonel Humphrey lifted his glass of whisky. "Cheers, Margaret. How did your meeting with Zinat go?"

I raised my wineglass. "Cheers. Very well, thank you, sir. The Queen was most hospitable, and I got to see much of two of the palaces." I took a sip of wine. "And, what's more, even though the Queen appeared quite healthy, she's asked me to return and treat her for some imaginary illness."

Commissioner Fraser smiled and lifted his glass, as well. "It seems the Queen's quite taken in by you, Margaret. How did you find the *zenana*? Anything like Fanny's comments?"

"In a poorer state, I should think. It looks like only the Queen's *mahal* sees a broom!" I sipped more wine. It was fruity, but pleasant.

"Now why cannot the zenana ladies do some decoration, once in a while? Like all good concubines should." Colonel Humphrey took a large gulp of his drink.

Mr. Frazer raised his empty glass to a waiter for another *burra-peg*. "My dear Will, if she did so, the poor woman might find herself in the servant's quarters! And no doubt it's against her faith to even touch a broom?"

The colonel guffawed. "Yes, I've heard of that strange behavior. And other things as well, like needing a servant of one's own caste to fetch even a glass of water! What a waste of Company's funds."

I felt amused at that statement, directed at others' religious practices. Besides, whose money was it, anyway? Was the Company not collecting taxes from these same people? I thought about remarking to that effect, but in the presence of the commissioner, restraining myself, took a deep breath. "So, Colonel Humphrey, does the Company expects the Mughal queens to sweep the floors?"

Humphrey guffawed again. "Good heavens, no, Margaret. I simply implied that if each of the women lent a hand, kept their own quarters clean I mean, those *mahals* should look decent enough."

"Hardly, sir." I took a sip of wine. "Those marbled palaces need constant attention to the floors, the pillars, all the nooks and crannies, the bedrooms, and not to mention the privies. I suppose the children make substantial mess." I took another sip. "I believe the queens could use more help."

The colonel looked at me, as if disappointed. "The Company has assessed the King's requirements. We are satisfied that his stipend is sufficient to lead a decent life. And if he can't manage, he can damn well … sorry Margaret … stop taking on more wives—"

Fraser interjected. "Did you meet many women, Margaret?"

I had finished my wine, and the attendant refilled the glass. "Yes, I saw quite a few, with numerous toddlers. I didn't keep a count, though." I smiled.

Fraser turned towards Humphrey. "Zafar has a number of wives, doesn't he?"

Humphrey ordered another whisky. "I know he has four wives, being a Mohammedan. But rumor has it, he's married some more. Can you believe that? At his age!" Humphrey accepted the glass presented by a waiter. "And, what's more, he has a number of concubines as well."

Fraser raised his eyebrows. "And how many offspring, that we know of?"

"We think over forty-five. I believe there are sixteen sons, all clamoring to be the next emperor!" The colonel smirked and took a swig of his drink.

"No wonder the GG is in a quandary over Zafar's successor."

Fraser smiled.

I took another sip of wine, which I was beginning to enjoy, and bit on a tasty *samosa*. "Hasn't that already been decided, Mr. Fraser?"

Fraser ate a *pakora*. "Woh! That is spicy. Oh, I don't know if any of the princes is fit to lead. But it's no secret that we prefer Fakhruddin."

I felt like asking about the secret succession agreement Fraser's predecessor, Sir Thomas Metcalfe, had made with the prince, but decided not to. "Why does the company prefer him?"

Fraser looked towards Humphrey. "Isn't Fakhru the senior most?"

Humphrey finished chewing some nuts. "That he is, and a poet too, like his father."

"But, sir, how can we select merely on seniority, when the King has a number of wives?" I reached for a *pakora*.

"Well, why not? Unless the eldest has some deficiencies or refuses the crown for any reason," Fraser responded.

"But surely, sir, the King should choose his heir apparent. Isn't it their practice?" I argued.

Humphrey laughed. "Ha! If we let him decide, we would soon return to the chaos Delhi was in back in 1802, when we liberated them from the Marathas."

The arrival of the butler prevented me from expressing my opinion on the 'liberation of Delhi'. He wished to take our dinner orders, and presented us with menu cards. There was mulligatawny soup, followed by deep-fried fish, roast beef, grilled partridges, and trifle for dessert.

"The soup and fish only for me, please. But could the cook sauté the fish?" I requested.

"Certainly. And would madam like the spicy sauce on the fish?" he asked.

"Yes, please." I smiled, seeing the staff by then knew of my preferences. I heard both Fraser and Humphrey order all the courses, except fish.

Soup was served, and I enjoyed a few spoonful of the savory broth. "But, seriously, Colonel Humphrey, seeing that the Company is fully in control here, why are they favoring Prince Fakhruddin? Is it only rank, or are there other reasons?"

Humphrey was silent for some time, and finishing his soup, put the bowl aside. "That was agreeable. My complements to your chef, Simon." While Fraser nodded, Humphrey turned towards me. "That's a good question, Margaret. And I don't claim to have the perfect answer. I do believe age is the key factor, among Fakhru's other qualities. And he appears to be the kind of fellow we can trust and deal with." He looked towards Fraser. "Is that not so, Simon? Unless you have something more to say?"

My order of fish, and theirs of roast beef arrived. The waiters left after refilling our wine and water glasses.

Commissioner Fraser glanced about to ensure none of the servants were within earshot. "We wouldn't really object to Zafar appointing his *bishti* if he wishes." He took a forkful of beef and chewed vigorously. After swallowing the morsel, he continued, "As you noted, Margaret, we are in-charge here. Zafar is a king, or an emperor as some call him, in name only." He paused to let his remarks have some effect. "So, don't you see this sham, of the 'Mughal Empire', has to end one day?"

We ate in silence. I was enjoying my delicately spiced fish, despite Fraser's comments. "So, when do you think this empire should terminate?" I responded.

He ate in silence for a while. "Upon Zafar's death would be an opportune moment, I should think." He put his plate aside and while waiting for a bearer to take it away, looked contemplatively into the distance. Humphrey, his head down, concentrated on his meal.

I drank some water. "And how might the Company achieve that? The Mughals would still be in the Red Fort. Are you suggesting they should be removed by force?"

"I don't think that would be necessary, for we have an ..." Fraser saw a waiter approach. The waiter picked up the plate and asked if Mr. Fraser would like the next course. Fraser looked at my plate. "The fish looks delicious. I'll have some as well, but without the spices, of course." He waited for the servant to leave and took a sip of wine. "As I was saying, Margaret," he moved his head closer towards me and dropped his voice, "we have a succession agreement with Prince Fakhru. But, could you please keep it to yourself?"

While I had heard of it from Captain Hereford, I feigned a surprised look. "Yes, of course. So, what's it all about?" I whispered.

When the colonel looked sharply at the commissioner, Fraser

said: "I think we should keep Margaret fully informed. Don't you, Will?" The colonel, after a slight hesitation, nodded. Fraser continued. "Upon accession, Fakhru has agreed to move his court out of the Red Fort, and we would occupy it. The Company would be taking other steps, as well, to reduce the Mughal's influence?"

"Such as?" I asked.

Fraser sipped some wine. "Fakhru agrees that there is no need to keep on the airs of Mughal superiority, and start meeting us as equals. We would discontinue the practice of formally sending presents from the Company to the King. We have already banned him from conferring titles on others, and might deny him the privilege of bearing his mark on coins. And perhaps their titles, his own of king, and of his family members, could be changed to other less traditional ones."

"And he can jolly well stop calling himself 'The Refuge of the World'. Hah!" Humphrey added.

I took another sip of water, amazed at the strategy of a bloodless and easy capture of the Red Fort, which the Mughals had built and occupied for hundreds of years, and to bring about their demise. "And what would the Company do with the fort?"

Fraser looked towards Humphrey.

The colonel nodded. He put his plate aside and took a sip of wine. "Use a fort, for what it's meant for. House soldiers and armaments." He waited while a waiter approached and took the plate away. Humphrey ordered fish, as well. "So, Margaret, did the queen say anything about the succession situation?"

"Yes, she did," I responded, wanting to be as candid as possible. "I understand she wishes her son, Prince Jawan, to be declared the heir apparent."

The colonel frowned. "She can wish it to her heart's content. But it isn't going to happen. We cannot make a fourteen-year-old, and the fifteenth in the line—"

A waiter arrived with their fish order.

Fraser ate a piece of fish. "It's all very well for Zafar to nominate a younger son as the heir apparent." He laughed. "But he's conveniently forgetting that, in 1807, when his father, Akbar Shah II wished Zafar's younger brother to succeed, the British had objected, and helped put Zafar on the throne!"

That was news to me. "Why didn't Akbar Shah want, his eldest son, Zafar to succeed?"

Fraser smiled. "In a letter to the Company, Akbar not only considered Zafar to be incompetent, but also accused him of committing … 'an offence against nature', as he put it."

"Oh dear," I said. "Was there any evidence of this 'offence'?"

Fraser sipped some wine. "None was presented. Hence, we saw no reason why Zafar should not have succeeded, and he eventually did."

We ate in silence. Upon finishing my delectable meal, I placed the knife and fork together on the plate. "Well, sir, the Company is at least consistent." A waiter arrived to take my plate and enquired if I wished any desert. I asked for only a cup of tea.

My tea and the next courses for Fraser and Humphrey arrived. Humphrey waited until the waiters had left, and then said: "Margaret, I'm glad that you're beginning to understand the situation here."

I sipped on the aromatic tea. "Yes, it's certainly devilishly complex. Thank you for bringing me up to date."

"I thought you should know our position, for you would hear the other side's views while visiting the palace," Fraser said, as if addressing one of his junior staff members.

Humphrey looked towards me. "About your palace visits, Margaret. Could you please keep your eyes and ears open? And do let us know, if you hear anything out of the ordinary?"

"Yes, of course, colonel," I said, although the idea of acting like a plant felt disgusting. I sipped more tea.

Fraser finished chewing a mouthful. "This partridge is delicious. If I may make one more request, Margaret. While at the palace, could you please not say anything about our succession agreement with Prince Fakhru?"

"Yes, definitely, sir. I shan't say a word about it," I responded.

"Good." Fraser looked relieved and smiled. "You do realize if they learnt of this accord, it might be putting Fakhru's life in danger."

"Good heavens! They'll never hear it from me. Besides, I have no desire to be part of a Shakespearean tragedy staged at the Delhi Fort!" I finished my tea amid their bursts of laughter. "Now if you will excuse me, gentlemen, I must go and see to my child."

They both stood and wished me a goodnight. But before I

turned to leave, Colonel Humphrey said: "And give a peck from me to the little one." I believed he was looking for an invitation to visit my room. Not to encourage him, I merely nodded and left the table. While walking up the stairs, I felt thankful that they had been candid with me. However, learning of the Company's heavy involvement in the affairs of the Mughals, bothered me. What might have happened if Zafar's younger brother had taken the throne, as his father wished? Would the current situation in Delhi—although peaceful for the citizens, yet the royals wallowing in an appalling state—have been any different? I tried to put those thoughts out of my mind. Nevertheless, I felt relieved that Humphrey had not suggested an after dinner turn around the gardens, which might have led to God knows what.

One morning at the CMH, while walking—and fanning myself with a notebook—along the corridor towards the Indian ladies' examination room, I spotted the tall and smartly uniformed sepoy, Sharif Khan. He stood in the long line-up of patients, and next to him a burka-clad woman sat on the floor. Upon seeing me, he salaamed; I nodded. Nurse Betty standing outside the room opened the door. Thanking her, I entered the office and sat at the desk. She ushered the patients in, one by one. Most of the women and their children had the usual cold weather complaints, severe coughs and fevers. There were some pregnancies as well. I examined them quickly and wrote prescriptions for medications they could obtain at the dispensary.

Soon it was Sharif's turn. He came in, followed by a short and slim but hugely expectant woman. She moved the burka's veil over her head to reveal an olive-complexioned, angelic face, having an apprehensive expression. I motioned at her to sit on the chair in front of the desk.

The nurse, in anticipation, started to prepare the examination bed.

"Gooden morning, Doctor Margaret. You remember, I Sepoy Sharif Khan?" He stood at attention, and hesitated, wondering whether to salute, but decided against it.

"Yes, Sharif. I remember you very well. I see you have brought your wife?" I stood and walked to the woman.

"Yes, my wife, Mumtaz Mahal." He patted her shoulder and

said, "*Arrey, salaam karo na.*"[come-on do a salaam] She immediately salaamed me.

"Oh, her name is the same as Shah Jahan's wife, and just as pretty as well," I said, to ease her anxiety.

Sharif translated, and her face burst into a lovely smile, but she covered it with her palms, as if embarrassed.

"I see she's with child, but is there any problem?" I asked Sharif.

"Yes, sometime she has bad pain."

I put my hand on Mumtaz's shoulder and asked, in what little Urdu I had picked up, "How long have you had this pain, and when does it occur?"

"For about two months, sometimes, pain bad at night." Mumtaz patted her ballooned belly.

"Any bleeding?"

She shook her head.

"All right, let me examine you." Nodding at Betty to prepare the patient for the examination, I proceeded to the washstand to wash my hands.

Taking Mumtaz by the arm, Betty asked her to come to the examination bed and undress. She then turned towards the sepoy. "Can you wait outside, please?"

Mumtaz, on seeing Sharif move towards the door, twisted her arm out of the nurse's grasp and ran to him. Holding him, she implored: "No, no. I don't like examination. Only get medicine, as you said."

"Arrey, begum, have you gone mad? How can the doctor *sahiba* give you medicine without check-up?" He guided her, gently, back towards the nurse, and left the room.

Betty said some words in Urdu, she had picked up, to soothe Mumtaz, and led her to the examination bed. She drew the curtain across, to provide the terrified woman some privacy.

I dried my hands and went to the bed to face Mumtaz; she lay there with a fearful look. Telling her that I was not going to hurt her, I gently lifted the bed sheet—she had wound it tightly about her—up to her very swollen belly. Her pregnancy looked to be well advanced. I inquired, and she responded that she thought she was in her seventh month. I prodded and probed carefully, asking questions. The inspection did not disclose anything unusual. The baby was positioned normally, except it seemed too large for her slender build.

Having finished my examination, I asked her to get dressed and requested the nurse to call Sharif back into the room. Rewashing and drying my hands, I sat down at the desk and wrote some notes.

Sharif came in, and I asked him and Mumtaz to sit on the chairs across the desk.

"Sharif, what type of diet has Mumtaz been following?"

Sharif looked towards Mumtaz. "Oh no, she no diet. She eat all the traditional food. Meat, chicken, lamb."

"Any fruits and vegetables, and fish?" I asked.

Sharif bent forward. "No, she don't like those."

I noted it. "Hmm … Mumtaz, do you eat a lot of *mithai*?" I asked her.

She adjusted the burka's top about her and smiled. "Yes, I like sweets."

Sharif had a worried look. "Is she all right, Doctor Margaret? I tell her all time. Not eat the sweets."

I made some more notes and closed the file. "Sharif, your wife is fine. There is nothing wrong with her. I think the pain is because the baby is a bit bulky, but not to worry. She needs to reduce meats and add more vegetables to her meals."

Sharif nodded. "Any medicine for her?"

I reached for a requisition slip. "I don't think she needs any medication, but she mentioned she's suffering from minor constipation. I'll prescribe something for it." I wrote a prescription for a mild laxative, an herbal tonic we gave to most patients.

I handed the note to Mumtaz. "And no more *mithais* for the next two months. *Maloom*?"

She took the slip and smiled. "*Acha*, Doctor sahiba." She rotated her head in the typically Indian style, meaning "yes".

Sharif started to get up to leave, but sat down again. "Doctor Margaret, did you get house in Daryaganj?"

"No, not yet. I looked at some, but didn't find a suitable one. I might have to search further away," I responded. The truth was that, with the cost of servants, and the high rents, made residing in that upper-class area beyond my means. Although, living further away from the hospital would have been inconvenient. "Didn't you say *you* live in Daryaganj?"

"Yes, we have big *haveli* we call Sharif Mahal. You like to stay there? You have baby too, yes?"

"Yes, I have a child, and his *ayah*, as well. Your offer sounds wonderful. But, no, thank you. I couldn't impose on you," I answered, although they looked to be decent people, and I wouldn't have minded dwelling in their *haveli*.

"It's no problem for us. We have many rooms empty. Also, house very close to hospital. It is respect for us, you stay with us," Sharif insisted.

Mumtaz also leaned forward and spoke in Urdu: "Doctor sahiba, normally we do not rent rooms. But we like you to live with us. Please come, see the house. All right?"

At their kind offer, and knowing that my welcome at the Residency would soon be running out, I could not help but reply, "All right. I'll come and see your Sharif Mahal."

Sharif looked pleased. "You come this evening?"

"No, I'm busy today. How about tomorrow, after work?"

Sharif stood up. "Good. I come to hospital in afternoon. Yes?"

"I'll wait for you." I stood, and they departed happily, thanking and salaaming me a few times.

While Betty went to fetch my next patient, I felt elated at having met such generous people, and at their genuine hospitality. Sitting in my chair, I closed my eyes and said a silent prayer to thank the good Lord for all his benevolences on me.

The next afternoon, having to attend to a difficult delivery, I was delayed for my appointment with Sharif Khan. However, when I stepped out of the hospital's main doors onto the garden path and in the bright warm wintry sunlight, I found him waiting under a shady tree, chatting with some *chaukidars*. He came forward immediately and salaamed. I apologized for my tardiness, and we walked to the front gates. He had a *tonga* waiting, and led me to it. I climbed onto the back seat and he sat at the front, beside the *tongawalla*. It was only a short drive through the crowded streets to the mansion. In a narrow lane, the *tonga* stopped in front of the grand entrance, with large wooden doors; I alighted.

While Sharif paid the driver, I looked up at the stone-front of the imposing two-story Sharif Mahal. It resembled a miniature palace having a number of balconies, latticed windows and intricate cornices. He opened the smaller wicket gate in the main door, and shouted our arrival to someone inside. He turned towards me. "Please come in, madam."

Bending down, I entered through the small door into the coolness of the marbled floored hallway that led to a courtyard in the middle of the building.

Mumtaz—followed by a number of women and children—came waddling towards me. "Welcome doctor sahiba. We are honored to have you come to our humble abode," she said, speaking slowly in Urdu, to assist my comprehension.

I exchanged greetings with her and the other excited ladies. They touched my temples with their palms, in their customary manner, giggling with delight. I was escorted into the quadrangle that had a lovely garden of colorful flowering bushes, fruit trees and a water-well at its center. I was made to sit on a *charpoy* under a shady tree. Mumtaz handed me a silver cup of cool water from the well, and plumped down beside me; Sharif sat on another *charpoy* across from us. Other ladies and numerous children, either lolled on *charpoys* or stood around in a circle, looking curiously at me. Several elderly women and men peeked from the windows of their chambers, on the second floor. On the roof, I spotted, what looked to be birdcages and saw some young boys tossing pigeons into the air, and calling out to the flying flocks.

"You will have tea? Yes?" Mumtaz asked, holding my wrist, and without waiting for my reply, shouted at a servant, "*Chai layaoo.*"

I took a sip of the refreshing water. "Your *haveli* is beautiful. How long have you lived here?"

"I came here only last year, after my marriage to Sharif Khan." She blushed. "But, his family have owned this house for a long time." She looked at Sharif.

"My great-grandfather, also name Sharif, receive it from the Mughal emperor, for service in his army. But, building not the same now. Grandfather make many changes." Sharif waved his arm around. "You like?"

I looked at the marble columns with artistic intricate carvings of vine leaves and flowers, and the intriguing latticed balconies of the flats around the courtyard. "Yes, very impressive. It seems he hired the same artisans who might have built the Taj Mahal!"

Both Sharif and Mumtaz laughed. "No, those workers long dead by Grandfather's time. But many copy the same designs. We have a nice apartment for you." Sharif pointed to a corner unit on the second floor. "We show you after tea."

"Yes, I'd like to see it. But I don't wish to create a problem for your family. You having to move someone out of the rooms, just for me."

"No problem." He shook his head. "The apartment empty now. My brother, also in army, lived there. He was transferred to Lucknow. He and his family gone there."

Maids arrived carrying trays of tea and refreshments. Mumtaz got up and quickly piling—with her fingers—on a plate the best pieces of sweets, samosas and other delicacies, handed it to me. I protested mildly, but accepted the platter, for I was getting fond of those tasty snacks. A maid handed me tea in an exquisitely engraved copper cup. Taking a sip I found it to be heavily sweetened. I politely asked her to pour me another cup, without any sugar. While we partook the victuals, Mumtaz and Sharif informed me more about the background of the *haveli* and their family. An elderly couple, dressed in plain white *kurta-pajamas*, entered the courtyard, from the back door. Through the open door, I spotted a small back-garden and white minarets of a small mosque beyond. Sharif introduced them as, Mr. and Mrs. Akbar Khan, his parents. They greeted me and apologized for not having received me earlier, for they were busy in their afternoon prayers. I salaamed them, and they sat beside their son.

"Are you in the army, as well?" I asked Akbar Khan.

"No, not like my sons. I no like fighting." He smiled. "I have small jewelry shop in Chandni Chowk. You come see someday. Yes?"

"Yes, of course. Chandni Chowk is close to my hospital. I'd love to have a look at your jewelry." I finished my cup of tea and put it and the snack plate aside.

Sharif took the last gulp of his tea and stood up. "You like to see your apartment now, Doctor Margaret?"

I nodded, and followed him towards an open stone staircase, built along the side of the back wall. Mumtaz and Sharif's parents came behind us. I was careful walking up the stairs, staying close to the wall, for although the steps were wide enough, there were no handrails, and one side was open to the floor below, which I though was rather odd.

On reaching the second floor, Sharif walked along the hallway, with rooms on one side and a latticed marble wall and windows on the other, to a corner apartment. He opened the door and ushered me inside.

It was a lovely room with dark red carpets, wall hangings, a divans with numerous flamboyant bolsters, and settees placed at the sides. Fresh air blew through a small balcony with latticed windows, facing the street and the river beyond. The setting sun's rays cast long fingers through the window's trellises. A small bed was at one side.

I thought this was all of the rental unit, but Sharif hurried over, and opened a door on the side to a second room. Going inside there, it was a pleasant surprise to see an exquisitely furnished bedroom. There was a dark-wood four-poster bed with mosquito netting, in the middle, a large dressing table and numerous wardrobes and a washbasin, stood along the walls.

I walked over to the window on the outside wall, and opening the shutters was thrilled at the view of the palatial buildings, the gardens along the river and the domes of the Jami Masjid and the Red Fort to the north. As I turned around, to face the others, I noted a small crib in one corner of the room. How considerate of them, I thought. They all had inquisitive expressions, no doubt wondering how I felt about the chambers.

Mumtaz came up to me and touched my wrist. "You like the rooms? Yes?"

The pleasant expression on my face must have answered her question, but I still had a concern. "The flat is wonderful … but I am not certain if I can afford the rent."

"Rent!" Sharif's father exclaimed. "No, doctor sahiba. We will not charge you any money. You will stay here as our guest."

"Oh, no," I said firmly. "I would not dream of imposing on your hospitality. I like your apartment very much, but would stay only if I pay rent. Please tell me how much you will charge me?"

Sharif took his father aside, and they conferred in low whispers. Finally he turned towards me, and stated a monthly rate that was a bit lower than the other landlords in the same neighborhood had quoted me earlier. No doubt he would have made some enquiries.

Just as I had thought, the rent was still higher than I believed I could afford, on my low salary. There were Elgin's wages to consider—that reminded me that I had not paid the poor girl for the previous month yet—other expenses, and not to mention the costs of food and clothing.

While the sight of the high quality furnishings, in the classical Mughal style, the elegant apartment in an enchanting *haveli,* and living among such noble people was so very tempting, I could not bring myself to accept their offer. The thought of the additional outlays, upon the arrival of my other two dear children from Canada, also crossed my mind.

True there was a small pension of my deceased husband that was being sent, with my approval, to his mother, Aunt Fiona. But she had not said a word about it—although its receipt was acknowledged in letters from Cousin Heather. I did not have the heart to ask Aunt Fiona for that remuneration.

As if reading my thoughts, Sharif's Mother said, in Urdu, "And you will dine with us. You like Dilli-Muslim food? Yes?"

This additional thoughtfulness from her almost brought tears to my eyes. "Alright, since you are being so kind. I will rent the rooms." I might have sounded barely audible. "But, on one condition. My *ayah*, Elgin, will help in the cooking."

"*Inshallah*," both Mumtaz and Sharif said, almost in unison. Sharif's parents had broad smiles on their faces.

"You come tomorrow to the apartment?" Mumtaz asked.

"Oh, no. It wouldn't be appropriate for me to leave the Residency so suddenly. The Commissioner has been very kind to me." In reality I was anxious to move at the earliest from the Residency, feeling that I had stayed there long enough. I thought for a moment. "How about this Sunday? Would that be convenient?"

"Yes, very convenient." Sharif beamed at me. "I come to Residency in a carriage and help with luggage. Yes?"

"That would be most kind of you." I took out my watch from my dress-pocket, and looked at the time. "My, it is getting late. I should go."

"You stay for dinner? Yes?" Mumtaz asked, looking at me with her dark eyes and nodding her head.

"No, but thank you so much. I must leave. My child would be crying for me. Could you please have someone fetch me a *tonga?*"

Sharif immediately went into the hallway, and opening a window, shouted the instructions to a servant down in the courtyard.

While we walked down the stairs, a thought occurred to me. "Sharif, why was your brother transferred to Lucknow? Did he request it?"

Sharif turned his head, slightly backwards, towards me. "No. He no ask for transfer. He got order to go. Many more soldiers going there also."

Reaching the bottom of the staircase, we walked across the garden in the courtyard towards the main doors. Sharif's response puzzled me. "Why are they sending more troops there? What's happening in Oudh?"

He shrugged his shoulders. He did not look directly at me, while responding, "We not know. But many rumors."

I could not question him any further, for the servant entering through the wicket gate, announced that the *tonga* was waiting outside. I thanked my hosts again for all their kindness and considerations, and particularly Sharif's parents for renting me their eldest son's apartment. They salaamed and thanked me in return, numerous times. Sharif wanted to accompany me back to the Residency, but I dissuaded him against it, saying there was no need for it. He however, paid the *tongawalla* the fare. I was soon seated in the two wheeler and its driver cracking his whip over the horse hurried him along towards the Cashmir Gate, through the congested narrow streets. From my small handbag, I took out my blue pashmina shawl and wrapped it around my shoulders. The evenings in Delhi were beginning to get cool.

After thanking and tipping the *tongawalla*, and while climbing up the curved steps to the Residency's stone veranda, I saw Mr. Fraser, dressed in his customary dark suit and cravat, walking up from his *kutchery daftar* next door. A *chuprassi* followed, carrying his large dispatch-box. I waited for them to draw close. "Good evening, sir."

He tipped his black hat. "Working late?"

"Hardly, sir. Have been house hunting."

We reached the entrance, and he waited for me to go inside. "Find anything you liked?"

"As a matter of fact, yes!"

He followed me into the hallway. "Where abouts?"

"In Daryaganj, of all places. And close to the hospital, too."

"In one of those *havelis*?"

"Yes. Sharif Mahal. Do you know it?"

"Hmm … yes. I've driven by there. A rather grand palace. Owned by a Mughal noble family, the Sharifs, I believe?"

"Yes, that's the one."

"Bet they'll charge a pretty penny for rent. Can you afford it?" He handed his hat and walking stick to the butler.

"I think I can manage it. And the rent includes room *and* full board!"

"Ah! And have you decided to take it?"

"Yes! May I say, Mr. Frazer, I cannot thank you enough for your kindness. But, would it be all right if I moved there this Sunday?"

"Not at all. It is my pleasure. But this weekend! You don't have to leave here so soon, you know, Margaret."

"Oh, but I must, especially with my children arriving shortly from Canada. I might not be able to find such a suitable place, particularly one I can afford."

"Yes, I understand. Ah, that reminds me. You had a visitor this afternoon." He fished in his pocket and taking out a card, handed it to me.

The name on the card read: *J. H. Taylor - Principal Delhi College*. "Oh! Mr. Taylor himself came to see me?"

"Yes. He did indeed. He has an interesting proposition for you. It would help you along with your finances, as well, I'd imagine. Could you see him tomorrow afternoon?"

"Yes, I would be most happy to."

"Good. I'll send word to him to expect you." The butler approached, carrying a whisky and soda on a silver tray. Mr. Fraser picked up the crystal glass. "Care to join me for a drink."

"Oh, no thank you, sir. I've had my tea at the Sharif Mahal. And I must go and see to my son."

He nodded. Picking up a side of my skirt, I scampered up the staircase towards my room, Principal Taylor's card clutched tightly in my hand.

Chapter Thirteen

The Delhi College

1855, November-December: Delhi, India

THE NEXT AFTERNOON, after seeing the patients all morning, and having completed the paperwork, collecting my reticule and putting on my bonnet, I prepared to leave the hospital. Earlier, I had peeked into Doctor Chaman Lal's office to inform him of my intention to be away soon after lunch, because of my appointment with Mr. Taylor. He had looked up from the file he was reading, and with a smile rotated his head, in his usual way. "Of course you may, Margaret. I am sure you will enjoy teaching at the College. Mr. Taylor is a good man. He often invites me to give lectures there too, you know." I thanked him and closed the door.

As I came out through the hospital's wrought iron main gates, holding an opened sun-umbrella, the first *tongawalla* in the line-up of the carriages along the street came hurriedly towards me. He was a burly chap, sporting a dark beard and moustache, obviously a Pathan. He recognized me. "Salaam, memsaab. You go to Residency, yes?"

"No, khan-sahib, not right now. But, can you take me to Delhi College, please?"

He nodded, and with a bow asked me to ascend his carriage. He drove at the usual fast-trot speed, winding in between other vehicles through the narrow streets. Soon the entrance gates of the college loomed ahead. Turning on the curved path through the picturesque garden, the carriage stopped at the front portico of the college's oriental styled red sandstone walls that complemented the Red Fort's fortifications, across the road.

I got down and paid the fare along with a generous tip to the *tongawalla*. He smiled broadly and salaamed me a couple of times. Obviously looking for more business, he asked if he should wait there for me. While I thought that it would be nice to have a conveyance available just for me, but knowing there were only a few coins left in my purse, I told him that it would not be necessary.

Streams of students were ambling out and hurrying in through the main doors of the arched entranceway. They looked curiously at me as I passed in between them into the coolness of the main hallway, and approached the front desk. An Indian lady, dressed in a red sari, sat there. She stood and came around the counter towards me. "Good afternoon. Are you, Doctor Wallace?" When I nodded, she said, "Welcome to Delhi College, Mr. Taylor is expecting you. Could you please have a seat? I'll see if he is available." She waved her hand towards a cushioned sofa in the corner, and proceeded up the stairs to the second floor.

I seated myself on the comfortable couch next to the latticed window, and enjoyed the cool breeze streaming in. Looking through the window, I spied a picturesque garden in a courtyard in the center of the college's complex, and beyond loomed three white marbled domes of what obviously was a mosque. Scholars, books and papers in hand, hurried about in the verandas around the garden, while others sat on benches or lay on the grass underneath shady trees. I did not have to wait long before the clerk came down the staircase, followed by an elderly gentleman. He was dressed in a dark suit, and from his deep-set blue eyes, grey hair and the short trimmed beard, I recognized him. It was Mr. Taylor.

"Welcome, Doctor Wallace. Good to see you again." Mr. Taylor approached me, with a smile. I stood, and we shook hands. "I am glad that you could come over on such a short notice."

"Thank you. Sorry that I wasn't at the Residency yesterday when you came to see me," I said. "I was free this afternoon, and I'm happy to be here."

He turned towards the lady. "Parvati, could you please have some tea sent up to my office?" She nodded. Mr. Taylor then asked me to follow him and we climbed up the stairs.

"Very impressive building," I said as we walked along the clean corridors, keeping to the shaded side of the passage. Sounds of teachers and students emanated from the classrooms. "Wasn't this Sir David Ochterlony's Residency? When did the College move in here?"

"The College was originally in the north of the city, at an old madrasa's location. We needed more space, and were allocated this vacant building in 1845. Yes it was the former Residency, and prior to that the Emperor Shah Jahan's son, Prince Dara Shikoh's library."

"This College began as a madrasa! I imagine they would have taught mostly in Arabic then?"

"Yes, and Persian as well. The madrasa was setup in the 1700s by Nawab Ghazi-ud-Din. I believe he was a general in Aurangzeb's army."

"When did English classes commence here?"

"Around 1828. I believe it was the former Resident, Sir Charles Metcalf, who recommended it. But, we have progressed much, and have instituted several new initiatives. Actually that's why I called upon you." We had reached his office. He pushed the door open and ushered me in.

I entered, wondering what he had in mind. While it was a large room, only a desk and some chairs and tables were at one end. Cabinets and bookshelves, which seemed to overflow with books, reports, and stacks of papers, took up the rest of the space. Mr. Taylor requested me to sit down. I hung my bonnet and parasol on a coat rack, and sat on a chair in front of his desk.

Pushing his coat tails aside, Mr. Taylor sat down on his chair. He put away some papers and files that were in front of him, and looked at me with his kind eyes. "I understand you are presently at the Civil Hospital in Doctor Chaman Lal's group?" I nodded. He continued, "And how are you getting along, working for an Indian … err … I mean someone not English?"

The question did not surprise me, for others had asked me the same previously. I smiled. "Quite well, actually. He is a knowledgeable and competent doctor and not only that, he cares for all his staff. I am happy to be reporting to him."

Mr. Taylor look relieved. "Good to hear that. As I was saying, we have initiated some new projects, which could use your help. The position I have in mind would be under the supervision of an Indian professor, Mr. Ramchandra. He's a compatriot of Doctor Chaman and teaches mathematics and science subjects. You might have heard of him?"

"Yes, I have. Doctor Chaman has mentioned him." Also, I remembered Papa telling me that both he and Doctor Chaman were baptized at the same time by Reverend Jennings, which had caused quite a stir within the Delhi's Hindu and Muslim communities. But, I did not think it proper to bring it up at that moment.

Mr. Taylor stroked his beard. "Good. So I take it you would not have any reservations working for Professor Ramchandra?"

Opening my fan, I fanned myself to get some relief from the warm ambience in the room. "Not at all. I understand he is learned in scientific matters. I have seen some of his articles in the local papers."

"Yes he is a proficient person, and indeed a valuable resource for our institution. He has even written a book on algebra. I believe I have it here." He got up and pulling out a leather-bound volume from a bookshelf, handed it to me.

I flipped through the book's pages. While it looked to be a professionally written mathematical tome, having numerous diagrams and formulate, I could not comprehend it. I handed the book back. "Mr. Taylor, I am afraid I am unable to read it, for it is in Urdu! I should mention that I am still learning the language, and can speak it only a little bit."

Mr. Taylor sat down in his chair, and smiled. "Actually Mr. Fraser told me that he's heard you speaking to the servants, and you can speak Urdu quite well."

I beamed. "I should thank Mr. Fraser for his high opinion. But it's only a few sentences. My vocabulary is very limited, really."

"I understand. So let me get to the point of calling you here. You might have heard that the College is involved in a program of translating English textbooks into Urdu, naturally for the benefit of our local students."

"Yes, I've heard of it."

"Professor Ramchandra is presently very busy translating the scientific books, and could use help from a learned doctor, particularly for the medical texts. I feel your assistance would be invaluable. Hence, would you be interested in working on the translations of some of the medical textbooks?"

The prospects of a job translating those types of textbooks, which I was familiar with, interested me. Not only for the money, but I thought I would enjoy that work. Nevertheless, notwithstanding Mr. Fraser's kind recommendation, I was still concerned about my lack of proficiency in Urdu. "I should be delighted in helping in any way I can. However, it bothers me that while I may be able to speak Urdu, I'm simply not able to write it yet."

"Yes, we had realized that, and professor Ramchandra has indicated that he could assign another colleague to assist you, in writing the Urdu. How would that suit you?"

I felt much relieved. "Oh! That would be wonderful. I'm certain that I'll require much help in the writing."

There was a light tap on the door, and a bearer entered the room carrying a tea tray and placed it on a side table. Pouring two cups of tea, he put them down on the desk in front of me and Mr. Taylor, along with small platters of milk and sugar, and biscuits. While I sipped on the refreshing aromatic tea, and nibbled on the tasty scones, Mr. Taylor and I conversed further. He inquired about my background, my days at the Women's Medical College in Philadelphia, my married life in Canada, and my experiences in the Crimea.

I brought him up to date, and was grateful that he did not dwell too much on the sad death of my dear husband. Remembering Crimea had already distressed me somewhat, and my eyes were getting moist. I dabbed them with my handkerchief.

Mr. Taylor, expressing his condolences, tactfully changed the topic. He proceeded to tell me a bit more about the workings of Delhi College. He informed me that Persian was replacing the Oriental curriculum originally taught in Arabic. The Western syllabus, delivered in English, comprised of humanistic subjects with greater emphasis on history, philosophy, mathematics, and sciences, such as astronomy. He proudly indicated that the college possessed a printing press that produced newspapers and books.

I smiled when he said, "Books are changing the ancient form of teaching, from the oral to reading and writing." We continued our discussion and finally, having tactfully satisfied himself of my ability, he offered me a part-time position at a generous salary, which I was happy to accept.

Having finished my tea, I put the cup and saucer aside. Mr. Taylor said, "May I take you to meet Professor Ramchandra, now?" I replied in the affirmative. Putting on my bonnet and parasol in hand, I followed him out of the room. As we walked along the veranda, students passed by giving me curious glances, and wishing us a good afternoon; we returned their greetings. We soon came before a door with a nameplate that read: *Professor Yesudas Ramchandra*. Following a knock, Mr. Taylor opened the door and waited for me to step inside. A dark complexioned and clean-shaven person, who looked to be in his thirties sat at a desk, reading some papers. Upon seeing me, and Mr. Taylor, he immediately stood and came around his desk towards us. He was dressed in the Western style—white shirt and dark trousers—and Mr. Taylor introduced us; we shook hands.

Mr. Taylor looked towards me. "Doctor Margaret, if you would excuse me, I have to teach a class shortly, and I will leave you in the good hands of Professor Ramchandra. But please do come and see me, if you have any more questions on your appointment in our College."

"Yes, I will, and thank you for having me."

"You are most welcome." Mr. Taylor bowed and left the room.

Mr. Ramchandra then ushered me to a chair in front of his desk. Sitting down, I could not help glancing at the numerous books with their titles printed along their spines, in Urdu and English that lined the bookshelves along the walls.

Mr. Ramchandra sat down on his chair and closing the manuscript he had been reading, put it aside. "Doctor Wallace, it is indeed a great honor for us to have you join our College," he said folding his arms.

"Thank you, sir. I am pleased to be in this notable institution. Did you not study here as well?"

"Yes, I did. And after graduating, in 1844, it was a privilege to have been appointed to teach science and mathematics."

"It would have been a shame if the College had let you go and tutor elsewhere," I said. "And, apart from lecturing I believe you publish scientific periodicals, and have also written an Algebra textbook!"

"Yes, thank you. Unfortunately, I've had to discontinue the journals." He sighed. "But, have you read the book?"

Although I had heard of the decline in readership of his journals, following his conversion, I did not mention it. "Mr. Taylor just showed me your book. But, I couldn't read it, for it's in Urdu! You should translate it into English."

"There is an English version, and I am in the process of improving it, with help from others. Also, I am happy to say that

Professor Morgan, of Trinity College at Cambridge, has offered to have it published in England."

"Oh, how wonderful! With Professor Morgan's recommendation, I am certain the book should be well received."

"It's most kind of him to give his blessing. I'll show you the English version when it's been revised. But, where we need your assistance is in translations of medical texts from English to Urdu. I understand from my friend Doctor Chaman that you can speak Urdu quite well."

I fanned myself and smiled. "It's kind of him to say so. I might be able to speak Urdu, a bit, but I can hardly write it."

"Yes, I can understand that. Hence, for the writing part I will assign a young man to assist you. His English might not be perfect." Mr. Ramchandra smiled. "But his Urdu is superb."

"That would be most helpful. Is he a student here?"

"He's a recent graduate. His name is Zaka Ullah, and being interested in science and mathematics, he teaches those subjects in my department."

"Oh, he's a science teacher! Then, he shouldn't have much difficulty in writing down my translations."

"That I am certain of. And of course you could use this good dictionary that I rely on." He got up and going to the bookshelf behind his desk, pulled out a worn volume and handed it to me. While I thumbed through it, he took down two more thick books and placed them before me. I recognized them as introductory medical texts, which took my mind back to my college days.

"These are the basic level textbooks. Perhaps you could commence translating these two first?"

I nodded. "Yes, certainly. I am familiar with these texts. Translating them wouldn't be much of a problem."

"Good. So, how about if I take you now to your office. It's right next door. And I'll go and fetch Zaka. He should be in his office or the library." I nodded.

I followed him out of his office, carrying the books, to the room next to his. After showing me inside, he went to look for Mr. Zaka Ullah. It was a small room with a table and four chairs, and a window that overlooked onto the courtyard and the garden below. Bookshelves lined the wall on one side. I placed the books on the table and opened the window, a crack, to let in some fresh air to ameliorate the stifling atmosphere in the room. Sitting down on a chair, I perused the medical texts.

It was not long before Mr. Ramchandra returned with the young man, who carried a file folder, and introduced him. He immediately salaamed me in the Muslim fashion. He was dressed in the Delhi Muslim tradition—a long knee length cotton white shirt, and a dark waistcoat over tight-fitting pajamas. He sported a trimmed dark beard on a fine featured and light-complexioned face. We sat around the table, and after some pleasantries, discussed the rewriting of the textbooks in Urdu. I was relieved to note that Zaka spoke English reasonably well and also pleasantly surprised to see that he had already started on the translations.

Opening the file, he showed me the books' table of contents and some of the front pages, which he had scribed so far. I was still getting used to the Urdu script, which similar to Arabic goes from right to left, and the book's pages are turned similarly—the reverse of one written in English. While I could not read most of the neatly written flowery script, it looked that Zaka had written the books' front end very well.

"Your handwriting is very good, Mr. Zaka Ullah. Have you had any calligraphic instructions?"

"No. Not taken any lessons," he responded with his eyes down on the manuscript.

"It's likely hereditary," Mr. Ramchandra interjected. "Zaka's father is a *munshi*, and a tutor to the Mughal princes."

I nodded, and noted some blank spots and a word in English written above them in pencil. "I see you have left some blank spaces."

"Yes. I want to know the meaning of those English medical words from you first, before writing them."

"Certainly. I'll help you with those. And as for some of the more difficult words, we could use this medical dictionary," I said, turning the pages of the manuscript. "Good. I see you have made a wonderful start."

Seeing that I was pleased with Zaka's work, Mr. Ramchandra remarked, "Well, in that case we should have the texts translated and published in no time. So, Doctor Margaret, how often would you be able to visit us?"

"It would depend on how busy I would be at the CMH. But, I

believe I should be able to work at the College on two to three afternoons a week. I'll send you a chit a day before, to advise you of my arrival. How would that suit you?"

"That would be wonderful." Mr. Ramchandra looked happy to hear that. After some further review and planning of the work, as it was getting late, I took their leave. Both the gentlemen accompanied me out to the College's front gate and hailed a *tonga*. Bidding them a farewell and a promise to see them the next week, I was soon in the carriage that clattered on its way to the Residency.

The butler must have heard the *tonga* arrive at the Residency, for he opened the front door and bid me a good evening as I ascended the steps of the portico. Entering the cool hallway, I heard voices, unmistakably those of Commissioner Fraser and Colonel Humphrey, from the drawing room. They appeared to be in a serious discussion. The butler waited patiently, as I undid my bonnet and handed it to him, along with my parasol. Walking further along I heard Humphrey mention, rather loudly, Wajid Ali's name who I knew was the Nawab of Oudh. I became curious and wishing to hear what it was they were talking about, walked towards the drawing room. However, as I appeared before the open French doors, they abruptly stopped talking and stood up, mumbling a good-evening.

"Ah, Margaret. Please do come in." Commissioner Fraser, dressed in his usual dark frock coat and a glass of whiskey in one hand, motioned to me.

"May I pour you a drink, Margaret?" Humphrey, wearing his smart red uniform jacket, raised his glass of wine.

"No, thank you, Colonel Humphrey. But I would love a cup of *chai*." I turned to look at the butler standing by the door. He nodded and proceeded towards the kitchen. I sat down on a comfortable wing chair placed close to the overhead swinging *punkah*. I pitied the young lad outside the room squatting on the floor in the heat, pulling the fan's rope. The two gentlemen sat down back on the sofa.

"*Chai!* Hmm… I hear you are becoming quite proficient in Urdu, Margaret." Humphrey took a sip of wine.

"Well, I spent the whole afternoon at Delhi College."

"Did you meet Taylor?" Mr. Fraser took a gulp of whisky.

"Yes. In fact he came down to the lobby to get me."

"Did he now! It would seem you fared better than Mirza Ghalib, when he went there for his interview," Fraser said, breaking into a laugh, and Humphrey guffawed as well.

I had heard of Delhi's poet laureate, Mirza Ghalib, but not comprehending their joke I looked quizzically at the two. "Oh, is Mr. Ghalib teaching there as well?"

"No, he does not," Fraser responded, still laughing a bit.

"Why not? I've heard he's a brilliant poet." I still must have had a puzzled look.

"I am sure he would have been appointed as the Persian Professor, a job I believe he badly needed, if only he would have gone inside the College's building and attended the meeting."

"Why did he not go in?" I asked.

Fraser smiled. "He kept waiting outside in his palanquin, for a formal welcome. Although, the secretary, Mr. Thomason, came out and explained to him that an official reception would not be appropriate, for Mr. Ghalib was there as a candidate for employment."

I was still confused. "So, what did Mirza Ghalib do?"

"He left in a huff," Fraser responded with a smirk. "Most unfortunate, I think, for I believe poets are usually short of funds."

Humphrey asked, "But, do tell us about your meeting, Margaret. What would you be doing there?"

A bearer brought in my tea and a plate of Indian hors d'oeuveres, which the cook knew I liked. I passed the plate over to Humphrey and Fraser. They took only a small piece each, saying the snacks would be too spicy for them. In between sips of the aromatic tea and bites of the delicious samosas and pakoras, I narrated the events of the afternoon to them; they listened intently. I concluded by saying, "Professor Ramchandra is doing a remarkable job in turning the English textbooks into Urdu. It would surely benefit the Delhi students immensely."

Fraser smiled. "Indeed, translated texts are helping to bring knowledge to the local population. Although, some have questioned the process."

"Really! Questioned on what basis, and by whom?" I asked.

"I was at a meeting where a Christian missionary had argued with Ramchandra on the value of the learning by Indians through translations of English texts," Fraser said. "But you know, to his credit, Ramchandra had responded remarkably well."

"Oh! And what did he say?" I was most curious.

"He said that translation is the medium through which knowledge has been shared by civilizations. He gave the example of Europe having learned from the translated Arabic texts, who had gained the information from the Romans and they in turn had obtained it from the Greeks, and so on." Fraser raised his eyebrows and sipped his drink.

"An interesting counter argument," I said. "But I think the missionary was likely promoting the use of English as the preferred teaching medium, and not Urdu."

"Spoken like a true missionary's daughter." Fraser smiled. "But, you know, the Company agrees with those views. We would be soon moving towards having our official correspondence written solely in English."

"Oh! Is that why I overheard you speaking about Nawab Wajid Ali? To have him agree to this proposal?" I took a sip of my tea.

"No, that's another matter," Fraser responded, and then looked quickly towards Humphrey as if to seek his acceptance on what he wanted to say next.

"Yes, we might as well let Margaret know of the developments in Oudh," Humphrey said shifting in his chair. "We'd agreed, earlier, to keep her abreast of all the events, hadn't we?"

"Quite so." Fraser took a sip of his whiskey and glanced at the door to ascertain none of the servants were within earshot. "You might as well know now, Margaret, for you'll hear sooner or later. Colonel Humphrey has received a dispatch from Calcutta. The GG wishes him to go to Lucknow and, along with Outram, have another word with Wajid Ali."

I knew General Outram was the Company's Resident for Oudh, having replaced Sleeman, and although I had an inkling of what this was all about, I asked looking towards Humphrey, "A word, about what?"

"I am sure you are aware, Margaret, that despite repeated warnings, some delivered by me personally," Humphrey responded, "the Nawab continues to mismanage his kingdom. The common populace of Oudh are living in a state of misery, at the mercy of the landowners. All the while he spends his time in a life of luxury and debauchery. We have to act." Humphrey took a sip of his wine.

"Yes, I have heard some gossips. But there are poor people all over India. What proof do we have of the Nawab's mishandling of his state's affairs?" I asked.

"Well we have Outram's report, and another one as well by the former Resident, Colonel Sleeman. They both suggested—"

"Yes. We were just discussing those reports, when you arrived, Margaret," Fraser interjected. "As I was saying, Sleeman wrote a couple of letters as well."

"I am aware of them," Humphrey said.

"Well, for Margaret's benefit, let me just read from these two letters." Fraser turned towards a side table on which lay his bulky wooden dispatch box. Shuffling through the stack of paper, he dug out two missives. "Ah, here they are. The first one was to Dalhousie, written in April 1852. Let me read the following portion. He proceeded in his deep baritone voice:

"...In September, 1848, I took the liberty to mention to your Lordship my fears that the system of annexing and absorbing Native States—so popular with our Indian Services, and much advocated by a certain class of writers in public journals—might some day render us too visibly dependent upon our Native Army; that they might see it, and that accidents might occur to unite them, or too great a portion of them, in some desperate act..."

While Humphrey looked on calmly, Fraser put the first letter back in the box, and glanced at the second. "And, here's the other one that Colonel Sleeman, less than a year later, in January 1853, wrote to Sir James Hogg, in London." Fraser looked towards me. "Sir James, you know, the Chairman of our Company's Board. Now, here's an interesting bit. Let me read it to you:

...I deem such doctrines to be dangerous to our rule in India, and prejudicial to the best interests of the country. The people see that these annexations and confiscations go on, and that rewards and honorary distinctions are given for them, and for the victories which lead to them, and for little else; and they are too apt to infer that they are systematic and encouraged and prescribed from home. The Native States I consider to be breakwaters, and when they are all swept away we shall be left to the mercy of our Native Army, which may not always be sufficiently under our control..."

"How interesting!" I said, feeling a surge of excitement run through my body. I looked towards Humphrey. "And what did the Governor General think of these remarks?"

Humphrey's jaw tightened. "Well I can't speak for him. But I dare say, he would have considered them."

"Yet he chooses to ignore them?" I said somewhat astonished.

"Margaret, despite what those letters say, the formal reports by the two Residents are quite clear. Annexation by the Company would be in the best interests of the people of Oudh." Humphrey took a large gulp to finish the last of the wine in the glass. "Besides, our GG has received approval of his missive to the Directors in London." He put his glass down on the side table, as if a judge would deliver his judgment.

Fraser also finished the whisky in his glass. "But, Will, what do you make of Sleeman's warnings about being left at the mercy of the Native Army, as he put it?"

"Pure speculation, I'd say. Although the native sepoys greatly outnumber us, they would never turn against their British officers. 'Having eaten our salt' as they say. I've seen our sepoys in action. I can vouch for the loyalty of every one of them." Humphrey looked towards me. "Don't you recall, Margaret, how fearlessly they fought off those rebels who ambushed us on our way to Delhi?"

And one of them took a bullet meant for you, I thought. "Yes, but don't you think, sir, annexation of a whole kingdom could be another matter?" I persisted.

"Oh, there might be some initial resentment. But when the populace learn they are rid of their corrupt ruler, and under our efficient administration, they will calm down. These minor unrests usually blow over. And just to be sure, we will have General Wheeler and his regiments camped just outside Lucknow," Humphrey responded in a confident voice.

I had heard of that mobilization from Sepoy Sharif Khan, for his brother was part of it, and whose apartment I was to occupy shortly. What a turn of fate I was thinking, when I heard Fraser say, "Why the army, Will, are you expecting any trouble?"

"No, not really. Dal is a reasonable man. He sincerely hopes that the Nawab will listen to reason."

"And what if the Nawab doesn't listen?" Fraser asked.

"Ah! That's when things might get interesting, but we trust not. Outram has instructions. He turned towards me, "And, Margaret, not a word about these plans to anyone, please. Especially in the Palace. You understand, don't you?"

"Yes, I do." I nodded. Although I wished to question the

proposed takeover of Oudh, some more, I thought it would serve no purpose. I felt tired, and finished my tea. Just then there was a knock at the door.

"Dinner would be served shortly," the butler announced. He then looked at me, as if to inquire if I was going to change.

"Oh, I must freshen up, and see my child before dinner. Thank you gentlemen, for enlightening me." I got up and proceeded towards the door. Humphrey and Fraser stood and bowed, murmuring that they would see me at dinner.

While climbing up the stairs, excerpts from Colonel Sleeman's letters still ran through my mind. I knew that he had travelled widely in India, and was well respected for being instrumental at having eliminated the Thuggees. Hence, it seemed preposterous for the Governor General to have disregarded the well-informed former Oudh's Resident's cautions. However, those troubling thoughts soon faded when I heard Elgin's baby talk, and the cooing of my boy. I hurried towards their room.

******

"Simon tells me you would soon be leaving us!" Colonel Humphrey blew a puff of cigar smoke up in the air, as we walked along in the rose garden behind the Residency. We had just finished a sumptuous four-course dinner, and Humphrey had invited me out for a stroll in the shrubbery. I had reluctantly accepted, for I was feeling rather full, having enjoyed the fish and the meat dish as well, since it was a spicy roast lamb—one of my favorite. Simon Fraser had gone off to an evening choir practice at St. James, and Humphrey and I were left alone.

"Yes, Mr. Fraser has been too kind to have put me up for so long. It is about time I found my own accommodations." I responded, admiring the lovely flowers.

"Where would you be staying? If I may ask."

"At a lovely *haveli* in Daryaganj, fairly close to the hospital. Most convenient for me."

"Oh, I thought most of the Europeans had moved from that locale."

"They might have, but I shall be residing with an Indian family."

"Really! Are they one of the nobles?"

"Not even that. I understand they have a jewelry shop in town and their sons are sepoys. One of them is named Sharif Khan. I believe you met him the other day when you dropped me off at the Red Fort."

"Oh yes! I remember him. But, Margaret, do you believe this is a sensible choice? Them being low class natives. What will others think?"

While his remark infuriated me, I simply replied, "It seems an appropriate choice for me, given my circumstances."

"Oh, come now, Margaret, you can do better than that."

"Better than what, sir?" It seemed the wind had picked up, for it was beginning to get somewhat chilly. I wrapped my woolen shawl tighter around me.

"We can discuss it. But I see it is getting rather cool. Shall we go inside, and may I have a peek at you lovely boy as well?"

I was getting tired, not only physically but of his company as well. I reluctantly agreed, perhaps also intrigued by what he wished to 'discuss'. We walked back into the Residency and up the stairs to my room. Elgin had placed Jan in his cot, and since he was sleeping soundly, she asked if she could go for dinner, and I had readily agreed.

"Ah, what a handsome boy." Humphrey approached the cot and gently moved a piece of the blanket from Jan's forehead, exposing his blond locks. Jan stirred a bit, and continued his slumber.

I was glad that Humphrey did not ruffle Jan's hair or stoke his cheek, for that would have surely woken him, and breakout in a howl. "That he is. An image of his father," I said standing beside Humphrey.

"I have always wanted a son. However, Providence favored us with three daughters," he said with a sigh and turned to face me.

"Daughters are a blessing too, sir. And can be more loving as well."

"That they can be, I am certain, and just as pretty as you." He put his hands on my shoulders and tried to draw me to him.

I resisted and gently pushed his hands down. "Thank you, sir. Anyhow, you wished to discuss something?"

"Why, yes. You know how fond I have become of you." He tried to look me in the eyes.

I turned my face towards Jan. "You have mentioned it often

enough, sir."

"Oh, please call me William or Will even, as you had started to."

"I am sorry, sir. I just cannot bring myself to do that anymore."

"I am sure you would, after you hear what I have to suggest." He tried to put his arms around my waist.

I stepped back and pushed his hands aside. "Yes, what is it that you are suggesting, sir?"

"My dear, Margaret, how shall I put it? I know your situation in Delhi is not the best as it could be—"

"Why, sir, I am quite happy here."

He put the palm of his right hand up. "Please hear me out, my dear. I know they have employed you at the CMH here, at about half the salary they pay Indian male doctors. You have responsibilities, not only for yourself, but your child and his *ayah,* as well. Furthermore, your two young ones are due to arrive soon from Canada. Simon tells me that he has persuaded Principal Taylor to take you on a part-time position at Delhi College. Even with that additional remuneration, you would hardly meet all your disbursements. Is that not the case?"

Not wishing to get into a detailed discussion of all my expenses, I simply stared at him. Finally I asked, "So, what are you suggesting, sir?"

"What I am proposing is, why don't you come with me to Calcutta?"

That submission stunned me. It was the furthest from my mind. "Why, sir, are you offering me to come away with you to Calcutta?"

"Well, why not. I have a large enough house. We would have servants and perhaps even engage a governess for your children. Also, I would get you appointed to a senior post at the Government Hospital there, at the full rate paid to a European doctor."

As I was standing mesmerized by his suggestion, he came forward swiftly and put his arms around my waist. I tried to push him away, but he only held me tighter, and pulled me to his strong chest. Murmuring, "Oh my darling, we could have such a wonderful life together." He tried to kiss me but I turned my head sideways, and continued to push him away. But, he managed to plant some kisses on my neck, and began to squeeze my bottom. I felt his hardness on my belly.

I felt enraged. "Please, sir. Let go of me," I said loudly.

"Oh, my dear. You are the most gorgeous woman I have met. Come let's go and sit on the bed."

"No, sir. Someone might come in. Kindly release me," I said a bit more loudly.

"Why? There is no one here." He tried to push me towards the bed. I resisted and twisted. My hips hit the side of Jan's crib, jolting it. He woke up and started whimpering.

"Please, sir. My baby is awake. I must tend to him."

Humphrey did not respond to my pleas and continued attempting to kiss and caress, my breasts, hips, all over. It looked as if he was struggling to pick me up and carry me to the bed. I kept trying to wrestle out of his hold.

My pleadings and stamping of our feet on the wooden floor must have raised quite a ruckus, for there was a knock on the door.

"Are you alright, memsahib?" It was Elgin. Fortunately, she had not yet left her room.

Hearing her, Humphrey immediately released me.

"It's all right, Elgin. Only Jan has woken up."

I glared at Humphrey, and whispered, "Will you, please, leave?"

"Why yes, my dear." However, he managed to hold my hand, and kissed it. "Will you consider what I have proposed?"

Knowing that he was an influential person, I did not wish to have him harm me. Hence, I responded, "Yes, yes. I will. Now please *go!*"

When Elgin opened the door and walked in, Humphrey left wishing me a goodnight, without even a glance at Elgin.

Later that night, as I lay in bed contemplating the events of the day and what Humphrey had said and tried to do, I wondered if I had acted inopportunely. For here was a wealthy man, although not titled—being the younger son of an earl—yet a senior military officer holding an influential position on the Governor General's staff, offering me, a lowly widow with three children, a life of luxury among the elite in Calcutta.

But what about beyond? Would he take me back to England? Likely not, for I did not hear the magical word 'marriage' or even a hint of it. Although he seemed to be infatuated with me and desired me a lot, but was it lust or love? One side of my brain warned me to be cautious, for I had heard of numerous cases of vulnerable women, such as myself, being taken on as mistresses and being left behind to suffer in silence in India.

However, my gentler soul whispered to me that perhaps I was judging Humphrey too harshly. The thoughts of all he had done for me flashed through my mind. I was told that isn't this the normal way most men fervently in love behaved? Also, hadn't my beloved Robert acted in a similar way, in Grimsby, during the earlier days of our meeting?

A suggestion flashed through my mind that perhaps I should approach the subject of marriage with him. But then why should I? I could perhaps bring myself to that level, if I loved him. I pondered that thought. But realized that while he is a likeable person, and has many good friends, there was something about him that did not sit right with me, and raised warning bells in my head. It did seem that, despite his affluence, he was not the person I could spend the rest of my life with.

But then again did I know him enough to judge him, perhaps too severely. Suddenly some words that Catherine had said to him, on our way to Delhi, reminded me that she seemed to know him well, even during his earlier assignment in India. I made a mental note to speak to her when I would see her next, perhaps at church.

The idea of seeking Catherine's opinion seemed to calm me. While I was formulating my questions to her, sleep embraced me and carried me off to a peaceful flowery meadow and lay me down on a soft bed of fragrant grass.

Chapter Fourteen

Margaret Moves to Daryaganj

1855, December-January, Delhi

"MEMSAHIB, DO YOU THINK it will be all right for us to live at Sharif Mahal?" Elgin asked, with a bit of a worried look on her face, as she sat on the seat opposite mine with Jan in her lap. We were in a carriage clattering along on the road towards the Cashmir Gate. As arranged, Sharif Khan had brought over the conveyance to the Residency that Sunday morning and was sitting up on the bench beside the *tongawalla*.

Earlier, while Sharif helped to load my sea chest and other baggage, Mr. Fraser had personally escorted me to the carriage. I thanked him profusely for all his kindness, to which he had responded in his usual refined manner, and offered that I could return back to the Residency anytime I wished. I also expressed my gratitude to all the servants who had come out to the terrace to see me off. Colonel Humphrey was nowhere to be seen, and I did not bother asking about him. He was likely sleeping a binge off at some *naatch* girl's *kotha* or some such place, I thought, for I was still upset at his appalling behavior the other evening.

"Why ever not, Elgin?" I responded, thinking her question rather odd. Although, I had noted some uneasiness about her, when I first mentioned our moving there.

"Do you know, memsahib, they are Muslims?"

"Yes, I am aware of that. But why should it make any difference?"

"Muslims don't like us Christians. Say we eat unclean pork and they don't believe Jesus is son of God. Also think we want to change them all to Christianity!"

"Oh, that is just nonsense and hearsay. We only preach the gospel, and if some of them, like your family, wish to convert the choice is theirs. I am not fond of ham and pork either, and won't miss it. You may know, they do believe Jesus was a prophet, and the educated Muslims don't question His parentage. You will see, the Sharifs are very nice people, and I am sure you will be happy staying there."

"Yes, I know, not all Muslim people are unfriendly. And I will be happy anywhere with you." Her smile looked comforting.

"I am glad to hear it. But do be careful when you'll be working in their kitchen. If anyone does or says anything improper, let me know immediately. Will you?"

"Yes, I will, memsahib." She smiled again, rocking my dear son sleeping in her lap.

"By the way, Elgin, I was wondering if you are missing your parents, and would like to visit Futtehgurh for Christmas? I could ask Mr. Fraser to arrange your travel and get another *ayah* to look after Jan, while you are away."

"Oh, no memsahib. I think of my parents, and write many letters, but I like to stay here for Christmas with you."

I was relieved to hear that, for I could not have trusted any stranger to care for Jan. "Thank you, Elgin. I truly appreciate your devotion. But, tell you what, on Jan's first birthday next May, we will travel back to Futtehgurh, for a month long visit. Would you like that?"

"Yes, memsahib. That would be wonderful. Thank you," she squealed delightfully.

Delhi's streets were relatively empty that mid-morning, and it did not take long for the carriage to traverse the thoroughfares and turn into a narrow lane to halt at the grand entrance of Sharif Mahal. Jumping down from the driver's bench, Sharif opened the wicket of the main gate, and hollered at the servants to come and get the luggage.

The colossal main doors of the *haveli* opened and I was ushered inside, Elgin following with Jan in her arms. A large group of mostly women, dressed in colorful garb and holding what looked to be garlands, waited in the hallway. Each of the ladies, in turn, salaamed and greeted me in their usual fashion—touched my forehead—and festooned me with the colorful and aromatic leis, almost up to my ears. Elgin received some as well. Such a delightful reception was most overwhelming. I felt almost like a bride entering her new home!

I was happy to see Mumtaz looking plump and well—she had a month or so to go before her delivery—and holding my hand she led me towards the courtyard. "Welcome, welcome, doctor sahiba, to our humble abode," she said, her face beaming with enthusiasm. I managed to mumble some words of thanks and followed her into the quadrangle. A large crowd of men, women and children, all dressed in mostly white *shalwar-kemeeze* stood around the central water well and repeatedly salaamed me their welcome. Sharif's parents, Mr. and Mrs. Akbar Khan, were also there, and greeted me warmly. They guided me to a *charpoy* covered with a colorful quilt. I noted Sharif leading a group of servants up the stairs carrying my luggage.

Mumtaz sat on the charpoy between me and Elgin, and introduced the people in the gathering to me. There were far too many names to remember, and I merely nodded to their salaams. Apart from the residents of the haveli some of the neighbors were also there. I remembered being introduced to one of them, a Mr. and Mrs. Ahmad Ali Khan. I recall Mr. Ali, a rather portly and dark faced fellow, dressed in a sepoy's uniform. Although he salaamed me, he did not smile, rather looked at me with a somewhat hostile stare. At that time I thought nothing of it.

Mumtaz asked me to have Elgin uncover Jan's head, for the others wished to see him. I nodded, and Elgin complied exposing Jan's fair hair and his chubby rosy cheeks. There were murmurs of delight from the audience. I was glad that Jan slept on, but dreaded that he might awake any moment and, being hungry, put an end to my welcome with his wails. Each of the elderly women came forward to admire Jan's handsome face and, after whispering a prayer, tucked in a rupee or more, into his blanket. I was most surprised, for I had never seen this done, and was unaware of this ritual.

"What is the money for, Mumtaz?" I asked.

"It's just to keep the evil eyes and spirits away from your beautiful child."

"Really! But how will that be possible?"

"Well, you may use the money to cook some cakes and distribute them to the poor."

"So, the poor will then pray for my baby?"

"Yes, they will do it," Mumtaz responded.

How interesting, I thought. I glanced towards Elgin, and she nodded, for she likely knew of this custom.

Maids arrived with tea and trays of the delicious Indian snacks. While most of the gathering sat down, on the numerous charpoys in the compound, with cups of tea—placed on the floor— and plates of food on their laps, I noticed Mr. and Mrs. Ali departing through the back door. Also, I could not recall Mrs. Ali having come forward with a blessing for Jan. Now that seemed rather odd, I contemplated. However, I enjoyed my tea and nibbles, and engaged in general conversation with those around me. Some were concerned about what was happening in the Kingdom of Oudh, and wanted to know what the Company was planning to do there. I feigned ignorance on that topic.

Soon, with the celebration of my arrival over, I was happy to be in my pleasantly furnished apartment. I rested, reclined on the comfortable divan. Bright sunshine and a cool breeze streamed in from the windows. The balcony offered a lovely view of the Jamuna River and the city. Earlier, Jan had indeed woken up and I had taken care of his hunger, while Elgin had gone down to the kitchen and fetched a tray of delicious chicken curry, beef kabobs and chapattis for my lunch, which I had relished.

In the adjoining room, while Elgin unpacked my sea chest, which the hard working girl had meticulously loaded just the day before, when it occurred to me that I should attend the evening service at St. James' Church. It was not only that I had missed the morning session, but I recalled Catherine mentioning that she and her husband usually joined the evening service, for they preferred to 'sleep-in' on Sunday mornings. Hence, I hoped that at an opportune moment, when we might be alone, to talk to her about Colonel Humphrey; he was still very much on my mind. This seemed like a good time to meet her, for although, Catherine did come to see me at the hospital, I was not certain when she might return.

I called out, "Elgin, could you please leave my evening gown out? We will be going to church."

"Yes memsahib," she acknowledged in her cheerful voice.

There was a knock on the door, and Mumtaz waddled in.

"Hallo doctor sahiba, are you settled in? Is there anything you need?"

I sat up on the divan—an elbow on a bolster—and she sat next to me. "Oh, please call me Margaret. You have been too kind. Everything I need is here." It then occurred to me to ask her about her neighbors. "By the way, I noted a person in uniform this morning. Is he one of your relatives?"

"Oh, no. They live next door. He subedar in the army and my husband's superior. But please excuse his behavior. He says he is from a *nawabi* family, and thinks highly of himself. But I don't know ..." She giggled, covering her mouth with a corner of her shawl.

"He seemed disturbed. Is it because I am now staying here?"

"Oh, no, Doctor Margareet. Not you. He don't like English people. He sold some land and property to the Company. But says they still owe him more money, and not pay him. Yes, he also tell Sharif to not invite a '*ferangi*-woman' in this house. But Sharif tell him, you no like the other English. You very kind lady."

On hearing that, I was somewhat alarmed, and offered, "I am sorry to have caused some difficulties for you with your neighbor. Perhaps I should leave?"

Mumtaz held my wrist. "Oh no, doctor sahiba, I mean Margareet. You very welcome here. Please ignore that fat Subedar Ali. I say to Sharif, to not bring Ali in our house again. He no bother you again."

I felt relieved to hear her assurance. "Well, if you think so. It's so generous of you to have me live here with your family. I'll be sure to stay out of Mr. Ali's way."

She smiled. "Good. We very happy you here. You come later have dinner with us, yes?"

Knowing how that Subedar Ali felt about me had bothered me, and I thought that perhaps it would be improper for me to become too familiar with the Sharif's family, so quickly. "Thank you, but we will be going to church this evening, and will likely dine out with some friends." I responded, also thinking that if I did not see the Herfords at church, I might drop in on them, anyway.

She got up from the divan, looking disappointed. "Good, have nice prayer at church. We see you when you come back," she said, and walked towards the door.

It was a fine early winter's evening, although still warm but comfortable, as the *tonga* with me, Elgin, and Jan, entered the curved driveway of St. James' Church. A few carriages were ahead of ours and gentlemen, dressed in dark coats and top hats, helped ladies in elegant gowns and bonnets down the vehicles, and escorted them into the church.

While Elgin took Jan with her to the back garden, where the other *ayahs* and governesses gathered, and no doubt engaged in gossip about their employers, I entered the church and searched for a place to sit. I was delighted to see, just as I had hoped, Catherine and Captain Herford seated in a pew up ahead, and there was space on the bench beside Catherine. I made my way there.

"Hallo, you two. Fancy meeting you here," I said sitting down beside Catherine.

"Margaret!" Catherine exclaimed, turning towards me. "So good to see you."

I nodded. She looked well, but I still asked, "How are you feeling, Catherine."

"Much better, thank you. That herbal concoction you gave me, the other day at the hospital, seems to be working."

I smiled, thinking that it might have been the medication, but given time and both mental and physical rest, particularly in her case, the body usually heals itself.

Captain Herford glanced towards me. "We heard you have shifted from the Residency. How are the new accommodations?"

"Most comfortable, thank you," I responded, and in a hushed voice told them all about my move.

"So did you bring all those coins, which Jan received, to the church? Might overflow the collection-plate," Herford teased.

"No. I am supposed to use that money to bake cakes and distribute to the poor."

"If you are going to make those spicy ones, can we have some too, please?" Catherine joked.

"I might, and you may come over to the *haveli* to get them," I responded.

"Yes, we would love to. But that reminds me. You have yet to visit our house. Would you like to come over for supper tonight?" Catherine asked.

"I would be delighted."

"Good. Would you like to accompany us in the carriage, after the service?" she offered, and I nodded.

Later, Catherine, leaned a bit towards me to whisper, "Oh, and I should mention, your Canadian friends, Nancy and Lieutenant Miller, will also be there. They live just a few bungalows down from us. I'm sure you will be glad to see them again, won't you?"

Hearing their names riled up my blood once more. I simply nodded, but thought of some excuse to beg off her invitation. However, just then Reverend Jennings arrived at the podium, shuffling his feet to get everyone's attention, to begin his sermon. The ensuing silence helped to calm me down. The long oration helped as well.

Following the service I ventured out into the garden to find Elgin. I spotted her sitting on the lawn under a shady tree, with Jan at her side. I walked there.

Upon seeing me, she shouted excitedly, "Look memsahib."

Worried, I hurried to her. But was arrested when I saw my child crawling! With tears of joy I lay down on the grass and let my Jan move gingerly, on all fours and giggling, up to me. I picked him up and rolling over, I held him to my bosom, and said a small prayer of thanks to our Lord for helping Jan to grow into a healthy child.

Entering the Herford's bungalow, felt like as if I was in my parents' home in Futtehgurh. Although the house seemed larger, the layout was similar. A narrow path led from the front gate through a well cultivated garden to the white painted verandah. From the front door the hallway, with rooms on either sides, took us up to the kitchen and dining area. From the back door we entered a large yard having a manicured lawn, and colorful flower beds at the sides, and shady trees at the back. Captain Herford's batman was busy there instructing the servants on setting up the dining table. Upon seeing us he bowed and pushed chairs aside for us to sit.

Jan was fidgeting in my arms and knowing he was hungry, I asked Catherine if I could nurse him. She immediately guided me to her well-appointed bedroom, and pointed towards a comfortable sofa. She left the room to allow Elgin help me get ready for Jan's nurturing. I took my bonnet off and sat on the sofa, with Jan on my lap. When he started his feeding, not needing Elgin anymore, I asked her to go and see if she could help in the kitchen.

Later, Catherine returned to the bedroom, to inquire if I required anything. I told her I was fine, and beckoned her to sit beside me. She did, and it gave me the perfect opportunity to talk to her alone, while I suckled Jan.

"Catherine, I have been meaning to ask, how well do you know Colonel Humphrey?"

She smiled, likely anticipating where this conversation was leading to. "Oh, not very well. Although, we knew him in Calcutta when he was there earlier, during the 1840s, serving on Sir Henry Hardinge's staff. My husband was just a young Lieutenant then." She laughed. "Why do you ask?"

"Well, he .... I don't know how to put it ... appears to be getting rather fond of me."

"I have sensed that. Has he proposed to you?"

"Not directly. At least not yet." I did not wish to tell Catherine about his atrocious behavior, at that moment. But added, "Although, he has asked me to move to Calcutta, and will help me get a better position at the hospital there."

"Hmm ..." She seemed to be in deep thought. "And how do you feel about his suggestion?"

"I am a bit confused. He was married, wasn't he, at that time in Calcutta?"

"Yes he was, with three lovely daughters. Then, most unfortunately, his wife died. Cholera, I think it was. He was naturally devastated. Although, he sent his daughters home, he remained in Calcutta hard at work, even when Hardinge left and Dalhousie took over."

"Didn't Humphrey leave India, later?"

"Yes, he did. A few years after Hardinge. In 1850, I believe it was. Left rather abruptly, it seemed to us."

"Oh! If he liked working here, why did he return to England?"

"I'm not sure. There are several rumors, of course. I don't believe it was work related, though. He is getting along rather well with Dalhousie, and the new Governor General Canning, due to arrive soon, wants him here."

"So, what was it then? Something personal? Another woman, perhaps?"

Catherine glanced back towards the door, to make sure no one was there and whispered, "Well, he's known a few women here, I believe. These officers all do when they are alone, away from home. Can't be helped, I suppose. But then in London ... listen I am telling you all this in confidence ... for you've been so good to me ... could you keep it to yourself?"

"Yes, certainly," I whispered. "Please, go on."

"In Calcutta, a year or so after his wife's death, he took up with a native lady. I saw her a few times with him. An attractive woman, Begum Zebunisah or some such name, from a noble Mughal family we understood. Even housed her in a grand *haveli*, with servants and all, would you believe!"

"Oh, really! Did he marry her?"

"Don't think so. Although, we all thought he was going to."

"So, what happened?"

"Don't know. Something must have, for their relationship ended rather abruptly. She left Calcutta for her home, somewhere in Oudh I think, and Humphrey returned to England—"

There was a tap on the door and Elgin entered. Jan had finished his feed and now lay smiling in my lap. I buttoned my blouse and handed him to Elgin. She held him with his head resting on her shoulder, and left the room saying she would take him outside to help him burp.

Catherine started to get up from the sofa, but I held her wrist. "Isn't there some more you were going to tell me? Something in London, was it?"

She sat down and leaned back on the couch. She rubbed her forehead, with the fingers of her right hand, as if wondering if she should say anything. Finally she spoke, "Yes, there is some more that I should mention. Did he not tell you anything about his past?"

"Not much. Just a bit about his deceased wife and his daughters."

"Well, if he wants you to live with him in Calcutta, I think he should have had the decency to tell you about his fiancé in London!"

I was shocked to hear that. I stammered, "Really! Cannot be true. Surely, it's just a rumor. Isn't it?"

"I think not. I know it for a fact. Read the announcement in the newspapers. I was in London, at that time."

"And who is she?"

"Lady Sofia, an earl's older unmarried daughter. Not very pretty, I think, but no doubt known to Humphrey's family. Humphrey's elder brother inherited the title and the Humphrey Estates, you know."

"Yes, he told me about his older brother, but nothing about his lady friend. Could it be that William is eyeing this lady's fortune?"

"It's possible."

"Will she be coming to Calcutta?"

"I'd imagine so. They all do. But, it might be that he's changed his mind about marrying her. He likely still owns that house in Calcutta, where his former *bibi* lived, and wishes you to stay there."

"I am not sure how I can trust such a man. What do you think?" I said, as tears welled in my eyes.

Catherine put her hand on my shoulder, and gave it a gentle squeeze. "It's up to you, really. Look, I'd suggest you be very careful. Ask him about his betrothed, and his intensions, before you decide moving to Calcutta. It's a major undertaking, I should think." Catherine obviously did not wish to divulge any more details. She simply added, "And, please, not a word to him, or anyone else, about how you obtained this information."

I nodded, dabbing my eyes with a handkerchief. We heard footsteps on the verandah.

"Oh, I believe the Millers have arrived. If you'll excuse me, I'll go and receive them. Take heart, Margaret, dear. I'm sure you'll make the right decision." She smiled and patted my shoulder.

I thanked her for her kindness. She left the room saying, "Come and join us when you are ready."

I sat on the sofa for some time, my mind in a daze. In a way I felt relieved, for Catherine's statement had confirmed my suspicion that Humphrey was not being honest with me. Of course gentlemen had their lady friends, and I would not have been surprised if he knew some in Calcutta, London or elsewhere. I would have even accepted that. But to be actually engaged, and not mention it to me, yet professing his love for me, was just beyond belief.

I dabbed my eyes, as tears started to drip down again. However, a little calm voice from the back of my head whispered what Catherine had also said. Something about him having possibly broken off with that woman. Well, if that was true, or he was in the process of terminating his engagement, then surely there was no need to tell me about it, at least not at that moment, was it? Anyway, I decided to first have a good talk with Humphrey, before responding to his suggestion to move with him to Calcutta.

Although my mind was still in a whirl, I got up from the sofa with a heavy heart. Even though it had been over a year since my beloved Robert's death, he was still very much in my mind. Furthermore, the thought of having to face his murderer, Albert, now in the garden, grieved me even more. Somehow, I managed to compose myself, and looking into the mirror over Catherine's dressing table, wiped the tears off my cheeks that looked flushed. It was a good thing that I did not wear any mascara or rouge, for my face would have been in a mess. Nevertheless, I had a quick wash at the washbasin, and straightening out the creases in my gown, and putting my bonnet back on, I walked out of Catherine's bedroom, towards the back yard.

Although dreading meeting Nancy and Albert again, I put on a brave face and my best smile, when I spotted them seated at the table with the Herfords. I had hardly take a few steps out of the back door, when Nancy immediately jumped from her chair and came swiftly towards me. She looked her usual radiant self, dressed in a pink silk gown with frills, and wearing expensive looking jewelry. "Hallo, Margaret, what a lovely surprise to see you! And we saw your handsome boy earlier, too! What a gorgeous baby!"

"Thank you, Nancy." We embraced and exchanged kisses on the cheeks. Albert also came wobbling forward, drink in hand, his red uniform jacket stretched over his protruding belly. He bowed and extended his arm towards the table. Captain Herford stood and pulled out a chair for me. I walked over and sat beside Catherine. Nancy and Albert sat opposite us.

"So, tell us, Margaret, about this wonderful apartment you have moved to, in a grand *haveli* I hear," Nancy squealed.

The batman arrived and I gave him my drink request of white wine. "Hardly an apartment. Just two rooms, in a crumbling old mansion, really." I proceeded to tell her about the place, but in lesser detail than I had mentioned to the Herfords earlier.

"Oh, I think it's an absolutely fascinating location. As if living in an Arabian Nights palace. I would love to see it."

Everyone guffawed at her crude attempted wit. I did not respond to her oblique request for a visit, and merely smiled.

"Are you paying any rent?" Albert asked, stone-faced.

I almost glared at him, at his implied transgression on my part. I thought that he is just the same old lewd Albert, always with wicked thoughts. "Of course I have to," I replied. "My family doesn't own mills around here," I said, with an obvious reference to Albert's lucrative family's business in Canada.

While others laughed, Albert turned red. Yes, squirm you rascal, my husband's murderer, I thought. I should have finished you off, with my Robert's revolver, that afternoon on that Turkish beach. Perhaps I might get another opportunity here, and hoped it would come soon, before he raped and killed me, for I believed that was his motive in coming to Delhi after me, was it not? Wild deliberations raced through my mind, until I noted the batman putting a glass of white wine before me. I took a large sip of the refreshing liquid. It calmed me somewhat.

"How is your family, in Canada, Nancy?" Catherine asked.

"Oh, all very well, thank you. Our children are with their grandmamma and grandpapa, Colonel Mitchell, you know, and ...." Just the mention of that Colonel's name, brought his fiendish face before my eyes. My mind wandered again. I recalled when, in Grimsby, despite my tearful pleadings, he had steadfastly refused to rescind his order to send my dear Robert to Crimea. Nancy rattled on and on about her family and my mind meandered to thoughts of my two lovely children with their granny, also in Canada.

Nancy soon captured my full attention, when I heard her say, "And, Margaret, I have been meaning to tell you. Guess what Father wrote to me, recently?"

"Why, has he got another promotion?" I responded facetiously, but I hoped what she was about to say, concerned my children.

"No, not yet, anyway. He wrote that at the request of Mrs. Wallace, your mother-in-law, he has procured passage for her, her two daughters, *and* your two youngsters!"

"Oh! Is that for their trip to Crimea?" I asked with excitement.

"Yes, to visit *our* dear Robert's grave."

I noted Albert look the other way, when she said *'our'*. Ignoring him, I asked, with elation, "And when will this happen?"

"This Spring. As soon as Lake Ontario unfreezes, likely in April. They will sail for Halifax and from there catch a ship for Europe. I am sure they will stop in London first, and ...."

I did not hear her other details. Just the thought of seeing my children again, in only a few months, set my heart fluttering. Nancy stopped talking only when servants started serving the first course.

While we ate and engaged in amiable conversation, my mind still reflected on my infants. Then another thought crossed my mind and I asked, "So, Nancy, did Colonel Mitchell write, when they might be in India?"

"Well, he did write that your cousin Heather had approached him to extend the trip to India. But it seems there is some difficulty in arranging that part of the journey from Canada. They might have to book the passage when in London."

Turning towards me, Captain Herford interjected: "I am sure they will be able to get aboard one of our Company's vessels. Perhaps I'll have a word with our friend, Colonel Humphrey. He's an influential person. He should be able to arrange their passage without much difficulty. Would it be all right with you, if I spoke to him?"

While Catherine looked at me uneasily, I felt I had little choice, but to respond, "That would be most kind of you Captain Herford."

Although I felt apprehensive about getting Humphrey involved in my affairs, particularly related to my children, I decided to put disturbing thoughts out of my mind. I enjoyed my meal and joined in the general conversation around the table.

The subject of the upcoming Christmas Ball at Metcalf House came up. Nancy elaborated on her choice of the gown for that evening, and again offered to lend me one of hers. Even though I did not have a suitable outfit, I politely declined her overture intended likely to demean me. A thought occurred to me to perhaps ask Mumtaz, if she could lend me one of her exquisite silk saris. I believed it would be quite appropriate to arrive there, with flair, dressed in an elegant Indian attire. After all the ball was in Delhi.

Later in the carriage with Jan and Elgin, on our way back to the Sharif Mahal, pleasing thoughts of having my children finally with me in India came back to me. I mentioned the possibility of their arrival to Elgin, and she was thrilled to hear it. I considered several options for the living arrangements. I might ask the Sharif's for another room, or perhaps move to another house, but could I afford to? And what about their clothing and education? I made a mental note to ask around for a suitable school and inquire about the fees.

But then, if I moved to Calcutta, with Humphrey, would not these problems disappear? These ideas, and future plans, churned in my mind, as the *tonga* jangled its way through the streets of Delhi.

Eventually, the Saturday of the Christmas Ball at Metcalf House arrived. It was another one of those lovely early winter days, and the evening was not too cold, but just balmy enough to enable gentlemen and particularly ladies to dress up in their fineries.

That afternoon, I finished a leisurely bath in the ladies' *ghusalkhana*—situated downstairs in the zenana wing of the *haveli*— in a metallic tub that was likely purchased by the Sharifs especially for me. I did not think the Indian ladies bathed in a bathtub, rather preferring to douse themselves, standing up, with cups of water from a bucket. Returning to my bedroom, I saw the exquisite red silken Indian dress having colorful flowery patterns with intricate golden embroidery, and white silk pajamas laid out on the bed. Elgin had just finished ironing the outfit.

Some days ago, when I had requested borrowing the dress from Mumtaz, she had immediately held my hand and led me to her storage room. There she had opened several chests and kept taking out outfits, each lovelier than the other, until I told her to stop, for with so many to choose from, it was nearly impossible to select one. Mumtaz thought the one I had picked was too simple, but I managed to assure her that it was elegant enough, and I normally preferred to dress modestly.

On seeing me, Elgin held up the silken *dupatta*, "Will you be wearing this, Memsahib? Should I iron it? European ladies don't wear it, you know."

I had seen most Indian women wearing that long scarf around their neck and over their breasts, but having difficulty keeping it on their shoulders, for it kept sliding off. Fearing I might have the same problem during the dancing, I responded, "I think I'll skip that, but will take my red pashmina shawl, in case it gets chilly."

"Yes, that should match the dress. Let me fetch it." She opened my sea chest and proceeded to look for it in there.

I slipped off my bath robe, and while drying myself with a towel looked in the mirror. I was glad to see that with all the work activity in Delhi, I had lost some of the weight I had put on, and was beginning to return to my slim figure. Although I still had to lose some off my breasts and hips, and noted that I would need to wear a corset. I asked Elgin to also fish it out from my coffer.

Elgin had just finished helping me dress, when there was a knock on the door and Mumtaz entered, carrying a jewelry box in her hand. "I bring this set, seeing that you go naked to a grand party," she said opening the red velvet case.

Although the sight of the glittering jewelry set—a necklace having a row of leaf-shaped diamonds and rubies, and matching earrings and bracelets—bewildered me, I murmured, "Oh, no, Mumtaz. No thank you. I could not possibly wear them."

"Why not? Look rubies match your red dress." She held up the necklace in her hand. "It complete your attire. Without jewelry is not good. Otherwise you look naked! Only for tonight. You return them tomorrow."

I was intending to wear the only pearl necklace that I owned, and it went with all my dresses, but thinking about the Indian costume, I realized she certainly has a point about the 'nakedness' and relented. "Alright, I'll borrow it. But only for tonight. You are too kind, Mumtaz."

While Elgin helped me to put on the jewelry, Mumtaz went over to Jan's cot and picked him up. "I take pretty Jan baba now. I look after him, as my own. You have good dinner party, and dancing too, of course!" She rolled her head.

"Thank you, Mumtaz. I am happy to leave him with you." I gave the sleeping Jan a kiss on his cheek. Mumtaz left the room, saying, "I get Sharif to fetch a carriage for you." Noticing that she walked with some difficulty, I thought she was likely close to her delivery date.

While I applied some mascara and rouge, Elgin put on a decent looking, but faded, blue dress—likely one of Mamma's hand downs. Elgin helped me with my pink cape, and I donned its hood to avoid getting my fair ringleted hair blown about in the wind. She wrapped herself in her usual grey woolen shawl that needed a wash. I made a mental note to buy the poor child a decent cloak. As we strutted down the stairs towards the entrance I noticed inquisitive eyes peeking at us from behind doors and windows. Ascending the waiting carriage, we were ready to attend the grand Delhi Christmas Ball at Metcalf House. I felt happy and was looking forward to it.

Chapter Fifteen

Christmas Ball at the Metcalf House

1855-6, December – January: Delhi, India
"HOW ARE YOU GETTING ALONG in the *haveli's* kitchen?" I asked Elgin, seated across from me in the carriage, as it clattered on its way through Delhi's narrow streets.

"Very good, memsahib. I happy working there. I like cooking the tasty food."

"Yes, I see you've learned to cook in the Mughal style. But is anyone bothering you there?"

"No. Even I am Christian, they are nice to me. But just this morning, one woman tell me something?"

"Yes, what was it?"

"She from the Gujjar tribe. Said, Mr. Metcalf's father took away their whole village and farms to build the grand mansion we are going to."

"That was Sir Thomas. But I am sure he would have paid for the land." I had heard that unlike other officers of the Company, he had decided to stay somewhat permanently in Delhi and had built not only this house but another one in the south of the city.

"The Gujjar woman say, the *goora*-sahib not pay enough. Her family now very poor. And Sir Thomas died soon, because of the curse."

"A curse! What nonsense. He was getting old, and in this climate, it was likely of natural causes." Then I remembered what Colonel Humphrey had mentioned. He believed Sir Thomas was poisoned, most likely at the behest of Begum Zinat Mahal. Not wanting to bother young Elgin with another rumor, hence on a lighter note, I said, "I am glad mangoes are not in season."

"Why, memsahib?" She looked puzzled.

"I understand Sir Thomas preferred ladies to eat them only in a bathtub! And now his son, Sir Theophilus, might carry on the tradition."

Elgin laughed. "I hope not, for you will surely get mango juice on your beautiful Indian dress!"

A cool wind blew in through the carriage window. I wrapped the pashmina shawl around my shoulders and wondered what the reaction of Delhi's gentry at the ball would be to my attire.

The carriage left the pandemonium of the city, and travelled on the road outside the Red Fort's wall towards Metcalf Estates. It soon turned into the long cypress trees lined driveway, through the main gates of the property. While I had seen Metcalf House previously, only from a distance, it appeared much grander as we drew nearer the mansion. I spotted gardens of colorful flower beds and orange groves that extended up to the banks of the Jamuna River. The coach stopped at steps leading up to the wide stone verandah. The row of marble columns, supporting the roof, shone in the evening sunlight. It looked they had been washed particularly for the occasion. A red drugget covered the bottom steps up to the front entrance. I felt as if we had arrived at a Gothic mansion.

Several Indian servants dressed in red tunics and white trousers busied about. One of them opened the carriage door and helped us descend. While Elgin took my cape and shawl, and was directed towards the servants' entrance, I joined the other invitees proceeding to the hallway. I glimpsed through the windows the impressive drawing room with alluring paintings on the walls, bouquet of flowers on side tables, and Christmas decorations on miniature bushes in the corners; all presented a festive atmosphere.

The aroma of perfume and alcohol, intermingled with smoke from the fire places, permeated the drawing room. The scent of wealth, I thought. A British sergeant announced the guests into the reception area, who were being greeted by a lineup of the hosts. Taking my invitation card from my reticule, I handed it to the sergeant. He barely looked at it.

"Begum ... err ..." Realizing his error, the sergeant quickly read my card. Red faced, he corrected himself in a louder voice, "Doctor Margaret Wallace," Some of the guests, standing nearby in groups drinks in hand, turned around and looked quizzically at me.

Before I could say anything, Sir Theophilus Metcalf, elegantly dressed in a formal dark suit and cravat, came forward and bowed. "Doctor Wallace, please allow me to apologize for my Sergeant-At-Arms' indiscretion. He mistook you for someone else."

I curtsied. "No apologies needed, Sir Theophilus." While the other invitees returned to their conversation, and no doubt commented in whispers on my dress, he led me to the first lady clad classily in a black gown, in the reception line. "Doctor Margaret Wallace ... my sister, Mrs. Emily Bayley."

She shook my hand. "Welcome Doctor Margaret. So pleased to meet you. Are you settling in nicely here?"

"Yes. I am."

"Glad to hear that. My, what a wonderful outfit! I've heard that Indian costumes are the rave in London this season. I've been meaning to get one myself, for we are to depart for home soon."

"Thank you. You are too kind," I responded, feeling happy that she, as the hostess, approved of my attire. I moved along to be introduced to her younger sister, Lady Georgina Campbell, and the other dignitaries.

At the end of the line stood my benefactor, Commissioner Fraser. "Good to see you, Margaret. Are they treating you well, at the *haveli*?"

"Yes. Thank you, sir. Very well." We shook hands.

"I can see that." He smiled. "Must admit I didn't recognize you, when you entered, in this lovely Indian dress."

Before I could respond, someone behind me said, "I would recognize Margaret in any outfit." I turned around to see a red coated officer, well-groomed and smartly dressed, in the full formal regalia—with medals—in a colonel's uniform. I was taken aback, for it was Humphrey, holding a glass of whisky in hand. It seemed he had been lurking around just waiting for the first opportunity to swoop upon me.

"Thank you, sir. But I am sure you must be very familiar with Indian clothing."

"If I may say so, the attire suits you." He seemed to have ignored my snide remark, and added, "We have been expecting you. Care to join us?" He motioned towards a group standing to one side of the fireplace at the back of the room.

I turned towards Baron Metcalf, still beside me. "Thank you for inviting me, Sir Theophilus. You have a lovely home. I've heard so much about it. Particularly the Napoleon room."

"That's part of my dear father's art collection. I'll be happy to show you around, later perha—"

"Oh, Theo, you'll likely be too busy. I'll be delighted to take Margaret around your impressive grange." Humphrey interjected.

"Certainly, Will," Mr. Metcalf bowed and left us.

Although annoyed at his butting-in, however not wishing to be impolite, I took Humphrey's arm and he led me towards the Herfords and the Millers. They stood around in a circle, drinks in hand.

"Margaret!" Nancy shrieked, no sooner than she saw me, and came hurriedly forward, nearly spilling champagne on her dark gown shimmering with silver inlays. We embraced and kissed like lost sisters. "Oh my, look at you. You've turned out like a mongol princess. I heard a "begum" being announced, but didn't realize it was you! You'll be the belle of the ball." I complimented her on her attire, but she went on and on about mine, as we joined the others.

I shook hands all-round, and they each commented favorably on my getup. I noted Albert, dressed in his too tightfitting uniform, glancing slyly at my thighs and legs that showed shapely through the silken fabric. He is still his same lecherous self, I thought. Picking up a fluted glass of champagne from a server's tray, I held it up. "Merry Christmas, everyone." They responded in kind. The sweet sparkling wine tasted refreshing, and put me at ease. The last few week had been stressful, with the move, and at work and College. I looked forward to an enjoyable evening. But a whisper in the back of my mind, warned me to be cautious.

Humphrey looked into his empty whisky glass. "I don't care much for champagne. I'll go get a refill." He sauntered off towards the bar.

Catherine, standing next to me, also dressed in an eye-catching dark evening gown and fetching pearl earrings and necklace, asked, "Any news from home?"

"Yes, I had a letter from my cousin Heather. They are all well, and would be sailing in the spring, with my dear children for London, and then on to Crimea."

"Yes. My father is organizing their trip." Nancy piped in.

You had told us that already, I wanted to retort, instead asked, "Any more on extending their passage to India?"

"No. Just what Father wrote. They will have to arrange that with the Company's offices in London," she responded.

What a half-baked arrangement. Typical of Colonel Mitchell. I fumed. It must have shown on my face, for Catherine said, "That reminds me." She turned towards her husband. "Jack, have you spoken with Colonel Humphrey, about getting them on a Company's boat?"

"No, not yet. But I will," he said.

"Thank you, I am so looking forward to having my children here," I said. But had a strange feeling in the pit of my stomach, wishing they wouldn't involve Humphrey in this.

"Whose children are we talking about?" Humphrey returned, his drink in hand.

Captain Herford looked towards Humphrey. "Margaret's, sir. Her aunt is due to leave shortly ...." He proceeded to explain the circumstances. I was talking to others, and heard him say in closing, "... Margaret is anxious to have her children here."

"I am sure she is." Humphrey looked at me and smiled. "I'll see what can be done."

Although it seemed his grin had a hidden message, I murmured, "That would be kind of you, sir."

The fate of my children having been taken care of—more likely left to the wind, I thought—Nancy and Catherine proceeded to talk about their children, with Humphrey also joining in, now and then, with a jovial comment about his daughters. While I listened and smiled politely, my mind was still on my two youngsters. I wondered if they remembered their mother, and what they now looked like. In my letter to Cousin Heather, I had requested their photographs. While she had written that she would send them, I was still waiting to see their cheery faces in every letter. The delay seemed to be another one of Aunt Fiona's malice towards me. She had likely forbidden it, for she still continued to blame me for her son—my dear husband, Robert—being sent off to die in Crimea.

At the sound of a gong, my mind was brought back to the ball. "Ladies and gentlemen. Dinner is served. Please take your seats." The butler announced.

"Our seats are in the main banquet room," Humphrey proudly whispered to me. I was certain he had had a hand in arranging it, as he seemed to have a say in most matters, and officials listened to him. But little did they know of his carnal desires. I mused. Nevertheless, he offered me his arm, and holding on to it we proceeded towards the banquet room. I noticed the Millers and Herfords were seated in a side dining room.

The place settings' silver cutlery, crystal glasses and china, on the long dining table, shone in the candlelight from the numerous chandeliers. Servants pulled back the polished mahogany chairs with carved eastern patterns. Humphrey waited till I sat. Mr. Taylor was seated next to me, and bid me a good evening. I was happy to see him for he was someone I knew and could talk to about Delhi College, and other literary matters. I noticed Annie Jennings sitting across the table smiling, in recognition, at me. I acknowledged her with a nod.

Following grace and a toast to the Queen, led by Reverend Jennings, the banquet commenced. Smartly dressed servants went about performing their tasks, promptly. I was happy to see, listed on the menu card, other than the usual turkey and roast beef, some Indian dishes, which I relished. All were washed down with an excellent complement of fine wines.

The general talk around the dinner table was the usual: politics and the conditions in India. Actually, there had been relative calm and serenity around, and the state of affairs in the country were generally good. Someone thought it was remarkable. Humphrey responded that the credit for the 'English peace' was due to the presence of the Company and the good efforts of the Governor General, Lord Dalhousie. There were murmurs of, "Hear ... hear." While, I smiled at that remark wishing to add a comment on how it had all come about, financially, but held my tongue lest I spoil the mood at the dinner table. Others did inquire about the situation in Oudh, and the nawab's dalliances. Humphrey responded in general terms and was coy about the Company's decisions and the direction he was about to participate in. When a junior officer indicated that he had heard of some unrest in the sepoy ranks, he was quickly put down by a senior officer with medals all over his chest, as that talk was "sheer nonsense."

I conversed a bit with Mr. Taylor, and was pleased to hear him mention that: "Professor Ramchandra is very happy with the work you are doing for him."

While savoring the trifle for dessert, I heard musical sounds coming from outside. Through the windows, I noticed musicians setting up under a large tent in the back garden.

"It's the regimental band tuning up," Humphrey informed me. "Are you up to some dancing, Margaret?"

"Yes. I haven't been to a dance since I left Futtehgurh."

"How are your parents, and sister?"

He forgot I had a brother as well. "My parents, my sister *and* brother, are all well. Thank you. They'll be visiting Delhi during the Christmas break."

"Ah, good. I hope I'll be here to meet them."

"When do you leave?"

"Early in January, I believe. Waiting to hear from Outram."

I knew he meant the Resident at Oudh, but before I could question him any further, hearing a chair scrape on the floor, I looked up and saw Sir Theophilus standing at the head of the table. He welcomed all, and mentioned some notable guests: Colonel Humphrey and others. Everyone turned their eyes on me, when he stated that it was comforting to finally have a lady doctor stationed in Delhi. I nodded my appreciation. He delivered a rambling speech on various topics, but was thankfully brief, for I wanted to visit the ladies room. He ended by inviting all to come out to the back garden, and enjoy the evening, drinks, and dancing.

On the way to the water closet I sent word to have Elgin fetch my shawl, which she did. The band was playing light tunes when I stepped down from the rear veranda steps on the path leading up to the tented enclosure. Although the sun had set, the garden was charmingly lit with Chinese lanterns held on strings from tree branch to tree branch. Since the wind had died down, it felt pleasantly warm, and I just let the pashmina rest over my shoulders. Tables were arranged, under the tent, around a wood dance floor. The band was located at one side.

I searched for my friends, through the groups of people milling around. Humphrey had commandeered a table for six and waved to me. He pulled out a chair for me. Jack and Albert were already there; Nancy and Catherine were delayed a bit, but soon joined us.

When Humphrey got up to go and meet someone he knew, Catherine sitting next to me, leaned and whispered, "Have you spoken to him yet about ... you know?"

"No, not yet." I whispered back. "But I am sure he will bring up the subject soon enough."

A waiter came by and took our drink orders. I requested white wine, and Catherine only water. I asked, "How is your health, Catherine?"

"I am feeling much better, thanks to your medications and rest suggestion. In this heat alcohol bothers me."

I nodded.

"And, how are you settling in Delhi, Nancy?" I asked.

"Oh, it's too quiet here. It was much livelier in Calcutta. Albert likes it here, though."

"We've just got here." Albert sipped his drink. "Haven't seen much of the city yet."

"Oh, I'd love to meet Queen Zinat." Nancy squealed. "I know you have been to see her, Margaret. Can you take me along next time?"

"You would be disappointed," I said. "They don't live as royally now as they used to."

The band began to play a lovely waltz tune, which got us tapping our feet. Couples started to move towards the dance floor. Nancy jumped up. "Come on Albert. Let's dance." Albert put his drink down and followed her.

Catherine and Jack, not wishing to leave me sitting alone at the table, started to talk to me about my work at the Delhi College, until finally Humphrey returned.

"Sorry to leave you alone, Margaret," he said, and taking a sip of his whiskey, put the glass down on the table. "My, what delightful music. Margaret, may I have the pleasure of this dance?"

"Of course, William." Although I had not intended to call him by his first name, I blurted it out, possibly because he was being so charming.

He offered me his arm, and we walked towards the dance floor. "I am glad we are on first name basis again, Margaret. Does it mean that I am forgiven?"

"I wouldn't be so sure of that." I smiled.

"I need to work at it some more, do I?"

"Perhaps."

We started to dance. "My very first dance with you, Margaret. I must say you dance skillfully."

"Have attended far too many officers' dance parties. I might be a bit rusty, though."

"Not at all. You glide gracefully." He was a nimble dancer as well, and drew me closer to him. I did not resist. We enjoyed the dance. I saw others watching us.

"Tell me, where did you obtain this beautiful Indian costume?"

"In Chandni Chowk. At my landlord's shop." I lied.

"It's lovely. Suits your exquisite figure."

"It might be a bit tight on me. But thank you William."

He asked me more about my new residence, and seemed to be satisfied, by saying, "Well, if you are happy there, it's all that matters. But, do keep your eyes and ears open."

"Always, do." I responded.

Completing the dance, we returned to the table. Nancy and Albert were still dancing. Humphrey went to get another drink and meet some more friends. I danced the next one with Jack. While he moved reasonably well, but danced very formally, keeping a proper distance between us.

When we came back to the table, and I had barely sat down and sipped my wine, when Albert jumped up and asked me to dance. I said, "No, thank you Albert. I'm a bit tired. Later perhaps?" He looked disappointed, and slumped back down on his chair. Nancy glanced sharply at me. I ignored her. In retrospect, considering Albert's mental state, I should have had that dance with him, for it's never helpful to aggravate such unbalanced persons. But I couldn't bring myself for him to touch me again. It would have brought back a flood of those dreadful memories from our past. I still wondered why he had followed me to India.

Some of the Delhi ladies passed by, and greeted me and wished me a Merry Christmas. I had seen a number of them at the hospital, and inquired after their health. While chatting with others around our table, I noticed Albert glowering at me. I took no notice of him.

Emily Bayley and Sir Theophilus came by and asked if we were enjoying the evening. I thanked them and also expressed my condolences at the death of their father, two years ago, and as well the passing of Sir Theophilus' wife in the same year. He sighed, and thanked me, saying that it was a dreadful year, one they have not quite recovered from yet.

Humphrey returned, and asked me to the floor again. We started to dance and he held me even closer, our thighs touching. It might have looked improper, but I did not care. Somehow I felt secure in his arms.

It was likely then that I made up my mind about accepting his earlier proposition. Nevertheless, I expected him to let me know about, if not all, most of his previous relationships, and of course his plans for our future. I hoped there would be an opportunity to discuss those with him that night.

It seemed he still had something on his mind, and asked, "How is Zinat? Have you seen her again?" Not addressing her as the 'queen' his disdain for her was obvious.

"No, not since the last time you took me to the palace. Although Doctor Chaman Lal mentioned to me, after his recent visit to tend to King Zafar, the queen wished to see me and will be sending for me soon."

"Hmm ... I wonder what's ailing her now." Humphrey chuckled. "As I asked earlier, could you please let me know if you hear or see anything odd over there?"

I only nodded, for I did not relish having spying added to my curative duties. By then a bright moon had appeared and lit up the Metcalf House. To change the subject, I said, "Look William. Doesn't the mansion appear magnificent in the moon light?"

"Yes, it certainly does. Sir Thomas must have taken great care and attention while having it built."

"It looks like he did. I've heard he loved collecting art and memorabilia."

"Yes, he was a connoisseur. He has a rooms full of relics. Did you not say you wished to see his Napoleonic collection?"

"Napoleon intrigues me."

"I know where those artifacts are. After this dance, would you like to have a look?"

"Yes, I'd love to. Especially when Sir Theo has given us permission to rummage around his home."

Humphrey laughed. "He has, indeed."

We danced, enjoying the moment. When the dance ended, we walked back to our table. Only Catherine and Jack were seated there. I collected my reticule and shawl. "I'm going to take Margaret around the house," Humphrey told them.

Catherine nodded, a knowing smile appearing on her face. We

started towards the mansion. "Don't get lost," Jack called after us. He was ignored.

We climbed up the stairs of the rear veranda and walked along the hallway. A long row of rooms were situated at one side. Each had a large door opening onto the patio. Humphrey seemed to know the place intimately. Although servants walked by, he did not ask for directions, and opened one door into a spacious chamber. "Here we are. The Napoleon Gallery room." Upon entering it I was amazed on seeing the walls covered with engravings and paintings, of not only Napoleon, but also his generals, and scenes of his famous battles. I was attracted by an object in one corner. On a pedestal stood an exquisite marble bust of Napoleon. I stared at it for it looked so real.

"Sculpted by the famous Venetian, Antonio Canova," Humphrey informed me.

I had heard of the renowned artist, and could only exclaim in admiration, "Oh, my. What a lovely figure! Very realistic."

"Come look at this." Humphrey directed me to the center of the room. A glass case covered some objects on a table. Placed in there were, Napoleon's Cross of the Legion of Honor, and his diamond ring. "Do you see his initials on it?"

"Yes, I do. How did Sir Thomas come to possess these?"

"He purchased them from Mr. William Fraser, the former commissioner. I understand they were gifted to Fraser by Napoleon himself. Sent during his exile in St. Helena."

"What a precious collection. How interesting."

We browsed around at other articles and the numerous leather bound books. "The house is just on one floor is it?" I asked. "Wondering if there was a second floor."

"Yes, one floor. But there are some *tehkhanas*, underground rooms. Used as billiards and games rooms. Would you like to see? I believe that door there opens to the stairs down below."

"Yes. Please lead the way."

We walked down the stairs to the passageway leading to the *tehkhanas*. Lanterns hanging on the walls lit the areas, likely in anticipation that some guests may wish to play billiards. Entering a room, I noticed billiards and card tables, chairs, and sofas were placed all around. But it seemed no one was interested in having a game. However, the dim light from the lanterns created a romantic atmosphere in the cavern like chamber.

Humphrey led me to a couch at one corner, and we sat down. I expected, we could then have a talk in private. He put one arm around my shoulders. "You do look like a princess, tonight, my dear."

"Oh, I'm certain you have seen many princesses in similar dresses. Haven't you?"

"Not as lovely as you."

That provided me the opening, I was waiting for. "How about Begum Zebunisah?"

He looked stunned, and straightened up, taking his arm off my shoulders. But soon regained his composure. "Who told you about her?"

"It's not important. It was common knowledge. She was living with you, wasn't she?"

"It was a long time ago, after the death of my wife, and my daughters returning to England. I was left alone in Calcutta."

I looked at him. "Why didn't you marry her?"

"How could I? It's not the done thing now. Besides, she wanted me to change my religion. But I'm no David Ochterlony, you know."

His explanation sounded odd, so I asked, "Did you love her?"

He averted my eyes, and looked towards the ceiling. "I might have initially, but I am not certain now. I also had to leave for home." He then turned towards me, and again put his right arm over my shoulder. "Believe me, Margaret. It's long over with her."

I did doubted that, for knowing she lived in Oudh, it did seem peculiar that Humphrey visited there often. Anyhow, I asked, "Is there anyone else you care about?"

He again stiffened. But kept his arm about me. "I am certain your source would have told you about my betrothal to Lady Sofia, in London?"

"Yes."

"It's all over with her as well." He pulled me closer towards him. "We are no longer engaged." But he did not look at me when he said it.

It sounded strange as well, so I inquired, "Why did you break it off?"

"She did. She wasn't inclined to live in India." He put his other arm around me as well, and hugged me. "It's only you I care about now, my dear Margaret." He tried to kiss me, but I moved my face away.

It did not sound convincing, for if it was true, Catherine would have known about it. "You never told me you wished to stay long in India."

"I'm telling you now. I know you like it here, and so do I."

"So, now you want me to come to Calcutta?"

"Yes, my darling. Wouldn't it be so wonderful, for us to be together? As I mentioned, I'll get you a better job, likely as the head of a whole medical department. And you can bring all your children there. We'll hire nannies and governesses for them. They'll go to the best schools. Just think of it. It would be a grand life for you."

While all his talk sounded sweet, he still had not said the magic words, I wished to hear: 'love', 'marriage', 'wedding', or even a 'betrothal'. He again tried to kiss me on the lips, but when I wouldn't let him, licked my cheek and nibbled on my ear.

"Please stop," I said.

He did not listen. "Why Margaret? Don't you care even a bit for me?" He murmured, and putting his hand on my bosom, tried to caress my breasts.

I pushed his hand away. "Kindly stop. Someone might come in."

"Alright, why don't we go somewhere else? I know a nice Indian dance house. We can sit and watch the dancing girls, have some wine. Would you like that?"

I knew he meant a brothel, where they likely also rented out private rooms. "No, thank you. It's getting late. I should go home now." I tried to break out of his hold, wanting to get up. But he held me down on the sofa.

"Oh, my dear, you are always pushing me away. What do you want from me?"

Although he might have expected me to, I was not about to stoop so low as to break out in tears on his shoulder, tell him that I loved him, and beg him to marry me. He disgusted me. Gathering all my strength I managed to jump up from the couch. He stared at me, as I stood looking at him.

"What I least want to do, is to become your *bibi*," I said calmly.

As I walked towards the doorway, I heard him shout, "Don't do anything you might regret later."

"What's there to regret." I shouted back. However, indeed, I would subsequently lament the consequences of that action. Nevertheless, I believe I had made the right decision.

Later, returning home in a buggy with Elgin, I felt happy, yet in a way concerned. I wondered if I had thrown away an incredible opportunity, to live the life of luxury, like those of the landed gentry, to have no financial worries and have servants at my beck and call, and all the needs of my children taken care of. However, what kind of a life was that with someone when there was no mutual love between the couples, and he merely desired you carnally? Suddenly, the thought of my children brought my mind back to reality. I was eager to see my son, Jan. For something in my head told me to reach home as soon as possible.

It was past midnight and the streets of Delhi were nearly deserted. The carriage drove speedily, and turned into the *haveli's* narrow laneway. But when it shot past the house, I looked inquiringly at Elgin. She thrust her head out of the window, and shouted up at the driver, "You have gone past Sharif Khan sahib's residence."

"Ahh, I thought you said, Saleem Khan's house," he hollered. "Okay I go back."

As he pulled on one rein, and cracked his whip, to force the poor horse turn in a tight circle; the creature darted forward. When the buggy spun around, one of its rear wheels fell into the drainage channel at the side of the lane, nearly overturning itself. Some passersby upon hearing the ruckus ran up to help. One of them held the steed by the bridle and tried to pull him forward. The horse attempted to move, but its shod hooves just scraped on the cobblestones. Fearing the vehicle might topple, I shouted at them to stop, and opening the door, Elgin and I jumped out.

In the dark street, I looked towards the *haveli* in the distance. There were lights shining from only one of its apartments on the second floor's corner. My heart began to beat fast, when I realized it was Mumtaz and Sharif's flat. I thrust some money in Elgin's hand, and asking her to settle with the *tongawalla,* I ran towards the house.

On reaching the massive doors, using the elephant-head metal knocker, I pounded it loudly.

Soon, Sharif opened the wicket gate. "Doctor Margaret! Please come in. We waiting for you." He looked curiously towards the carriage stuck in the gutter down the lane.

I hurried inside to the courtyard. "Is anything the matter? How is my son?"

In the moonlight, I saw his nervous look. But it was most relieving to hear him say, "Jaan baba all right. Not to worry, he sleeping good." My concern returned, when he added, "It is my wife Mumtaz. Not well."

"Oh! Is she having her baby?"

"I think so."

"Did her water break?"

The young man—he was hardly twenty-years-old—looked puzzled. "What do you mean?"

"Never mind. Is the *dai* here?"

"Yes, but she say, baby no come. Something wrong. Also no *hakim* available. They all out of home. That's why we waiting for you."

"Alright, let me take a look. Is hot water available?"

"No. Do you like tea?"

"No, no, for washing. Can you ask someone to bring, to Mumtaz's room, hot water in a bowl? And, yes, also tea for me please."

"Yes, I get a girl to do it." He walked towards the kitchen.

Elgin had also arrived in the courtyard. We sped up the stairs. Reaching the second floor, I asked, "Elgin, can you fetch my medical bag, please?" While she rushed towards my rooms, I hurried to Mumtaz's apartment. A group of Sharif's relatives stood outside in the corridor, looking apprehensive. Some prayed, reciting verses in Arabic. I knocked, and was surprised to see their neighbor, Mr. Ali, open the door. Without any greeting, and with a stern face, he gestured at me to come inside.

I went straight up to Mumtaz, lying curled up in bed. Mrs. Ali sat beside her. Sharif's mother sat on the other side, mopping Mumtaz's brow. The *dai* sat cross-legged on a carpet at one side of the bed; she gave me a baffled look.

"How are you feeling, Mumtaz?" I asked.

"Ohhh .... doctor sahiba. I too much pain. I happy you come."

"This is your first baby, isn't it?"

"Yes, my first one. Dai say I no can have. Baby too big!" She started to sob. Sharif's mother comforted her. Her belly certainly looked huge, and visions of my experience while delivering Jan passed before my eyes.

"Stay calm, Mumtaz. I'll see what can be done. Where is Jan?"

Mumtaz pointed towards the next room. I went there and saw him, wrapped comfortably in a blanket, lying on a couch. Upon seeing him sleeping soundly, I felt reassured. Elgin had arrived with my medical bag. Putting the bag on a table, she gently picked up Jan and took him back to my apartment.

Sharif also came in the room, with two servant girls in tow. One carried a steaming bowl of hot water and the other a stack of towels and a cup of tea. They put them on the table. I told them in broken Urdu, "Need more hot water. Bring up kettle. *Maloom*?" They nodded and left.

"Is my wife going to be all right? What about the baby? He come?" Sharif asked anxiously.

"Calm down. I will examine Mumtaz, now. First, I would like you, your father, and Mr. Ali to stay out of her room."

Sharif motioned at them, and they reluctantly followed him out of the apartment. Taking off my rings and other jewelry, I washed and dried my hands, and took a gulp of the hot tea. The women stood to one side of Mumtaz's bed, when I approached her.

"Mumtaz, I need to examine you," I said pulling down her bedsheet and lifting up her *kameez*. She nodded. I asked her some more questions about her pains and symptoms, which confirmed that she was indeed in labor and was going to have her baby that night. She still wore her *shalwar*, and undoing its string I removed it.

My examination confirmed, what I had suspected. The baby, although positioned normally, was too large. Its head was lodged a bit high in the vagina and was having difficulty moving down. This was exactly what had been in my case, and I recalled Doctor Fleming having to use a mediolateral incision in the perineum. It seemed to be the only way to save her life and deliver her baby. But will the Sharifs agree to it? I did not think they approved of surgery, particularly during childbirth.

I put the bedsheets back over Mumtaz; she was still crying in pain. I rewashed my hands, and took a sip of the refreshing tea. Then opening the apartment's door, I motioned for Sharif and his father, Akbar, to come in. Mr. Ali also barged inside, and I could not stop him.

With the men standing around me, I explained Mumtaz's condition and the situation in simple terms, as well as I could. It took some time, for there was also the language barrier to overcome. They finally comprehended, what I was suggesting doing, and looked horrified at me. The women, standing beside the bed appeared to also understand and covered their mouth with their *duppatas* to suppress their exclamation.

Mrs. Ali explained my proposal, to the *dai*, as well as dramatized it by clenching her fist, as if holding an imaginary knife, and thrust it downward. The *dai* shrieked and waved her hands, "No, no, no. Don't do it memsaab."

"Let's wait till the morning for *hakim* sahib to come," Mr. Ali interjected.

I turned towards him. "I'm afraid, waiting until the morning would be too late." I then looked at Sharif. "What do you think?"

"I say we ask Mumtaz, what she want." He looked at her. "*Jaani*, what you like Doctor Margaret to do?"

Mumtaz help up both her arms and beckoned to me. I went up to her and held her hands. "Are you sure Doctor Margareet, you need to cut me to make baby come?"

"Yes, I am certain Mumtaz. Any delay will endanger both you and your child."

"Is it safe?" she asked.

"Yes, it is. The cut will heal nicely. And, if it is any consolation to you, a doctor did the same operation on me to deliver Jan."

"Ohh, Jaan baba born this way! Then I am happy. Please do the same to me." She squeezed my hands. I squeezed them in return to reassure her.

I looked towards Sharif and Akbar Khan.

Sharif looked at the floor.

"If the doctor say it's safe, and Mumtaz *bahu* wants it, then I agree. Let us follow doctor sahiba's suggestion," Akbar said in an authoritative voice. Being the eldest of the household, he had the final say.

Sharif nodded. However, Mr. Ali angrily persisted, "I still

disagree. What does a ferangi woman know ... she wants to butcher our girl ... is she really a doctor .... and ...," he kept babbling on and on. Sharif gently took him by the arm and led him outside the room, whispering, "*Areyy bhai* ...", and calming words to him. Akbar followed.

The maid returned with a boiling kettle of water. I asked her to replace the water in the basin. Taking out of my bag the sharpest scalpels and other instruments, I dropped them in the steaming water. I asked the dai to place some clean towels under Mumtaz's hips. But she stood in one corner with her arms folded, as if to say that she wished to take no part in the process. Sharif's mother stood, and removing the bedsheet placed the towels. Rewashing and drying my hands, I laid the instruments at one side of the bed and requested Mrs. Ali and Sharif's mother to hold Mumtaz's legs wide apart. They complied.

I got on the bed between Mumtaz's thighs, and recalling the procedure Doctor Fleming had used on me, I made the incision. Mumtaz screamed. She appeared to have fainted, but I was ready with the bottle of smelling salts that revived her. Looking down to see if there was much blood, I was gladdened to see the baby's head just protruding from the pudendum. I asked Mumtaz to push. She did, and the baby gently slid out onto my receiving hands. It was a girl. The dai seeing the successful birth, eventually decided to help, and coming forward with a clean towel, took the child from my hands.

I am not certain which sounds were louder, the baby's screams or the cheers of the Sharif Mahal's residents, gathered outside the door. I heard shouts of *Allah-ho-Akbar*. I finished my procedures on Mumtaz, and let the dai take over. She did her job, which she was good at. She took care of Mumtaz, and after washing and bundling the child in a cotton wrap, presented her to Mumtaz.

Tears ran down Mumtaz's cheeks as she cradled her whimpering baby. She looked up at me with eyes that expressed her gratitude. "Thank you, very, very much Doctor Margareet," she whispered. I asked if she felt all right, and she nodded.

Sharif opening the door, rushed in, followed by all those waiting outside. He asked how the mother and child were, and I told him they were well. While they all stood around the bed, trying to have a peek at the baby, I went to the adjoining room. After washing my hands and instruments, I repacked by medical bag, and with it in hand I walked quietly towards the apartment's door. I felt tired and did not wish to stay there and revel on my successful operation. Sharif's Mother and father, on seeing me leaving, came forward. Both expressed their gratitude. She embraced me and put her palms on my head; her way of saying thank you.

The false dawn light shone through the windows, as I trudged in wearily into my apartment. I was relieved upon seeing that Jan lay sleeping in his cot. Elgin, still dressed in her evening clothes, lay curled up on the couch. It seemed she had fallen asleep waiting for me. On hearing my footsteps, she woke up with a start. I told her the good news, and that everything was fine.

She was thrilled to hear it. "You like tea and breakfast, memsahib?"

I smiled, upon her remembering my hearty appetite for breakfast. "Yes, some chapattis and spicy omelet with masala chai, would be lovely."

While Elgin scampered down to cook and fetch my tea, I washed and changed. Since it was Sunday, I felt like sleeping the whole day. I walked back to my bedroom, took a peek again at my slumbering boy, and stood by the window. It was still early, for the morning cannon from the Ridge had not fired as yet, and a refreshing cool breeze blew in from the dark blue waters of the Jamuna River flowing at one side of the awakening city. While smoke from cooking fires curled up from a few mansions, I had been informed that some of the elite residents, having reveled all night in singing and *naatch* parties, would be just about going to bed.

As I breathed the refreshing air I heard the melodious sounds of a *muezzin's* call for prayer from one of the tall minarets of the nearby Jami Masjid towards the left. Listening to it indeed put one in a calming trance. Looking farther to right side, beyond the Red Fort and nearer the river, I noticed the pink dome of the St. James' Church. Although it was too early for the church bells to be ringing, I had a strange sensation; I heard them toll. The combination of these two forms of calling to prayer produced a most extraordinary resonance in my head.

I clasped my palms, got down on my knees, and resting my elbows on the window sill, bent my head in prayer. I thanked the

Lord for all His bounties He was bestowing upon me. I thanked Him for the courage, strength, and spiritual assistance He had provided me in the successful operation and delivery of Mumtaz and Sharif's child. I thanked Him for keeping me safe from evil. Lastly, I spent some time in expressing my heart full desire and wish that I hoped He would grant me. It being the arrival of my two children from Canada to be here with me.

My thoughts also turned to my parents. It being Sunday, how Papa would be getting prepared for the church service, and Mamma would be planning her usual sumptuous Sunday meal. I recalled reading in her recent letter that they were planning a trip to see me in Delhi, after Christmas, when things were quieter at the Mission. I missed them very much, and looked forward to their visit.

I knelt in prayer for some time, until I heard the door open and Elgin entered with the breakfast tray. She placed it on my small dining table. The delicate aroma of the masala tea drew me to it.

Chapter Sixteen

Annexation of Oudh

1856, January – February: Delhi, India

WITH THE ARRIVAL of the new year, while cold weather took a firm hold of Delhi, the cold season festivities continued. Although chilling winds blew through the streets, making the common natives walk about bundled in blankets, and heat their homes with small braziers, the elite's mansions and bungalows glowed from their blazing fireplaces within, and the European gentry drove in carriages, dressed in elegant gowns and suits. While I received numerous invitations for parties, dinners and theatrical events, being busy at the Hospital and in College work, I did not attend many. I did go to the Herford's New Year's Eve party, since Catherine had visited me expressly at the Hospital to deliver the invitation card. I inquired whether Humphrey was invited. She mentioned they had not seen him for a while, and asked me about him. I indicated that the Christmas Ball was the last time I had met him. She smiled knowingly when I confided to her the events of that night in the *tehkhana*, and that it was all over between us. She, however, cautioned me to be wary of him. After Catherine left, I wondered what she had meant by that remark.

Subsequently, at a church social, I overheard someone say that Humphrey had departed Delhi for Calcutta, on account of the arrival of the new Governor General, Lord Canning. I felt relieved, for I was expecting my parents any day, and hoped that Humphrey would not come around to see them. The Sharifs had kindly offered them a room in the *haveli*, and it was already cleaned and three new beds placed in here. When I offered to pay for the couple of week's accommodation, the Sharifs would not accept it, saying that it was all in indebtedness of my having brought Mumtaz's child safely into this world, which was truly a Heavenly bequest. I did not press too hard, and accepted their offer graciously, for I knew in their culture it was not proper to refuse such gratitude.

A few days later at the Hospital, I was returning to my office following a round of the wards, when opening the door, I saw a young blond man, dressed in a beige suit, sitting in my chair leafing through a medical book. Thinking, what the devil, I said loudly, "Excuse me, can I—," but halted, when he looked up with a wide grin. It was my brother, David.

"Hallo Sister!" He jumped up and came to me. Tears of joy ran down my cheeks, as we embraced. Although at twenty-one, he was four years younger than me, but at nearly six feet, was already a head taller.

He stepped back, still holding my hands. "Well, look at you. Have you been dieting, Sister?"

I likely blushed. "No, no. It's all the walking I have to do here. But my, I didn't recognize you. You have grown. Where are the others?"

"We went straight to the *haveli*, as you had written. They are reposing now. It was an exhausting three days drive. Thankfully the carriage didn't throw a wheel."

"I'm glad you are here safely. How is Amari?"

"Good." He turned red. "Busy at school. She wants to be a nurse."

"That's nice. Perhaps we can have her here." I did not press further about his Indian girlfriend, for no doubt he would tell me more later. "Good that you came here to fetch me. It's nearly time for me to leave." I collected my things and we walked down the hallway towards the main door. I did stop by Doctor Chaman Lal's office to inform him of my going home a bit early. He rotated his head, agreeing readily.

Entering my apartment, it was a thrill for me to see my parents again. I ran to them and we hugged and kissed. Mamma's eyes were filled with tears as well. My younger sister, Elizabeth, stood by a window with Jan in her arms. She came to me and putting an arm around me, kissed me.

"How are you Liz?"

"Fine," she said.

She had written to me about Ronald, a nearby Indigo plantation owner's relative, she had been seeing. I asked her about him.

"Ron is well. He wanted to accompany us, but some unexpected work came up on the plantation."

"Too bad. But you should bring him here another time, soon," I said thinking that it seems to be getting serious between the two.

She nodded. I was happy to observe that she, and in fact they all, looked well.

"My, how much Jan has grown." She tickled his chest. He giggled, moving his arms and kicking his feet.

She moved towards a corner of the room. "Look, Sister, what we have here for Jan." She pointed to a wooden contraption, like a small child's buggy on three wheels, standing there. She went to it and placed Jan on the seat. He wiggled a bit at first, waved his arms wanting to be picked up, but settled down comfortably on the leather chair.

"Is that a perambulator?" I had seen pictures of it in The New York Times.

"Yes," Papa said, dressed in his usual dark suit and cravat. He walked over to the pram, holding its handles, moved it around. The smaller third wheel at the front enabled it to be turned effortlessly. "See, how easy it is to carry your child around!"

"Goodness, how wonderful. I've heard they are the rage in New York. Where did you buy it, Papa?"

"Had it made in our workshop. Showed one of the carpenters its picture, and he put it together in no time. Those Indian workers can perform miracles." He chuckled.

"Thank you. You think of everything." I kissed Papa and Mamma, again.

David took hold of the handles and moved the pram forward and backwards. "A clever invention. But it won't catch on here."

"Why, David?" Elizabeth asked.

"Might put the *ayah's* out of work." He looked slyly at Elgin. She merely smiled.

"Never." I went to Elgin and put my arm around her shoulder. "I wouldn't know what to do without Elgin."

"What a grand mansion!" Mamma exclaimed. "How did you manage to find such luxurious accommodation, Margaret?"

"Can you afford the rent?" Papa interjected. He had been eyeing the plush furnishings.

"It's a long story. I'll tell you later. But first, I'd like to hear all about yourselves. How are things in Futtehgurh?" I made them sit down and asked Elgin, if she could fetch tea.

It did not take long for Elgin to bring up a tray, for in the kitchen they had tea ready throughout the day. Over hot refreshing *chai* and Indian snacks, Mamma and Papa brought me up to date about themselves, and I told them about my life in Delhi. I noted their happy smiles when I mentioned that my job at the hospital was going well, and I was even doing some part-time work at the Delhi College.

"Oh, I'm so happy for you, child. But tell me, how is Colonel Humphrey? When do we get to meet him?" Mamma probed. She was obviously more interested in matters not related to my work.

"I don't know. He has left Delhi."

"Really! But didn't you write, dear, that he wished to meet us?"

"Yes, he'd said so. But was called away to Calcutta."

"Couldn't he have waited for us?" Mamma persisted.

"Seems he wasn't able to. Lord Canning is due to arrive any day now."

"Ah, and there's the situation in Oudh he is helping to sort out. Is he not?" Papa asked.

"That too, I believe," I responded.

Both Mamma and Papa nodded. I felt relieved that I did not have to go into details of how things stood between Humphrey and me, and his devious overtures. "But, you will meet Mr. Fraser. I received a note from him inviting us for dinner at the Residency, next Saturday."

"Oh! Meet the Delhi Commissioner." Mamma clasped my arm, excitedly. "Dinner at the Residency! How wonderful." She turned towards Papa. "See James, how right I was to have packed my evening gowns you were objecting to, saying the luggage was becoming too heavy."

Papa simply smiled. I was happy to hear that she would wear something elegant, than the simple and plain dresses she usually put on.

"How are Nancy and Albert Miller? Your friends from Grimsby, you'd mentioned are also here," Elizabeth asked.

"Good, I think. I haven't seen them since last Christmas. They don't come to Church much."

"Didn't I meet Albert in Grimsby, when we were there?" Elizabeth said.

Yes, and you prattled about him and me, to Aunt Fiona, I wanted to say, but held my tongue. I simply replied, "You must have. We might call on them." Although I dreaded the thought of visiting them.

The door opened and Mumtaz walked in. She looked well after her ordeal, last month. "Welcome, welcome, to my humble home," she said to Mamma and Papa. Then turned towards me, "Margareet, you happy your parents come?"

"Yes, Mumtaz. I am, very much so."

"Thank you for having us in your grand palace," Papa said.

"Oh, no palace. Just a small house, padre-sahib. You like room?"

"Yes, we are very comfortable there." Mamma responded.

"Now, we make special dinner for you tonight. You come down to dining room after you rest. Alright?"

"We will be delighted to try your dishes. But less spicy for us, please," Mamma said.

"I understand. I go tell cook." She noted the tea tray. "You like wine? I have servant bring for you up here. Downstairs, we no have wine. Only sherbet."

"Oh, no thank you." Papa hastily responded. "We are not too fond of wine. We will drink whatever you'll serve with dinner." The others nodded in agreement.

"Alright. We see you later," she said and left the room.

I was glad that Papa had respected the abstinence practiced in a Muslim house. "You'll get plenty of wine at the Residency," I said, and noted their smiles.

That evening, dinner was indeed an extravagant affair. The main banquet room, on the ground floor was especially freshened up for the occasion. While there were tapestries and colorful patterned hangings on the walls, the room was devoid of furniture, except for small tables in the corners holding hookahs. Seating was in their traditional fashion, on the floor. A large white cotton sheet was laid over the thick rouge Persian carpet. Plates, cutlery and glasses were arranged, as if on a dining table, but instead of chairs, cushions with colorful silk covers were placed alongside.

Aroma of grilled meat and fresh chapattis was wafting from the kitchen, when we descended the stairs and arrived at the dining room. Mumtaz, Sharif, his parents, and other relatives were already at the door. Most wore their usual white silk *kurta-pajamas* and colorful waistcoats. Sharif introduced them and they salaamed their welcome to my family.

After the customary hands washing, assisted by servants standing by with pitchers of water and towels, we were led to the dining room. I was glad I did not have to remind my family about the no-shoes rule, for they immediately took theirs off, leaving them outside the door. I was also relieved to see they had clean stockings on. Furthermore, I was amazed at the ease with which my family sat cross-legged on the cushions. It seemed they had been long enough in India.

While maids busied around us, filling glasses with aromatic fruit juice and placing bowls of nuts, only the male members of the household sat down for dinner.

"Where are the women?" Mamma whispered in my ear.

"They always eat after the men," I murmured back, and noted her surprised look. It seemed there were some customs she was not yet aware of.

Sharif's father, Akbar Khan, sitting next to Papa, moved a bowl of nuts towards him. "Padre-sahib, this your first time in Dilli?"

"I've only passed through here, on my way to our mission in Ludhiana. This is a first visit for my wife and children, though." Papa sipped his sherbet. "I hear you have a shop here, sir?"

"We have jewelry store in Chandni Chowk. You come and see, yes?"

"I'm not certain if I should take my wife inside a jewelry store." When others looked blankly at him, he quickly added, "She may not wish to leave." Mamma playfully slapped Papa's wrist. While it took some time for Akbar and others around him to catch on, they finally did, and broke into smiles and nods.

"No, no. Bring memsahib and children. You no buy, only look." Akbar sipped some sherbet. "Then I show you around the Chowk. Have you seen Jami Masjid?"

Papa was eating some nuts, and shook his head.

"Masjid just opposite my shop. I show you. Then we go see Kutab Minar."

"Oh, no Khan sahib. I wouldn't think of taking you away from your shop."

"No problem. My wife and servants look after store. I am sitting all day reading newspaper. I have carriage. I take you all over Dilli."

"Well, that's very kind of you …"

While Akbar continued to discuss with Papa, his proposed tour of Delhi, servants started to serve dinner. The first course was a delightful chicken soup. I particularly enjoyed the way they delicately flavored it with herbs. Knowing that soups do not feature much in Mughal cooking, it seems they had prepared it especially for their European guests. This was followed by a delicious array of grilled chicken, beef kebobs on long skewers, and lamb shanks. There were several dishes of curried vegetables, and of course complemented with pilaf rice and mouthwatering hot naan bread and chapattis.

Mumtaz came in and asked Mamma if the cooking was not too spicy. Mamma thanked her and said it was to her liking. Although, I noted some of the others adding, onto their plates, an extra bit of pickles and crushed chilies from the condiments' tray.

I asked Sharif, who sat beside me, "How is your brother? Is he still in Oudh?"

"Yes. Last time he is writing, he is in camp outside Lucknow."

David, sitting across from us, was curious. "That would be near Cawnpore. What are they doing there?"

"I do not know, David baba. But big army there under General Wheeler."

"Sounds strange, to have a large force camped in the middle of nowhere," David said.

One of Sharif's cousins responded, "They have to keep those soldiers busy, to do something for their pay." He obviously was not in the army.

There was laughter all around.

"People say they waiting for some orders. But what, no one can tell," another cousin opined.

It seemed Sharif knew more, but when others looked at him, expecting him to elaborate, he did not. The conversation moved on to other topics.

Finally, desert arrived in the form of those exquisite looking and heavenly tasting Indian sweets. I had to force myself to hold my hand back. Nevertheless, I had a second helping of the delicious *rasmalai*. Finally, wonderfully aromatic and lovely tasting, Turkish coffee was served. It was another treat for us.

Dinner being over, we stood up, with some difficulty, and thanked our hosts for the superb meal. They said it was the least they could do in the honor of my family's first visit to their city. Papa asked, obviously having overeaten, if there was a park or somewhere we could go for a stroll. Akbar Khan suggested we go down the lane, and just beyond the Daryaganj Gate to the river and a nearby *ghat*. It would be pleasant to watch the sunset from there, he said. He apologized for not being able to accompany us, for he, and the other men, had to go for their prayers to the Masjid. We had heard the call for prayer earlier.

After, the traditional, rewashing our hands, we thanked Akbar and Sharifs again. David went up and helped Elgin bring Jan and his pram down. She also brought our shawls and jackets—for it was beginning to get a bit chilly. With Elgin rolling Jan's pram, we started our walk down the laneway, towards the river. Mamma and Papa admired the imposing mansions and their gardens, on either sides of the gully, each one more impressive than the other. Some of the passersby looked curiously at the pram, but upon spotting the bundled up baby, smiled and nodded knowingly.

The river was hardly a ten minutes' walk away. I felt happy to be with my family again. Although it was less than a year since I left Futtehgurh, it seemed longer, for there had been changes and new beginnings. It was apparent they were glad to have made the long journey.

We arrived at the river walk in front of the steps of the *ghat* leading into the blue river water. The steps were virtually deserted, for not only it was getting late, but the Hindus usually bathed and performed their pujas in the mornings. The setting sun cast orangey rays that reflected off the water, creating an enchanting atmosphere. We walked along the banks for a while, taking in the views of the temples and houses, and watched the boats sail by. At a clearing, Papa stopped and asked us to gather around in a circle, and hold hands. As he did often, he recited a prayer. He thanked the good Lord for all his blessings, and having saved us from evil, and shown us the virtuous path....

He continued on, and I myself said a silent prayer. I especially thanked God for having saved me from the sinful future that, having greed overwhelm me and nearly giving into temptation, I had foolishly considered following.

When we broke from our meditation, Mamma whispered to me, "Who is that man?" She pointed with her eyes towards someone standing on the other side of the street. "He has been standing there watching us."

I turned around and saw a soldier, dressed in the red and white sepoys' uniform. He was the Sharif's neighbor, Mr. Ali Khan.

I might have nodded my recognition, for he came forward. "Salaam, doctor sahiba. I returning from work. This your family, yes?"

Glad that he had finally acknowledged me as a doctor, and although he had not been civil the last time I saw him, I introduced him all around. He shook their hands.

"You liking Dilli, padre-sahib?"

"Yes, from what I've seen so far."

"You do preaching at St. James' Church?"

"Oh, no, sir. I am here only on a social visit," Papa responded. "To see my daughter and grandchild." He pointed to me.

"I think Padre Jennings need you help."

"Oh, I'm sure Reverend Jennings is managing quite well," Papa said.

"But you can help him in Dilli Kallij. No?" Ali looked at Papa mischievously.

"I don't understand, sir." Papa looked perplexed. "What kind of help?"

"Teaching Bible and make more convert to Christian. Yes?" Ali looked as if he knew a secret.

"I am doing no such thing." Papa looked a bit annoyed. "Besides, I don't believe Reverend Jennings would hold Bible classes at Delhi College. It's a secular institution. Is it not Margaret?" Papa looked at me.

I nodded. "I haven't heard of such lessons there."

"Oooh ... you don't know of the secret Bible class," Ali said rotating his head. "You padres want to pollute our children's mind."

"We are doing no such thing." Papa looked sternly at Ali. "Now if you will not stop bothering us, we will have to report you to your superior."

Ali appeared to be taken aback, but was about to retort with another slur, when we heard a voice from the other side of the street. "Salaam, Ali *bhai*. Is anything the matter?" It was Sharif, waking towards us.

"No, Sharif *bhai*, no problem. I just welcoming padre-sahib and family, to Dilli."

"That was, indeed, a fine welcome," Papa said.

Ali did not seem to comprehend Papa's sarcasm. "I go home. Late for dinner," he said and left us.

When Ali was out of earshot Sharif said, "I come looking for you, see if you are all right. I hope Subedar Ali did not say anything bad to you."

"No. He did not say anything mean, personally, to us. Appears to be upset about our teaching the gospel," Papa responded.

"Please excuse him. He has dispute about his lands with the Company."

"No point in taking his frustration out on us," Papa said.

"I tell him. Please come, my father want you to smoke hookah with him. Yes?"

"I'll be delighted. Haven't smoked one for a while."

The sun had set, and it was getting dark. We walked back to the *haveli*. While Papa had a smoke with Akbar, the rest of us went to our beds, for a restful night.

For the next few days, during the week, I was glad that Akbar took my family around to see his beloved city, Delhi. Every evening, I heard them tell me of their visit to a famous landmark, and also some other obscure monument of historical significance, which Akbar showed them, with pride. And he had good reason to love and be proud of the metropolis, for his ancestors, the Mughals, had come centuries ago from Northern and Western Asia. Having established their kingdom, they made Delhi their capital. They truly considered this to be their "home," not some distant city or land in Persia, Arabia or elsewhere they wished to return to someday.

The following Saturday, we spent the whole afternoon, bathing, grooming, and dressing. Finally, in the evening, wearing our best gowns and suits, we were ready for the dinner party at the Residency. Soon, squeezed three abreast on the two benches, and Jan in Elgin's lap, we were on our way in a landau clattering and jolting through the streets. The carriage travelled through the Cashmir Gate, on the all too familiar road, out of the city. I pointed out the landmarks, up on the Ridge to the left and those on the right along the river. Mamma looked admiringly at me when I indicated the Metcalf House where I had attended the Christmas Ball.

"Too bad Colonel Humphrey is not here to accompany you tonight, dear," she whispered to me. Not wishing to spoil her and others evening by telling them the facts, I simply nodded, and directed their attention towards the Ludlow Castle looming in the distance.

As we climbed up the steps onto the wide patio, the butler, opening the front door, came out to greet us, and bid me a special "welcome back." I thanked him. In the hallway, he collected our capes, shawls and overcoats. Elgin quietly took Jan upstairs to a room she used previously as his nursery, and we were announced into the spacious drawing room.

Mr. Fraser, dressed in his usual formal dark suit, and another couple were seated there, drinks in hand. They rose and bid us a "good evening." The other invitees were Reverend Jennings and his daughter Annie. Following introductions, all around, we settled down on the comfortable sofas and chairs. The butler took our drink orders. Upon my inquiry, Annie informed me that Miss Clifford had gone out with some friends.

"So, Margaret, are you settled in Sharif Mahal, or ready to return here?" Mr. Fraser asked jovially.

I laughed, slightly. "I am quite comfortable there. But thank you, sir, for asking. You were so kind to have housed me here for such a long while."

"Wasn't any problem at all, Margaret." Fraser looked towards Mamma. "How about you Mrs. Wallace? Enjoying the city? Nothing like New York, is it?"

"Oh, the streets of Manhattan!" Mamma clasped her hands, not correcting him that we were actually from New Jersey. "Hardly, sir. But it's quite pleasant here, and I dare say, much livelier than Futtehgurh."

Our drinks were served, and Mr. Fraser toasted our arrival.

"Have you seen much of the city, Brother Wallace?" Reverend Jennings, wearing a brown suit and white collar, asked. He sipped his sherry.

"Yes, nearly all of it. In just the last few days." Papa sipped his whisky, while Fraser and Jennings looked at him puzzled. He hastened to explain. "Akbar Khan ... Margaret's landlord, has been showing us the city. Knows it intimately. Says he was born here."

"Didn't he say he is related to the Emperor?" Mamma added.

"Hah! They all claim to be." Jennings interjected. "And if you let them, they will trace their lineage to Babur, and even all the way to Timor!"

I was glad Papa did not comment on that cynical remark, and proceeded to talk about all the landmarks they were taken to. He finished by saying: "We did stop by your lovely church, but had time only to explore the picturesque garden and the cemetery. We expect to see the inside tomorrow, of course."

"After the service, I'll be delighted to show you around, especially, James Skinner's crypt," Jennings offered.

"We'd love to," Mamma said. "Goodness, Mr. Skinner lies buried inside the church!"

"That's the least we could do for the builder of this great church." Jennings sipped his sherry.

"I've heard, he was born in Calcutta, was he not?" Papa asked.

"Yes. His father was a colonel, in our army, and mother a Rajput princess," Jennings responded.

"May I have a look in your stables, sir?" David, likely bored, asked the commissioner.

"Yes, please do, while there's still some sunlight."

"I'll join you." Elizabeth jumped up and walked behind David towards the door.

"I love horses, I'll come too," Annie said and followed them.

"Don't be too long children," Mamma said. Then as soon as they were out of the door, she turned towards Fraser. "Talking about colonels, any news of Colonel Humphrey?"

Fraser likely knowing Mamma's motive for the question, responded: "Er ... yes. He went to Calcutta to receive Canning." He sipped his whisky. Upon seeing we waited for more, he looked towards me. "Have you heard from him, Margaret?" When I shook my head, he continued guardedly. "I understand, he's in Lucknow now."

"In Lucknow! Whatever for?" Mamma wanted to know.

"Er ... well ... he's with Outram. They have to deliver some letters from the Company, to the Nawab, personally."

"Personally! The missives must be of some importance then?" Papa asked.

"Yes, I believe they are," Fraser said. Jennings looked out of the window, straight-faced, for he likely knew of their contents.

"It might be inappropriate, but are you at liberty to share with us their subjects, sir?" Papa asked, with a concerned look.

You are pushing your luck Papa, I thought, when unexpectedly, Fraser responded, "I think you should know, Reverend Wallace, for you'll hear soon enough. And, besides, Margaret was fully briefed earlier." I nodded.

Fraser moving forward in his chair, continued in a low voice, "Please keep this to yourselves, for the moment. The first letter, along with a new treaty, has just been presented to the Nawab." Fraser gulped the last of his whiskey. "The Company, particularly our Directors in London, wish to bring some order into the chaotic manner Wajid Ali has been governing Oudh. We are asking him to handover the control of all civil and military administration to the Company."

Despite Sleeman's warnings, I thought, and took a sip of my wine. But I did ask, "How did the Nawab respond?"

Fraser smiled. "To be honest, the fellow surprised us. Did not sign the treaty, made some disparaging remarks and gibberish that treaties are between equals. Obviously doesn't consider the Company as his equal! Can you believe that?" He called for the butler to replenish our and his drinks.

After the butler had poured another round and left, Jennings remarked: "I say, the chap has a spine after all! Any news on what the playboy is up to?"

"He's been given a few days to think it over," Fraser responded.

"If he still doesn't sign over his kingdom, then what?" Papa asked.

"Then he will have the second letter placed in his hands," Fraser said.

"Which says?" Papa persisted.

"That the Company is taking over Oudh, regardless," Fraser said somewhat proudly, like a conqueror might.

Mamma clasped her hands, the way she usually did when excited. "Oh! I trust there won't be any war."

"No fear of that Mrs. Wallace," Fraser said. "The Nawab has hardly any army, only a few palace guards. We have been providing him protection, established in an earlier agreement. Besides, we have General Wheeler and his regiments camped outside the gates of Lucknow."

"What I hear from the chaplain there," Jennings said in a low voice, "it is the Nawab's wife, Begum Hazrat Mahal, whom we should be worried about."

Fraser nodded. "I've heard something similar. She is his third or fourth, or whatever number, wife. She thinks she can start a revolution. Hah!" He took another large gulp of whisky.

"How will the Company govern Oudh?" Papa asked, for being a clergyman, he was interested in management of people.

"The same way we do most other Indian states. I believe Dalhousie planned to subdivide the land into four divisions, each with a commissioner, reporting to the chief commissioner in Lucknow. The divisions would be subdivided into three districts, each to be administered by a deputy commissioner. Of course, there would be judicial and financial officials appointed as well."

"Quite a comprehensive organization. Is most of it in place, already?" Papa looked towards Fraser.

"Yes, most of it is. On paper, anyway—"

"What lovely horses!" Elizabeth exclaimed, as she burst into the room. While Mamma looked crossly at her, Annie and David followed behind.

"You are welcome to come and ride here, any time, young lady," Fraser offered.

"I'd love to," Elizabeth said.

Likely upon hearing the youngsters were within, the butler entered the room and announced: "Dinner is served."

We took our seats at the table. The food was just as delicious as ever. I was pleased to hear the butler mention that the cook had added herbs and spices in my servings in the way I preferred. I asked him to thank the chef for remembering me.

During dinner Frazer, sitting beside me, asked: "How is Begum Zinat? Have you been to see her again?"

"No, not since my first visit. But Doctor Lal mentioned that she'll send for me soon. He had been to treat King Zafar."

"Oh, is she the queen? I'd like to meet her," Mamma said.

"That's one queen you wouldn't want to have tea with, ma'am," Jennings said.

While others smiled, Mamma looked puzzled. "Why is that Reverend Jennings?"

"Well ... there have been some unfortunate incidences." Jennings did not elaborate. "In any case if you do visit, I'd feed whatever she serves to the cat first." There was laughter all around.

"She is unwell, Mamma, and may not be seeing visitors," I said. It seemed to satisfy Mamma.

"But do let us know if you see any dead cats around the palace," Fraser said. I smiled and nodded at his witticism, and the veiled instruction. Earlier Humphrey had also said something similar. They really want me to spy on the royals. I thought.

Later, returning home in the carriage, having enjoyed the lovely evening and having thanked Commissioner Fraser profusely for it, we were deep in our thoughts. I felt Mamma press my arm. "Did you really know about those letters to the Nawab?" Not wishing to elaborate, I simply nodded. "Was it Colonel Humphrey who told you?"

"Yes," I said, and looked outside the window.

"Oh, my. What a fine gentleman. Has such high regard for you. Has he said anything ... I mean in the form of a proposal, or a letter perhaps?"

I shook my head, and continued to gaze out of the window. Thinking about Humphrey brought back a flood of memories mainly of those awful times when he had clumsily tried to seduce me. And finally that vile proposal where he wanted me to live as his mistress in Calcutta, a bit magnificently perhaps, but in depravity none the less. He certainly did not have a "high regard" for me, as Mamma believed. I felt like opening my heart out to her, and inform her of all those events I was keeping bottled up inside. I worried for my and my children's future prospects. Was I to spend the rest of my life in spinsterhood? Tears welled in my eyes and started to drip down. I quickly pulled out my handkerchief from my sleeve, and dabbed my cheeks.

Mamma must have noticed my tears and putting her arm around my shoulder hugged me to her. "Do not fret, dear. He will call, or write soon." I wanted to tell her that my tears were not for what she thought, but could not.

That Sunday at St. James' Church, following the service and the tour of the relics as promised by Reverend Jennings, we attended the social, in the adjoining hall. While pouring our teas, a feminine voice behind me said, "Hallo, Margaret. We heard, your parents are here!"

I turned around and saw Nancy and Albert. From their disheveled appearance it seemed they had rushed to get to church. Being late, they had stood in the doorway, hence I did not notice them earlier. I was about to say, good to see you made the effort, but merely responded, "Good to see you. Yes, my family is here." I introduced them.

"Elizabeth! Didn't I meet you in Grimsby, ages ago?" Albert exclaimed.

"Yes, you took me out riding. I remember you," she said. Which was a surprise revelation to me, and wondered what they might have been up to. I hoped it was not what he had wanted to do to me, when he had taken me out.

"And I recall seeing you marching with the militia, as the drummer boy, on the beach," Papa said.

"Yes, with Robert as well," Albert said. But, quickly realizing his insensitive remark in my presence, looked away.

Yes, that was when you pulled my pigtails and punched my beloved Robert, I thought, but remained silent.

Mamma and Papa conversed with them about their parents and other New Jersey émigrés living in Grimsby. It was also a good opportunity for my family to meet some more Delhi's Christian residents, who circulated about. Papa was very pleased to meet Doctor Chaman Lal and Mr. Ramchandra. He shook their hands, saying, "I've heard so much about you."

Having finished our teas, I asked David to hail a carriage for us to return home, but Nancy interrupted, and invited us over to their house for dinner. When I tried to gently dissuade her by saying we did not wish to impose on her, she responded, "No, no problem at all. I have left instructions with the cook to have dinner ready. And the Herfords will also be there, as well." Realizing she had made the arrangements already, and in the presence of Mamma and Papa, I could not refuse her invitation.

The Miller's residence was a typical cantonment bungalow, virtually identical to the Herfords, and similar to my parent's. It being a warm afternoon, we were directed to the back garden, to a table setup under a shady tree. Although only early February, it seemed Delhi's brief winter would soon be over, for spring like weather was already in the air. Albert quickly prepared drinks for everyone, and we sat down and talked amiable on various subjects.

Dinner was served. Although it was the standard roast beef and potatoes, but with liberal helpings of horse radish, it was palatable. Sipping wine and listening to the bird songs, I was enjoying myself, until the topic of my children in Canada, came up. It was Nancy who initiated it.

"Margaret, have you heard anything more from your Aunt Fiona about their trip to Crimea?" Nancy asked.

"Yes, Cousin Heather wrote they would be sailing in May."

"With your children?" Nancy asked.

"Yes, of course. I was going to ask, if Colonel Mitchell has made any further arrangements for continuing their journey to India?"

"No. Nothing more than what Father wrote earlier." She turned towards Captain Herford. "Unless Jack has talked to someone?"

Captain Herford finished his mouthful of beef. "Yes, I spoke again to Colonel Humphrey, to remind him. He said he'd been busy, but would look into it. I haven't heard any more from him."

"Has he written to anyone in London?" I wanted to know.

"He might have, but he should have passed on a copy either to me or to you, Margaret. Did you receive anything?"

"No, I haven't."

"It's likely this business in Oudh that's taking his time. I'm sure he will act on your request for a passage for your children. After all you are an employee of the Company as well," Hereford said, and took a gulp of his beer.

"Perhaps, I should apply to the Governor General?" I said.

"No, no. Don't do it yet," Herford said. "It will likely get bogged down in the bureaucratic mess over there right now, during the changeover. Let Humphrey handle it. He will come through. You'll see."

I did not find Captain Herford's words comforting, and

wondered if Humphrey would do anything to assist me, especially after our last encounter. But my thoughts were interrupted.

"Oh, I am certain Fiona will manage somehow to secure passage on some passenger, or even a cargo vessel to Calcutta, or Bombay," Papa said in his preacher's optimistic voice. "Your Aunt Fiona is a very resourceful person, Margaret."

I would not be too certain of that, I thought but said, "I should hope so, Papa."

The conversation moved on to the Herford's and Miller's children. Catherine said her children, being older now and well settled in schools in London, would only come on visits to India. Nancy said she would not bring her kids to India even for a holiday. She went on and on berating the Indian's way of life, and how it was full of disease and evil. There were no proper schools or facilities. Papa tried to reason by saying that conditions were improving, in every area, and more so in the higher education field. He cited the example of my brother, David, who would be attending that fall, the recently established Thomason College of Engineering at Roorkee. However, Nancy kept complaining about the attitude of the natives, and they did not want the British to be there anyway.

Captain Herford responded by saying, "They may want us or not, but we are here to stay."

"Well, I am not." Nancy snapped. "I can't understand how I got talked into coming here. I've been imploring Al to return home, as soon as we can."

"You have only just got here, Nancy. Do give it some time," Catherine tried to pacify Nancy.

"I've had a constant headache, ever since I've arrived." Nancy rubbed her temples, and turning towards me said, "Do you have any medication for it, Margaret."

"None with me, Nancy. But if you would care to come to the Hospital, I'll see what I can do. It might be something more than a headache, you know."

"Can you take me there, Al?"

"Yes, I will," Albert said, and added sheepishly, "And when we are there, perhaps Margaret might examine me? I've been having these chest pains. I wouldn't want to see any native doctor."

"Yes, certainly," I responded, thinking those chest pains are more than likely from too much booze.

While it was still only the middle of the afternoon, I wished to go home, for I felt tired and all the talk of children's absence had depressed me. Using the perfect excuse that my son was alone, although with his *ayah*, I suggested to Mamma and Papa that we should return to the *haveli*. They agreed readily. While David beckoned a carriage from down the road, we took our leave of the Millers, thanking them for a superb lunch and a pleasant afternoon. I asked them, and the Herfords as well, to come for a visit to the *haveli*. They said they would.

Later in the carriage, staring silently out of the window, I felt Mamma's comforting arm again around my shoulder. "Do not fret child. Your children will be here with you, soon." At her words, tears welled again in my eyes. "Humphrey, or Fiona, will see to it," she tried to cheer me.

I put my head on her shoulder. Somehow I did not feel assured of either of Aunt Fiona's or Humphrey's assistance. I resolved, if I had to, I would scrape together enough funds for their and a chaperon's passage to Delhi. But, how would I be able to accomplish that, on my meagre salary. I wondered.

I enjoyed my parents' and sibling's all too brief sojourn. Much as I wished for them to have stayed longer, they had to return to their respective jobs. Papa to his preaching, David to his work in the tent making factory, and Mamma and Elizabeth to their teaching in the Mission School.

On account of my work, I was unable to accompany them to the many picturesque locales in and around the city they visited, and heard their tall-tales every evening over dinner. However, I loved most our long after dinner walks. We usually went to the nearby Daryaganj Gate's river walk and watched the sights from the steps of the *ghat*. It was also a wonderful respite for me, following a stifling day at the Hospital.

On the last evening of their holiday, we walked out of the *haveli* on the laneway. Papa, David and Elizabeth strolled ahead of Mamma and me. I pushed Jan's pram, since Elgin was having her dinner with the other servants. Mamma held my shoulder to slow me down, and to let the others walk on out of earshot. I knew she wanted to tell me something.

"We will be expecting you soon in Futtehgurh, Margaret," she said.

"Oh, I don't know, Mamma. Not sure how soon I will be able to get away," I responded. "My patients' list is growing daily."

"I know. But I am sure they will give you time off to attend your sister's wedding!"

I stopped the pram. "Really, Mamma!" I hugged her. "How wonderful." Mamma nodded.

We resumed our walking. "It is a pleasant surprise. Liz hasn't mentioned it to me. Have they set a date?"

"No, not yet. But soon I hope. They seem to be deeply in love. Ron rides over, nearly every day. She will let you know when they are ready."

"Liz wrote that Ron works on a plantation. But who is he, and how did they meet?"

"Do you recall that Nawab of Furrukhabad's brother's wife, who once came over to see you?"

"Ah, I remember her. Nur Jehan you mean?"

"Yes, Harriet Birch. That's her real name isn't it?" I nodded. Mamma continued. "About three months ago, one Sunday, she visited us again in her royal carriage, and invited us to her parents' plantation. Of course your papa and I refused, but Elizabeth went with her. It was there she met Ron, and they have been going out ever since. I am happy for them."

"Is Ron, Harriet's brother?"

"A cousin actually. Has recently come over from England, to help his uncle, Mr. Birch, run the plantation."

"Does he plan to stay on here?" I was curious, and wondered if he was just having a holiday fling.

"It looks like he's here permanently. Seems to be enjoying his work. Since Mr. Birch is getting old, Ron might end up taking over the whole operation."

"Hmm ..." I mused, feeling happy for my sister.

We reached the river bank and found the others waiting for us. From my smile, Elizabeth must have guessed what Mamma and I were talking about.

I went up to her and hugged her. "I am happy for you, Liz," I whispered in her ear.

"Thank you, Sister," she whispered back.

We walked along the river and relished the sight of the setting sun that cast a mesmerizing orange glow around us.

After a tearful goodbye, and my promise to visit them soon, they departed the next morning. Since the days were already beginning to get hot, Papa had decided to proceed before sunup, to get a good head start on the long and dusty road to Futtehgurh.

******

In a way I was glad that my family had returned to Futtehgurh when the news of Oudh's annexation, by the Company, finally reached Delhi like a storm. Although there were none of the public protests and demonstrations, which some officials—including Commissioner Fraser—had feared. Nevertheless, they had increased the number of security guards, all over Delhi. However, from the glum faces in the streets it was evident that the populace were not happy. There were far fewer smiles and salaams, from the natives to the Europeans, as we drove around in our buggies. Although the officials stressed, in the English press and in speeches, that the takeover was for the good of the *Lucknowies*, I was not certain, if the locals paid any heed to it.

However, the situation at the CMH was normal as ever, and the Indian nurses, orderlies and other staff went about their business, respectfully. I suspected it was more out of fear for their jobs. They knew, if they showed the slightest discontent or criticized the Company's actions in Oudh, it would result in dire consequences for them. Things were pretty much the same at the *haveli* as well. All treated me with the same veneration, as before, and I heard nary an unkind word.

The only person who showed any resentment, was Mr. Ali. Usually, Elgin and I took Jan out in his pam for our evening walks, and Mr. Ali invariably passed us in the laneway. However, he always crossed the street to the other side and looked away. But if he did glance at us, it was a chilling look with his glaring dark eyes. I always ignored him and advised Elgin to do the same.

One evening, I sat in the courtyard on a charpoy, conversing and having tea with Mumtaz. She rocked her daughter—they had named her Jahanara, after the Empress Mumtaz's daughter—and I kept an eye on Jan crawling on the bed. Akbar Khan passed by.

"Salaam Margareet. How are you?" he said.

Mumtaz hurriedly put her *dupatta* over her head, and I did the same with my shawl. I returned his salaam, telling him I was well, and asked, "How are things in Oudh?"

"Ah, not good. Nawabsahib and his family all thrown out of their palaces."

"Did they put up any resistance?"

"No. In fact Nawabsahib ask his troops and palace guards to put down their weapons!"

"Really. So where is he now?"

"He go to a big house in Calcutta, with his mother, three wives and children."

"What about his fourth wife?"

"Begum Hazrat Mahal, she decide to stay in Lucknow, in a small house with her son."

"Interesting. Why didn't Begum Hazrat want to go with the Nawab to Calcutta?"

"Don't know. But perhaps Nawabsahib no take her because ..." Akbar bent down and said in a low voice, "Nawabsahib planning to go to London. Talk to Queen Victoria. Tell her of all the bad things Company doing in Oudh. You see. Now Queen Victoria will take care of the Company's *badmashes*."

I did not quite believe it would happen, knowing the little effect similar petitions, by other Indian kingdoms' representatives, had had. However, being more interested in our city, I asked, "What about Delhi, Khansahib? Have you heard or seen any disturbances here?"

"No. Everything quiet here. What can we do for Oudh, from so far away? *Dilli door est!*" He salaamed and hurried away towards the prayer room.

I felt relieved upon hearing from—one of Delhi's elders—that the city was calm. I smiled when I remembered the Persian saying, he had recited: 'Delhi is far.'

As the weeks rolled by, and with the sun increasing its warmth daily, Delhi returned to its normal jovial self. Smiles reappeared on the dark faces, and the calamities in Oudh it seemed were forgotten. I was not only busy at the Hospital, but during any free moment, my thoughts were for my children's arrival. I was hoping to hear from

Humphrey, for it was the least he could do, if he cared even faintly for me. Also, I anticipated a letter from Cousin Heather. I looked forward to her advising me of their departure date from Grimsby, and more importantly their anticipated arrival date in Calcutta. Of course I longed to be at the Hooghly docks to receive them, and hoped that I could, in the same trip, also attend my sister's wedding in Futtehgurh. Earlier, while saying goodbye, she had whispered that the nuptial might be sometime in the summer.

However, an unfortunate occurrence in Delhi, shook the city, and was to disrupt my plans, and to change my life forever.

Chapter Seventeen

Begum Zinat Mahal's Illness

1856, March: Delhi, India

ONE MORNING at the Hospital, while I was still having my tea, Doctor Lal himself, dressed in his usual white coat over blue shirt and black trousers, came to my office. Normally he asked his nurse, Gita, to fetch me. I immediately stood up from my chair. He beckoned me to sit, and sat on the opposite chair.

"Last night while I was at the palace, rubbing oil on King Zafar's feet, Mahbub Ali came into the chamber." I knew he referred to the queen's chief eunuch. "He said, 'Queen Zinat's health is getting worse, and she wishes to see Doctor Margaret.'"

"What's wrong with her?"

"I understand she is experiencing pains in the abdomen. Has been complaining for a while. I don't believe she is expecting. But, I hope it's not an inflammation of the appendix, we have been reading much about, recently."

"Yes, I read that report in the Medical Gazette, about a new operation to remove a swollen appendix, performed in London." I wondered if we could do it at CMH. "Did you examine the queen?"

"No." Doctor Lal smiled. "She won't see me, nor Hakim Ahsanullah. Want's only you to attend to her. It seems you have made quite a favorable impression on her. Our Civil Surgeon is very pleased to know that."

"I'm happy to hear it. When does she wishes to receive me?"

"The palace guard's sepoy Sharif Khan, your landlord," he chuckled, "will be over later this morning. He will escort you to the Palace."

"All right, good. I don't have many patients this morning. I will be ready shortly."

We talked a bit, regarding some of my patients, and after asking about my child and my parents visit, he left my office.

Later that morning, Betty informed me that Sepoy Sharif was waiting for me at the Hospital's gates. I hurried out to meet him. He salaamed, and I boarded the *tonga* he stood beside. We arrived at the Fort's Lahore gate—the main entrance—and Sharif guided me to a waiting palanquin. Just as on my previous visit, he walked beside the dolly, making sure that I reached the queen's residence, the Rang Mahal, safely. The same pretty ladies were waiting at the terrace, and came hurriedly down the steps to the palanquin to help me out. One of them ran in to fetch Mahbub.

He came waddling onto the terrace. "Welcome, welcome, doctor sahiba. Begum Zinat waiting for you," he said in his squeaky voice.

Sharif left, saying that he will stay at the Lahore Gate to take me back to the Hospital.

Medical bag in hand, I followed the chief eunuch along the marbled floored hallways, admiring the walls patterned with lapis lazuli and colorful stones, to the queen's chamber. He waited, while I took my shoes off, then opening the door ushered me inside.

Queen Zinat, dressed in a white silk kurta-pajama and some jewelry, was seated on a divan, her back resting on a multicolored bolster. Several ladies sat on the carpeted floor. I salaamed and she beckoned, "Come, come." Mahbub also followed me in, and sat down cross-legged at one side of the room.

One of the women quickly fetched a chair and placed it alongside the divan. Putting my bag down, I sat and asked, "How are you feeling, Your Majesty?"

"I feeling not good. Having bad pain," she responded, her pretty face twisted in a sorrowful expression.

"Where is the ache?"

She pointed to her stomach.

"Let me have a look." I was about to stand, when maids placed a tray of tea and snacks on a small foot-stool beside me.

"Have tea first," Queen Zinat said.

Since it was nearly mid-morning, feeling hungry and putting Reverend Jennings caution out of mind, I enjoyed the tea and the delicious *samosas* filled with spicy vegetables. Maids brought a basin, a pitcher of water, and clean towels. After washing and drying my hands, I was ready for examining the queen.

Four ladies held a cotton curtain around the divan, and going around it I approached the queen. I was glad that she smiled when I pulled up her kurta to expose her belly, for I knew eastern ladies were uncomfortable with that procedure. I prodded and probed with my fingers, particularly in the vicinity of the appendix, but did not feel any swelling, nor did Queen Zinat express anguish at my touches. As Doctor Lal had thought, she did not look pregnant either. Upon my questioning for the exact location of the pain, she moved her fingers all around her belly. I asked if the pain was most severe during her monthly period. She nodded. I pulled her kurta down and went back to my chair.

Rewashing and drying my hands, and taking my note pad out from the bag, I made some notes. I believed I knew what her problem was. Considering her thirtysomething age, it was most likely a mild case of menstrual pains and gastrointestinal disorder, possibly due to inactivity.

"Your Majesty, have you been going for walks in the garden?"

"No, no. Very cold for walking outside," she responded.

I did not wish to inquire about her bowel movements, in front of her ladies, but believed she could use some help for those. "There doesn't appear to be anything seriously wrong. I would suggest you should go for daily walks."

"I go when warm weather comes. I like to look at trees with fruit. But now I have much pain. You give me some medicine, yes?"

Thinking that a mild stimulant and pain-killer would help her, I responded, "Yes, but I don't have it with me. If you would send someone to the Hospital, I'll gladly make a mixture for you."

"Mahbub," she called out. He stood up. "Go with doctor sahiba. Bring my medicine."

"*Ji huzoor.*" Mahbub bowed.

"Make it strong medicine, yes?" she said to me.

I smiled. "Yes, Your Majesty." I collected my bag.

"Wait," she said to me, and gestured at a lady.

A side door opened and Prince Jawan Bakht walked in. He wore his usual: gold and silver brocaded regal jacket, white silk tight-pajamas, golden curved-toed shoes, and a turban. He looked well, and a bit taller, since the last time I had met him. But I was still amazed knowing that he was married off, four years ago, when only eleven!

"Salaam, doctor sahiba. I happy to see you again."

"I am glad to see you too." Remembering his half-brother, the heir-apparent, I had not yet met, I asked, "How is Prince Fakhruddin? Is he around?"

"He resting."

"He always sleeping, or talking with English people. I no see him." The queen sneered.

Prince Jawan carried, with both hands, something wrapped in a red cotton cloth. He came up and presented it to me.

I put the parcel on my lap and, opening it, was delighted to see an eastern dress. I held up the silk kurta and admired the gold and silver patterns on it. Also, the bundle contained a red velvet covered box. Opening it I noticed a matching necklace and earrings set made of gold and precious stones. "Thank you very much, Your Majesty." I bowed to the queen. "But I cannot accept it." Although my heart said otherwise to me. "This is too much in payment for my services."

"No, no. This not in payment to you. We pay Company separate."

"But Your Majesty ..." I searched for the right words.

"I hear you like Mughal dress, yes?"

I nodded, thinking she would have heard about my attire at the Christmas Ball.

"Then you keep. This gift from me to you, not to Company."

These were expensive items, I could have hardly afforded. I forced myself to agree with my heart, and not my conscience. "All right, Your Majesty, as you wish."

"Do you remember, what I asked you to speak to Commissioner sahib, about my beautiful son?" The queen looked lovingly towards Prince Jawan.

"Yes, Your Majesty. I did."

"Please do again, yes?"

"I will." I salaamed the queen, and left her chamber. Mahbub followed behind, and I handed him the heavy parcel.

Upon entering the Hospital's main doors, with Mahbub behind me, I remembered what Humphrey had told me about him. Hence, not wanting him to see where I kept my medicines, I intuitively told him to stay in the waiting room. He, somewhat reluctantly, sat down on a chair.

Passing by Doctor Lal's office, and observing that he was not busy, I walked in.

"How was your visit with the queen?" he inquired.

I gave him the details of my examination, and concluded, "I think she likely has menstrual difficulties, indigestion, and possibly a minor intestinal blockage. I would recommend Belladonna mixture. What do you think, sir?"

"Yes, Belladonna sounds appropriate. We have had good results with it." He thought for a moment. "But do make it a mild blend."

"Yes, of course."

Back in my office, I unlocked my medicine cabinet and opening its glass door took out the large amber colored bottle of Belladonna tincture. Taking the bottle to the service table behind my desk, I carefully measured—the recommended dose—a tea spoon and poured it in a small flask of water. After stirring it with a glass rod, I poured the mixture into a clear white-glass prescription bottle and corked it. On the blank label, pasted at one side, I wrote the prescription:

For Queen Zinat Mahal Only
Belladonna – take one table spoon with a glass of water – 3 times daily.
Caution – harmful if dosage is exceeded.

I took the bottle out to my nurse. "Betty, can you please give this prescription bottle to Mr. Mahbub Ali, sitting in the waiting room?" She took it. "Also, tell him that Begum Zinat is to be very careful with this medication. No more than three times a day. Just as the label says."

"Yes, Doctor Wallace." She walked towards waiting room.

Nurse Betty returned shortly, carrying a parcel. "Mr. Ali gave me this, for you. Gift from the Queen?" she said, giving me an admiring look.

"Yes, it is. He was carrying it for me. Thank you." I took the parcel and placed it on a chair near my cloak.

Some days later, Doctor Lal come to see me again, in my office. He was smiling brightly, and I wondered what he was so pleased about.

"King Zafar is happy. Told me that Queen Zinat is feeling well. They even spent a night together!" he said with another broad smile.

"I am glad to hear it," I likely blushed.

"Thanks to you." He then moved closer and said in a low voice, "Part of our job is to keep these royals contented, lest they stir up trouble for us."

"I understand, sir." I nodded, thinking how nice that Doctor Lal is helping to smooth relations between the Delhi's various communities.

"Oh, and another thing, the queen has nearly finished the medicine. Can you please prepare another mixture bottle? Mahbub will be over to collect it."

"Yes I will," I responded. Doctor Lal left my office, wishing me a good day.

I found a new bottle, and poured the identical strength, as earlier, of Belladonna extract and water mixture into it. The bottle had a blank label affixed, and writing the same prescription on it, I locked it inside my medicine cabinet.

That afternoon, I was writing reports of the day's examinations, when there was a tap on the door, and Nurse Betty entered. "Captain Miller, is here to see you."

Although annoyed at the unexpected arrival, but thinking that Nancy's condition must have deteriorated and Albert had finally brought her over, I said, "Yes, please show them in."

"Hallo, Margaret." Albert entered, removing his hat. He looked well, and appeared to have lost some weight.

I motioned towards a chair. "Hallo. Where is Nancy?"

He sat down. "Left yesterday for Calcutta. Sorry that she didn't have time to say goodbye to you. A *dakgharry* was departing, with another officer and his wife. There was room for her. She jumped right in."

"Goodbye, did you say?"

"I'm afraid so. She is adamant about returning home. Misses our children and her parents. Don't blame her, really."

"How is her health? Is she up to this long journey?"

"Possibly not. She has those recurring headaches. Perhaps the Calcutta air and the gay life will do her good. She'll be staying with friends. Might even return here, who knows." He laughed.

Thinking, one's wife's illness in no laughing matter, I asked, "Why didn't you take her for a holiday? Perhaps to the hills?"

"I can't leave now. I've got a new job."

It was then I noticed his new dark green uniform, and around the arm a white band with initials: MP. Also there were three stars on the lapels. "You've become a policeman, I see. And a captain too. Congratulations."

"Not a promotion, really. Got my old rank back. With all that problem in Oudh, they were increasing the police force here. So I volunteered."

"Do you like your new job?"

"Very much so. Keeping the city's *badmashes* in control."

Yes, that's the kind of occupation you would relish, I thought. "So, what can I do for you? Did you say you were having chest pains? Does the pain rundown your left arm?"

"No, not down the arm. Stays mostly in the chest."

"Let's have a look. Can you please undo your shirt buttons?" I picked up my stethoscope and went around the desk. Bending beside his chair, trying not to breathe his foul body odor, I moved the stethoscope's head over his hairy chest, listening to his heartbeats. Also, with my fingers, tapped his ribs. Straightening up, I said, "Your heart sounds well. Good that you've lost some weight. I would suggest taking more off."

Suddenly, putting his arms tightly around my waist, he pulled me down on his lap. "My dear, Margaret. I'd do anything you say." He whispered in my ear, and tried to kiss me.

I moved my head away, and attempted to get up by pushing on his shoulders with my hands. "Albert! Release me, or I'll call the nurse."

"Alright, alright. I want to say something. Please hear me out." He relaxed his arms, but still held me on his lap.

"Yes, what is it?"

"You know I love you very much. Now with Nancy and Humphrey gone, why don't we move in to another house? I'll write to Colonel Mitchell, and get your children here. He will listen to me. He always does."

"Albert, how can I live with—" There was a knock on the door. Albert moved his arms away, and I jumped up. Straightening out my skirt, I said, "Come in." Albert buttoned his shirt.

Nurse Betty entered. "Sorry to disturb you. Mr. Mahbub Ali is here for the queen's medicine."

Picking up the chain of keys from my desk, I went to the medicine cabinet. I was opening it, when Mahbub also came in the room, holding something in his hand.

"I told you to wait outside," Betty said.

Mahbub salaamed. "I bring something for doctor sahiba. Queen say to give personally to you." He held a small blue velvet box out towards me.

"*Behenchood*, get out," Albert shouted at Mahbub.

Wanting to defuse the tension, I held up my palm. "It's all right Albert." Then taking the mixture bottle out of the cabinet, I went to Mahbub and accepting the gift, handed him the bottle. "Please thank the queen from me."

Mahbub salaamed me, and after glaring at Albert, left the room.

Albert kept sitting, ogling curiously at the expensive looking blue velvet box, I had placed on my desk. I sat down and picking a patient's examination report form, started to fill it.

"Is there anything else I can do for you?" I asked, while writing.

"You must be giving the queen special treatment. She is showering you with royal jewels," he tried to banter.

"Just some trinket, I imagine." I did not open the box, which he likely wanted me to do.

He got up, and put on his cap. "Will you think of what I've offered?"

Wishing to get rid of him, I simply nodded. He left my office.

That evening I walked, with Elgin pushing Jan in his pram, on our usual stroll up to the river. As we stood at the *ghat's* steps looking out on the glimmering waters of the Jamuna, Albert's appalling words came back to my mind. I fumed thinking that he had the audacity to call it an 'offer'. It was no better than life as a *bibi* that Humphrey had suggested. At least in Calcutta I would have lived in some splendor, but what would be my existence here as the mistress of a junior police officer? I wondered, if I was relegated to exist as a lowly widow, with children to support, and give in to the fancy of these designing men? Become their plaything?

My thoughts were diverted towards some bonfires burning down the road. "Elgin, are they having a cremation, at this time of the day?"

"No, Memsahib. Start of Holi."

I had forgotten that it was a holiday the next day, on account of the Hindu spring festival. "But is it not tomorrow, when they will throw colored powders at each other?"

"Yes, but tonight they celebrate the burning of the witch, Holika, and killing of the demon king by god Vishnu."

"Ah, the celebration of victory of good over evil, and wishing for plentiful spring harvests. What else happens tonight?"

"They apply the fire's ashes to their foreheads. Some people drink *bhang*, and have fun."

"Perhaps we should return home before we get smeared with ashes by those intoxicated men." I turned towards the *haveli's* laneway.

While we hurried home, knowing there would be the colors and water throwing carnival in the streets the next day, I was concerned about the safety of our Hospital, from those *bhang* crazed *badmashes*. But I imagined the security guards would prevent any looting.

The next morning, I was awakened by the sounds of revelry in the streets below my apartment windows. I saw young men and women, shrieking and laughing, as they chased each other holding containers of colored powder, which they threw or smeared on each other's faces. Some of the residents stood in the balconies of their homes, and from buckets, threw water on these in the street below. It looked as if the whole city had gone wild.

There was a knock on the door. Thinking it was Elgin, with my breakfast, I opened it. Mumtaz stood there holding a copper tray with tumblers of colored powders.

"Happy Holi."

I was surprised at her greeting. "This is a Hindu festival, is it not?"

"Yes, but we Muslims celebrate it too." She then smeared my face with some red dust."

"Oh, no," I said. "I'll have to wash rabbain."

"Do not wash today. The powder bring you good luck."

"All right." I quickly dipped my fingers in a red and yellow bowl, on her tray, and daubed the powders on her face. "I bring you happiness too."

She ran away squealing with delight.

The following morning, while riding in a *tonga* to the Hospital, I observed the streets and the houses' walls streaked with paint from the merriments. Walking up the Hospital's garden path, I saw similar paint strewn over the bushes, the walkways and even inside the hallway. Sweepers and servants were busy cleaning up the mess. In a way, I felt happy that the populace had celebrated their festival with passion and forgotten, at least for a day, their conflicts and worries.

Nurse Betty opened the locked door of my office. We exchanged greetings and joked briefly about the Holi gaiety; I went inside. Taking off my bonnet and hanging up my cloak, I sat down at my desk. The neat pile of patient's files, I was to see that day, was stacked on one side. My eye caught sight of the blue velvet box that lay next to them. In the commotion of Albert's visit, I had forgotten to take it home.

I reached over, and opening the box was delighted to see inside a pair of shiny gold bracelets. How kind of the queen, I thought. I took one out and was examining its intricate patterns in the sunlight shining from the window, when my eyes caught sight of the medicine bottles, through the glass door, within the cabinet. Something was odd, for they were not placed in my preferred order. I got up and, taking the key chain out of my reticule, opened the glass door. My heart skipped a beat when I saw the amber colored large bottle of Belladonna extract was nearly half empty. The bottle was almost full earlier, as I had only used a little bit of it for making the mixture for the queen.

Thinking some other doctor might have used it, I stepped outside and went to my nurse's desk. "Betty, did someone take nearly half a bottle of Belladonna from my cabinet?"

"No, Doctor Wallace." She looked astonished.

"Did anyone go in my office, yesterday?"

"I don't think so. Yesterday was holiday. I was not here. Perhaps somebody from the admin did. Shall I go and inquire?"

"Yes, please do." She walked towards the general office.

I had hardly sat down at my desk, when the door suddenly opened, and Doctor Lal entered. He looked disheveled, as if he had not slept the whole night. I stood and we exchanged good mornings.

He saw, on my desk, the Belladonna container and the open velvet box with the shiny bracelets in it. "Nice *karas*. A gift from the queen?"

"Yes." I mumbled, still confused about the missing medicine.

"Are you sending more Belladonna to her?" He pointed at the bottle.

"No." I mentioned the disappearance of half of the bottle's content, and having Nurse Betty inquire who might have taken it.

"We'll get to the bottom of this, later. But can you please come with me? Some persons in my office wish to talk to you."

I followed him into the corridor, and we walked over to his office. He opened the door and ushered me in. To my surprise, the Civil Surgeon Doctor Balfour, and Commissioner Fraser were seated on chairs around the desk. They stood, and wished me a good morning, with solemn faces. Mr. Fraser pointed to an empty chair beside him. I sat down, thinking what could be the matter.

Doctor Lal sat down on his chair and, clearing his throat, looked towards me. "Late last night, I was called by King Zafar to attend to his son, Prince Fakhruddin. The messenger had said, he was gravely ill. But, unfortunately by the time I reached his chamber, the heir apparent had already passed away. There was nothing I could do. Most unfortunate."

The news shocked me. "Oh! I'm so sorry to hear that. What was the cause of his death?"

"From what I was told, by Hakim Ahsanullah, the prince had shown Cholera like symptoms: diarrhea, vomiting and such. But one can never be certain. Could have been something else, even food poisoning."

"Cholera has been going around the city, as you may know, sir. We have many cases here." I said.

Doctor Lal mopped his brow. "Yes, I'm aware of it. Naturally, I immediately advised our officials. These gentlemen wish to see you. They have some questions."

"Doctor Wallace," Doctor Balfour turned towards me. "I understand you are treating Queen Zinat?" I nodded. He continued, "What have you prescribed her?"

"Only a mild mixture of Belladonna, within the limits, sir. It's in my reports," I responded.

Doctor Balfour looked towards Doctor Lal. "You said the

prince died of food poisoning. Could it have been from Belladonna?"

"Difficult to say, sir. The symptoms are very similar," Doctor Lal said nervously.

Mr. Fraser looked at me. "Margaret, did you prescribe anything to the heir apparent?"

"No, sir. I've never even met the prince," I replied.

"But, could someone have given him the Belladonna?" Fraser looked at me in the eyes, as if wanting to see if I replied truthfully.

Knowing what he was implying, not averting his eyes, I responded, "I did prepare the Belladonna mixture bottles. They were intended for the queen, and picked up by her trusted servant, Mahbub Ali. I have no knowledge of what happened to them inside the palace. I'd presume the queen took the medicine."

"You are certain of that?" Fraser persisted.

"Yes, sir." I looked towards Doctor Lal. "Didn't you say, the queen was feeling better after consuming the medication?"

Doctor Lal nodded. "King Zafar mentioned it to me." Then he looked towards Doctor Balfour. "I have some more information, sir. Doctor Margaret told me, just this morning, that half a bottle of Belladonna extract is missing from her cabinet."

Doctor Balfour's face grew red with anger. "How on earth is it possible?" he bellowed. "Isn't it under lock and key?"

"Yes, sir. It is," Doctor Lal quickly responded, uncomfortably. "Even the office door is locked. But yesterday was the Holi holiday. There was much merriment going on. So we are not sure who took it. Nurse Betty is asking around."

"I would like a report, immediately," Doctor Balfour said loudly.

"Now that's an interesting twist to the riddle," Frazer said. "Gentlemen, I propose we adjourn this meeting, until we learn more about the missing Belladonna."

"Yes, I agree," Doctor Balfour said. "And, Doctor Lal, kindly also interview any visitors to Doctor Margaret's office in the last few days. I'd like a full report, *jaldysay*, please."

"Yes, sir. I will sir." Doctor Lal nodded a few times.

Thinking the meeting was over, I stood. The others did the same. It was then Doctor Balfour uttered those words to me. They still ring in my ears: "Err ... Doctor Wallace, under the circumstances, it would be advisable if you would take the next few days off. At least until we have completed our investigation. We will advise you when you may return. It will be up to Commissioner Fraser, if he wishes to hold a formal inquiry or not."

On hearing those words, tears welled in my eyes. I quickly dabbed them with my handkerchief. "Have I done anything wrong, sir? Why can't I continue performing my duties?"

While Doctor Balfour looked straight ahead, hands clasped at his back, as if not wanting to discuss his decision, Mr. Fraser said in a soothing voice, "Margaret ... I am sure this sad news has distressed you. A few days rest will do you good. It is no reflection on your abilities. You'll be back at your job soon. You'll see."

"Also, please leave the keys to your medicine cabinet with Nurse Betty," Doctor Balfour added.

They bowed, as I turned and walked towards the door.

Back in my office, I sat quietly for a while contemplating the sequence of events. How quickly people can turn against you, I wondered. Finally, having dried my eyes, I collected some of my personal items, including the jewelry box, and stepped outside the door. Seeing Betty was back at her desk I approached her. "Did you learn anything about the missing Belladonna?"

"No. I asked everyone. No one acknowledges having taken it."

"Did anyone enter, or see someone go into my office yesterday?"

"I asked around. Nobody went in or saw anyone enter. But there were lots of street people here celebrating Holi. Your office door was locked. Except for the cleaning staff, they have the master key, no stranger could have gone inside. I can't imagine any hospital staff taking it, without informing you, or me at least."

My head reeled with disbelief. I put one hand on her desk to steady myself. "The disappearance is most peculiar. Anyhow, please keep inquiring. I'm going home now, and can be reached there in case of any emergency or any urgent matters." She nodded sheepishly. It seemed she already knew that I was being sent home. I handed her the keys, and did not need to tell her anything more.

As I walked on the garden path towards the main gates, to hail a *tonga*, I wondered if I would ever return to that hospital.

After descending from the carriage, I was about to use the elephant-head knocker on the *haveli's* door, when its wicket opened and Sharif stepped outside. I believe he was on an afternoon shift that day, and was likely going out on a social visit, for he was dressed in mufti.

He looked surprised to see me returning so early. "Salaam Doctor Mar—" He stopped in mid-sentence upon seeing my teary face. "Is anything the matter?"

"It's all right," I said trying to suppress a sob, handkerchief over my nose.

"No, no. Not all right. Please come in, tell me what happened." He ushered me inside and we went into a small sitting room, the *bethak*, next to the entrance. It was used mostly by menfolk, and they being at work, was empty. Sharif shouted at a maid to bring tea for memsahib. Upon hearing my name, Mumtaz came over hurriedly, and sitting by me put her arm over my shoulder.

I thought I might as well tell them everything. In the event of losing my employment, I feared I could not have paid them even the next month's rent. Over tea and snacks, and in between sniffles, I told them about the crisis I was in, which, like a quicksand, was about to swallow me to disgrace and perhaps imprisonment.

While both Mumtaz and Sharif expressed their sorrow on hearing of Prince Fakhruddin's death, but they did not look surprised. They stared at a wall for a while. Mumtaz broke the silence. "Of course she killed Fakhru. She want her son, Jawan, to be king. So now with Cholera in city, she has perfect opportunity to poison the *waliahad*."

"Yes, Mumtaz, it might be so, but the Hospital thinks that I provided the poison," I said.

"Did anyone see you give the medicine to Mahbub?" Sharif asked.

"Yes, lots of people. But it was only a weak mixture. No one could have died, even if they drank the whole bottle."

"That Mahbub very clever." Sharif rubbed his chin. "I am sure he steal the strong medicine."

"But if no body see Margareet give poison to Mahbub, then how can Hospital say she give poison?" Mumtaz demanded.

I was somewhat relieved on hearing that. "Yes, Mumtaz, you might have a point. I will just have to wait and see. It could be that some other doctor might have taken the liquid and forgot to record it."

"Yes. You will see everything will be all right, soon." Mumtaz hugged me. However, from the corner of my eye I noticed Sharif still staring out of a window. It seemed he was not so sure of Mumtaz's supposition.

I stood. "Thank you for the tea. I must go and rest. It has been a most tiring morning."

Some days passed, and I did not hear anything from the Hospital. It seemed as if they had forgotten all about me. I was tempted to go and see Doctor Lal, but decided against it, thinking they were likely still investigating. I spent the time, with my dear son, taking him out for long strolls in his pram, with dutiful Elgin at my side. We discovered some delightful used bookstores, in the market along the river. I purchased a boxful of old classics, which I was told had been donated by departing British residents. These helped greatly in whiling away the hours. I also spent time in mending and altering my old dresses, a task I had let slip by.

Some days later. One morning, as I lay on a divan by the window, enjoying the cool breeze and reading Charlotte Bronte' *Villette*, and comparing my unhappy life to Lucy Snowe's, Elgin came excitedly into the room.

"Colonel Humphrey is at the main door."

I wondered why he had come. It then occurred to me. Of course he is here to personally bring me the good news of him having arranged my children's passage to Calcutta. "Oh! Ask him to come in, then."

"No. He wants to meet you outside. Wishes to talk in his carriage."

That sounded odd. "Alright." I bookmarked the novel's page, and stood. I straightened out my dress, and looking into the mirror, I made sure my hair was in place and wiped away any mascara that had smudged below my eyes. Not that I cared much for Humphrey, I merely wished to look decent.

I found him waiting beside his carriage, looking as smart and trim as ever, in his red uniform jacket. His escort sepoys kept the curious onlookers at bay. A footman opened the carriage door.

"Good morning!" Humphrey touched the brim of his cap, and motioned towards the carriage. "Shall we?"

I entered the carriage. Humphrey followed and sat next to me.

"So good to see you again, Margaret. You are looking radiant as usual." He tried to hold my hand, but I moved it aside. "Such terrible news. The death of a Mughal prince. I've returned straight from Lucknow."

"While his death is unfortunate, but why does it distress you so much, sir?"

"He was the heir apparent."

"I am sure the King will appoint another one."

"But Fakhru was the one we favored."

It was then I remembered the 'Agreement' that some Company officers had made with the prince. It was likely Humphrey was part of that group. It also dawned on me that most of those officers had died mysteriously, and perhaps Humphrey was also on the list! However, not wanting to bring it up, I simply asked, "Did you wish to see me about something, sir?"

He reached again for my hand, and this time managed to grab it. "Margaret, dearest. You know how much I care for you ... ever since I saw you ... I cannot stop thinking about you ..." He went on and on with his adulations, which I hardly listened to, and gazed out of the carriage's window, waiting for him to speak about my children. My mind was brought back when I heard him say, "And now my dear you have gotten yourself into this pickle."

"What 'pickle' are you referring to, sir?"

"This business of the poisoning of the prince."

"Poisoning! And you think, I did it?"

"It's not what I think, it's what the CMH believes."

"Really, sir. Who in the Hospital?"

"Doctor Balfour, Lal, your Nurse Betty, and others too."

"How interesting. And do they have any proof?" I thought he was simply bluffing to get me to agree to whatever he sought me for, again.

"Yes, I'm afraid they do. Have witnesses and lots of evidence, as well. I've seen the report."

"What evidence dand witnesses?" I was beginning to get angry.

"My dear Margaret, I am not at liberty to say. But Fraser is convinced. He will be holding a formal Inquiry, in a few days. You will likely get the summons later today. So, I thought I should come and see you immediately."

I felt as if I had been thrown out of the carriage and lay in the street, with Hospital's officials, in white coats, standing around and pointing their fingers at me. I must have fainted, but came to when I felt Humphrey stroking my arm.

"Margaret, Margaret. Are you all right? Would you like some water? Some brandy perhaps?" Humphrey said in a concerned voice.

"No, thank you Colonel. I am fine now. I feel weak. I should go and lie down. Is there anything else you can tell me?"

"Yes, there is, my dear." He continued to stroke my arm. "You know Fraser is an old chum. With one word from me, and if he wishes, I can even get a telegram from Canning, your Inquiry will be cancelled."

"Really, sir. And will I go back to my old job at the Hospital?" I asked, thinking Humphrey really did care about me, and was actually willing to get me out of the 'pickle,' he said.

"Oh no. With all this publicity it may not be possible now for you to work there. Here's what I propose we do. I get Fraser to postpone the Inquiry. You come and stay with me at Calcutta. I get you a senior job at the hospital there. After a few months, a year at the most, when this storm has blown over, I get Fraser to cancel the Inquiry permanently. What do you say, my dear?"

On hearing that despicable "proposal" again, brought back memories of all those qualms I had about living in sin, particularly, with a devious individual like Humphrey. He sickened me. I felt distraught. Tears started to stream down my cheeks. Humphrey immediately pulled out a clean handkerchief and handed it to me.

"Sorry Humphrey. I told you earlier. I cannot live with you as your mistress in Calcutta."

"You know I cannot marry you."

"Why is that?"

"My brother wishes me to marry Lady Sofia, for her inheritance. He needs the money. He's lost a lot of our family fortune in foolish business ventures. I'm planning to go to London, marry her, and return back to you in Calcutta. What do you say, my dear?"

Although hearing that surprised me, but it did not convince me, for he had told me differently earlier. I felt it was another one of his devious ploys, to get me to Calcutta. "Well, sir, you should do what you have to do."

"But what will you do?"

Not hearing those 'magic words,' what else could I have said, except: "I'll take my chances at the Inquiry." I opened the carriage's door.

"But they have proof of your collaboration with the queen!"

"I am innocent." I got down from the carriage.

Humphrey slammed the door, and glared out of the window at me. "Have you considered your children's passage to India?"

I did not respond, for I did not comprehend. But while walking back to the *haveli*, I understood what he meant. It brought on more tears. I wiped them with his handkerchief, and blowing my nose in it, threw it in the sewage gutter flowing in the alleyway.

Humphrey was not bluffing. That afternoon, a *chaprassie* delivered a summons, signed by the City Magistrate, Sir Theophilus Metcalf. I was to appear for an Inquiry at the Delhi City Courts, in two days, on Thursday the twentieth day of March 1856, at ten o'clock sharp.

Sharif would have heard about my summons, for in the evening he knocked on my apartment door. Elgin let him in. I asked him to sit on the chair. I sat on the sofa. I asked if he would like some tea. He declined. Elgin took Jan outside. We conversed again about my situation. I told him what little Humphrey had confided in me.

"So, they say they have witnesses and evidence?"

I nodded.

"I think they make it up."

"I'll have an opportunity to explain myself. It will be for the judge to decide, whether the evidence is believable."

"I fear for you. They all the same, Company English men."

"Well, I think Doctor Lal will be there. I am certain he will be fair."

"Doctor Lal. Hah!" Sharif smirked. "He more English than English!"

"Well, Sharif, what choice do I have?"

Sharif then moved forward in his chair. "I have choice for you," he whispered.

"Whatever do you mean?"

"I tell you after Friday prayers, *inshallah*. After your court. If you no like their decision, you decide if you like my choice."

Although I was certain the Hospital had no case against me, and all that 'evidence' would be thrown out of the court, I felt happy that Sharif had a plan I could fall back on. "Alright," I said. "We will speak again on Friday, how you say ... *inshallah!*"

He nodded, and getting up salaamed, and was about to leave the room, but halted at the door. He took something out of his shirt pocket. "Ah, this letter come for you in this evening *dak*. Sorry, I should give you before, but we start to talk." He handed me the envelope bearing the red Canadian stamps having the solemn face of Queen Victoria on them.

I thanked him and flew to the divan, and resuming my comfortable prone position, opened the envelope. It was the long awaited letter from Cousin Heather.

Dearest Margaret,

Sorry about the delay in my reply to your last letter of months ago. We are all well, and so are your lovely children. We will be celebrating Brucie's fourth birthday soon, and you will be in our thoughts all that day. While Brucie has begun to talk—you wouldn't believe the things he says—his sister, Vicky, while only a year younger, tries to imitate him a lot. They have been told, through pictures of sailing ships and our crude imitations by crawling on the rug, that we will be soon going on a sea voyage. They seem to understand, for they jump up and down with joy, and crawl behind us, as if on a ship. Mother is most anxious, as are Kirsten and me, to get to Crimea and visit our dear Robert's grave. Also, we are concerned that there should be a proper monument marking his resting place, or else his mound would be obliterated over time.

With regards to our extending our trip to India, I have approached the subject with Mother and Colonel Mitchell, who is kindly making the arrangements, and we are happy to learn, part of the expenses as well. The good news is that he has heard back from the P&O Steamship Line, and they want, payment up front for the tickets to India. The additional cost they are quoting is £30 per person, one-way fare (first class and full board, of course), with the children at half price.

From Mother's facial expression, upon hearing of this, I could tell that she was not too happy about spending the extra money. She is now citing numerous reasons—such as, "Too long and tiring ... have to return back to my canning business ..."—for not wishing to extend the journey to India. However, upon my insistence that your children have been far too long away from you, she has relented saying, "If Margaret is willing to pay, you can take them to India."

Now, dearest, wouldn't it be wonderful if I were to bring them to you? But I won't be able to stay too long, for as I wrote earlier I have managed to have my fiancé, John, to agree to postpone our wedding till after my trip. This brings me to the other reason for writing to you. A matter of financing your children's and my voyage to India. The additional fare would amount to £90. Not having any money of my own, I have to rely on you. So, my dear, if you were to wire me this amount, I will immediately deliver it to Colonel Mitchell, so that he can purchase our tickets' extensions in a timely manner.

On a lighter note, I've read somewhere that the East India Company is offering free passage to young women, from Britain to India, as part of a special program (The Fishing Fleet, the writer jovially called it). Also, if a lady was unable to find a husband, she would be provided a return passage as well (a Returned Empty, again as the writer put it!). But seriously, my John would hit the roof, if he heard that I'd opted for this option!

So glad to read that you are enjoying your medical work at the Hospital and at the College as well. And also socializing and attended the Christmas Ball at the Metcalf House! Everyone here was so impressed on of hearing it. By the way who is this Colonel Humphrey you keep writing about? Do tell more. Has he ....

I could not read any more, for tears of happiness filled my eyes, thinking my children would be here with me, soon. I folded the letter and put it back in the envelope. Nevertheless, my euphoria quickly evaporated when I realized that I had only a couple of pounds in my savings account at the Delhi Bank. Although I was not surprised, it still distressed me that Aunt Fiona, while happily receiving my Robert's pension—albeit a small amount—was unwilling to pay for my children's fare. Furthermore, there was a good chance of my losing my job, and I could end up scouring the country seeking employment. I thought about asking Mamma and Papa for the money, but considered it unfair, for they were earning hardly enough to live respectably, which they were expected to do. I felt at a loss and was staring at the ceiling when Elgin entered, baby talking to Jan.

"What is it Memsahib? Some bad news in letter from Canada?" She looked at the envelope.

"Yes, and no, Elgin. I have to send ninety pounds to Cousin Heather for her and my children's tickets. And I don't know where

I am going to get that much money. It's nearly two months of my salary."

"You can take from my wage. Pay me when you have money."

"Come now, Elgin. Don't be ridiculous. I am paying you only two pounds per month, and you send most of it to your parents, who need it. I could never even dream of taking your money."

She must have thought of something, for she put Jan in his crib, and went into the adjacent room, to my dressing table. She returned with the small blue velvet box in her hand, and gave it to me. I opened it and saw the gold bracelets shining inside.

"Elgin, you are not only a hard worker, but a genius as well!"

"Thank you Memsahib. Your children more precious than these *karas*."

"They certainly are. I know just the jewelry shop who will buy them. We will go there early tomorrow."

That night before going to bed, it occurred to me that no wonder the thought of disposing something came immediately to Elgin's mind. For it was how the poor survived, by selling off the family jewels. In my prayer I asked for God's help that I may never have to resort to such an act again.

Although Chandni Chowk was a fair distance from Sharif Mahal, Elgin and I decided to walk over there. With Jan in his pram, we carefully traversed the streets avoiding not only the carriages' wheels and horses' hooves, but also the horns of the Brahma bulls that freely roamed in the lanes.

We reached the shop with a large sign board that read: *Sharif Emporium*. Akbar Khan, wearing his usual white shalwar-kameeze, a black waistcoat and matching *topi*, sat on a chair outside under the awning, reading a newspaper; a glass of tea steamed on a side stool.

Upon seeing us approach, he immediately stood. "Salaam memsahib. Welcome, welcome, to my humble shop. Please come inside."

While Elgin waited outside, with Jan in the pram, I followed him into the spacious store, with glass top counters and glass door cabinets on the walls. All were full of exquisite looking jewelry sets. He led me to a sitting area in a corner with cushioned stools and a table, set up for the more serious clients. While some customers looked around, a couple were at a counter examining some items, being served by Mrs. Khan. I salaamed her and sat on a stool. I was glad that no one I knew was in the shop. Akbar sat on the opposite stool. He asked a servant to bring tea.

"You want to see some jewelry?"

I shook my head, and looked away, too ashamed to say what I wished to do. The servant put two glasses of steaming hot tea on the table. Knowing it was the regular Delhi sweet *chai*, I was too distraught to ask him to change it.

Akbar seemed to get the message that I was not there to purchase anything. He sipped his tea. "I hear bad thing happen to you at Hospital. But don't worry, my son will help you," he whispered.

I finally picked up courage to whisper, "But, this morning I need *your* help, Khan sahib." I pulled out the blue velvet box, from my reticule, and placed it on the table.

He opened it and his eyes lit up on noticing its content. He took one of the bracelets out and examined it in the sunlight, rotating it between his fingers. "Belong to queen?"

I nodded. Then suddenly I thought it was a mistake to tell him the truth. For knowing that, he may not purchase it.

Akbar stroked his beard, then finally whispered, "How much you want for it?"

"Ninety pounds, for my children's tickets to Calcutta," I murmured.

He got up and with the bracelet in hand, went to his wife. They moved to a corner and spoke in whispers. I tried to take a sip of the tea, but put the glass down for it was too sweet. I saw Mrs. Khan glance towards me. Goodness, I thought, it seems she doesn't wish to pay ninety pounds. Likely thinks she can grab them cheaply, for I am in difficulty. Finally I saw them nodding.

Akbar returned to the table and sat down. "Alright, we can pay you one hundred pounds. Is it enough? Or you need more?" he whispered.

I felt ecstatic. "It's more than enough, Khan sahib," I whispered back.

He put the bracelet back in the box. "Wait a minute, please." Picking up the box he went to the cash counter. Opening a drawer he counted out some bills. He returned and placed a small multicolored pouch on the table. "Here you are memsahib. Thank you very much. Please come again."

Glad that no one else looked in my direction, I put the pouch in my reticule. Thanking him, and salaaming Mrs. Khan, I exited the shop. Elgin was rolling the pram up and down the street, and come up to me. In answer to her questioning look, I nodded. She smiled broadly.

"Let's walk up to the Delhi Bank, over there." I pointed towards the large building.

We entered the impressive iron gates of the Delhi Bank building's boundary wall, and strolled on the winding path through a small garden. This was a former palace built by Begum Sumru, the wife of a German mercenary employed by a Mughal Emperor, another one of Delhi's aristocratic families. Elgin preferred to amble, with Jan in the pram, in the garden. I ascended the curved stone stairway onto the patio that led into the palladium like building of Delhi Bank.

The Bank's manager, Mr. Beresford was just walking out, likely for a stroll. He recognized me and tipped his hat, bidding me a good morning. I returned his greeting and inquired after—my patients—his wife and five lovely daughters. Pleased to hear they were well, I asked if I could wire some money home. He pointed out the desk and the clerk who would look after me.

I walked up there and made the request to wire ninety pounds to Canada. The Anglo-Indian clerk handed me a form, saying, "There will be a one pound fee." I nodded, and filled out Cousin Heather's name and address as the recipient. Taking out nine £ 10 and one £ 1 notes from the pouch, I gave them to him. He wrote out a receipt, and rotating the curved wooden blotter over the ink, passed the paper to me, saying: "There you are memsahib. Your money will be there in a few days."

I thanked him and walked out onto the stone patio bathed in bright sunshine. I felt so happy that I wanted to spread my hands and do a pirouette singing: my children are coming here ... my children are coming here. But I restrained myself, for there was a constant stream of people going into and out of the bank, and I had had enough odd looks for the day already.

I found Elgin sitting on a bench under a shady tree, gently rocking Jan's pram while he slept peacefully inside.

"Nearly all done, Elgin. We have to make just one more stop."

We strolled over to the nearby Post Office building. While Elgin again waited outside, I walked up to the telegraph counter, and sent out the following telegram to Heather:

Money wired. Please advise arrival date in India. Love. Margaret.

While walking back to our *haveli*, we were arrested by the mouthwatering display, outside the Gantewalla's Sweets Shop. Elgin and I looked at each other, and we both nodded simultaneously, with smiles. "Yes, let's take home some *barfis, jalebis* and *rasmalais*," I said. "Let's celebrate."

Although later that night, after dinner, while enjoying the delicious Indian sweets, I wondered if my celebration was premature. Sadly my premonition turned out to be true.

Chapter Eighteen

Mini-Judgement Day

1856, March: Delhi, India

ANOTHER ONE of my mini-judgement days on Earth arrived on Thursday the twentieth. I woke up early at the sounds of the morning *azan*, from the nearby mosque, and the six am firing of the cannon, from the Ridge. Knowing that I liked to bathe, Mumtaz had a hot bath ready for me in the ladies *ghusalkhana*. After a leisurely soaking and a light breakfast, Elgin helped me dress in my best gown, the grey one, I had purchased in London. She straightened out the ringlets of my fair hair, and asked if I wanted any mascara or rouge? Knowing the court house would likely be crowded by the curious, I responded, "Why not. Let them all have a good look at the medicine woman of Delhi."

Before departing, alone in my room, I knelt before a window. With my clasped hands resting on the window sill, and with the dome of St. James' Church in the distance before my eyes, I prayed to my Lord. I prayed that He would give me courage and strength to face the day. I prayed that although He knew I was innocent, but I would accept whatever judgement he wished to deliver onto me. I rose with a clear heart and conscience.

It was just after nine o'clock when Elgin and I descended the steps from the second floor. Mumtaz had earlier collected Jan and taken him to her apartment. We found Sharif waiting in the courtyard, all dressed up in his sepoy's uniform, even though he was on the afternoon shift.

He approached us and salaamed. "Doctor Margaret, your carriage is waiting. I come with you to court, yes?"

"No, thank you, Sharif. I will be fine. Elgin is accompanying me," I responded not wishing others to think he was somehow involved in my case. He wished me good luck with a bow, and we boarded the conveyance.

It did not take long for the carriage to reach the Court House located in another palatial building in the city center. At the entrance I spotted several of the Delhi's European gentry, in their smart dresses and suits, walking in, without even a glance towards me. However, just outside the doorway several Indian youths stood chatting. I recognized them as students from Delhi College. Upon seeing me they immediately turned, some salaamed and others *namested*. I nodded in return.

Inside the foyer, I handed Elgin my bonnet and cloak, but kept my white silk shawl about my shoulders; I waited, while she hung them in the cloak room. She kept her grey woolen robe wrapped about her. The receptionist directed us towards the room, where the Inquiry was to be held.

Entering the court room, I felt relieved to see that it was only about half full. Some of the seats on the main floor were occupied, and most of the students sat on chairs in balcony. Nothing to worry about, for I am innocent, I thought. Wrapping by shawl around me, I walked up the aisle, Elgin following me. A clerk came hurriedly forward. "Are you represented?" He looked bewildered when I shook my head. He then directed us to the reserved seats in the front row. Most of the gathering's faces turned around to look at me. I ignored them.

While bending down to sit, I saw Catherine and Captain Herford sitting in the second row, behind me. Both nodded and smiled encouragingly. I returned their smile. Then I noticed Albert, in his uniform, sitting beside them. How strange that he is here, and hasn't he got anything better to do, I thought. He also smiled and nodded. I unheeded his gesture and sat down.

On the stage, at the front, a long table with a red covering stood in the center. Behind it were placed, five high back mahogany chairs. The court clerks sat at a lower table, below the stage. Uniformed security guards stood around. I noticed a prisoner's dock at one side. I wondered if I would be made to sit in there. The witness box was situated at the other dend of the stage. I was certain that I would be cross examined in there.

Promptly at ten o'clock, the court clerk rose to state, for the record, the place, date, time and so on, and that this was a formal Inquiry into certain incidences at the Civil and Military Hospital, with Magistrate, Sir Theophilus Metcalf, presiding. "All rise."

Five officials dressed in dark tail coats, black cravats, and grey trousers, entered the stage from a side door. They were led by the City Magistrate, Sir Theophilus, who took the center chair. He was followed by Doctors Balfour and Lal, who walked over and sat on chairs at his right. Commissioner Fraser and Colonel Humphrey, trailing behind, sat on chairs at the Magistrate's left. Although I knew them all well, they did not smile or make eye contact with me, rather kept shuffling papers in files in front of them.

After the audience sat down, Sir Theophilus looked towards Doctor Balfour and nodded.

Doctor Balfour clearing his throat, started speaking. It was a long winded account of how he was informed one morning, by Doctor Lal—he glanced towards him—of the sad death of Prince Fakhruddin. And Doctor Lal suspected the mortality might be as a result of food poisoning, and could have been due to an overdose of Belladonna. He went on and on about how concerned he became, especially knowing that Queen Zinat was being treated by a lady doctor from his hospital and Belladonna had been prescribed, and that he became additionally alarmed upon being informed that nearly half a quart, from a full bottle of Belladonna pure extract, was missing from that lady doctor's office.

Following murmurs of unease from the audience, Doctor Balfour continued into a lengthy discourse of how the queen was demanding more and more Belladonna, which the lady doctor was happily providing, and in return was seen to have received gifts, likely of considerable value.... Balfour deliberated at length.

On hearing these statements, my mind went numb, and I stared out of the open side doors into the picturesque garden. It was also beginning to get warm, and I fanned myself.

Finally Doctor Balfour completed his speech, and looking towards me, asked, "Is Doctor Margaret Wallace present?"

I stood.

"Please come to the witness box."

I went there, and after the usual swearing in, and stating my full name, date and place of birth and other details, sat down.

"Are you the doctor who had been treating Queen Zinat?"

"Yes, sir,"

After some standard questions of her health and so on, he asked,

"How much Belladonna had you prescribed?"

"As in my report, sir. Only two bottles of a weak mixture."

"And who do you believe took the almost half a quart of the extract from your office?"

"I have no idea, sir. Didn't the Hospital find anyone?"

"No. There is no record of anyone from the Hospital taking it. Also, there is no evidence of any unauthorized person entered your office."

"Then why Mahbub Ali go into her office?" Someone from the balcony shouted. The gathering mumbled. The Magistrate banged his gavel, and looked up towards the balcony. "Quiet. Any more comments and I shall have you thrown out of this court. Doctor Balfour, please continue."

After some more mundane inquiring, Doctor Balfour said, "I do not have any more questions." He looked towards the other members on the panel. "Does anyone else wish to question the witness?"

"Yes, I do," Colonel Humphrey said.

"Doctor Wallace, what were those gifts you received from the queen, and how much would you say they are worth?"

While surprised at his line of questioning, I remained calm and described them, and said, "I am not certain of their value."

"Now those Indian garbs are very expensive, are they not?"

"Perhaps. How do you know, sir, have you purchased any?"

The audience tittered. Humphrey asked angrily, "Did you not ask the queen for that fancy costume you wore at the Christmas Ball?"

The spectators hummed. "I did not. It was borrowed from an Indian lady friend. I can provide the details," I calmly responded.

"Yes, please deliver the court clerk her name and address," Humphrey said, trying to control his temper.

"I have a question," Mr. Fraser said, leaning forward.

"Margaret, do you think the Belladonna mixture in those two bottles, you sent to the queen, could have poisoned anyone?"

"Hardly, sir. The mixture wasn't strong enough to even kill a cat." I was certain he would have caught on to what he had said earlier to me.

The gathering burst out in laughter. Sir Theophilus rapped the gavel. "Order, order." There being no more questions I was asked to step down, and I returned to my seat.

Doctor Balfour then called a number of Hospital staff, including Nurse Betty, as witnesses. All corroborated the information that I had been giving medicine bottles to Mahbub Ali and had received several gifts.

It was getting close to noon. Sir Theophilus seemed to be getting a bit impatient. He looked up at the clock, and asked, "Doctor Balfour, your report says that it is very likely the Prince was poisoned by the Belladonna extract taken from Doctor Wallace's office. What evidence do you have of it?"

"Yes, I was coming to that," Doctor Balfour responded. He mopped his brow. We have a witness. I now call upon Captain Albert Miller, to please come forward."

On hearing Albert's name, I fell into a state of disbelief. My head swam, as if in a haze. I searched my brain, wondering what he would say against me. I did not hear all his swearing in and introduction, but my mind began to register when he commenced his testimony: " ... I was experiencing chest pains and had gone to see her that day."

"Was anyone else with you in Doctor Wallace's office?" Doctor Balfour asked.

"The nurse had let me in, then Mahbub Ali came in and the nurse left the room."

"Then what happened?"

"Doctor Wallace, opened the medicine cabinet, and handed Mahbub Ali a bottle full of Belladonna."

The audience oohed. "Are you certain of that?" Doctor Balfour wanted to confirm Albert's statement.

"Yes, absolutely, sir."

Doctor Balfour glanced at the others on the table.

"I have a question." Mr. Fraser again leaned forward.

"Captain Miller, have you had any medical training?"

"No, sir."

"Then how are you certain that it was Belladonna extract that Doctor Margaret gave to Mahbub Ali?"

"Because she poured it out of the big bottle, with a label, into the small bottle. I can read, sir."

While pandemonium broke out in the court room, and Sir Theophilus banged the gavel, I sprang up and screamed, "It's a lie!" Catherine came around quickly and embraced me. I sobbed on her shoulder.

When order was restored in the room, at Catherine's pleading I sat down, while she still kept her arm around my shoulders.

"Doctor Balfour, are there any more witnesses?"

He shook his head. "No, sir."

"Since it is past noon," Sir Theophilus began, "we will have a short recess for lunch. Following that, I will meet with the Inquiry committee members in my chamber. I trust we will come to a recommendation. This Inquiry is adjourned till two o'clock." He banged the mallet and rose. The other committee members also stood and followed the magistrate out of the side door, clutching files to their chest. The spectators rose.

While Albert quickly left through a side door, Captain Herford came around to where Catherine and I sat. "The gall of that man. I just cannot understand why he would tell such a lie!"

"And Doctor Balfour, accepts it!" Catherine said.

I continued to dab my eyes, too distraught to speak.

"There's a tavern round the corner. Let's go there for some lunch, shall we? Join us, Margaret?" Herford asked.

Having recovered, a bit, I responded, "Yes, thank you. I could use a drink."

Elgin said she had some shopping to do, and should return to the *haveli*, since Jan was likely hungry. We had started to feed him some goat's milk and solid food mashed and softened up, which he seemed to enjoy. I agreed, and gave her some rupees for the goods and *tonga* fare.

While walking out of the court house, I noticed more students standing around in groups. No doubt they are debating my case, I thought.

We entered the tavern and sat down in a booth. The waiter came over. I asked for a glass of white wine and some snacks, for I was not too hungry. The Herfords ordered whisky, gin and beef kebabs with naan for themselves.

"Seems you have some supporters here, Margaret," Catherine said.

"Delhi College students I believe. Who listens to them anyway," I commented.

"Oh, I wouldn't dismiss them. Students can stir up quite a bit of trouble." Hereford sipped his whiskey. "Tell me Margaret, how well do you know Albert?"

"He was more my deceased husband's friend."

"Seems he has a bone to pick with you?" Herford said.

"He might. I know something about him," I said, but did not elaborate.

Catherine seemed to understand, and nodded. "I'd be very careful of him. No wonder Nancy's left him."

"Yes. Stay away from him. Heard rumors about him having seduced some Indian girls," Herford finished his drink.

I sipped my wine. "Really! And were there any charges laid?"

"None. How could we? No one came forward. Frankly I am happy he's left my unit, and joined the police."

Our lunch arrived, and we ate while discussing my case some more. Both thought the Hospital's report looked more like a cover-up of their management processes, and Humphrey's cross-examination was most inappropriate. Furthermore, they were certain that, despite Albert's testimony, I would be exonerated and no charges will be laid against me. "I'll be your first patient after your return to your job, Margaret," Catherine said. Her cheering up had its effect, and I smiled at her.

Walking back to the court house, we observed more people had gathered outside. There were not only additional students, but Indian men and women workers had joined the crowd. The women, dressed in colorful saris and shalwar-kameezes, stood apart from the men. They were led by Mumtaz. Elgin must have informed her, I thought.

Upon seeing me, she waved. "Good luck Margareet," she shouted. I waved back, pleased to see her come out in my support.

"Daktar Margareet, ki jaay," someone in the crowd shouted.

Others in the throng joined in, and a chant began.

Daktar Margareet, ki jaay .... Daktar Margareet, ki jaay ....

I ducked my head in embarrassment, and along with the Herfords, quickly walked into the court house. I noted extra security guards, bamboo sticks in hand, were posted outside. They kept the onlookers at bay.

The court room did not resemble the same as when I had left. Nearly all the seats in the main hall were occupied, and so were the ones in the balcony. The new arrivals were mostly Indian men and women, gesturing and chatting excitedly. Their voices filled the room. The court staff were having difficulty keeping the front row seats clear. I informed them that the Herfords were with me, and they let us pass. I sat between Catherine and Captain Herford. I was happy for their backing. Some other Europeans, their earlier seats having been occupied, were allowed to sit in the front row. I saw Albert enter and take a chair at the far end. Good, stay away from me you devil, I said to myself.

Close to two o'clock the court clerk stood and raised his both arms in the air. "Quiet, please. Quiet. Silence in the court. The proceeding is about to restart. All rise."

When the noise ebbed, and the attendees rose, Magistrate Sir Theophilus and his entourage entered the stage, again from the side door and took their seats. We sat down.

Sir Theophilus, leaned forward and surveyed the gathering. He waited for complete silence. When he could not hear even a faint whisper, he began his summary: "Ladies and gentlemen, this morning, you heard the Civil and Military Hospital's Chief Surgeon's report. It indicated that Doctor Margaret Wallace was assigned to attend to the health of Her Majesty, Queen Zinat. Doctor Wallace did so, and the Hospital received good comments of her performance, from His Majesty King Zafar himself. This feedback was passed on to her by her supervisor, Doctor Lal. And ..."

While the Magistrate continued his brief, a recount of the hospital's report and my and other witness's testimony, my mind again wandered. Believing in my innocence, I felt as if I was back in my office, and reviewing my patients' files. I thought about some of the important cases, and whether other doctors had looked after them, and if so whether my patient had been provided the proper medication. I made mental notes to inquire with Doctor Lal about those and other cases. I wondered how the Delhi citizens were faring from the Cholera epidemic, and whether there were there any more patients in the hospital. My mind returned to the court room, when I felt Catherine's gentle squeeze of my wrist.

"This committee has reached its recommendation. I shall deliver it now," Sir Theophilus said, looking at the others on the panel. They nodded.

The court clerk said, "Would Doctor Margaret Wallace, please stand."

I stood.

"Doctor Wallace," the Magistrate began, "this committee is of the opinion that you should not be held responsible for the death of Prince Fakhruddin ..."

There was polite clapping from the Europeans, but the Indians, particularly those in the galley, broke out in cheers. I thought it was all over. I was free, and was about to sit, when I heard the Magistrate bang the gavel.

"Quiet, please," Sir Theophilus continued. "However, in view of the Hospital's report that Doctor Wallace willfully prescribed poisonous medicine—"

"Even if she did it upon the instructions of her supervisor?" someone shouted from the gallery.

"Who said that?" The Magistrate looked up angrily towards the gallery. "Remove that man, immediately."

The man, shouting and screaming, was taken away by two guards. He could still be heard ranting outside.

Others in the masses outside began chanting, once again, which could be heard faintly within the room.

Daktar Margareet, ki jaay .... Daktar Margareet, ki jaay ....

Captain Herford, looking towards Catherine and up at me, muttered, "Told you. That student will rile up the crowd."

Sir Theophilus waited another moment, and silence having been restored, continued, "However, the Hospital believes Doctor Wallace was negligent in her duties in ensuring the safe administration of the poisonous medication and its safekeeping in her office."

What on earth he is driving at, I thought. Then I heard his next words that rooted me to the spot. I felt Catherine hold my hand, and squeeze it gently, as if to give me some strength.

"... hence this committee agrees with the Hospital's recommendation that Doctor Wallace be dismissed from her employment. With the additional stipulation that, for a period of five years, she not be permitted to take up employment at any of the Honorable British East India Company's sponsored hospitals, as well as she be removed and not return within the Delhi City limits during this period."

I could not believe my ears that I heard those words: 'dismissed', 'removed from Delhi'. Bedlam broke out in the court room. While the Magistrate continued to bang the mallet, most of the Indian audience stood up shouting obscenities at him and at other members of the head table. There were shouts of: "It's a cover up ... punishing a helpless innocent woman ... typical British justice ..."

The protesters, who would not sit down, were driven out by the guards waving their bamboo sticks. I stood mesmerized, looking ahead. I might have fainted into Catherine's arms, but I saw the bearded image of our Lord, hovering above the stage close to the ceiling, like in a church. He smiled and seemed to be saying to me: not to worry, for He would look after me. That provided me immense courage to face whatever was to follow. I remained standing.

Order having been restored, once more, Sir Theophilus resumed: "Doctor Wallace, do you have anything further to say?"

What could I say? I simply responded, "No, sir. Except that I am innocent."

He nodded, as if he knew. "Now, as you are required to be removed from Delhi, would transportation to your parent's home in Futtehgurh be acceptable?"

Was there anything for me to choose? I simply nodded.

"Very well." The Magistrate turned towards Humphrey. "Colonel Humphrey could you please arrange for transportation of Doctor Wallace?"

Colonel Humphrey leaned forward. "Captain Albert Miller."

Albert jumped up. "Sir."

"How soon can you be ready to transport Doctor Wallace to Futtehgurh?"

"Any time, sir. Immediately, if the court wishes."

Sir Theophilus, quickly interjected. "Er ... no need to act right away. Let's see ... tomorrow is Friday ... it's the Mohammadan's holiday, and then we have the weekend coming. How about Monday?" He looked at me. "Would Monday be suitable for you, Doctor Wallace?"

Still in a daze, I again nodded.

"Good. Transportation date for Doctor Margaret Wallace is set for Monday the twenty-fourth of March at ten o'clock." He banged his gavel. "This Inquiry is adjourned." Those still remaining in the room rose, as the Magistrate and his committee filed out.

I slumped down on the chair and remained seated, gazing at the floor for a long time, while Catherine sat beside me with her arm around my shoulders. Some people did pass by expressing what sounded like commiserations, but being in a stupor, I could not respond. The room had nearly emptied, when I again heard the chanting, still continuing outside:

Daktar Margareet, ki jaay .... Daktar Margareet, ki jaay ....

"Come Margaret, your supporters are still outside. Waiting for you."

I nodded. With Catherine holding me by my waist, I walked slowly behind Captain Herford.

No sooner than I had stepped out of the court house doors when the large crowd gathered at the front broke into loud cheers. The ladies group, carrying garlands of jasmine and marigold, ran forward to me, Mumtaz in the lead. They bedecked me with so many leis around my neck that they reached almost up to my ears. Mumtaz and the other women hugged me, expressing their unhappiness at the decision.

The students changed their chant to:

Reinstate Daktar Margareet ... Reinstate Daktar Margareet ...

Overcome with their concern for my welfare, tears started to flow down my cheeks.

"Come, I have carriage waiting to take you back to Sharif Mahal," Mumtaz said. I nodded. I wanted to hold my son.

With Catherine and Mumtaz at my sides, holding me by the waist, and Captain Herford clearing a way through the throng, we made our way towards the carriage.

The crowd was so riled that despite the guards' warnings, they did not disperse. The police, fearing the agitators might enter the court building and destroy government property, charged the student lines striking them with their sticks. Some of the students resisted, shouting and screaming. For a moment it looked like the students might break through the police lines, but likely fearing for their lives, they fell back.

Upon hearing the rioters yells and the police warnings, we scampered towards the carriage. Upon reaching it I quickly bid a tearful thank you to the Herfords, for their comfort and support during the proceedings. They said it was the least they could do, and expressed their sympathies again. Hurriedly, promising to meet them again at church on Sunday, and accepting a farewell dinner that evening at their house, I swiftly boarded the coach. Mumtaz was already seated inside, and we were instantly on our way. Through the windows I observed groups of students running in the side streets, being chased by baton waving policemen. I think I saw Albert leading a police chase after some students. I wished I would never set eyes on that court house again.

When we had recovered sufficiently from the excitement of the commotion, Mumtaz asked, "You go to Futtehgurh, yes?"

"I don't have any other choice, Mumtaz, what can I do."

"No, you have choice. Sharif tell you."

I then remembered that Sharif had hinted about something. "What 'choice' is it?"

"Sharif speak to friend, tell you tomorrow."

She sounded very secretive, and thinking it would likely amount to nothing, I simply responded, "Alright. I'll talk to him tomorrow."

Entering the *haveli* through its wicket gate, Mumtaz and I walked quickly into the courtyard. I spotted Elgin sitting, on a charpoy under a shade tree, with Jan in her lap, chatting with some maids. She stood and came towards me. The other women scattered to their tasks, upon seeing Mumtaz. I took Jan from Elgin and hugged and kissed him. He gave me a delightful smile that cheered my sorrowful heart.

"Everything alright, Memsahib? You like lunch?" Elgin asked.

"Everything's fine. I've had lunch, but would love some tea. Can you bring it up please?"

She immediately went towards the kitchen. Thanking Mumtaz and hugging her again, I trudged upstairs.

Placing Jan in his cot, I washed and changed into a loose-fitting comfortable dress. Elgin brought a tea tray as I lay on the divan by the window enjoying the cool breeze from the river. From her sad face, I knew she had heard about the Inquiry's decision, likely from Mumtaz.

"Are we really returning to Futtehgurh, on Monday?"

"Yes, Elgin I am afraid so. But I am sure you will be happy to see your parents again."

"Yes, I happy, but we travel with Captain Albert?"

It then suddenly dawned on me, that it was Albert who was

appointed to escort me. Thinking of travelling with him and spending those nights in the *dak*-bungalows worried me. The Herford's warnings to stay away from him played in my mind. They need not have cautioned me, for I knew him all too well. "I'm glad, Elgin, you pointed it out. I don't think he should travel with us. I'll go and see the magistrate and have him replaced."

"Yes, Memsahib, I wouldn't like to travel with him, either."

Then something occurred to me. "Did Albert do or say anything to you?"

She was quiet for a while. I waited patiently, and she finally said, "I did not tell you before. But at the night of the Christmas Ball at Metcalf House, he came over to the servant's area and told me that you wanted to see me. He then took me to an empty room ... and ... kissed me and tried to seduce me. But I managed to free myself and run away."

I noted tears in her eyes. I stood and hugged her. "Elgin, I am sorry. You should have told me immediately. I would have taken some action."

"I did not wish to bother you. Also, Nancy memsahib is your good friend."

"You should not have worried about upsetting Nancy. I am glad nothing much happened. But next time anyone does anything like this, tell me right away. Alright?"

"Yes I will Memsahib." She dried her eyes. Jan had started to squirm, making noises. She went and picked him up. "It's too early for him to sleep. I'll take him for a stroll in his pram."

"Yes, he likes that. Sorry I can't accompany you, for I am too tired. Take some other maid friend of yours along. Do not go out alone. The rioters may still be out in the streets."

"Yes, I will, memsahib." She left the room, carrying Jan in her arms.

I went to bed early that evening and, being exhausted, slept late into the next morning. After breakfast, I wanted to visit the City Magistrate's office. But Mumtaz informed me that it being a Friday, the office would be closed, and said, "But you should stay home. Sharif go see a friend then talk to you." I agreed, also remembering he had mentioned that he would see me after the Friday prayers. It dawned on me that it was after the Friday prayers, friends met to socialize, similar to what we did at church, following a service.

While Elgin puttered around packing our meager possessions, with a heavy heart I sat down to complete the translation of the last few chapters of a medical textbook for Delhi College. I expected to complete it that or the next day, and hand in the manuscript on Sunday, on my way to church. I made steady progress, even working while having lunch, which Elgin brought up on a tray.

Being engrossed in my work, I did not even hear the call for the Friday prayers, and it was mid-afternoon when there was a knock on the door. Elgin answered and let Sharif in.

He salaamed. "Sorry, Doctor Margaret. I hear your very bad news. Very shocking for you, yes?"

"Thank you Sharif. I have just about recovered from the disbelief. Please sit down." He sat on the chair and I reclined on the sofa. "Would you like some tea?"

"No thank you. I just drink it." He waved his hand.

Elgin, tactfully, picked up the babbling Jan and went out from the room.

"So, you decide to go to Futtehgurh, what you do for work?" he asked, looking concerned.

"They have barred me from working at a Company hospital, perhaps I could find a job in a mission clinic. But I am not certain if even they'll have me."

"And I hear, mission clinic, no pay good."

"Yes, that as well." Then remembering that my children were due to arrive from Canada soon, I again vexed about how I would provide for them. But remained silent.

He let me think for a while, then said, "I have a choice for you. You get a good job, with good money."

On hearing that I brightened up. "Really! What 'choice' is that?"

"You know the kingdom of Jhansi?"

"Yes, I've heard of it."

"My friend has lands there. His father working for the Rani. He tell me the Rani looking for European lady doctor. Her only son very sick. She ask the Company, but they no help. Are you interested in working for Rani?"

"Hmm ... and you said the salary would be good?"

"Yes. Although the Company take her lands, but she live in the palace there, has good pension and her own family money too."

I then remembered about the annexation of Jhansi by the Company, on some flimsy excuse. I thought: well, Jhansi is not far from Futtehgurh, and I will be closer to my family there; the job may not be permanent, but if the remuneration is generous I could take it for a while; I also planned to appeal the Delhi Magistrate's decision, to the Governor General; it might take a year or so, but I was certain Lord Canning would over-rule that silly decision. "However, Sharif, how certain are you the Rani will hire me?"

"I am sure. But you can ask my friend. He come this evening. You meet him, yes?"

"Alright. No harm in me speaking with him."

"Good. I call you later." He got up, salaamed, and left the room.

I returned to my work, and did not notice the hour that slipped by. Sharif returned to say that his friend had arrived and was waiting for us in the *baithuk*. Sharif stood outside the door while I washed and tidied myself. Wrapping a shawl about me, the way Indian women did, to look modest, I followed him down the stairs. I had meant to ask him who this person was, but had forgotten. As I entered the men's sitting room, the three men lounging there jumped up, and salaamed. It was a surprise when I recognized one of them as the neighbor, Ali Khan. They all wore the usual: white shalwar-kameez, black waistcoat and a dark *topi*. Their short beards, trimmed in the Muslim fashion, gave away their religion.

"Sorry doctor sahiba. I hear your very very bad news," Ali said and introduced the other two as his cousins, from Jhansi.

I thanked him, and sat down on a chair, and according to their custom, a couple of seats away from the men. Without being asked, as usual, a maid brought tea in glasses and put them in front of us. I took a sip of mine, and put the glass back on the table, for as customary it was too sweet.

Ali told me, all what Sharif had mentioned earlier, about the Rani wishing to employ a European lady, particularly for her son, who was gravely ill.

"But, Mr. Ali, are you certain the Rani will hire me? And how much will she pay?" I wanted to know.

"I am sure she give you job." He looked towards his cousins. They nodded. "For money and other conditions, you can speak to Rani. But I sure she pay you good money and good apartment in her palace."

"I want to be certain, for it would be a long way to travel to Jhansi from Futtehgurh, and then return back if the conditions are not suitable to me," I said.

"I have suggestion." Ali leaned forward. "My wife and I go with my cousin-brothers to Jhansi, for holiday, on Sunday. My cousins ride in their carriage. My wife and I travel in our carriage. We have space for you. Why don't you come with us? And, if you no like Jhansi, we take you to Futtehgurh. You like, yes?"

I must admit his offer sounded like a gift from Heaven. Something which my Lord had promised me in the courtroom, to arrange for me. I was hopeful that the conditions and the salary at Jhansi would be even better than what little I was being paid in Delhi. Also, Ali's plan would help me secure employment with the Rani without Humphrey getting wind of it, for I feared he might scuttle it. And most of all, Elgin and I would not be travelling with that fiend, Albert.

I noted the men were looking at me, anxious for my response. I smiled. "Mr. Ali, you are being so kind to me, with such a generous offer. How can I refuse it? Of course, my son his ayah and I would gladly travel with you to Jhansi. At what time do you propose to depart on Sunday?"

"Very good. I happy you come with us." Ali beamed. "We like to leave, early morning. Also, if you have luggage ready tomorrow afternoon, my cousin come and pick it up and put it on carriage." He looked at them, and they nodded again.

It was getting late, and the slanting rays from the sun shone through the windows of that small *bethak*. I rose. "Thank you gentlemen. Now I must take my son for his stroll along the river." They also stood and salaamed.

From the courtyard, as the others did, I shouted up towards my apartment, for Elgin to bring Jan down. She heard me and came down with him in her arms. We placed him in the pram, which was kept in a corner, and went out of the *haveli*.

While walking, I informed Elgin of the change in plans and that we would be departing for Jhansi, early on Sunday morning. I asked if this was alright, and she readily agreed, saying she is happy that Albert would not be around bothering us. I also mentioned that, too bad, we were not going to Futtehgurh, but as I had promised earlier, we would visit there next May, for a month, to celebrate my Jan's birthday. She was delighted upon hearing it. I made a mental note to put the manuscript of the translated book in an envelope— addressed to Professor Ramchandra—and give it to Sharif with a request to please hand it in at Delhi College, on his way to work at the Red Fort. I also decided to write to the Herfords, but much later from Jhansi.

We soon reached the road that ran along the bank of the river. I preferred walking there at that time of the day. It being the evening hours the market shops were closed, and the *ghats* were nearly empty, except for some people performing special *pujas*, half submerged on the steps in the water. I felt happy and so elated that I wanted to do the same.

We walked along and reaching the same deserted stretch, where we used to pray with Papa, I asked Elgin to please stop. While she held the pram's handles, and looked curiously at me, I took off my shoes and socks. Barefoot I tiptoed onto the first steps of a *ghat*. Then hitching up my skirt, and folding it such that it stayed above my knees, I walked onto the second step that was partially submerged in the river. I stood there, for a moment, ankle deep in water. Then, bending down, I scooped the sacred water in my cupped hands and straightening up, let the water flow down over my face and onto my bosom. Clasping my hands, I looked out over the Jamuna River flowing serenely on, and the setting sun's rays casting an orange glow on its ripples. I felt at peace.

It was then the image of my Lord appeared on the horizon. I prayed and thanked Him for opening a new path for me to follow, just like the river, towards Him, into Heaven.

Chapter Nineteen

Escape From Delhi

1856, March: Delhi, India

THE NEXT MORNING, I awoke from the sound of the six a.m. cannon fire from the Ridge. After a quick breakfast, and while Elgin proceeded to finish packing my sea chest, portmanteau, a small box of Jan's things, and her holdall, I decided to pen a short note to Magistrate Sir Theophilus. I was worried that he might become concerned on my unexplained departure from Delhi. I wrote:

> *... abiding with you decision, sir, I will be leaving Delhi, and since I have managed to secure my own conveyance, I would no longer require the escort nor transportation by Captain Albert Miller.... etc ... etc.*

Putting the note in an envelope, sealing, and addressing it, I requested Elgin to deliver it to the City Magistrate's Office. After finishing packing, she left with the letter. She also planned to stop at the post office to wire some money to her parents, and at the river market to purchase a few victuals for our long journey. I got busy finishing and editing the translation of the medical textbook.

I had just finished inserting the completed manuscript in a large envelope and addressing it to: *Professor Ramchandra, Delhi College,* when there was a tap on the door and Mumtaz entered.

"Good morning, Doctor Margareet. I see you pack your boxes, already! Good, because Ali *bhai's* cousins are here to pick up your luggage."

I returned her greeting. "Yes, the baggage is ready. Please have them come in and take them away. Also, tell them not to forget taking Jan's perambulator from the courtyard." I also handed her the large envelope, requesting her to have Sharif deliver it.

"Yes, I say them." After making some baby talk with Jan, who sat on the divan playing with toys, she went away to find the young men.

Elgin returned from her trip into the city center. She placed her purchases on a table and picking up Jan, rocked him in her arms.

"Did you have any difficulty delivering my letter to the Magistrate?"

"No, memsahib. I give it to Metcalf sahib's *chaprassie*. He say he will give it to the Magistrate. But when I coming out of the Court House, you no believe who I saw."

"Who did you see?"

"Captain Albert!"

"Really! Did he say anything to you?"

"No. He standing taking to some people. As I pass by, he saw me. When I go in the street and look back, I see he follow me."

"Did he catch up to you?"

"No. I walk fast to the market. Lot of crowd there. I go between people and into shops. I lose him. I no see him again."

"I'm relieved to hear it. For I'm certain he would have wanted to know, why you had gone to the Court House."

"Yes, me too. I bring you tea now?"

"Yes, please. Also can you have them put hot water for my bath in the women's *ghusalkhana*?"

"Yes, I tell them." She went down to the kitchen.

Following a refreshing cup of tea and snacks, I went down to the ladies washroom for a leisurely bath. I was glad for it, knowing it would be a few days carriage ride to Jhansi. Although we would be stopping at caravansaries, I did not trust the washrooms there. They were usually full of snakes, I had heard. Elgin came in and helped to wash my long fair hair with the coconut milk soap she had purchased at the market.

Later I dried my hair in the hot sun, on a small terrace, at one corner of the second floor, looking out towards the garden. Due to the high walls on the sides, covered with bougainvillea vines with red and yellow flowers, it was a private area. While sitting on a chair reading a book, my hair flowing down and exposed to the sweltering sun's rays, I noticed a small gate in the wall adjoining the neighboring mansion, the Ali Khan's *haveli*. It opened to a similar terrace, on the other side. How convenient, I thought, to drop in on your neighbor for tea.

That evening the Sharif's household had gone to much trouble and prepared a lavish farewell dinner for me that included most of my favorite dishes. While I enjoyed the cuisine, my heart was dejected for leaving Delhi, a city I had come to love. It would have shown on my face, and everyone in the household tried their best to cheer me, with pleasant talks, of my children, my family, and I would have a marvelous time working and living in Jhansi. It was not only an appealing city, they said, but the Rani was known to be a most kind hearted lady, one who revered her populace.

Following the sumptuous meal, it was time for me to say goodbye, for the Ali's wished to depart very early, prior to sunrise, the next morning. Everyone, including Mumtaz, Sharif's mother and the other ladies, came to me and embraced me. Each wished me a safe journey, and in their usual manner, touching my temples and reciting a prayer. They also—likely knowing that I was insolvent— pressed money into my hands, despite my reluctance to accept it. I could not thank them enough for all their hospitality and kindness.

Akbar Khan salaamed and said, "Doctor Margareet, you come back soon to our hose." I thanked him again for his hospitality and kindness, and said I would return one day.

Sharif, uncharacteristically, shook my hand with both his palms, and bowed. "Doctor Margaret, I see you again in Jhansi. I go there sometime. Take message from King Zafar." I thanked him, and told him I would look forward to his visits, and he should bring Mumtaz as well.

That night before going early to bed, I knelt and said a prayer to my Lord and expressed my deepest gratitude for all His benevolence and opening the doors to a bright future for me.

It felt as if I had slept for hardly a few minutes, when I was awakened by loud hammering of the *haveli's* front doors. I looked at my gold pocket watch—I kept at bedside—and noted the time. It was just past midnight. Instinctively, gripped by fear, I jumped out of bed. Throwing on my housecoat and opening the apartment's door, I walked out into the hallway, and peered through a window onto the courtyard below. Sharif had already gone downstairs and walked towards the entrance. Mumtaz also came running from her flat and stood beside me.

"Who is there?" Sharif shouted.

"Open up. It's the Chief Inspector of police," an English accented voice shouted, still thumping the door.

My heart sank, on hearing that voice. It was unmistakably, Albert's. I moved away from the open window, but continued to look down through the marble lattice openings in the wall.

"What you want?" Sharif opened the wicket door.

Albert barged in, followed by four other policemen. They ran into the courtyard. "Where is she?" Albert bellowed at Sharif.

"Who you mean?"

"Your white mistress."

"I no have any mistress."

"Yes, you do. Margaret Wallace. I have a warrant for her arrest." Albert pulled out a piece of paper from his uniform jacket's pocket, and displayed it before Sharif.

"Ah, you mean Doctor Margaret." Sharif read the name on the paper. "She no here. She gone."

"*Behanchood*, don't lie to me," Albert roared. "Take me to her room."

"Who you call *behanchood*? You get out of this house." Sharif stood in front of Albert, blocking his way.

Without warning Albert punched Sharif, hard on the jaw. Sharif fell on the floor. When he tried to get up, a policeman pointed his rifle at him, telling him to stay down. The other three policemen levelled their rifles at some of the residents who had emerged onto the courtyard.

"Arrest this bastard." Albert ordered a policeman. Then waved at another policeman. "Come, we search the rooms. You go this way, and I that way. Look in every room. When you find the bitch, tie her up." Albert pulling out his revolver from its holster, started towards the rooms.

A policeman making Sharif stand, proceeded to tie his hands behind his back. Sharif looked up towards Mumtaz who peered out of a window, her *dupatta* over her mouth. Sharif motioned with his eyes at Mumtaz. She understood the veiled message.

Mumtaz came hurriedly to me, and whispered, "Get your clothes and boy. I take you to Ali's house. I get key." She ran towards her apartment.

Elgin stood peering through the partially opened door of my apartment, her woolen shawl over her nightdress. I ran towards her. "Elgin, collect our things, we have to run."

Spreading a bedsheet on the floor, we quickly threw our travel clothes, shoes, and other items on it. While I picked up Jan, who thankfully slept despite the rumpus, Elgin tied up the bedsheet's corners into a knot and hoisted it over her shoulder, without much difficulty. She was a strong girl.

"Ready?" Mumtaz was at the door. I nodded. "Come follow me," She whispered. We moved swiftly, down the corridor, towards the private terrace.

"The bitch is upstairs." I heard Albert bark. And when I looked backwards, through a window, I saw him coming up the stairs, revolver in hand.

We reached the terrace. Mumtaz turned the key in the small gate's lock, and opened it. We scrambled onto the similar patio of the Ali's mansion. Closing and relocking the gate, Mumtaz led us to the Ali's apartment, and gently knocked on the door.

It seemed they had also heard the commotion in the Sharif Mahal, and were already up, for Mrs. Ali opened the door, immediately. Mumtaz hurriedly explained the situation to her, in her rapid fire Delhi Urdu that was too difficult for me to comprehend.

Mrs. Ali nodded, and embraced me. "Good you come, *beti*. We can depart early on our journey. Come change your clothes here." She led me and Elgin to a side room.

"I go tell my cousins to get carriage ready." Mr. Ali hurried out of the door.

Having changed into our travelling outfits, we sat on a divan gulping down hot and refreshing tea; it helped to calm my agitated state. Mr. and Mrs. Ali had also dressed and scurried about collecting the last of their items for the journey.

There was a knock on the door and one of a cousins entered. "The carriages and horses are ready. But waiting at the back laneway, because the police are still in front of Sharif Mahal."

"Come quietly. We go from back door through the *baghicha*." Ali motioned to us and we followed him, out of the apartment and down the stairs to their courtyard, making as little noise as was possible. Elgin carried Jan. One of the cousins had picked up our knotted bedsheet of clothes and other items.

While the others went out of the rear door into their *baghicha*, I bid another tearful goodbye to Mumtaz. I hugged and thanked her for saving me from Albert's clutches. I also expressed my apprehension at Sharif's arrest, and hoped he would be released directly, and if not she should let me know and I would write to the Magistrate and the Commissioner.

"Don't worry," Mumtaz said confidently. "We take care of that *daroogah*. Who does he think he is, the caliph of Dilli?"

I wondered what she meant by that. Promising to keep in touch through letters, I gave her a final hug and hurried out of the door to join the others who, I noted in the darkness, were half way on the garden path leading to the back alley. A quarter moon glimmered barely enough pale yellow light for us to stumble along.

Before we reached the garden gate, we were rooted to the spot when we saw an Indian policeman standing at the gate, rifle in hand. Ali motioned at us to stop and went ahead, with his two cousins, to the policeman.

It looked as if the policeman knew Ali, for he salaamed them. He is a Muslim, which might be a good thing, I thought. They conversed in whispers. The policeman glanced around to ascertain if any of the other police constables were around, then nodded and opening the gate stood at one side. Ali waved at us to come along.

"Put your shawls over your heads," Mrs. Ali whispered to Elgin and me.

We complied, and followed Mrs. Ali. While exiting the garden gate, the policeman hardly glanced at us. I breathed a sigh of relief when I heard the garden gate clang shut behind me. Walking along the foggy lane, we soon reached the two carriages waiting ahead, their side oil lamps casting a faint glow. The two cousins were already seated in one, with most of the luggage. Ali opened the door of the front carriage for us and we clambered inside. He entered and sat beside his wife on one bench. Jan had started to whimper, and I took him from Elgin who sat next to me. At Ali's command, "Chaloo," the *tongawalla* cracked his whip and the carriage rolled forward with a jolt.

Happy that we were finally on our way, and thinking the danger of my being recognized was over, I took off my shawl from over my head. However, I was wrong, again. Since, we were to take the southern road that led to Jhansi, the carriages had to exit the city through the Delhi Gate. Looking out of the window I saw it looming up ahead. But my heart sank, when I saw that it was closed.

The carriages stopped. A British sergeant and two Indian sepoys, wearing their scarlet uniforms, ambled forward. "We 'ave instructions to search all carriages," the sergeant told the *tongawalla*.

I quickly re-covered my head.

"I go talk to him," Ali said and descended from the carriage.

I heard them talking. Ali told the sergeant that he was a subedar and going to his home village for a holiday. They argued a bit.

"Oi don't care if you are the baddyshah 'ere. We 'ave to search," the sergeant said. He then told the two sepoys to go and look though the carriage at the back. "O'll examine this one."

My heart started to beat faster, as the sergeant opened the door and with one foot on the step looked inside. In the carriage lamp's dim light I recognized him. It was Frank Willoughby, my sea voyage cabin companion's husband.

Despite my attempted disguise, he recognized me immediately, "Mornin, Doctor Wallace."

"Good morning Frank," I whispered.

"I 'eard about your court case. 'orrible decision, if you ask me."

I nodded, as tears welled in my eyes.

"Oi see no reason to stop you from goin' where ever you want to go. Me wife would never forgive me if oi arrested you. You bein' so kind to 'er all durin' the long voyage an all. Also, oi met your Father in Futtehgurh. A fine gentleman 'e is."

"Thank you Frank. Please give my regards to your wife," I said trying to suppress a sob.

"Oi will. 'ave a safe journey." He stepped down. The two other sepoys had finished their inspection and were walking up. Sergeant Frank waved at the gate keepers. "No one in 'ere. Open the gate."

Ali jumped back inside the carriage. The Delhi Gate's massive wooden doors opened and the carriages moved through them. Soon we were clattering on the south road out of Delhi.

"Good, they let us go," Ali said. "But how you know this man? He is only a sergeant."

"Mr. Ali I make an effort to know people from all walks of life. And usually it is the common folks who will help us in our time of need. Is that not so?"

Ali smiled and nodded. "My experience, also. But it is all in the hands of Allah. I pray for you and your children too. He is your God as well." He raised his palms and recited a verse, possibly from the Quran, in Arabic.

When he had finished, I said, "Thank you Ali *bhai,* for changing your mind about me, and deciding to help me. I will remember you and your family in my prayers as well."

"It is Allah's wish," Ali said.

With all the turmoil of our departure finally over, we settled down and rested our heads on the padded leather seat's head-rests, to catchup on the lost sleep. However, repose did not come to me easily, for my mind still churned about Albert's actions, particularly how had he managed to secure a warrant for my arrest? And on what charge? It then dawned on me that it would not be beyond Albert to have forged the Magistrate's signature. I resolved to write, from Jhansi, to Sir Theophilus requesting an explanation.

A month or so later, after I had written to the Delhi Magistrate, I received a reply. The Magistrate wrote that there appears to have been some misunderstanding, and expressed his apologies. He clarified that upon receipt of my note, delivered by Elgin, advising him of my departure independently from Delhi, he had cancelled the previous warrant that ordered my transportation. However, simply as a precautionary measure to ensure my departure from Delhi, he had issued another warrant ordering my arrest and forcible transportation, but specifically had written at the bottom of the warrant: *to be enforced only in the event Doctor Margaret does not travel on her own accord, out of Delhi – signed Sir Theophilus Metcalf, Magistrate.*

The cancelled and the second warrants were both sent over to the Chief Inspector of Police's office.

Sir Theophilus also informed me that, Captain Albert Miller was reprimanded for acting prematurely in executing the warrant. Furthermore, no charges were laid on Mr. Sharif Khan, and he was released unconditionally.

Hence, while Albert had not forged the Magistrate's signature, he had tried to use the revised second warrant to hoodwink Sharif into 'arresting' me. Thankfully Sharif, although not being able to read English well, had not been deceived. I wondered, if in the event Albert had imprisoned me that night, likely at a secret location, what horrific torture he would have subjected me to.

Nevertheless, on that night of my 'escape from Delhi' as the carriage clip clopped and rolled speedily in the night on the road towards Jhansi, I felt at peace and fell into a slumber, thinking I had finally evaded Albert's clutches. However, future events would unfold to reveal how wrong I was.

Epilogue

Walli and Alexandra's home

[Na Iran ne kiya, na Shah Russ ne
Angrez ko tabah kiya kartoos ne]
It was neither the Shah of Iran, nor the Russians, that did it
It was the cartridges to the British, that did it
--Bhadur Shah Zafar, Delhi (1775 – 1862)

1967, July: Baltimore, Maryland
ALEXANDRA YAWNED. "Goodness just look at the time."
She glanced at the baroque clock on the mantel above the fireplace.
"Nearly two o'clock, Walli dear! Don't you have a busy day at the
hospital tomorrow?"

I placed a bookmark and shut Doctor Margaret's journal that lay
on my lap. "Mondays are always busy. And I am sure for you too,
honey. All those rich clients would be waiting in your law office's
reception room."

Alexandra got up from our living room sofa we had been sitting
on for the last six hours, sipping wine and reading Volume III of
Margaret's journal. "Well, dear, you be sure not to accept fancy gifts
from your patients, else you might face an Inquiry by your hospital,
just as Doctor Margaret had to."

I stood up as well, and stretched. "Not sure if I could refuse an
Indian silk dress and jewelry!" We both laughed, and hugged and
kissed.

Alexandra looked at the thickness of the unread pages in the
journal. "Seems we are only about half way through. Why don't we
call it a night, sweetie?" I agreed and we, arms around each other's
waist, walked up the staircase towards our bedroom. Alexandra
leaned a bit on me. "I wonder if our Grimsby friends, the Wallaces
and the Barinowskys, have reached Florida yet. Greg's information
that Nancy returned to Grimsby from India is substantiated by
Margaret. It would be nice to read Nancy's diary or journal, if she
left any. It might throw some more light on Albert's abuses of other
women, apart from Margaret."

"Yes, and I'm looking forward to reading Greg's daughter,
Katya's story about her great-grandmother. And it would be

wonderful to meet her again, if Greg is able to bring her out of Russia," I said, being a fan of thriller mysteries.

"That would be lovely, but first I want to know what happened to Margaret when she arrived in Jhansi."

"Yes, let's read that part of her journal during the next week."

THE END

Glossary

Almirah: wardrobe
Arrey: hey
Azadi: freedom
Badmash: hooligan, trouble maker
Baghicha: a small garden
Bahen: sister
Behenchood: a very bad word
Bhawaj: sister-in-law
Bahu: daughter-in-law
Bara karoo : make big
Barra-peg: a double shot of liquor
Beta: son
Bethak: sitting room (usually for men)
Bhadur: brave warrior, a title
Bhang: a narcotic mixture from the cannabis plant
Bhag jaoo : run away
Burj: tower
Chai: tea
Chaloo: let's go
Chapatti: leavened bread
Chaprassie: peon, clerk
Charpoy: a bed comprising a wood frame and four legs, with netting of jute
or cotton
Chaukidar: gatekeeper (security guard)
Choti-hazri: light breakfast
Dada: grandfather
Dai: midwife
Dakgharry : mail coach
Daroogah: police chief
Darzi: tailor
Dilli-wallahs: Delhi residents
Divan: a low, wide, four-poster platform for sitting in living rooms
Diwani: tax
Duppata: a narrow shawl

Ekka: a two wheeled horse carriage

Ghats: steps with landing (dock) to a river or sea

Ghusalkhana: bathroom

Gulab-jamun: sweet made with cottage cheese deep fried

Gully: side street

Goora: white man

Hakim: physician

Haveli: mansion

Hookah: a tobacco smoking pipe where the smoke is drawn through a water base

Huzoor: sir or madam

Inshallah: God willing

Jaani: darling

Jaldhysay: quickly

Ji: yes

Kahani: story

Kameez: shirt

Karas: wide golden bracelets

Kotha: brothel

Maalis: gardeners

Maidan: open ground

Moazzen: the caller to prayer, usually in a mosque

Maloom: understand

Munshi: clerk

Naatch: dance

Nameste: I bow to you (Indian/Hindu greeting)

Paisa: the smallest Indian currency (like a penny)

Pakoras: battered and deep-fried vegetables

Punkha: fan

Rani: queen

Rasmalai: cottage cheese-balls fried and sweetened in honey

Sahiba: Mrs. or mistress

Salaam: peace be on you (Muslim greetings)

Samosas: deep-fried patties of either vegetables or minced meat filling

Sarkar: government, used to reference the East India Company

Sepoy: Indian soldier

Shikar: hunt

Shalwar-kameez: a long shirt and baggy trousers

Sowar: cavalryman

Subedar: sergeant
Taj: crown
Talwar: a curved sword, like a sabre
Tehkhana: basement room
Tiffin: lunch
Topi: a cap shaped like a boat
Wallah: person
Waliahad: heir apparent
Zemindar: land owner
Zenana: women's area

About the Author

Waheed Rabbani was born in India, near Delhi, and was introduced to Victorian, Edwardian and other English novels, at a very young age, in his father's library. Most of the numerous books had been purchased by his father at 'garage sales' held, by departing British civil service officers, towards the end of their terms in India, during the Raj.

Waheed was educated at St. Patrick's School, Karachi, Pakistan, and graduated from Loughborough University, Leicestershire, England. He received a Master's degree from Concordia University, Montreal, Canada. While an engineer by profession, Waheed's other love is reading and writing English literature. Waheed also obtained a Certificate in Creative Writing from McMaster University, Hamilton, Canada, and embarked on his writing journey.

Waheed and his wife, Alexandra, are now settled on the shores of Lake Ontario, in the historic town of Grimsby.

Note to the Readers

Dear Readers, thank you for reading this novel, and for following this series. For some more information, background, and news about the series, please visit my Facebook Page, or my website: http://wrabbani.ca/author

Also, I would be most grateful if you could please post a review at your favorite on-line book store. Thank you very much.